MURDER-OKE!

And Other Spooky Cape May Tales

By Terry O'Brien

ISBN 978-0-9799051-2-4

Cover design by Mike DeMusz

Book design by Jack Wright

Illustrations by Mike DeMusz

Exit Zero Publishing ★ Cape May, NJ ★ www.exitzero.us

Welcome

HIS is the first of what I hope, nay promise, will be a series of Cape May-inspired anthologies brought to you by the people who publish *Exit Zero* magazine, a funny-yet-useful guide to America's Original Seaside Resort. When I launched the magazine — on July 4, 2003 — it was my ambition to seek out, and publish, new talent. First of all, though, I had to figure a way to pay the bills. And now that our little boutique publishing company has more or less managed that, it's with pride that I introduce this book, which I think might be the hottest read on the beach this summer. (It better be — truth be told, not *all* the bills are paid.)

Four of the five stories featured in this collection were published in serial form in the pages of *Exit Zero* over the last few years, the exception being "The Jetty," which is making its publishing debut.

The writer of these stories is Terry O'Brien, who is responsible for *Exit Zero*'s Undertow column, which has sometimes provoked controversy in the Cape May community, usually because Terry writes with the uncorrected honesty that any writer needs if he or she is going to make anyone pay attention. Terry often makes fun of people in his column. Okay, Terry sometimes actually *insults* people in his column. But no one comes in for more abuse and inspection than he himself. He's self-deprecating to a fault. (He's other things to a fault, too, but there's no need to get into that.)

He's also a very talented writer. In my previous life as a magazine editor in New York, I had the pleasure and privilege of editing literary heavyweights such as Bret Easton Ellis, Jay McInerney, William T. Vollmann and Jim Harrison, along with dozens of accomplished, award-winning magazine writers. I only boast to illustrate the fact that I think I know good writing when I see it. And Terry is a very good writer. His tight, economic prose, allied to a wicked imagination and a mischievous sense of humor, combine to produce stories that are true page-turners.

Usually, I hate book blurbs that say "I laugh, I cried." (I hate the "tour de force" cliché even more). But every time I read the title story *Murder-Oke!* I laugh out loud. A lot. Every time I read *The Celestial*, I cry twice and get goosebumps three times. In the same places. (The same places in the story, AND on my body.) *The Reindeer, the Elf and the Attic Vent* made me cry once (again, in the same place); *The Five Stages Of Death* is in the best tradition of pulp fiction... a fast-paced thriller with quite a few twists and turns; while the final story, *The Jetty,* is spooky and sentimental in fairly equal measures.

Read the book (after buying it) and see if you have the same reactions. And then buy copies for your friends and family. If they love Cape May, they'll love YOU for it.

I also want to give a shout-out to our staff artist Mike DeMusz, who penned the drawings in these pages. I wanted the book to have the feel of a classic pulp fiction novel or one of those old adventure books for boys that feature heroic cowboys, soldiers, airmen... you know the type. Thanks, Mike, for doing such a bang-up job — on the usual tight deadline that you always seem to handle without drama.

PS: The little "sticker" on the cover is no joke. Movie rights to the *Murder-Oke!* story were purchased, and shooting is/was (depending on when you read this) due to start in Cape May in the fall of 2008. Terry O'Brien has written the screenplay and is hopefully starring in the movie, too (as well as being a talented waiter, karaoke host, singer and writer, he's also a trained actor). I can't wait!

Enjoy the book.

— *Jack Wright, Editor/Publisher*

For Cath

Contents

Murder-Oke!...Page 8

The Celestial..Page 92

The Five Stages of Death.................................Page 130

The Reindeer, the Elf and the Attic Vent........Page 196

The Jetty ....Page 226

Acknowledgments..Page 250

MURDER-OKE!

With a deranged serial killer on the loose, It's not just the songs that are being mutilated!

CHAPTER ONE
Sal At The Ugly Mug

Although all the names of people and places in this story are real, this is a work of complete fiction. Any and all actual people and places have given express permission to be used in this story. The mayor is a fictional character.

T WAS a little after 2am on a brisk Monday morning as Sal Riggi pushed his way out the heavy glass door of the Ugly Mug and on to the Washington Street Mall. The air was a little crisp for this late in May, but he didn't care — it felt good on his face, made him feel alive. Everything seemed to feel better since he started working out regularly at North Beach Gym and shed some pounds. The air tasted better, his feet felt better, his clothes fit better. It was just... better.

So with a deep breath and a smile he made his way across the red brick-paved mall (*nice job they did of that mall renovation*, he thought happily) and toward his car. The mall, a three-block stretch of Cape May's finest storefront realty encircled by metered parking, had been a symbol of the town's resurgence when it was built in the 1970s. Before that, the street had been a dying little part of a dying little town. In the 30-plus years since, Cape May had become, once again, one of the most beloved seaside resorts in the country. And the Ugly Mug, one of Cape May's oldest and most visited drinking establishments, had been through it all, thick and thin, a beacon to all thirsty fisherman and tourists, a port in the storm.

Stinkin' smoking ban, Sal thought, as he lit up his little cigar/cigarette thing and inhaled deeply. The baby cigar was terrible. It smelled terrible, it tasted terrible, it *was* terrible for him. But, at 300 (formerly 600) lbs and the survivor of two heart attacks, a stroke and diabetes (not to mention being 90% deaf), he had eliminated just about every vice in his repertoire and, aside from the occasional Johnny Walker Blue, these stinky sumbitches were all he had left.

So he hummed and smoked as he walked to his car, which sat parked near the public restroom on the outside circle of the mall, literally a 30-second walk from the Mug.

Unfortunately for Sal, they would be his last 30 seconds.

"Here's my story, sad but true..." he crooned, "'bout a girl that I once knew..."

Under his breath he continued to sing "Runaround Sue", his favorite Dion song. And his favorite karaoke song. "She took my love and ran around." A plume of vile smoke circled his head. "With every single guy in town... Hey!"

The song in his heart and the bounce in his step were partly attributed to the good scotch, but mostly due to Sunday night being karaoke night at the Mug. And if there was one thing Sal loved, it was karaoke. The host, a squat, bald guy named Terry was the new karaoke guy in town (Terry-Oke! he cleverly called it), and presented a nice alternative to the mobs that swarmed Carney's every Tuesday night during the summer. Terry's following was faithful, yes, but, thus far, sparse. Four hours at a Terry-Oke! show and you could sing 10-12 songs. Four hours at Carney's yielded two, maybe three. Good for Joe Carney, bad for Sal.

So, over a few months and a few cocktails, Terry and Sal had become good friends. Sal was attending five to six karaoke nights a week, anchoring Terry's local following. But not for much longer.

"Well, I should have known it from the very start..."

It was dark in the area between the shops and the parking spaces, the only real unlit part of the mall.

"This girl would leave me with a broken heart..."

Behind the public toilet the dark figure waited, club in hand, waiting for the right moment.

Sal turned, retrieved his car keys from his satchel, and bent to open the door. "So if you don't wanna cry like I do..."

The dark figure leapt from the shadows, silent, determined.

"A-keep away from a-Runaround... GACK!"

The dark figure jumped on Sal's back and wrapped an arm around his throat, squeezing tightly. The air in Sal's lungs swiftly evaporated. He thrashed, spots spreading before his eyes, the panic of impending doom gripping him.

"There, there, it'll all be over in a minute," the dark figure whispered into his ear in a voice Sal thought he recognized.

But Sal wasn't that easy. From the heft on his back he could tell he outweighed his assailant by at least 100lbs. That knowledge in hand, he turned as quickly as he could, legs quivering, and began slamming himself against the car with a zeal borne of desperation. Once, twice, a third time... contact.

"Gah!" the dark figure spat as the rearview mirror exploded against his rib cage. The dark figure released his grip and fell to the ground, dazed.

Raising the small club in his hand, the dark figure advanced further, and with his free hand pulled off the black ski mask.

Precious air seeped back into Sal's lungs as he pulled himself off the ground and turned on the dark figure. "All right you son of a bitch, now I'm pissed. Let's go!"

Sal, though not a small man, was nimble and learned not only in the ways of karaoke, but in karate. In a defensive stance he waited for his attacker's move. The dark figure shook his head, bits of glass tinkling to the ground, and rose to his feet. The dark figure was not especially tall or big, but moved with a robotic determination. He rolled his head, worked a kink out of his neck, and advanced.

"Bring it," Sal challenged, his Italian temper rising.

The dark figure was unfazed: "It ends now."

Raising the small club in his hand, the dark figure advanced further, and with his free hand pulled off the black ski mask.

Sal was stunned: "YOU?"

The now not-so-dark figure nodded. "Me."

Sal dropped his hands, "But... why?"

"Not important."

"Please?"

The now not-so-dark figure shrugged, "All right."

With grim purpose he closed the distance between them, cocking the club, "Because I..."

Whap!

"HATE!"

Whap!

"KARAOKE!"

Whap!

The first blow sent him to the ground, head bleeding. The second split and emptied his skull. The third blow sealed the deal.

As Sal lay dying, the not-so-dark figure calmly wiped a few bits of flesh and bone from his face. He caught his blood-smeared reflection in the remains of the shattered rearview and smiled.

"Thank you and good night."

Behind him, the life ebbing from his broken body, Sal hissed, "I knew it was you. You broke my heart..."

"Shut up, you," the not-so-dark figure said, giving Sal a swift kick in the ribs, "and *The Godfather* is overrated tripe."

Putting the ski mask back on, the dark figure disappeared into the night.

★   ★   ★   ★   ★

A SHORT time later, Terry O'Brien, he of Terry-Oke!, had just finished wrapping up his gear — a bunch of CDs, a couple of speakers and microphones, a half-dozen cords and wires, and "The Beast," a 200lb, 3ftx3ftx3ft rig that powered and ran the whole thing. In it was a power amp, a three-disc karaoke changer (top of the line!) and a fairly kick-ass mixer board. Everything, it seemed, except one cordless microphone, which had disappeared at some point during the previous six hours. A $150 expense he really couldn't afford, but broken/stolen mics, busted speakers and scratched CDs were all part and parcel of karaoke — the price of doing business.

And the price, all told — the system and its various accessories (song books, pencils, printing costs) — cost about $5,000, a chunk of change for someone so poor. But a living had to be made, and when one is qualified for little more than singing or digging ditches, singing wins every time. In fact, Terry was making a decent living at it.

Within a week of purchasing the system he had lassooed four gigs a week in four different bars and had absolutely no idea how to run the system. But a weekend spent hunkered down with the various owner's manuals had given him at least a working knowledge of rudimentary electronics and an even vaguer notion as to the voodoo of Japanese technology.

After years of being a pretty decent rock-and-roll singer for some of Cape May's most popular bands, karaoke wasn't quite the same. In fact, every time he fired up his fake band-in-a-box, he died a little. But the Cape May music scene wasn't quite what it was in the early-to-mid '90s (and honestly, at 36, it would be a little unseemly to still be covering Justin Timberlake songs).

With the Jersey Shore economic recession of the last few years (which, oddly enough, came on the heels of an unprecedented 10-year real estate boom), bars and clubs were less willing to shell out $1,000 for a live band, but were quite happy to pay $200 for a DJ. And because Terry-Oke! was a little of both, he got paid ju-u-u-u-st a bit more. Not *much*, but a little.

For years Terry had made his living as an actor or singer, or both. The previous year was the first in many that he had done neither, so karaoke seemed a logical transition. Painful, but logical. And honestly, it wasn't SO bad. He'd made a lot of great new friends and got to drink for just about free. And though there was something just a little soulless in being a karaoke guy, with a wife and three kids counting on him at home a living was a living. And he still got to sing a lot in front of people, which was all he really wanted anyway.

He stacked the last box on top of the last crate on top of the TV. Done for another night.

"Be right back, Dwight!" he yelled across the bar to the manager of the Mug. "Gotta get my car!"

Dwight grunted with a nod and a wave.

"Nice talking to you," Terry joked as he stepped into the night. It was almost 3am now, and the unseasonable chill had grown unseasonablier as Terry's breath plumed before him. "Chilly," he said to himself, then felt a bit silly for thinking out loud.

It had been a three-beer, two-Jameson's night, which dulled the cold a little, but his nose began to run anyway. He fished through his much-derided fanny pack for his keys and approached the public restroom, behind which his car, a piece of crap '93 Honda Accord on its third transmission that burst at the seams when laden with all his karaoke gear, was parked.

Concentrating on the mess of keys in his hands and still feeling the fine Irish buzz in his head, he didn't notice the shattered glass crunching beneath his feet, the pool of crimson liquid staining his shoes, or the dead body of his friend feet away.

"Gotcha!" he exclaimed, finding the right key, then felt silly again for thinking out loud. He got in the car, turned the key, blasted the heat and put it in reverse. Swinging the wheel around and flipping on the headlights, he noticed the carnage before him.

"The hell?"

Putting it in park he stepped out, surveyed the scene, then very much wished he'd had a third Jameson's.

★　★　★　★　★

THE dark figure watched as the police and ambulance crews arrived at the grisly scene. Step one of his plan had been executed, along with that insufferable doo-wop singer. In a few weeks it would all be over, but for now there was more work to do — an hour or two to celebrate, perhaps, then back to the grindstone.

"One down," he whispered to himself, then felt a little silly for thinking out loud.

Off into the night he went, the plan spun itself around in his head, over and over. It was ruthless and flawless, but most importantly...

TERRY-OKE! HAD TO BE STOPPED.

CHAPTER 2
Officer Steve On The Scene

ERRY O'Brien (Terry-Oke! to his followers) sat on the bumper of the police cruiser, wrapped in a thick blanket, a cup of coffee steaming before him, the shock of the night's grisly discovery still fresh on his face. It wasn't every day one discovered one's good friend lying dead in the handicapped parking spot.

It was just past 5am, about two hours since he had blindly (and a little drunkenly) stumbled through the crime scene. Morning hinted at the edge of the night sky. A police officer approached him from near the body which was now, thankfully, covered. Terry noticed, a little perturbed, that a small crowd had begun to form on the fringes of the DO NOT CROSS police tape cordoning off the area. He frowned.

"Pascal," the police officer said, startling him a bit, "Officer Steve Pascal. Pleased to meet you."

Terry shook the hand offered him and answered, "Terry O'Brien."

Officer Pascal smiled. "I know who you are, you're all over the place with this karaoke thing. What do you do, five nights a week now?"

"Six," Terry corrected wearily.

"Wow, six, that's a lot of karaoke."

"You're telling me."

Cape May Police Department Officer Steve Pascal was not an intimidating figure as cops went — 5' 6", maybe 5' 7" — but his sleek, sinewy build and flat-top haircut made an unmistakable impression: underestimate at your own risk.

Hitching up his pants and thick officer's belt, Steve cast a sideways glance at Terry. "You know I'm a bit of a singer myself."

"Really," Terry responded without joy.

"Sure. Why, back in high school I…"

"Do you have any idea who may have done this?" Terry interrupted a little brusquely, trying to nip this 10,000th "I'm a singer, too!" story in the bud.

A little crestfallen, Officer Steve answered, "Actually, I was hoping you might be able to help me out with that, Mr O'Brien."

Terry was stunned: "Me? What could I possibly know?"

"Not sure," Officer Steve answered, handing him an object he'd been holding all along, but that Terry had just noticed. "Any chance you recognize this?"

He did at once — black, cylindrical, about eight inches long. "Sure I do. It's a cordless microphone. In fact, I think it's *my* cordless microphone. I was missing one when I packed up last night... I mean this morning... I mean... after work. Sorry, it's been a long night... morning."

Officer Steve nodded. "I understand, the shock and all. Must be tough."

"Yeah," Terry replied. "Anyway, luckily the cordless system came with two mics, otherwise I'd a been screwed. Hey, what's this gray stuff stuck in the on/off switch?"

Officer Steve hesitated. "Oh that, that's nothing."

Terry fixed a stink-eye on him, "Bull — what is it?"

Clearing his throat Officer Steve answered, "Brains."

Terry blinked, "Pardon?"

"Brains. Sal's brains."

"I... don't think I understand."

Officer Steve spoke slowly, loudly. "Those are Sal's brains. He was beaten to death with this microphone last night... I mean this morning... a little while ago. You're right, it *has* been a long night."

"Indeed," Terry said. Then he fainted.

★　★　★　★　★

MOMMY!" he shouted and bolted upright, pulling an ab. Officer Steve put a hand on his shoulder. "Easy, Mr O'Brien. You just fainted."

"D-d-d-didn't faint."

"You did," Officer Steve corrected. "I know it can be traumatic. Take a moment to..."

"D-d-d-didn't faint," Terry tersely replied. "Vaso-vagel."

"Come again?"

"Vaso-vagel Syndrome... blood pressure spikes... under stress... body shuts down... not faint... Vaso-vagel."

"Sure," Officer Steve replied, helping him up. "Vaso-vagel Syndrome."

An EMT, having witnessed the spell, trotted over. "You guys okay?"

Officer Steve waved him off. "We're fine, he just had a panic attack."

Terry glared at him.

"Your call, officer," the EMT offered and went away.

Officer Steve slowly led them over to the main strip of the Washington Street Mall, to a bench just outside of the Ugly Mug restaurant and bar. Just seeing the place gave Terry a bad feeling.

After a long sit, Officer Steve asked, "Feeling better?"

Terry took a deep, calming breath. "Yeah, a little."

To someone who'd never vageled, it was difficult to describe exactly how horrible an experience it was. First, one had to do or see something traumatic, like get a needle in the eye or witness the birth of a child, both of which had set Terry off in the not-too-distant past. Next, the stress of the trauma spikes the blood pressure. The brain, not knowing why the blood pressure has spiked, assumes something terrible has happened to the body and shuts down the whole operation until things normalize. Thus the loss of consciousness... or fainting, as it were. When one wakes up, one is covered in a tart, cold sweat, and if one is lucky, one hasn't soiled one's pants.

"Neat trick," Terry said.

Officer Steve beamed. "Yeah, sorry about that, but I really needed to see your reaction to the murder weapon."

"I figured."

"And seeing as how most murderers don't faint..."

"Vagel."

"...Vagel upon seeing their handiwork, I believe I've eliminated you as a suspect."

This caught Terry's attention. "I was a suspect?"

Officer Steve answered, "Well, you know, first on the scene, last person to see him alive, opportunity and, well, he *was* killed with your microphone."

Terry nodded. "Sure, makes sense. I've seen enough *NYPD Blue* episodes to know how it works. I'd expect you to ask the same of Sal if that were me lying over there with my head... never mind."

A second officer brought them fresh cups of joe from the Bank Street Wawa.

"Thanks, Gus," Officer Steve said to him.

"No problem," Gus answered and went back to work the crime scene.

Steve gave Terry a coffee. "So, think I can ask you a few questions now?"

Terry took a sip, burnt his tongue. "Sure." Ouch! Dammit!

"How long had you known Mr Riggi?"

Terry sighed. "About a year, since I started my business last May."

"I see," Officer Steve scribbled in his cop's notebook, "and in that time, have you ever known Mr Riggi..."

"Sal."

"Pardon?"

Terry choked up a bit, the loss of his friend now settling in. "His name was Sal. Everybody knows... *knew* him as Sal. He was loved."

"I see." The officer gave him a moment. "So, Sal, ever known him to have any enemies?"

"Well," Terry considered, "he was a Republican."

"I see," Officer Steve nodded and made a note.

"Other than that," Terry continued, "I just don't know."

Officer Steve tried a different tack. "Okay, Sal was loved, nice guy, that I get. But let's just throw all logic out the window and take any possible idea to its illogical end."

Terry was confused... and hungry. "I'm afraid I don't follow."

Officer Steve explained. "Is there anyone, anyone at all, in the most ridiculously minute way, that would benefit from Sal being gone? Anyone?"

Terry considered this. Sal was a nice guy, but he wasn't without his quirks. He "owned" a lot of very popular karaoke songs, meaning no one but Sal was "allowed" to sing them. It was a courtesy Terry had extended to a number of singers who supported him regularly, but none more so than Sal.

"I suppose..." he started.

"Yes?" Officer Steve prodded.

"I suppose if I were a mentally deranged karaoke singer who wished he could sing "Runaround Sue" or "Mack the Knife", I might want Sal out of the way."

"I see," Officer Steve said. "Anyone you know fit that description?"

Terry answered, "Well..."

From the notebook of CMPD Officer Steve Pascal...

Potential suspects, Riggi homicide, as per T. O'Brien, friend of the victim:

Will Knapp — Local musician, karaoke singer. Had mildly inappropriate attachment to "Mack the Knife," a song performed exclusively by Mr Riggi. According to Mr O'Brien, had more than one verbal conflict with Mr Riggi over said song, most ending with Mr Knapp proclaiming Mr Riggi a "doody-head."

"Well, that's a start. Anything, anyone else you can think of?"

"Hmm," Terry hmmed. "If we're going to really stretch things, I guess that anyone who was really tired of hearing "Mack the Knife" or "Runaround Sue" might want to do away with him."

"I see," Officer Steve offered, "and what kinds of people might those be?"

"Oh, you know, people who are at my shows a lot. My regulars, bartenders, wait staff... I could see how they might, you know, go a little crazy hearing the same songs over and over again."

"Uh-huh," Steve made a note, "and would... you... be one of those people?"

"Would I what?"

Officer Steve explained, "Well, as the host you hear these songs more than anyone right, almost every night? Isn't it conceivable that it could drive you a little crazy?"

Terry sighed deeply. "I suppose, but that's a dirty trick. Hey, what are you writing?"

From the notebook of CMPD Officer Steve Pascal...
Terry O'Brien — karaoke host, fat. Doesn't seem dangerous, but eyes a little shifty... and quite a lovely shade of green. Note to self: look into tinted contacts. Mr O'Brien had the opportunity and now a motive, though he doesn't look to be in any kind shape to actually kill someone. Note to self: no more McDonald's.

"Just exploring every avenue," Officer Steve said.

Terry tossed the coffee into a trash can. "Wonderful."

"Now, is there anything, *anything* else that comes to mind?"

"Let me think," Terry answered, a little too curtly, then really began to let two-plus-two equal 22.

Sal had been pretty militant in his opposition to the recent New Jersey smoking ban, claiming it to be a violation of a smoker's basic civil rights. Terry happened to agree with him, but was not quite as vociferous. Sal also happened to recently join North Beach Gym in North Cape May, where he endeavored to continue a remarkable weight-loss effort that had seen him drop from almost 600lbs to a shade under 300lbs. But the gym was owned and operated by a militant non-smoker and left-wing liberal — Sal's polar opposite.

Terry answered, "Let me ask you, Officer Steve, if you owned a gym and were an anti-smoking advocate and leaned a little to the left of Ted Kennedy and one of your new members was a big Ronald Reagan nut and constantly complained about the hypocrisy of a smoking ban in front of your health-conscious clientele while sweating all over your cardio machines... would that bother you a little?"

From the notebook of CMPD Officer Steve Pascal...
Mark Chamberlain — owner, North Beach Gym. According to Mr O'Brien, he and Mr Riggi had butted heads repeatedly over politics, religion, the usual. Also bald, which might further fuel rage. Note to self: if Mr Riggi and Mr Chamberlain had a child, I think it might look a lot like Mr O'Brien.

"We're wrapping it up here, Steve," Officer Gus announced.

"Thanks, Gus."

"Can I go now?" Terry asked.

Steve reviewed his notes. Terry noticed a little smile as he finished.

"What's so funny?"

"Uh, nothing," Steve lied, "but to answer your question, yes, we're done here."

Terry stood up, handed him the blanket. "Fantastic."

Officer Steve gave him a card, "My work, home and cell numbers are on there. If you think of anything, feel free to call me."

"Sure thing, no problem." *Is he hitting on me?*

"Stay reachable," Officer Steve said then walked away.

Relieved, Terry wasn't quite sure what to do next, so he pulled his cell-phone from his fanny-pack. Forty-five minutes later, having called Sal's karaoke buddies, he went back to his car. Two police cruisers were still there, but Sal was not.

What a shame, he thought.

Getting into the Honda he realized that, in all the excitement, he had forgotten to pull around to the Mug and load out his karaoke equipment.

"Dammit!"

Cursing himself, he swung around and backed the car on to the mall's brick pavers to within a few feet of the Mug's front door (quite illegally and in the presence of several police officers). He popped out and knocked on the door. The Mug's cleaning service was there to let him in.

"I'll just be a minute," he said to the man sweeping the floor.

"H'okay," the man replied.

The Beast (the main karaoke rig — about 200lbs) always went first. Heaviest to lightest he had trained himself, figuring if he did the opposite he'd never have the strength to lug The Beast to his car. Plus, if he was going to have a heart attack, The Beast is what would trigger it, and why die after carrying everything else out? A waste of energy.

He grabbed The Beast's silver handles and girded himself — one, two, three... *hoit!*

The permanently pulled muscles on his left side popped again, but he'd grown relatively accustomed to that, as he had with the shooting pain now flaring down his left leg and the dull ache in his right achilles. The pain in his left elbow was new, but not yet excruciating, so he didn't worry about it as he inched his way to the door. The phrase YOU'RE NEXT, etched into the top of The Beast by a very sharp object, on the other hand, was quite alarming.

"Gah!" Terry shouted as The Beast crashed to the floor and spilled its electronic guts.

Holy crap, I'm next! he thought first. *Holy crap, I need a new karaoke system!* he thought second.

IVE days had elapsed since Sal Riggi's murder had rocked the small beach town of Cape May. Happening as it did right outside the Ugly Mug restaurant and on the town's most famous thoroughfare, the Washington Street Mall, more than a few brows were knitted. Cape May witnessed a few random acts of aggression every year, most of them stemming from tourists (and more than a few locals) getting their beer muscles on and flexing nuts. But real acts of violence, like murder, were rare. Cape May was a ridiculously safe place to live.

But the "Riggi Homicide", as it became known, made the headlines of all the local papers, made page three of the *Press Of Atlantic City*, and even rated a mid-section paragraph in both the *Philadelphia Inquirer* and *Daily News* (home of the best sports section in the country) because it was such an odd thing to happen in Cape May. But beyond that, nobody seemed too concerned, figuring it as just an act of heartless violence, by a drifter, probably, and nothing more. Philly, of course, saw more murders in a week than Cape May did in a decade, but that's neither here nor there.

This theory was, in its own way, good for Cape May — the summer season was just ramping up and the last thing the townspeople and Mall merchants needed were rumors of a serial killer floating around. God forbid...

So by the time Friday came, no one in nearby Rio Grande gave much of a rip about what had happened to one rich guy in Cape May. Anything bad happened to anyone there in Snootyville, they probably deserved it.

Rio Grande was the literal rock in a hard place, lying almost exactly between the Victorian grandeur of Cape May and the backwards-baseball-cap-wearing Wildwood (Cape May's younger brother who never listened and always seemed to get into some kind of trouble). Rio Grande had no shore and no beachfront property to foist upon the unsuspecting public at hundreds of times its actual value, but it did have the only Wal-Mart within 30 miles, and it had the Rio Station restaurant.

Rio Station ("The Rio" to the locals) was an excellent, family-owned joint that offered a little of everything, but leaned slightly towards the

Italian. After more than 20 years of being surrounded by an abandoned factory, rusted-out railroad cars and general squalor, it now sat squarely in the middle of Cape May County's newest (and biggest and best) shopping center as the slow, steady creep of gentrification swallowed South Jersey, bite by bite. Not that there was anything wrong with having a gleaming new shopping center in Rio Grande, but like many New Yorkers who now reflect fondly on the sin and decadence that was Times Square, so, too, did many Rio Grande-ites deem it somehow more noble to live in a slum.

To each their own.

Word on the street was that Rick, the owner of the Rio, was considering selling to one of the big chain restaurants like TGI Friday's or Applebee's, which would make his partners very happy, but would take away yet another family-owned business from an area that was losing them rapidly (hello Home Depot, goodbye Mom and Pop). But Rick told anyone who would listen that the rumor was false. No matter how tempting it might be, the Rio was not going anywhere.

The dark figure stood off to the side, observing carefully. If he was going to continue his plan tonight he would have to be wary — the Rio Station was buzzing, the dining room full, the bar three-deep. But he could care less about the diners — hungry people had to eat. The people in the bar, though, were there for one reason and one reason only — karaoke. And there was simply no excuse for that.

"Get you something?" the bartender, Tammy, asked cheerfully despite the noise and the heat.

The dark figure shook his head.

Tammy sensed otherwise. "You sure? It's going to get hot in here tonight."

The dark figure considered this. "A pint of anything light... and a Jameson's neat."

Tammy winked and went to it.

Just one, the dark figure thought, *to calm my nerves*.

Five hours later the bar was still packed and hot, the karaoke was still going full-blast, and the dark figure was dead-ass drunk.

★ ★ ★ ★ ★

ONE week later the dark figure sat at the bar at Rio Station, sipping club soda, chewing on the ice, biding his time. The karaoke clowns sang song after ear-piercing song as the clock approached midnight. Karaoke (Terry-Oke! the idiot called himself) was only scheduled to go till 11pm, but a full, steady bar and a never-ending supply of people willing to embarrass themselves in front of an audience made for a target-rich environment, so the bastards added an extra hour.

But the dark figure wasn't worried — what was 60 minutes more when making the world a better place, one dead karaoke singer at a time? Then he saw her, his mark for the evening.

The host announced, "And now, for your listening pleasure, Brandi, Brandi, Brandi!"

The attractive brunette stepped up to the mic to enthusiastic applause as the opening chords of David Allen Coe's "You Never Even Called Me By My Name" belched out of the speakers.

The dark figure hated this song, as he did most country and western, but this song deserved a special place in hell's jukebox, because this song, for whatever reason, compelled people to say unspeakable things.

And not just say them, but SHOUT them, at the top of their lungs, in a public place.

The dark figure steadied himself as the chorus approached.

Brandi sang, "And you don't have to call me darling..."

The crowd chanted, "B____! C___! S___!"

"Darling..."

"You f_____ wh___!"

Brandi finished, "You never even called me by my name!"

The crowd screamed, "What's my name, what's my m_____ f____ __ name!"

Four minutes later the song ended and the crowd went berserk. The dark figure could hardly stand it. He watched as Brandi waved to the crowd, exchanged a few words and a peck on the cheek with the host and walked out the door.

This was his cue. Heart pumping, adrenaline spiking, he rose, dropped a few dollars on the bar, and followed her out.

★ ★ ★ ★ ★

BRANDI Fossett loved the Rio Station for several reasons — it was not Cape May, so one could order three drinks, hand the bartender a $20 note and actually get change; the clientele, mostly hard-working Joes out to blow off some steam after a hard week's work, was more up her alley (as a Maine girl she knew the value of an honest day's pay for an honest day's work); and because they went apeshit when she sang David Allen Coe.

She tilted back the last of her Coors Lite and waited anxiously, as she always did, for the host to call her by her name. Brandi was a charter member of Terry-Oke! Nation (host Terry O'Brien's most loyal followers). To achieve citizenship one had only to do three things: come to at least three gigs a week, spend a little money when you did, and bring a friend or two. Those who did received "Most Favored Nation" status and were afforded such perks as "owned" songs, "cut-in-line" privileges and the occasional drink "on Terry" — okay, so Terry also got those drinks for free, but what his constituents didn't know wouldn't hurt them. After all, the appearance of magnanimity was almost as important as the magnanimity itself.

Sure, it was all a little silly to the outsider, but the people of Terry-Oke! Nation appreciated it, and every society needs a little order.

Finally, he announced, "And now, for your listening pleasure, Brandi, Brandi, Brandi!"

The brief rush of euphoria that enveloped her every time her name was called lifted her from her seat and to the stage, though it wasn't so much a stage as a corner of the bar where all of the karaoke crap would fit — but beggars couldn't be choosers.

Taking the microphone from the stand, she watched the TV screen and waited for her cue. She was dressed modestly — jeans and a white V-neck tee, but no matter what she wore, the eye was always drawn to the ornate antler-like tattoos that adorned her cleavage and, as far as anyone could tell, points nether.

Yes, Brandi had a rack on her rack.

The little yellow blocks on the monitor counted down and she began to sing. She wasn't an especially trained or accomplished vocalist, but what she *was* was fun; a rowdy bar singer in a town with too few of them. When it was over, the crowd was hooting and hollering, stomping their feet, banging their beer mugs on the bar.

Yes! Brandi thought and turned to Terry.

"You're a hit," he said, smiling, setting up the next song.

"Why thank you," she said with false modesty. "I do what I can."

"Just a sec," he said, "and now, ladies and gentlemen, let's have a warm, warm Rio Station welcome for Steve, Nate and Johnny B!"

Three men staggered to the stage.

He said, "Sorry, still gotta work. You out?"

She nodded, a sneaky little smile on her face. "Yeah, I've got... someone waiting for me at home. And I have early work tomorrow."

She leaned in and gave him a peck on the cheek.

"See you at the Mug!" she yelled into his ear over the din of the several drunken Coast Guardsmen sing-shouting "Friends in Low Places."

Terry returned the peck. "Cool, thanks! It was a fun night! That Black-Eyed Peas song is a hoot!"

Brandi laughed. "I can't believe you made me sing 'My Humps'!"

Terry shrugged. "Like to mix things up once in a while! And with humps like those, why not? 'Night!"

"'Night!" she answered, grinning, then quickly grew solemn and held a hand over her heart.

Terry understood at once. "Sal."

"Sal," she replied, then left.

Sal's loss two weeks prior had been a minor news story everywhere north of Exit 4, but to Terry-Oke! Nation it had been devastating.

Terry watched her leave (not an altogether unpleasant activity) then cast his eyes back to the bar, where Officer Steve Pascal, lead investigator on the Riggi homicide, sat in dark plain clothes, sipping O'Doul's from a glass, looking for all the world like just another guy out to tie one on at the end of the week. His presence was comforting to Terry, but also a little disquieting — a reminder of the words YOU'RE NEXT etched on to his karaoke machine the same night as Sal's murder.

But he hadn't been next — yet — and if he and his undercover friend could help it, he never would be.

At that moment Officer Steve caught his eye and mouthed, "Gotta whiz." Terry nodded and watched him leave (not an altogether unpleasant activity, if so inclined). It was a few minutes before midnight, almost quitting time. Terry loved his Fridays at the Rio. At 7-11 (or 12) it was his earliest gig and allowed him to get home early for a decent night's sleep, or, more likely, to get out early enough for drinks with friends at Martini Beach. And now that he thought of it, he had to take a whiz, too.

★ ★ ★ ★ ★

BRANDI strutted out of the Rio Station, her step lightened by the appreciative crowd, and lit the cigarette she'd been dying to have for the last 45 minutes. The side exit of the Rio emptied into a small parking area where there were no lights. This pleased the dark figure.

Not wanting to stink up her new truck, Brandi sat on the short brick retaining wall and puffed on the Marlboro Light. It was still a little cool for June as a chill shot through her, but she knew that soon she'd be begging for nights like this.

"Spare a smoke?" the dark figure asked out of nowhere.

A little startled, Brandi answered, "Uh... sure."

The dark figure took the cigarette. He knew that by standing backlit by the only floodlight, Brandi would be unable to see his face. That, and he was wearing a black ski mask.

"'Preciate it," he said and lit it, dragged deeply. "Nice night, eh?"

Brandi was wary. "Very."

She wanted to snuff out her smoke and leave, but didn't want the stranger to know she was nervous. So she sat and silently willed her cigarette to burn faster.

"Mind if I sit?" the dark figure asked.

The dark figure uncapped a small bottle, snatched Brandi by the hair, and poured the contents down her throat. Whatever the liquid was, it burned.

"Umm..."

Without waiting for an answer he sat, uncomfortably close to her on the retaining wall.

"I'm sorry," she said, "do I know..."

The knife plunged twice into her chest before she knew what was happening. Surprised, she looked down as the blood stains bloomed, "My... my humps..."

"Please," the dark figure said, ripping off the ski mask, "your last moments on Earth and that's what you say? You karaoke people... I'm doing the world a service."

Brandi recognized the dark figure at once and it all started to make a little sense.

"And a little something for that dirty little mouth of yours."

The dark figure uncapped a small bottle, snatched Brandi by the hair, and poured the contents down her throat. Whatever the liquid was, it burned.

"Why?" she managed to whisper, heat and fire spreading through her mouth and throat.

"Because..." the dark figure answered, raising the knife, "I!"

Slikt!

"HATE!"

Slikt!

"KARAOKE!"

Slikt!

And it was done.

"Thank you and goodnight," the dark figure said to himself, then felt a bit silly for thinking out loud.

The evening's task completed, the dark figure tossed the ski mask, knife and small vial into the bushes and skulked back into the bar, the last few measures of Garth Brooks blaring from the speakers.

It made him just want to kill everybody...

CHAPTER 4
The Usual Suspects

RIO GRANDE, NJ—For the second time in three weeks, Cape May County was shocked by a murder. Last night Brandi Fossett, US Coast Guard member and aspiring hairstylist, was stabbed to death outside the Rio Station restaurant in Rio Grande. This shocking event follows the murder of Villas resident Salvador Riggi, who was bludgeoned to death outside the Ugly Mug restaurant on May 22.

Police investigating the deaths do not believe the two are linked, despite the so-called "karaoke connection" (each was killed shortly after leaving a karaoke bar, and they were acquaintances). Ms Fossett recently graduated cum laude from the prestigious Cape Cosmetology School. Mr Riggi, an entrepreneur, was on the verge of a new patent in geological engineering at the time of his death.

Said lead investigator Steve Pascal of the CMPD, "We are positive the two are unrelated. Without going into detail, the crime scenes are different enough that we believe one had nothing to do with the other. Most serial killers have a certain M.O. These show none of those characteristics."

Rumors have been swirling since the discovery of Ms Fossett's body that a "Karaoke Killer" may be on the loose. Officer Pascal denies any such claim.

Said Officer Pascal, "This is not, repeat, this is not the work of one man."

HIS is the work of one man," Officer Steve told the mayor. The mayor, an unkempt sort stuffed behind his desk, was confused. "But you told the paper..."

"A lie, sir," Officer Steve confessed, "to make the killer think we're not on to him, but he probably already knows that we are. Probably wants us to be."

The mayor was flummoxed. "But..."

"Do you want a panic right before summer, sir?"

The mayor's face turned an unhealthy shade of red. He stewed silently before standing up and pacing before his enormous oak desk. He was a first-term Cape May mayor, and as such he wanted what every first-term mayor wants — a second term.

"This is bad, Steve."

"I'm aware of that, sir."

"I mean, Riggi... did you read the hospital report? Strokes, heart attacks, diabetes... he had death on speed dial. But this girl, young and pretty... not good."

"Yes, sir."

The mayor swept a beefy hand across his balding pate. "Okay, so... do we have any idea who's doing this?"

Steve hesitated. "A few, sir."

"Is that a no?" the mayor asked.

Steve shrugged. "More of a maybe."

"So," the mayor said, folding his thick arms in front of his chest, "tell me what you have on the Riggi thing."

"It's all right here," Officer Steve said, popping a cassette in the small boombox on the mayor's desk. He pressed "play".

The following is a transcript from an interview conducted by Officer Steve Pascal with Riggi homicide suspect Mark Chamberlain...

STEVE PASCAL: So you know we're being recorded.

MARK CHAMBERLAIN: Yes, I know. George Bush is still in the White House, isn't he? We're all being recorded, man.

SP: Nonetheless, where were you on the morning of May 22, at approximately 2am?

MC: *(Pause)...* I was out — with friends.

SP: Okay... names? Addresses?

MC: *(Pause)...* I'd rather not say. The CIA is listening, I wouldn't want to get anyone in trouble.

SP: Right, but... you understand this is a homicide investigation, Mr Chamberlain?

MC: Of course, duh.

SP: Don't you "duh" me. Did you hate Sal Riggi?

MC: Hate is a strong word.

SP: Would you mind, then, telling me then the nature of your relationship with Mr Riggi?

MC: He was a valued customer.

SP: And a Republican.

MC: *(Swallows hard...)* It's a free country, for now. George Bush is just shredding the Constitution, warrantless wiretaps, false intelligence...

SP: Right, right... but you didn't like that Sal was a Republican, did you?

MC: Sal paid for a three-year membership up front, in cash. I loved him.

SP: But not his politics.

MC: Doesn't mean I killed him. *(Under his breath)*... As much as I may have liked to...

SP: Pardon?

MC: Nothing.

SP: No, please, share.

MC: Look, Sal and I did not see eye-to-eye on a lot of things, but he made a commitment to losing weight and bettering his health. Politics aside, I respected that.

SP: But?

MC: *(Explodes)*... But he just wouldn't shut up about the goddamn smoking ban! Smokers' rights this and civil rights that... and he always smelled like a cigar... you know what that does to a place full of sweaty people? It isn't pleasant, I'll tell you that.

SP: So you didn't get along, he was a threat to your customer base and you won't give me an alibi. Ever hear of opportunity and motive, Mr Chamberlain?

MC: I watch *Law and Order*.

SP: Then you can see where this is going?

MC: *(Begins sweating profusely)*... I... I... I...

SP: It's okay, Mr Chamberlain, you can tell me.

MC: I... I... I...

SP: Did it?

MC: No! I was at McDonald's! The Cape May Courthouse McDonald's, okay? The damn thing is open 24 hours — how could I *not* go! I mean, it's like the siren's song from Hercules...

SP: *The Odyssey*...

MC: Whatever, one of those stupid Norse myths.

SP: Greek. But I think I see what you're getting at.

OFFICER Steve turned off the tape player and told the mayor, "I checked both employees working at McDonald's that morning and they said they recognized him. Said they'd never forget him. He had four Big Macs, three large fries, two hot fudge sundaes... and a Diet Coke."

The mayor sighed, "Skinny people, so angry inside."

Officer Steve continued, "He asked me to keep this confidential. If his clients knew he was binging and purging McDonald's four times a week, it might take a little gild off his lily."

"Understandable," said the mayor, perplexed. "You can count on my discretion. Anyone else?"

Steve pushed "play".

The following is a transcript from an interview conducted by Officer

Steve Pascal with Riggi homicide suspect Will Knapp...

WILL KNAPP: What the hell is this? I have to get to work. I only get 45 minutes for lunch.

STEVE PASCAL: Who do you work for?

WK: Whom.

SP: Pardon?

WK: *Whom* do you work for.

SP: My apologies, Mr Knapp. Whom do you work for?

WK: Myself.

SP: Then maybe you can talk to your boss.

WK: Funny.

SP: You know why you're here?

WK: Maybe.

SP: You know Sal Riggi?

WK: Yes, I know Sal "Hog All the Good Songs" Riggi. Sal "No One Else in the World Can Sing Mack the Knife" Riggi. Sure, I know him, Mr Sal "Enough With the Doo-Wop Already" Riggi.

SP: I sense a little tension?

WK: It's just... would it kill him to let someone else sing "Mack the Knife" every once in a while?

SP: *(Drops Polaroids on table)*... Apparently it would.

WK: Oh my god!

SP: Did you do this, Will?

WK: What? Me? I would never...

SP: You were heard, in public, calling Mr Riggi a doody-head because he wouldn't let you sing "Mack the Knife", weren't you?

WK: Well, yeah, but...

SP: You did do it, didn't you? Sal told you "No!" one time too many, and in your screwed-up little karaoke world you snapped, and you killed him didn't you? Didn't you?! Admit it!

WK: *(Calmly)*... A little theatrical, no?

SP: *(Pauses)*... A little. Just for effect. No good?

WK: No, no, it was good, but the whole good cop, bad cop thing really needs two cops, otherwise it's just, you know... one schizophrenic cop.

SP: I hear you. So, did you kill Sal?

WK: No.

SP: Want to prove it?

WK: Sure. Here. *(Officer Steve examines the evidence.)* So I guess I get to sing "Mack the Knife" now.

SP: Looks like.

WK: Huh... funny, not that I can't sing it. I don't really want to. Guess it was that whole "want what you can't have it" thing that made me want it so bad.

SP: Pfft... such a baby.

Officer Steve turned off the tape player. "That's when he handed me this ticket stub from the midnight showing of *The Da Vinci Code* at the Bayshore 8."

The mayor didn't quite get it. "But the murder took place a little after 2am."

Steve said, "Have you seen *The Da Vinci Code*, sir? It's a wee bit, shall we say, sloooooooooooow."

"So where does that leave us?"

Officer Steve pressed "play".

The following is a transcript from an interview conducted by Officer Steve Pascal with Riggi homicide suspect Terry O'Brien...

TERRY O'BRIEN: Haven't we been over this?

STEVE PASCAL: Just a formality, get it on tape.

TO: *(Annoyed grunt)...* Okay.

SP: So please, tell me, where were you at 2am on Monday morning, May 22?

TO: Inside the Ugly Mug, packing up my karaoke equipment.

SP: And, as far as you know, the words "You're Next" were NOT yet etched into the lid of your karaoke case?

TO: I'm positive. The lid was under a table, three feet from me, from the time I started until the time I packed up, about 9:15 to about 2:05.

SP: And it was about this time, 2:05am, that you realized your cordless microphone, which turned out to be the murder weapon, was missing?

TO: Yes. We've covered this several times, Steve.

SP: Officer Steve.

TO: Come again?

SP: It's Officer Steve. I didn't put myself through the Police Academy and train my body into an electric jolt of unholy whoop-ass to be called "Steve".

TO: Ooookay...

SP: Now, there are witnesses to your actions?

TO: Yep.

SP: But there was no one who saw you after 2:05?

TO: No, that's when I discovered the body, called 911 from my cell, and stayed on the scene until you arrived.

SP: Thank you, Mr O'Brien.

TO: It's been a pleasure.

SP: We're going to catch whoever did this.

TO: Whomever.

SP: Pardon?

TO: *Whomever* did this.

SP: Of course. Whom. Why don't you see your own way out.

TO: Why don't you go and f... *CLICK!*

Officer Steve cleared his throat and shut off the tape.

"Tough nut, that one," the mayor smirked.

Officer Steve answered, "We'll see."

The mayor asked, "So this 'You're Next' business?"

Officer Steve explained, "After Mr O'Brien discovered the body, he called 911. Witnesses inside the Ugly Mug say he stayed on the scene until we arrived, but that just means they didn't see him after 2:05am. We arrived, interviewed and released him. When he went back to get his equipment, he allegedly found the phrase scratched into the plastic."

"But you don't believe him?"

Officer Steve paused. "Not sure. Right now he's the closest thing we have to a suspect."

The mayor continued, "So let me get this straight. You think he left the Mug, killed Mr Riggi, left the murder weapon on the scene, called the police and waited for you to arrive? All this after scratching 'You're Next' into his machine sometime earlier in the night?"

Out loud like that it did seem pretty implausible, Officer Steve had to admit. "That's one theory we're exploring. Yes, sir."

"I see," said the mayor. "Do you really like any of them for Riggi?"

Officer Steve thought a moment, then shook his head. "No. Chamberlain and Knapp have solid alibis, and O'Brien has no real motive. Why kill his most prolific singer?"

The mayor sighed. "So anything on the Fossett case yet?"

Officer Steve flipped open his cops' notebook. "I'll re-interview O'Brien — he was there when it happened, again. And he's actually pretty good at making existential leaps and creating suspects."

"How nice. Maybe I should put him on the case," the mayor joked.

Officer Steve did not see the humor. "There's one, fairly gruesome aspect to the Fossett case we haven't told anyone about yet, sir."

The mayor cocked an eyebrow. "Which is?"

"It seems the last song she sang that night involved quite a bit of foul language. And though the official cause of death is still the five stab wounds to the chest she received, this didn't help." Officer Steve dropped some Polaroids on his desk — the mayor went white.

"The killer, whoever he is, poured a liquid down Brandi's throat — we found an empty vial, the knife, and a black ski mask in some bushes near the scene. We believe the liquid was some kind of acid, burnt away her tongue and larynx. The killer, he was..."

The mayor looked faint. "Don't say it..."

Officer Steve nodded grimly. "He was washing her mouth out with soap, sir."

The mayor took a hard swallow, "We have to find this guy, Steve, and fast."

"I couldn't agree more, sir. We're looking at a couple other potentials."

"Go on."

"The woman, Janis, manages the Rio Station, we think she may have had a financial reason to do it. And an Edward Kohl, Cape May guy, cuts hair at Artizan Salon and Spa — he could have had good cause as well."

"Okay," the mayor said with finality. "Keep it up. And I want in the loop on every step of this investigation. Am I clear?"

"Crystal, sir."

"And for God's sake, Steve," the mayor fixed him with a hard stare, "Keep a lid on this damned thing, will you? The last thing we need is the press getting wind of it. That damn Jack Wright has had it out for me since five seconds after I got elected."

Officer Steve laughed derisively. "Elected? Please, sir. We are men of action — lies do not become us."

The mayor blanched. "I promise you, son, you'll make detective by August."

"I should hope so, sir," Officer Steve replied. "Until then... I'll catch who... whomever did this."

"Good man," the mayor said, and shook his hand vigorously. "Remember: no press."

Steve wiped his hand on his pants. "Absolutely, sir."

Exit Zero *headline the following morning:*

KARAOKE KILLER TERRORIZES CAPE MAY!

CAPE MAY, NJ—Sources tell Exit Zero *that the recent killings of Sal Riggi and Brandi Fossett are the work of one man, a man being dubbed "The Karaoke Killer." Though details are scarce, sources have confirmed to us that the karaoke connection is real, and the killings are the work of a serial killer, the first in Cape May's history. This paper will do its level best to bring you any and all information as it comes along. Visit our website (www.exitzero.us) for breaking news. And visit the* Exit Zero *shop for a lovely T-shirt or baseball cap. At Perry Street in Congress Hall, before Uncle Bill's Pancake House. — Jack Wright, Editor-in-Chief.*

CHAPTER 5
Edward Kohl at Cabanas

DWARD Kohl sat in Cabanas, a popular beachfront bar in Cape May, and took a cool drink from his sweaty bottle of Coors Lite. He enjoyed his beers, but this particular beer on this particular night tasted this much better. Having spent the last six hours in police custody, he had been looking forward to this beer for approximately five hours and 59 minutes. Officer Steve Pascal, the pitbull cop with the Brill-O haircut, had grilled him over and over about the death of Brandi Fossett, Edward's friend and fellow karaoke singer. In the end he finally convinced Officer Steve of his innocence, but after six hours locked in that room with him, even Edward wasn't sure anymore.

"Another?" Jon King, the tall, good-looking bartender with the unfortunate receding hairline, asked.

Edward nodded yes, "And a black Sambuca. Chilled. Up."

Jon cocked a handsome eyebrow, paused, and then began making the drinks. Jon saw more tail in the summer than the average horse-and-carriage driver, but this is not Jon's story. Edward wasn't much of a shot-and-a-beer guy, but whatever he could do to hasten the departure of the day's memories he would do, even if it meant a nasty hangover and a screaming need for McDonald's in the morning.

"That damn Steve Pascal..."

Six hours ago...

EDWARD drew nervously from the Winston 100 as he sat at the small metal table in the small room in police headquarters in City Hall. It had been over an hour since Officer Steve Pascal pulled into the parking lot at Artizan Salon & Spa, where Edward worked as a hairstylist, and asked if he could "come with me for a minute."

It was Wednesday and Edward had a full book. However, Artizan owner Suzanne Spiegel had given him the rest of the day off. He took a sip from the can of Diet Coke and took another deep drag from the cigarette. In front of him, Officer Steve paced, flipping through a folder, brow knitted.

The tension grew as the seconds ticked by. Unable to stand it, Edward blurted out, "I really don't know anything. Brandi was my friend. I had nothing to do with her getting... with what happened to her."

What happened to her was — after leaving the Rio Station she had been repeatedly stabbed, then had acid poured down her throat, the perpetrator's demented way of washing her mouth out after a profanity-laden karaoke performance.

Officer Steve shot him a look. "But there are a few things I'm still not clear on, so..."

Edward looked at his watch: 4:15pm.

Officer Steve saw this. "I wouldn't do that. Technically I can keep you here for 48 hours without cause. Clock-watching will only make it longer."

Edward blanched at the thought of two days in this spartan, poorly-decorated room. "But I've told you everything..."

"Sure you have," Officer Steve cut him off and pulled out his cop's notebook, "but from what I can see here you have no alibi for the time of the murder, and after talking with a few people, we think we know why you may have wanted Ms Fossett out of the way. So you can see why I'm a little vexed."

Edward's face grew red. He did, in fact, have an alibi, just not one he was willing to share with anyone at the moment. "What possible reason could I have to kill Brandi?"

Officer Steve smiled a bit. Edward had taken the cheese without noticing the giant metal spring about to snap on his neck.

"Well," Officer Steve answered, "we understand Ms Fossett had just finished cosmetology school at the time of her death. Is that right?"

Edward fidgeted. "Yeah, so?"

"We talked to her former instructors and a few of her ex-classmates, and you know what they told us?"

"No," Edward replied, unable to look him in the eye.

"They told us that she was a pretty damn good hairdresser, a regular prodigy her teacher called her. Let me look in my notes... here it is: A natural gift for cutting and fixing hair, like she was born with a blowdryer in one hand and scissors in the other." Officer Steve closed the notebook.

Edward took another swig of the Coke. "So, what does that have to do with me?"

"What indeed."

"Spiegel on line two," a second cop, Officer Gus, said as he popped in and out.

Officer Steve held up a finger. "Just a moment, please." He hit a button and they were on speakerphone. "Miss Spiegel?"

"Yes?" said Suzanne Spiegel, owner of Artizan Salon and Spa.

Officer Steve held a finger to his lips — Edward knew to keep quiet.

"Miss Spiegel," Officer Steve continued, "we have your employee, Edward Kohl, down here at the police station, asking him a few questions about some recent... events that have taken place."

"You mean the Karaoke Killer?" Suzanne asked.

"Is that what they're calling him?" Officer Steve chuckled, then lied, "Trust me, Miss Spiegel, there is absolutely no connection between the murders of Mr Riggi and Ms Fossett."

"Whatever you say," Suzanne replied.

"Anyway, Miss Spiegel, how long has Edward been in your employ."

Suzanne answered, "About five years."

Officer Steve continued, "I see. And in those five years, how would you rate Edward's performance as a hairstylist."

There was a pause. "We're not on speakerphone, are we?"

"Of course not," Officer Steve fibbed again.

Suzanne sighed deeply. "The thing is... I love Edward as a person, but as a hairstylist, he's just... I'm not sure how to put this..."

"Go on," Officer Steve encouraged, "it's just us two talking." He winked at Edward.

"Well," Suzanne continued, "when he first started out he was fantastic. People booked him six months, a year, in advance. He was the fresh, hot new thing. Like a rock star."

Officer Steve didn't quite get it but... "Okay..."

"But in the last year or so he's been... not quite as good as advertised. His client book has shrunk 60%, I've had to fight off three lawsuits from unhappy brides, and he takes a cigarette break every five minutes!"

"Any idea why the sudden change in him, Miss Spiegel."

She answered, "There's something different about him now, like something is missing."

At that moment it all clicked for Officer Steve, but he said nothing. "I see. And this is why you were planning on hiring Ms Fossett and firing Edward, correct?"

After a long pause, Suzanne quietly said, "Yes."

Edward looked like someone had smacked him on the ass.

"But it was the hardest decision I've ever had to make," Suzanne continued. "I love Edward."

"I understand," Officer Steve told her. "So... any idea why his performance dropped off so dramatically?"

Suzanne pondered this. "None. Except..."

"Yes?"

"Well, he did turn 40 last spring. He's no kid anymore."

Edward gasped.

"What was that?" Suzanne asked, panicked.

"Nothing," Officer Steve lied a third time. "Sip of coffee, burnt my tongue."

Suzanne paused, suspicious. "Okay, um, I should get back to work now."

"Sure," Officer Steve said, "and you know that contraband Guatemalan lizard-tongue Faux-Tox you've been selling to rich old ladies out of your back room? Get rid of it, it doesn't work."

Suzanne asked, "But how would you..."

"It. Doesn't. Work," Officer Steve replied firmly and hung up the phone. Fixing Edward with a stare he said, "Seems to me keeping one's 'rock star' status and hot reputation would be two pretty good reasons to do away with an up-and-coming young hair-cutter like Ms Fossett, wouldn't you agree?"

Edward said nothing. He knew he was cornered, but if he told the truth he'd be ruined as a stylist forever.

Officer Steve said, "Admittedly, I don't have enough to hold you on right now, Mr Kohl, but I'm going to keep you here anyway. We're going to go over and over this until you convince me you didn't do it."

Officer Steve knew he didn't do it, but he had five hours left on his shift and it was hot outside.

Edward sagged in his chair. "Okay."

"But before we start, Mr Kohl," Officer Steve finished, "may I just say... that is one beautiful head of hair."

Edward grinned like a schoolgirl.

Nine hours later...

ON STAGE at Cabanas, Edward was singing the last few notes of his signature song, "Love Changes Everything" by Andrew Lloyd Weber. The medical plight of his ex-boyfriend, Bob, added a little extra emotional heft to the already emotional song for Edward. But tonight his heart was even heavier with a secret hurt, one that he could never divulge or he'd never work again.

Next to him, ever vigilant at the karaoke machine, stood Terry O'Brien, who was also hurting at the loss of his friends. Two in three weeks — it was almost more than they could bear.

Edward was a relative newbie to the karaoke world, only a year ago discovering that not only did he indeed have a voice but he had quite a good one. But there was very little karaoke in Cape May, so the chance to show off and hone his pipes came few and far between. But then... Terry-Oke!

Edward was singing the last few notes of his signature song... tonight his heart was even heavier with a secret hurt, one he could never divulge.

Edward was a charter member of Terry-Oke! Nation, and as such was afforded all the luxuries that came with it —"owned" songs, favorable rotation position, and the occasional free beer.

He and Terry had been acquaintances for a number of years — they once waited tables in the same restaurant, Henry's on the Beach, for a summer (if you go, have the chicken mascarpone), and Terry had long since trusted only Edward to cut his balding pate, a job Edward could do in about 90 seconds, but in order to charge his full rate play-acted into 30 minutes. But it wasn't until the birth of Terry-Oke! that they had become true friends, Terry even allowing Edward to "steal" a few of his "owned" songs — one of which Edward was singing right now.

It had happened slowly, subtly, Edward first asking permission to sing along with him, having fallen in love with the lilting Broadway tune. A few weeks later it was, "Do you mind if I try it by myself?" A few weeks after that and all pretense of seeking permission was gone, and it had simply become Edward's song. The song Terry absolutely adored, the reason he futilely pursued a stage career for 18 years, the reason he bought the damn karaoke machine in the first place... gone!

But such was the life of the karaoke host. It seemed every song Terry acquired specifically for himself eventually got co-opted by somebody else. Sal Riggi had done the same with Bruce Springsteen's "No Retreat, No Surrender." Jerks.

"Love will never, never let you be... the saaaaaaaaaaaaaaaaaaaaaaaaaaaame..." Edward sang, the last note impossibly long and high, sang it out, to Bob, to Sal and to Brandi. The song ended, the crowd erupted, and Edward handed the mic back to his friend.

"Nicely done," Terry said, a thin smile pressed on his lips.

"Thanks, man," Edward replied, a hitch in his throat. "I better get going. I've had too much too drink."

"Be safe," Terry said, then in his best Jon Lovitz voice added, "The Karaoke Killer is on the loose!"

Edward smiled ruefully.

"Sorry, bud," Terry offered. "Guess it's too soon for that. I miss them, too."

Edward nodded. "I can't believe they're both gone..."

"For the record," Terry continued, "I think all this talk about a karaoke serial killer is insane. It's just a coincidence."

Edward said, "You're probably right. You still have a bodyguard?"

Terry nodded furtively towards the bar: at the far corner in a ridiculously obvious fake mustache and black turtleneck sat Officer Steve Pascal.

"How lame is that?" Terry asked, "and a freakin' turtleneck in June."

Edward said, "It worked. I spent all afternoon with him and didn't recognize him."

"Real ball-breaker, isn't he?"

Edward nodded. *But he likes my hair!* "Well, I better go. See you at the C-View tomorrow."

"Chin up, dude," Terry told him, kissed his cheek, then turned his attention back to work. "Steve Axelsson, it's your turn. Let's give him that warm, warm, Cabanas welcome!"

The crowd was silent as Edward shuffled past the tables and out the front door, to be replaced at the mic by Steve Axelsson. Steve was a handsome, affable young fella, a fisherman by trade and a closet karaoke junkie. Closeted in the hard-bitten, fish-stained company he usually kept, where it would never do to be an outed karaoke singer. He'd never hear the end of it.

He stepped on to the stage, "Thanks, Terry."

"No problem, m'man." Terry answered, handing him the mic. "Listen, I gotta take a whiz and catch a smoke, so I put some Skynyrd on for you."

"Cool!" Steve exclaimed and Terry walked away. The rubes were suckers for "Freebird."

★ ★ ★ ★ ★

THE dark figure watched Edward leave the stage and shuffle, oh-so-sadly, towards the front door. The baby. Edward had a secret, a secret the dark figure knew all about, despite Edward's pained, futile machinations to keep it hidden. He followed as Edward turned left down Decatur Street, towards the Mug and along one of the darkest stretches of sidewalk in town.

Just before the Merion Inn Edward stopped, lit a cigarette, flipped open his cellphone, and began tapping out a text message. As Edward puffed on the cigarette, his face bathed in the pale blue light of the cellphone, the dark figure saw his chance.

"Edward!" the dark figure called.

"Who is it?" said Edward.

"It's me," the dark figure said.

Edward saw the face. "You... what the heck? What are you... is that a fake..."

The scissors flashed across his throat. Jets of blood sprayed from his ruined neck. He tried to speak.

"Shhh..." the dark figure hissed, "it'll all be over soon," the dark figure said. And there, in the night, the life running out of him, Edward understood.

"W-w-w-why?" he managed through his mangled vocal chords.

"Come, you must know by now," the dark figure answered, wiping the scissors on his coveralls. They gleamed in the moonlight. Edward looked up at him with pleading eyes.

"Because I..."

Snip-snip!

"HATE..."

Snip-snip!

"KARAOKE!"

Snip-snip!

T LEAST we know he didn't kill the Fossett girl," Officer Steve, a sinewy figure, said to the mayor, a beefy man of about 60 with balding gray hair.

"At least there's that," the mayor agreed.

Officer Steve handed him a folder. "Here's what I have so far on the Fossett and Riggi murders..."

What he had wasn't much — a short list of possible suspects (one of whom, Edward Kohl, had been crossed off in red ink, as he was currently dead), a vague report on possible motives and alibis, and a receipt from Gecko's, Cape May's southwestern restaurant.

The mayor eyed the receipt, "You're really going to claim that?"

"Sure," Officer Steve answered. "Technically, it was a business lunch. And the enchilada was outstanding."

"I've heard," the mayor said, then more quietly, "Steve, is what I've been hearing true? Did the killer mutilate Kohl's body like he did the others?"

Officer Steve measured his words. "In a manner of speaking."

The Karaoke Killer, as the press had dubbed him, had bludgeoned Sal Riggi to death with a microphone, splaying open his skull, and poured acid down the throat of Brandi Fossett as a means of washing her mouth out. But what he did to Edward Kohl was, in Officer Steve's mind, much worse.

"He cut off his hair," he said, "that beautiful head of thick, wavy hair... gone. It's tragic."

"Okay..." the mayor said.

"Sorry," Officer Steve replied, running a hand over his short, spiky locks. "I just really enjoy a good head of hair. But this bit of mutilation makes me think we should look into his workplace for a disgruntled former customer or co-worker."

"Good thinking," the mayor agreed, "but we're sure he didn't off the Fossett girl?"

Officer Steve nodded. "Positive."

"How?" the mayor asked.

Officer Steve smiled. He loved when people asked the perfect question. "As I suspected during my interview with Mr Kohl yesterday afternoon,

I deduced that he had nothing to do with her murder. His boss, Suzanne Spiegel of Artizan Salon and Spa, mentioned to me a recent downward turn in Edward's hairstyling abilities."

"So," the mayor said, "a hairstylist, means he musta been..." the mayor gave the international limp-wrist sign for "gay."

"Not at all, sir."

The mayor was confused. "But I thought they all were. I don't understand."

"You will if you'll give me five seconds," Officer Steve said, taking a swig of water as the mayor harrumphed. "Edward was gay, until about a year ago when, according to Ms Spiegel, he started his artistic decline, which is right about the time a young girl named Brandi Fossett was stationed here by the US Coast Guard."

The mayor looked like he smelled something funny. "So you're saying..."

"He met and fell in love with Brandi and was no longer a homosexual. What that had to do with his hairstyling prowess, I'm not sure. Sometimes these things are genetic."

The mayor whistled. "That Brandi, she musta been..."

"A fine girl," Officer Steve finished.

After a moment the mayor said, "So when a hairdresser turns straight he loses his mojo? Or his homojo, as it were."

The mayor chuckled heartily, but Officer Steve was not amused.

"Sorry, go on," the mayor said.

Officer Steve said, "A picture found on Mr Kohl's cellphone confirms the fact that, at the time of Ms Fossett's murder, he was, shall we say..." Officer Steve gave the mayor a badly Xeroxed photo of Edward, nude but for a few well-placed rose petals, his hands and feet bound by fuzzy pink handcuffs, on Brandi's waterbed, "... tied up at the time."

"Goodness gracious," the mayor said with a blush.

Officer Steve continued, "We believe Mr Kohl never alibied himself for fear that word would leak he was no longer gay, destroying the last remaining shreds of his already-declining reputation as a hairstylist. But there's one more thing..."

"Go on," the mayor urged, taking one last, curious peek at the picture.

"An unsent text message to Edward's former partner, a Bob Quigley, indicated that Edward was worried about something he may have stolen. We're not sure exactly what yet."

The mayor clapped a hand on his shoulder. "Well, stay on it, Steve. We've got to catch whoever it is..."

"Whomever," Officer Steve corrected him.

The mayor gave him the stink-eye. "Yes, sorry... WHOM-ever it is that's doing this. July is just around the corner, people need to get their season in, and that's not going to happen with stories about a Karaoke Killer playing on the Philly news every night. Atlantic City, Maybe. Wildwood, sure. But not Cape May, you understand me?"

"I'm on it, sir."

The mayor nodded. "Good man. Keep me informed."

"Will do, sir."

"You know," the mayor started as Officer Steve left the room, "another time, another place, this might all make a hell of a movie."

Earlier...

IT WAS warm, a little breezy, as Officer Steve and Terry O'Brien lunched at Gecko's, near the Washington Street Mall.

Over enchiladas and (sadly) non-alcoholic margaritas they discussed the case of the Karaoke Killer. Their relationship, at first tentative, then mildly friendly, had turned toxic since Edward's murder the day before.

"Let's get this over with," Terry requested.

"I'll do what I can," Officer Steve answered. "Where were you when Brandi Fossett was killed at the Rio Station."

"Taking a whiz, same as you."

"But I would have seen you..."

"I used the one by the bar, you went into the restaurant."

Officer Steve made a note. "Did you do it because you were sick of hearing her songs?"

"You going to ask me that every time someone in Cape May County gets offed?" Officer Steve glared at him as Terry continued. "No, I didn't do it for any reason because I didn't do it!"

"You know the killer washed her mouth out?"

Terry burped up a piece of tortilla. "Yes, thanks."

Officer Steve continued, "Did you do it because she sang songs with dirty words and as the dad of three young boys that offended your sensibilities as a parent?

Terry squinted at him. "Do they make you take a test to get into cop school?"

"A simple 'No' would have sufficed."

"Then no."

Officer Steve made a note, then said, "I believe you, jackass, but you were there... again. So I have to clear you before I can move on... again. Okay?"

Terry pondered this a moment, then softened a bit. "Okay."

"Let's get down to it." Officer Steve took out a second notebook. Terry thought he saw the word 'Movie' written on the cover. "Why would the killer scratch 'You're Next' on your machine if he wasn't going to kill you next?"

"Disappointed?" Terry asked. Officer Steve glared at him again.

Actually, this had bothered Terry, too. The night of the first killing, someone had etched those words into his equipment, making him the focus of an intense police protection scheme. He was not bothered at not being next, but rather, why would the killer do it?

"A distraction," he said, "a way to keep you focused on protecting me instead of looking for him."

Officer Steve nodded. "Not bad. Tell me, why do you always wear black?"

"Why do you always smell like cheese?"

Officer Steve wilted a bit, but kept his stare fixed on Terry.

"I wear black because, as nerdy as it may sound, I like to try to blend in at my shows, like a theater stage hand. I have a huge theater background. Why, back in high school I was..."

"I get it," Officer Steve cut him off, trying to nip this 10,000th I'm an actor, too! story in the bud. "You wear black to be unobtrusive. Gotcha."

Terry looked a little hurt. Officer Steve felt the mildest twinge of remorse. "And I smell like cheese because of a certain... foot odor condition."

Terry smiled. "Why do you care that I wear black?"

Officer Steve answered, "We have a few witnesses that reported seeing a quote-unquote 'dark figure' in the area on the night of the murders. Don't think it means much. Frankly, I think people are letting their imaginations get the best of them. That damn *Exit Zero* magazine is driving people batty with this Karaoke Killer stuff."

Terry said, "So, you really think this is one guy, not a copycat?"

Officer Steve thought for a moment. "A copycat killer copying a killer who kills copycat singers?"

Terry chuckled. "Does he use his own weapons or borrow a more famous killer's weapons? The mind boggles."

Officer Steve chuckled, then almost imperceptibly said, "But... if it were more than one person, that would explain..."

"What?" Terry said. "I can't hear you."

"Oh, sorry," Officer Steve recovered, "I was just thinking out loud. I always feel silly when I do that."

Terry answered, "Yeah, me too."

"Look," Steve said as he paid the bill. Their waiter, Sean Conners, looking haggard and more than a little hungover, took the fistful of cash, "Why don't we try to start over. You seem like a decent guy, and in other circumstances we probably could have been friends."

Terry lied, "Probably."

"So, even though I've conducted two interviews with you, I don't think you did it, so why don't we at least try to be civil?"

Terry considered this. Befriend a cop? *Eh*, he figured, *there were worse friends to have.*

"Okay," he said, "clean slate. Besides, why would I kill three of my most prolific singers? They sang, like, 30 songs a night. four minutes a song... that's two hours of time I have to fill now. It sucks."

Officer Steve raised an eyebrow.

"What? Don't look at me like that. I still have a business to run. I have to be a little pragmatic for chrissakes... I was just thinking out loud is all."

"Silly, isn't it?"

Terry stood, red-faced, ready to leave as waiter Sean brought back the wrong change. "Anyway, two out of three ain't bad, eh?"

"Pardon?" Officer Steve asked, pulling a fiver from the tip.

"You interviewed me about Brandi and Sal, but not Edward. Two out of three; not bad."

"Oh no," Officer Steve downed the last of his coffee, "you're on my list for Edward. I just need to gather more evidence."

Terry froze him with a cold stare. "Slate full."

★　★　★　★　★

JANIS Quiggle, General Manager of the Rio Station restaurant, was a fairly quiet type, scarlet hair framing a pretty face. She sat now with Officer Steve at a corner booth in the Rio's dining room. She was neither nervous nor placid, but even when standing still she seemed to be moving. Managing one of the busiest restaurants in the county will do that. She sat, fingers drumming on the tablecloth, as Officer Steve approached.

"Thanks for sitting with me Miss Quiggle."

"Oh, not a problem," she said with her sing-songy voice.

"I understand you can't verify your whereabouts at the time of Ms Fossett's murder."

Janis paused. She could verify them, but only if she wanted to go to jail. "As I told you on the phone, I really don't remember where I was at that particular time."

"I see," Officer Steve made a note. "Moving on. You hold a fairly substantial interest in the Rio Station, is that correct?"

Janis was feeling warmer. "Yes it is."

"How big a stake do you own, Miss Quiggle?"

Janis swallowed hard. "Roughly 30%."

Officer Steve cocked an eyebrow. "Roughly?"

"Okay, 40... but it should have been 50... stupid lawyer..."

"Come again?"

Janis sighed. "Rick, the owner, and I were once married. As part of our settlement I got 40% of the restaurant, which means zero until he actually sells the place, which he never will, which my lousy lawyer failed to foresee. So basically, I got nothing."

"Uh-huh," Officer Steve grunted. "Word on the street is that TGI Friday's is interested."

"Mmm hmm," Janis answered bitterly, "and so is Applebee's, Outback Steakhouse, Chik-Fil-A…"

"Ooh," Officer Steve drew in a sharp breath. "God a Chik-Fil-A would *kill*. The Waffle fries?!"

Janis agreed. "I know, but Rick isn't selling."

Officer Steve was crestfallen. "Really? A shame."

"You're telling *me*."

As much as Steve was now salivating at the thought of a hot Chik-Fil-A sandwich (with cheese!) and a box of salty waffle fries, he was more pleased that Janis had walked into his trap.

"So," he said, "you stood to make a pretty decent chunk of change if Rick sold. How much do you figure?"

Janis shrugged uneasily and felt like she'd made a terrible mistake. "Low seven figures."

Officer Steve whistled. "Wow. So, if you were a person who stood to make a lot of money from the sale of this place, would having an insanely busy and profitable Friday night of karaoke do anything to help you?"

"No, not really." A bead of sweat glistened on her brow.

"And," Officer Steve continued, "if one desperately needed money, wouldn't a highly publicized homicide drive down business, destroy its reputation, and force the owner to sell?"

"It might." She was freely perspiring now.

"So," Steve continued, "you can see how it might seem like you may have had a hand in this."

"What?" Janis was livid. "Why I never…"

Officer Steve stood, a finger in her face. "You killed Brandi to drive down profits and force Rick to sell! You poured acid down her throat because her language offended your customers! And you are the one trying to make it look like there's a serial killer loose!"

Janis stood and put a finger in his face. "I did no such thing! I could give a rat's ass about what somebody says in a bar! And I was going to burn the place down to get my share of the insurance money!"

She slammed a piece of paper down on the table. It was a Wawa receipt for three gallons of gas. Super.

Officer Steve sat. It wasn't the confession he was hoping for, but it was a good one nonetheless. "Want to come downtown with me, Ms Quiggle."

Janis stood. "Um… do you think I could call my lawyer first?"

"Use my cell."

Janis sank back into the booth and did just that.

CHAPTER 7
A Harpooned Henry

From Exit Zero magazine...

CAPE MAY, NJ—As panic grips the normally quiet seaside resort of Cape May, the summer days burn away with increasing alacrity. The season, already hampered by rumors (proven by THIS paper to be true) of a serial killer, may get worse before it gets better. Inside sources say Cape May police are no closer to solving these crimes than when the whole bizarre saga began with the murder of Sal Riggi, of Villas, outside the Ugly Mug on Cape May's Washington Street Mall, three weeks ago.

In the days following, Brandi Fossett, an aspiring hairstylist, and Edward Kohl, an aging lothario, were also murdered. The connection? Terry O'Brien and Terry-Oke!, a bustling Cape May karaoke business. Though present at each crime scene, Mr O'Brien is not considered a suspect at this time, though he is a "person of interest" according to lead investigator Officer Steve Pascal of the CMPD.

This magazine vows not to rest until the Karaoke Killer is caught and Cape May can breathe easy once again. Until then, be sure to visit the Exit Zero shop on Perry Street in Congress Hall, just across the road from the Pink House. Now selling Terry-Oke! T-shirts, $15 or two for $30. — Jack Wright, Editor/Publisher

D HENRY, owner of Harpoon Henry's (and Henry's on the Beach and parts of outer Mongolia), stared in happy disbelief at the gigantic throng that surrounded his bar. It was Tuesday night and the place was jammed. Harpoon Henry's (formerly The Whaler's Cove) had always done a brisk dinner business, but late nights were generally reserved for a few, hardcore local drinkers and the occasional lost tourist seeking the Cape May-Lewes Ferry. (How easy was it to miss the most sign-posted mode of public transportation on the eastern seaboard? Very, apparently.)

But several weeks ago, in a move of stunning prescience, Ed had decided to give karaoke a shot. The kid running it, Terry O'Brien, was a little dodgy, but what the hell? Tuesday nights were his slowest of the week, so any coin brought in by this fake music huckster would be a bonus. But then "The Karaoke Killer" came and, along with him, hordes of the morbidly curious.

This bizarre surge in Terry-Oke!'s business had been going on for eight days now, since Edward Kohl's murder outside Cabanas the previous week. His crowds, usually meager to decent, were now barely containable. Like people slowing down to rubberneck a car accident, they were showing up in droves at Terry-Oke!, hoping to see... who know what, exactly, but *something*. It all made Terry a little sick.

"Busy night!" Ed yelled at him above the din.

Terry looked up, two CDs on his pinky fingers, a third in his mouth, little white song slips littering the table and nearby floor. "Yeth," he said, CD in his teeth, "it'th fantathtic."

Ed chucked him on the shoulder. "Keep it up!"

Terry nodded. As Ed walked away, Terry cast a jealous eye at Ed's Terry-Oke! T-shirt. It looked like a regular Terry-Oke! T-shirt — "Terry-Oke!" across the chest and a big "O'ke!" on the back — but Ed Henry, never one to miss a marketing opportunity, had altered the design in the slightest (a different font) and added the words "I Survived" to the front, but not before quickly and quietly securing all the licensing rights to the design.

The "I Survived Terry-Oke!" T-shirt was the hottest-selling article of clothing in Cape May — shops couldn't keep them on the shelves, the Flying Fish Studio couldn't print them fast enough, and Terry, whose car, house and body were falling apart, wasn't getting a nickel.

Ed knew it was a bastard move, but he didn't make (then lose, then make) a fortune in Washington, DC real estate by worrying about the little guy. When one saw an opportunity one had to strike. Besides, he gave the kid a $25 a week raise and a free shirt. What more could he want? Taking one last, satisfied look around, he strolled out of the bar, on to the deck, and closer to his death.

★   ★   ★   ★   ★

THE dark figure couldn't believe it. Not only were people not NOT going to karaoke, they were coming in gigantic numbers. It was inconceivable! The plan was perfect, but now... no, no doubts. The plan will work, he thought. It just needs some more time... and more blood. Further examples would have to be made.

He sipped his drink and watched Ed, the pompous windbag owner, stroll out on to the deck. He was certainly more than worthy of being Victim #4. The dark figure hated people with money, but especially real estate people with money. Sure, Ed had given it all up 15 years ago to open Zoe's and flip burgers, but once a real estate parasite, always a real estate parasite.

Across the bar was the manager, Roger Furlin, the guy who brought Terry-Oke! to Ed's attention to begin with. "Let's give it a try!" Roger urged him, "they're making money hand-over-fist everywhere else he works!" Also definitely worthy of a pencil in the throat. But from the looks of him — bloody, stitched-up eyeball and missing digit on his right hand — Roger seemed to be doing okay all by himself, thank you.

Jay Bush, the head chef, would be an impressive kill, since he was tall and the killer was not. And not only did Jay work at Harpoon Henry's, the bastard also had a background as a dinner theater chef. If there was one thing on earth the dark figure hated as much as karaoke, it was dinner theater. But the dark figure loved the ribs at Harpoon Henry's and they were Jay's own secret recipe, marking perhaps the first time Jay's cooking ever saved him from anything.

Or maybe Tim Shriver, longtime Harpoon Henry's bartender and (world-class) ball-breaker. The dark figure loathed Tim for the lousy jokes he told and weak drinks he mixed. But bad bartending aside, the dark figure knew it had to be someone of influence, of import, someone who sat on the boards of so many local committees that his loss would be felt throughout the community. It had to be Ed Henry. The people had to get the message — Terry-Oke! must be stopped.

"Hey," yelled the bartender, "how was your drink?"

The Stoli Screwdriver had been fine, except that the dark figure had ordered a Stoli O and club.

Breathing deeply, the dark figure thought, Easy... focus... breathe...

"It was fine," he said, dropped a quarter on the bar, and stalked away. Dropping his cup into the trash, the dark figure stood and followed Ed Henry outside to the deck, where one could catch the most spectacular sunsets, if one dug sunsets.

★ ★ ★ ★ ★

IT WAS pushing midnight, Terry's usual cut-off time at H-Double, as he liked to call it. But, as had become customary this last week, there was no way he'd be able to quit at midnight. A three-deep bar, rollicking crowd, and three dozen song slips meant 1am, probably 2am. So with a resigned sigh he put a new disc in the player, shuffled the slips, and stepped over to the bar for a drink.

"Here you go," the bartender said, putting the drink on the bar, "Stoli Screwdriver!"

Terry sighed. "Thanks."

He wanted a Stoli O and club, a bad habit picked up from *Exit Zero* magazine editor Jack Wright at a launch party some months earlier. But apparently the only thing harder than getting a table at Harpoon Henry's was getting the drink you ordered. Since Terry rarely paid for drinks, he didn't bitch. Sipping the cocktail, Terry caught a glimpse of Ed Henry making his way to the deck in his damn "I Survived Terry-Oke!" shirt.

"Just business, son," Ed had told him the week before. "I'm sure you understand."

"Sure," Terry had answered with a wave of the hand, "I understand." *I understand a greedy, selfish bastard when I see one. I understand you making a fortune while three boxes of my regular shirts rot in the trunk of my car. Sure, I understand.*

But Terry stuffed the anger as Ed disappeared on to the deck, which was just as full as the bar. Which was just as full as the inside dining room. And the new outside bar.

Morbid, Terry thought, frowning at the idea of his friend's deaths making him a floating tourist attraction. *Someone should really teach them a lesson.*

A scruffy-looking fisherman-type in a black slicker and bucket hat nudged Terry.

"Yahr," he growled, "tell me lad, what time do it be?"

Terry sighed again. "Steve, you're supposed to be a fisherman, not a pirate."

Officer Steve wheeled on him, the orange 99-cent sticker still on his plastic eye patch. "Yahr, that be Officer Steve to you, me boy. I didn't put me bones through cop school and train me body into a remorseless killin' machine so that a landlubber like you could call me 'Steve.' That'll earn ye a one-way ticket to the bone yard!".

"Whatever you say, Popeye," Terry retorted to Officer Steve's scrunched-up face and squinky eye, "I've got work to do."

Terry went back to his equipment and, in desperate need of a cigarette, flipped through the song slips. Big Joe and Lauren were up next with Kid Rock and Sheryl Crow's tortuous paean to booze and infidelity, "Picture."

This song... Terry thought... *that Karaoke Killer might be on to something.*

But as much as he hated it, it was five minutes long and afforded him enough time to catch a whole smoke. So, with a pained grimace, he spoke into the microphone, "Thank you, Jessica Rose for that, um... *different* version of 'Total Eclipse of the Heart.' Up next we have Big Joe and Little Lauren singing my favorite song in the history of recorded music."

Without a word he handed them the mics and beat feet to the deck, where a nice surprise awaited him.

At the bar, Officer Steve plucked at the fake beard and mustache spirit-gummed to his itching lip and chin. Little beads of sweat dripped off of it and into his O'Doul's. As he eyed the packed bar it occurred to him that Terry had drifted out of sight. Not good. It was Steve's job to protect him, and letting him sneak away for a whiz was not going to get it done. He got up off the bar stool, no mean feat for a guy with a fake peg leg, and tick-tocked out to the deck.

★　★　★　★　★

ED HENRY, of the West Philadelphia Henrys, having pushed his way through the crowds, finally stepped into the parking lot. It was reasonably well-lit by several high, glaring floodlights, but Ed was parked two blocks away — the lot had been impossibly full since 5pm in anticipation of Terry-Oke! or Murder-Oke! as *Exit Zero* magazine began calling it. That insipid Jack Wright. It escaped Ed why the Scottish thought so highly of themselves, but Jack had a pretty good thing going with his magazine and gave Ed a hugely-read local platform in which to advertise his business ventures — so he could excuse the occasional grandiose editorial.

He crunched across the broken seashells to the far end of the lot, stepped over the telephone pole stumps, and on to the street. A block to the right, one left, and he'd be safely in his Lexus on his way home, visions of tonight's receipts dancing in his head.

He heard something behind him. He turned.

"Hello?"

Nothing. Peering into the dark he thought he saw something move, but chalked it up to his imagination.

Still, he thought, *not the brightest idea... walking out here by myself with a killer on the loose. Probably should have thought of that before I left.*

Picking up his pace he rounded the corner and turned left and half-jogged the last 20 yards to the SUV. *Whew!*

Someone tapped him on the shoulder. Ed spun, heart hammering. "What the... oh, it's you. What are you... Shouldn't you be... is that a fake... oh. Oh dear."

The dark figure raised his weapon.

Resigned, Ed quietly asked, "Why?"

The dark figure smiled inside — this was getting to be his favorite part.

"Because I..."

Zip-Thunk!

"HATE..."

Zip-Thunk!

"KARAOKE!"

With an explosion of glass and metal the SUV came to rest on top of the bar at Harpoon Henry's, tires spinning, engine coughing.

Zip-Thunk!
And it was done.

★ ★ ★ ★ ★

TERRY stuffed the cigarette into the little smoke-butt pyramid in front of the restaurant. He had about a minute until Joe and Lauren finished, so he slowly made his way up the ramp, the crowd thicker with each step. By the time he got to the door he was politely shoving people out of his way. Someone tapped him on the shoulder.

Terry spun. "Cath!"

"Hi honey!"

Terry hugged his wife, gave her a peck on the cheek. "What are you doing here?"

She had to shout over the raucous crowd, "I called Carlee to watch the boys, thought I'd come see what all the hubbub was about."

Terry chided her. "You shouldn't have come alone."

"I'm fine," she said, waving him off, "I'm parked right out..."

But Terry didn't hear the rest of the sentence. A pair of headlights moving up Beach Drive caught his eye. The vehicle seemed to be moving fast for such a pedestrian-rich neighborhood, and looked to be making a beeline towards...

"RUN!!!" Terry screamed and yanked his wife over the rail as a gold Lexus tore through the few small trees and hit the wooden ramp. In seeming slow-motion it sailed through the air and toward the huge bay windows that (at least for 1.3 more seconds) afforded the best view of the sunset in New Jersey.

CRASH!

With an explosion of glass and metal the SUV came to rest on top of the bar, tires spinning, engine coughing. Smoke drifted in a low haze, shattered glass tinkled to the ground. The dazed crowd milled about in shock. The music was gone.

From the smoke, Terry and Officer Steve emerged. They looked at each other, then, with mounting dread, to the hood of the car. There, perfectly held in place by three long harpoons, was Ed Henry — one through the chest, one through the gut, one through the... lower regions.

"Jeez Louise," Terry whispered.

"Yahr, shiver me timbers..." Officer Steve muttered. Terry smacked him in the back of the head. "I mean... wow."

Standing 18 inches from the bumper of the SUV were Big Joe and Lauren, microphones in hand, mouths agape, eyes wide. Terry took the mics from them, the severed cords sizzling, and dropped them on the floor. The KJ system was buried beneath the front end of the SUV, shooting sparks. He looked up at the slack, dead, one-eyed face of his former employer, wondered if anyone caught the irony of the "I Survived Terry-Oke!" T-shirt, and thought...

Great, another goddamned karaoke machine.

CHAPTER 8
Quigley Down Under

From Exit Zero magazine...

THE KARAOKE KILLER STRIKES AGAIN!

CAPE MAY, NJ—The usually sleepy seaside burg of Cape May was stunned again last night by the murder of Ed Henry, local restaurateur and multiple-committee member. He was found brutally murdered near his newest place of business, Harpoon Henry's, in North Cape May. Sources confirm that Mr Henry's body, like those of the previous victims of the Karaoke Killer, was mutilated. Though police are not releasing any details, this paper has learned that Mr Henry, who was harpooned to death, was missing his right eye. This fits a pattern established by the first three victims, Sal Riggi, Brandi Fossett and Edward Kohl, who were missing their brains, tongue and hair, respectively.

Anonymous sources tell Exit Zero that police are baffled. Extra personnel and overtime have done little to aid them in catching this heinous fiend. Rumors continue to swirl that the FBI may soon be brought in to take over the case. Said lead investigator Officer Steve Pascal, "We can handle it. I didn't put myself through cop school and train my body into a thousand different ways to die so that some punk college kid with a badge could take my place."

Big words from a small man. In the meantime, This paper will do its level best to bring you all the breaking news, fair and balanced. Until then, visit us on the web at exitzero.us and buy a subscription for $30/year. Next 10 subscribers get a free "I Survived Terry-Oke!" T-shirt! — Jack Wright Editor

OW where in the hell did he get three harpoons?" the mayor blustered.

Officer Steve shrugged. "Internet?"

The mayor looked at the clunky metal device on his desk. "Did he make this thing himself?"

"Not sure," Officer Steve answered, admiring the apparently homemade harpoon launcher. "Looks like something out of *Aquaman*."

"Jesus, Steve," the mayor continued, running a hand over his white mane. "Fourth of July weekend is right around the corner, our season is going to hell. We've got to stop this, you understand?"

Officer Steve stiffened. "Or what? Is the paper right? Are you bringing in the FBI?"

The mayor turned red and began sweating, "Now look, Steve..."

"OFFICER Steve."

"Pardon?"

"Officer Steve. I didn't put myself through cop school and train my body into an electrified ass-kicking machine so that a ham-handed low-life like you could call me 'Steve.'"

The mayor looked ready to explode. "Now look, here..."

"No," Officer Steve cut him off, "YOU look here. I covered for you on the election thing for one reason and one reason only: a promotion to detective that you promised."

"Look, I'm letting you lead this Karaoke Killer investigation, aren't I? Isn't that enough for now? I'm catching a lot of heat for that from the council, letting a beat cop lead a homicide investigation."

Officer Steve scoffed: "Screw the council and screw you."

He turned on a heel and was gone before the mayor could catch his breath.

God, the mayor thought, *he is going to make one GREAT detective.*

Outside Artizan Salon and Spa, later...

ARTIZAN founder and owner Suzanne Spiegel puffed nervously on the Parliament 100 as she waited for Officer Steve to ask his first question. The wiry policeman looked a little off today, his face a bit too red, his demeanor a bit too agitated. Suzanne had known Officer Steve only a short time, but she'd never seen him like this.

"Are you all..."

"MISS SPIEGEL," he cut her off. "Please, a moment."

"Sure," Suzanne said softly. Freak.

A moment later and Officer Steve seemed to have righted himself. His face was now pale and calm.

"Ms Spiegel," he started, "Edward Kohl, your employee..."

"Former employee," she corrected.

Edward Kohl had, three days prior, become victim #3 of the Karaoke Killer.

"Of course, my apologies, former employee... last time we spoke you mentioned a decline in his hairstyling abilities?"

Suzanne nodded. "Yes."

Officer Steve made a note. "And you also mentioned something about fending off several lawsuits from unhappy brides that Edward worked on. Am I right?"

This time she nodded silently.

"Seems to me," Officer Steve said, "that that might be a pretty good reason to get him out of the way: eroding skills, potential loss of thousands, if not millions of dollars. Do you agree, Ms Spiegel?"

Suzanne made a face like she just stepped in something. "You think I killed Edward?"

"I'm not sure. Convince me you didn't."

Suzanne flicked the cigarette away. "First of all, I loved Edward. He was one of my best friends. Second... well, that's all I really have. But I didn't do it. You wouldn't catch me dead near a karaoke bar."

Officer Steve replied, "I might... if you don't start cooperating."

Suzanne pondered this. "Okay, I was considering having him roughed up a bit, just as, you know, a wake-up call. But when I found out he and Brandi were in love... I just couldn't bring myself to do it."

Officer Steve was surprised. "You knew about he and Brandi and didn't tell me?"

Suzanne met his unwavering gaze. "A person's sexuality is their own business."

Officer Steve shrugged. "Fair enough. And what do you mean you were going to have him 'roughed up.' Leg busted? Knee-capped?"

Suzanne chuckled. "Oh, no, no... nothing like that. In the hair dressing world roughed up means something along the lines of... switching out his Paul Mitchell for a generic shampoo, slipping cheap scissors in place of his Bonika shears, booking him more elderly clients... that kind of stuff, but all without his knowledge, of course. He wouldn't have known who was doing it, but he'd have known something was up."

Officer Steve shook his head. "I will never understand this crazy, mixed-up shampoo world."

"It's okay, you're not supposed to."

Officer Steve turned to leave. "Thank you, Ms Spiegel."

"You're welcome, hey..." she answered, noticing something, "Is that a bald spot?"

Officer Steve's face grew red once again, and his shoulders rose to his ears. He got in his cruiser, and sped away, bits of gravel pelting Artizan's main window.

"Hey!" Suzanne shouted, covering her face from the barrage, as he took off. "Sheesh, sensitive..."

Bacarach Rehab Center, Cape May Court House, later...

FOR a guy who recently suffered a debilitating stroke, Bob Quigley was still pretty imposing in his Star Trek-type wheelchair, which was attached to a huge computer network that looked like Big Blue, the chessplaying computer, along with an armada of tubes and IVs. Somewhere,

Steven Hawking was spitting green with envy.

"Thanks for meeting with me, Mr Quigley. This shouldn't take long."

Bob, Phillies cap atop his still ruggedly handsome face, tapped a few words into the keyboard.

"NO PROBLEM DUDE," answered the flat, synthesized computer voice.

This unnerved Officer Steve a bit, but he pressed on. "How long had you and Edward been a couple before he... before his conversion."

Tap tap tap. "TEN FREAKING YEARS... THE JERK."

Officer Steve swallowed a laugh. "I see. And how did you react to the news that he was leaving you for a woman?"

Bob looked at Officer Steve as if to say, *Do you not see the wheelchair, giant computer and 37 tubes coming out of me?* But Officer Steve wasn't picking it up. So...

Tap tap tap. "NOT WELL."

Officer Steve made a note. "And you're aware we recovered an unsent text message Edward was sending to you at the time of his demise."

Tap tap tap, tap tap tap, tap-tap. "YES."

"Now this text message indicated Edward was worried about something he had stolen. Can you elaborate?"

Bob tapped for the next 15 minutes. Officer Steve tried to keep up. By the end he knew, sadly, who the killer must be. Quietly, he rose to leave. "Thank you for your time, Mr Quigley. You've been a great help."

Bob started to type something, then stopped. And with a Herculean effort for someone in his condition, he painstakingly lifted his left arm, raised his hand, curled it into a fist... and extended his middle finger.

"You have a good day, too, Mr Quigley."

Officer Steve left. Bob smiled wider than he had in months. It was crooked, but it was wide.

Gecko's, later...

"IT'S our second time here. Are we dating now?" Terry asked Officer Steve.

"It was you, wasn't it?" Officer Steve said abruptly.

Terry nearly spat out his mesquite-grilled salmon, "What? No! Why would you ask me that?"

Officer Steve hunched over the table. "I had a little chat with Bob Quigley today."

Terry was flustered. "Edward's ex? So?"

"Besides being one of the creepiest half-hours of my life, he shed a little insight into your screwed-up, little karaoke world."

Terry was defiant. "Well do tell."

"Edward had a partial text message on his cellphone: *He's mad I stole...* I HATE when people skip punctuation. Anyway, I had no idea what that meant until I talked to Bob, but I should've known, considering how sick you karaoke bastards are."

"What the hell are you talking about?"

Officer Steve was livid. "Edward stole one of your songs, didn't he?"

"Sure," Terry answered, "but lots of people steal my songs."

"But this wasn't just any song, was it?" Officer Steve continued, "This was 'Love Changes Everything' from *Aspects Of Love*. According to Bob, that song was the reason you wanted to be an actor in the first place, AND the reason you started your own karaoke business — so you could sing that song in front of an audience every night. But Edward stole it and that infuriated you, didn't it."

Terry answered, "It was rude, sure, but hardly worth killing anyone over. It's a *song*, dude."

"You sure about that?" Officer Steve asked, almost shouting. People began to stare. "Are you really sure?"

"Yeah, I'm sure," Terry shouted back. "You ever hear Edward sing that song? You should be interrogating Andrew Lloyd Weber, the way he murdered that song."

"Don't be a wise-ass!"

Terry raised his hands. "Look, Steve..."

"OFFICER Steve. I didn't put myself through cop school and train my body into ninja-fied spark of unholy whoop-ass..."

"Ninja-fied spark of unholy...?"

"...so that a slimy little karaoke nerd like you could call me Steve."

He was standing over the table now, face beet-red, breath ragged. The other diners had fallen silent and now stared at him like, well, like a Ninja-fied spark of unholy whoop-ass. Crazy whoop-ass.

Terry calmly took a sip of water. "Um... something bothering you?"

Officer Steve took a slow look around, realized the scene he'd just made, and sat. "Sorry, sorry... just, when I got out of the shower this morning the drain was full of, it was full of..."

He choked up and broke off.

"Hair?" Terry finished.

Officer Steve closed his eyes, a single tear ran down his right cheek, then he took a deep breath and tried to gather himself.

Terry leaned in close and said, "I know, it's hard, especially in the beginning. But it's not so bad. After a while you get used to it."

Terry took off his hat, revealing a bare dome that shone dully in the candlelight. Officer Steve looked at him for a moment. Terry smiled widely.

Officer Steve burst into tears. Annoyed, Terry put the hat back on.

The surrounding tables were growing more uneasy with every passing moment. Several asked for their checks, still more were reaching for their coats.

"It's okay!" Terry said loudly, "his, um, his mother just died!"

Their waiter, Sean Conners, walked over. "Dude, I just *saw* your mom, how sad is *that*? Um, dude... is that a bald spot?"

Officer Steve sobbed harder, Terry stared hot death at Sean.

Sean muttered, "I'm just saying..."

Outside the Merion Inn, midnight...

IT HAD been a beautiful night of fine food, delightful spirits, and fantastic jazz piano as Craig McManus and his friend Willy Kare stepped out of the Merion Inn and into the cool night. As anyone who's ever been there could tell you, the Merion was one the best fine dining establishment in a town full of them. One thing that gave the Merion a slight edge was the nightly, seemingly non-stop ivory tickling of George Mesterhazy, Cape May's premiere jazz pianist.

George shook Willy's and Craig's hands as they exited the building: "Good night, guys, thanks for coming."

Craig answered, "No, thank *you*, George... a treat as always."

Willy nodded.

"G'night!" Craig said a little loudly, the second bottle of wine just starting to settle in.

Craig had a natural-born gift for summoning the paranormal, to see and hear the spirits that walked among us. His Ghost Writer column in *Exit Zero* magazine was among the most popular in the paper, and chronicled the exploits of the shadow world in old Cape May. Craig was a living conduit to the walking dead. Especially when he was liquored up.

"Let's go home," he said to Willy, who nodded and took him by the elbow. They shuffled across the bricks towards the car when Craig saw something in the corner of his eye: a group of people, standing across the street, bathed in the dim light of a street lamp.

"Hold on," Craig mumbled and ambled across the street.

Without his glasses it was hard to tell who was who, but from all the recent TV and newspaper reports, Craig knew at once who they must be: Sal Riggi, Brandi Fossett, Edward Kohl and Ed Henry.

Craig made it to the corner, Willy stayed a good distance away: it always creeped him out when Craig did his spook thing.

Craig put on his glasses, took a deep breath and said, "Hi."

They said, "We need to talk."

Craig nodded. "I gathered."

CHAPTER 9
Terry Gets It

EOPLE were packed into the The C-View Inn, Cape May's oldest and most local-friendly drinking establishment, and famous for its wings. To be sure, there were many good wing joints in Cape May, but only the C-View's had the perfect meat-to-bone ratio and ju-u-u-st a little breading to give it a bit of crisp. Wednesday Wing Nights at the C-View were a required part of Cape May living.

But tonight wasn't busy because of the wings — tonight was busy because Thursday was Terry-Oke! night. C-View owner Mark Platzer sat at the bar, grinning from ear to ear as person after person walked in the door and tried to squeeze in. Until last week, Terry-Oke! had struggled to find a groove at the C-View, but as everyone was learning, any publicity was good publicity. And with a cloud of suspicion swirling about him as the Karaoke Killer continued to stalk Cape May, Terry O'Brien and his Terry-Oke! had become the hottest ticket in town.

The murders were hard on the general population, but great for business

The Karaoke Killer, dubbed so by *Exit Zero* magazine, had just claimed his fourth victim — Harpoon Henry's owner Ed Henry, an important and influential local businessman and member of many committees. The three previous victims, Sal Riggi, Brandi Fossett and Edward Kohl, had been mere karaoke singers and of little import, but with the harpoon slaughter of Ed Henry, the Karaoke Killer had moved up a few weight classes. It was clear he meant business.

What was not clear was what *exactly* that business might be.

In the meantime, Mark Platzer sipped his beer and smiled. The wait staff slalomed through the elbow-to-elbow crowd. It was stuffed, and they were all spending money to be there. This made Mark happy.

What made Mark unhappy was the fact that it was 9:50pm. Terry-Oke! was scheduled to start at 10:00, and he hadn't loaded in a single piece of equipment. Sure, the tables were all full and space was tight, but that was his problem, not Mark's.

Terry was standing by the corner door, looking sweaty and exasperated (his general state of being), talking with steadfast C-View bartender Paul Farnan.

Mark approached them. "Let's go, Terry, get your stuff in here and let's get started."

Mark watched with bemusement as Terry grew even more flummoxed.

"Mark, I know I'm late, but there's nowhere for me to put my gear."

"Not my problem," Mark answered. He could hear Terry trying to stutter out an answer as he walked away. It was cruel, but he loved seeing the chubby little jerk go into full-blown panic mode.

"Paul, help me out here," Terry begged.

"Ah," Paul said with the wave of a giant mitt, "he's just yanking your chain. They'll be done soon, you can move the tables and everything will be fine."

"But..."

"Relax," Paul advised, "it'll be okay."

With that he went back behind the bar to serve the teeming masses. Natalie, the other bartender, tall and pretty, shot Paul a look of hot death for leaving her alone. She now knew how chum felt.

Terry, pulse rising, sweat pouring, stepped out on to the patio, had his seventh cigarette in the last 30 minutes, and waited frantically for the tables to clear.

★ ★ ★ ★ ★

THE dark figure watched Mark Platzer strut cockily across the bar. He hated the way rich people walked and talked, like they owned the world. But even the dark figure had to admit — they were the best buffalo wings he'd ever eaten. He watched Mark talking, nose slightly upturned, unearned sense of entitlement oozing from every pore. The dark figure was going to enjoy doing away with him.

Since killing Ed Henry two days prior, he knew he could no longer go back to killing simple karaoke singers. If people were to get the message, the stakes must continue to rise. And rise they would.

He watched Mark take out his wallet, drop a few bills on the bar, and sit back down to sip his beer.

The fool, if he only knew how near the end was perhaps he'd be a bit more generous with the help. Maybe the dark figure would have to do it for him.

★ ★ ★ ★ ★

"I WOULD love to help you, man, but I don't wanna blow my cover, dude." It was 30 minutes later and Officer Steve stood on the patio in a ridiculous get-up of plaid board shorts, zebra-striped Hawaiian shirt, and a long, platinum-blonde, surfer-dude wig — a shrinky-dink version of Jeff Bridges in *The Big Lebowski*.

"Sure," Terry puffed, lugging a speaker up the corner steps, "I understand."

But Terry was used to moving his equipment solo — it was a curious fact that Terry-Oke! Nation, for all their loyalty, never failed to leave just before or arrive just after he had to move his stuff. It was his gig, and moving and setting up were ultimately his responsibility, but would it kill them to help every once in a while?

Ten minutes later the gear was all in — it was now just a matter of plugging in, taping down cords, stuffing songbooks and running a sound check. He looked at the clock — 10:30pm.

Great, he thought, *I'm already a half-hour late and I haven't plugged in a damn thing. I'm never going to get started.*

Stoically he began the process of opening up the big, black Gator case that was the central nervous system of his karaoke business. It contained the power amp, mixer board and karaoke player. It was his third in three weeks — the first was destroyed when he dropped it after seeing the words YOU'RE NEXT etched into the lid. The second was obliterated in spectacular fashion when Ed Henry's Lexus SUV, with Ed Henry harpooned securely to the hood, landed on it at Harpoon Henry's two days ago.

That made over $12,000, $8,000 of it in the last three weeks. The bank, the wife, and the UPS guy were getting a little fed up. And this, in fact, would be the last one he ever purchased. If another one got broken he simply did not have the cash for a fourth. It was like the killer was intentionally trying to...

It hit Terry like a ton of bricks.

"Offic... um, hey dude, come outside with me for a minute!" he half-yelled at Officer Steve, then took him by the elbow and all but dragged him outside to the C-View's patio.

"What? Let go!" Officer Steve protested.

"I got it!" Terry said excitedly.

"Got what?" Officer Steve asked.

"The reason behind... the why... how come..."

Officer Steve put a hand on his shoulder. "Take a deep breath and speak slowly."

Terry did so. "The killer... it's not about hurting my singers, it's about hurting me!"

"How do you figure?"

"Think about it, scratching 'You're Next' into my machine, then NOT killing me."

"But I've been protecting you..."

"Yeah, and we see how well that's going."

"Jerk."

Terry continued, "'You're Next' was meant for the machine, for karaoke itself. The killer knew I'd drop my rig and break it. He knew Ed Henry's car would crush the second one. The killer is trying to put me out of business."

Officer Steve pondered this for a moment. "You may have something. But... who would want to hurt you?"

Terry grimaced. "Who *wouldn't* might be an easier question."

Officer Steve pressed on. "Come on, can you think of anyone who might have a beef with you?"

Terry sighed deeply, "Let's see, people who don't like me... not a very exclusive club."

"How do you mean?"

Terry answered, "I've lived here for 14 years, had 22 jobs, 36 romantic entanglements, 35 of which ended badly. My business undercuts the live music scene and now my clients are getting killed."

Officer Steve struggled to keep up with his notes.

"Other than that," Terry concluded, "I can't think of anything."

"So you think," Officer Steve said, "that the killer was hoping to do away with your karaoke business because he, what, hates karaoke?"

"Sure," Terry said.

"And that the murders were an attempt to ruin your business, keep people away?"

"Why not? But I've never been so busy in my life."

"That must be driving him crazy, and if so, it's probably why he upped the ante with Ed Henry this week."

"Would make *me* nuts. It *has* made me nuts."

"And you think he knew destroying your equipment would eventually become too expensive for you to maintain?"

"Uh-huh."

Officer Steve finished writing, rubbed his cramping wrist. "Why don't we take these one at a time..."

★   ★   ★   ★   ★

MARK Platzer had seen enough. It was 10:30pm, the karaoke guy was outside chatting with a weird-looking surfer dude and the natives were getting restless. He made his way to the patio, his ire rising with every step. He opened the door. "So, you planning on working tonight or not?"

"Mark," Terry replied, "I'm glad you're here, we need to talk. You might be in terrible..."

Mark cut him off. "I don't want to hear it. Right now all I'm worried about is you getting inside, plugging in your crap and making me some money."

Officer Steve tried. "Look, Mr Platzer, my name is Steve..."

"And you," Mark turned on Officer Steve, "surfer guy or whatever you're supposed to be, this is none of your business, so butt out. Get in there and get to work."

Terry threw him a mock salute. Mark went back inside.

"You heard the man," Terry said, "I've got work to do."

"Okay," Officer Steve answered, keeping a squinty eye on Mark, "but I really don't like that guy."

Terry offered, "Good wings, though."

"Forgetaboutit!"

★ ★ ★ ★ ★

A MINUTE later, Terry was back to plugging in. For some reason, even though the hard work of loading in was already done, Terry always perspired profusely. His thin, black Nike hat was soaked through, drops of sweat fell from his chin and nose and to the floor. His white undershirt was nearly transparent. Good thing he always brought two.

As he ripped off a piece of duct tape and began securing the TV wires to the floor, his friends Skip and Bobbi Schwester entered.

"Hey Terry!" Skip said in that booming basso profundo. Skip was about 6' 4" with a full head of silver hair and a lovely woman attached to his arm. "How's it going?"

Terry looked up, as a bead of sweat dripped into his right eye. He blinked. "I'm good, but I'm really swamped, can we..."

Skip continued, "Did I ever tell you about the time I was at Daytona Speedway? One one-thousandth of a second from being the open-wheel record holder. And I didn't even know I was being timed..."

Terry had, indeed, heard the story before. Several times, actually. But Skip was a nice guy, new to Terry-Oke! Nation, and he helped fill the void left by the losses of Sal, Brandi and Edward. So Terry squatted and listened.

"Buy you a drink?" Skip finished.

"Sure," Terry answered. *Anything to get you to stop talking.* "Stoli O and club. Thanks."

Skip and Bobbi moved away, Terry went back to work, but not before seeing Mark tap annoyingly at his watch.

Yeah, yeah...

The taping done, Terry stood to start plugging in all the accessories — speakers, microphones, cordless system, etc. The door opened again. This time it was Richard and Mary Heminway. Richard, better known to the karaoke-going public as Rico Suave, was, like Skip, a relatively new member of Terry-Oke! Nation and one hell of a sweet guy, but the last thing Terry needed right now was a distraction, so he pretended not to see him.

"Terry!" Rico called out.

Crap. "Hey, Rico, what's going on?"

He shook Rico's hand, knocked Mary one on the cheek.

"Just out for some wings and some Oke," Rico answered.

"Cool," Terry said. "Look I'm *so* late, can we pick this up later?"

Rico and Mary glared at him.

"What? What did I do?"

"Look," Rico started, "if you don't want to talk to us just say so, but don't lie and tell us you're late..."

"But..."

"We'll be at the bar. Just watch yourself. Jerk."

And they were gone.

These people really are truly crazy, Terry thought, and went back to work.

★ ★ ★ ★ ★

IT WAS almost 1:30am and Terry-Oke! was wrapping up. "And for our last song of the evening," Terry announced, "Skip Schwester with some Frank Sinatra for you."

As Skip sang the first few notes of "My Way" Terry went over to the bar where Mark Platzer sat, not drunk, but a few beers shy of sober.

"Turned out okay," Terry told him.

Mark nodded slowly. "Yep. Look, I hate to be so hard on you, but we got to strike while the iron is hot here. Know what I mean?"

"Absolutely."

"Good. I'm gonna get out of here. Paul will take care of you when you're done. I'll see you next week."

He wouldn't, but it was a nice sentiment.

★ ★ ★ ★ ★

THE dark figure watched Mark half shuffle out the door and to the parking lot. It was, as usual, dark and unpopulated. The majority of the crowd was gone by now. Only a few hardcore karaokers still remained.

Mark whistled "My Way" and pulled his keys from his pocket. He heard a noise behind him but thought nothing of it. He figured the Karaoke Killer would have to be crazy to attack him so close to the bar. He figured wrong.

"Hey Mark," the dark figure said.

Mark turned, annoyed at the sight. "You? What are you doing out here, I thought you were..."

Then he saw what the dark figure was holding and it dawned on him.

"YOU!? Really? But... why?"

The dark figure answered with a smile, "Because I..."

Whizzzzzz-flikt!

"HATE..."

Whizzzzzz-flikt!

"KARAOKE!"

Whizzzzzz-flikt!

"Ow!" Mark cried, "What the f***?"

The dark figure gave a hard yank.

"AHHHHHHHHHHHHHHH!!!"

And it was done.

From Exit Zero magazine...

KARAOKE KILLER STRIKES AGAIN... AGAIN!

CAPE MAY, NJ—The body of C-View Inn owner Mark Platzer was discovered this morning outside his restaurant. Though details remain sketchy, indications are that he was found suspended by several fish hooks and strung up with fishing wire. This marks victim #5 of the Karaoke Killer, and police appear to be no closer to finding the culprit than when the sordid affair began.

C-View bartenders Paul Farnan and Natalie Summa reportedly found an inordinately-sized gratuity in their tip jar at the end of the night. Where the money came from is still a mystery.

This paper vows to not stop asking the tough questions until this threat is eliminated and the killer or killers are caught. Until then, please peruse our index of advertisers and support our patrons. — Jack Wright, Editor-in-Chief

CHAPTER 10
The Séance

From Exit Zero magazine...

CAPE MAY, NJ—In another twist on one of the most bizarre sagas in Cape May history, desperate police are turning to Craig McManus, the "Ghost Whisperer", to aid in tracking down the Karaoke Killer. McManus, a respected member of his field, has published several books and writes a regular column for this publication. Allegedly, Mr McManus had a brief encounter with the recently deceased "spirits" of Sal Riggi, Brandi Fossett, Edward Kohl and Ed Henry. No word on the attendance of victim #5, C-View Inn owner Mark Platzer, who was found dead late last night.

As the involvement of federal authorities seems imminent, Cape May police are making one last stab at solving the case, the most infamous in South Jersey history. This paper vows to keep you informed at every step. As we do so, please visit our Exit Zero shop and enter our Karaoke Killer dead pool — 25$ a slot, deadline 9pm Monday. — Jack Wright, Editor-in-Chief

ID HE mutilate Platzer?" the mayor asked.

Officer Steve shook his head. "No, but his wallet was missing."

The mayor paused. "So what does that mean?"

Officer Steve shrugged. "Not sure, but there must be a connection."

The mayor nodded. "You're probably right."

"Plus," Officer Steve continued, "according to several employees and a borderline obscene photo on the C-View wall, Mark Platzer was an avid sport fisherman. Explains the whole fishing motif."

"Motif?" the mayor cocked an eyebrow.

Officer Steve cleared his throat. "M.O., I meant M.O."

The Mayor went on, "This needs to be handled, Steve."

"That's Officer Steve, I didn't..."

"Yeah, yeah, yeah," the mayor interrupted, "you didn't put yourself through cop school and train your body into a billion-kilowatt lightning strike of kinetic ass-kickery or some such so that a jerk like me can call you 'Steve', right?"

Officer Steve brooded. "Well, it's true."

The mayor continued, "And what's all this about a psychic?"

"He's not really a psychic, he's more like a ghost... a ghost..."

"Buster?"

"Finder," Officer Steve finished.

"Well," the mayor said dryly, "I'm so relieved we've finally got a true professional on the job."

There was nothing Officer Steve could say to counter the mayor's withering sarcasm, for every bit of it was earned. This had been Officer Steve's investigation from the jump, and so far he had turned up nothing but false leads and empty promises. And it was their prime suspect, karaoke host Terry O'Brien, who pointed the investigation in the right direction — these killings weren't about hurting karaoke singers, they were about hurting Terry. And now a paranormal investigator? It was becoming a circus. But he knew, he just knew, that that was all about to change.

He said, "I'll have the killer by Tuesday morning, sir."

The certainty of the comment took the mayor by surprise. "Well, that's what I like to hear."

Without another word Officer Steve left, a newfound determination in his step, his bald spot nicely camouflaged by a can of brown spray-on hair.

The King Edward Bar in the Chalfonte Hotel, just before midnight...

A LIGHT, salty mist blew across the street lamp as Terry and Cathrine O'Brien got out of the car in front of the Chalfonte, because going to a haunted hotel in the middle of the night wasn't eerie enough.

"You ready for this?" Cathrine asked her husband who, even in the gloom, looked pale.

He nodded. "Sure, why not."

So he took her hand and they walked around the old hotel to the King Edward bar, "The King Eddie" to the locals, where fate awaited. The King Eddie was not the most popular bar in Cape May, but it had a fiercely loyal clientele.

The pub itself was relatively small: an L-shaped bar adorned with an over-sized suit of armor and sword, a dozen stools, six small tables. But its rustic charm was undeniable. Rather, its rustic charm *would* have been undeniable if it were not now presently plunged into near darkness, illuminated only by a burning score of candles.

"Creepy," Cathrine whispered as they walked in.

Terry squeezed her hand. "Understatement."

"Terry!"

"Gah!"

"Sorry," Officer Steve whispered, "I thought you saw me."

Terry clutched at his chest. "S'okay. That's your best disguise yet, by the way."

"Ha ha," Officer Steve said. He was, of course, in his regular cop uniform.

"You remember my wife Cathrine? We almost died together."

"Of course, how do you do, Mrs O'Brien."

She answered, "Still a little shaken from almost getting flattened by a flying Lexus SUV, but otherwise fine."

Officer Steve said, "Glad to hear it."

Terry continued, "Who else is here?"

Officer Steve answered, "Everyone."

He flipped on his cop flashlight and did a slow circle of the room. Terry's stomach dropped. There, gathered in the darkness, were Mark Chamberlain, Will Knapp, Janis Quiggle (in an orange DOC jumpsuit), Bob Quigley, Suzanne Spiegel, and Jack Wright from *Exit Zero*. In the opposite corner stood an unknown cadre of others.

"Who are they?" Terry asked.

Officer Steve answered, "Paranormal psychologists, a biographer, assorted hangers-on."

"Groupies?" Terry asked.

"Actually," Officer Steve replied, "they call themselves Zombies."

Terry suddenly felt very sad for them.

Cathrine asked, "The Eurotrash guy with the notebook... Jack Wright?"

Officer Steve answered curtly, "Yeah, cantankerous little foreigner."

"I've had problems with him, too," Terry offered.

"How so?" Officer Steve prodded.

Terry answered, "Last year when he started the magazine, he threw a launch party but he didn't have any money. So I donated Terry-Oke! in exchange for a free ad in perpetuity. Guess he didn't know how successful he was going to be or how much that quarter-page would end up being worth. He's been trying to buy me out all summer. I said 'No way,' the exposure I'm getting from the paper is priceless."

Terry could feel Officer Steve's hot glare through the darkness.

"What?" he asked.

Officer Steve said, "And you didn't think to tell me this when I asked you who might be interested in hurting your business?'"

"Um... no. Why?"

"You're costing him a lot of money. That's a pretty good motive for killing karaoke. Didn't that dawn on you?"

"Um... no."

"Idiot," Cathrine whispered.

"Hey!"

"Quiet everyone!" Jack Wright announced from the other side of the room, "Mr McManus is on his way in"

The room, already deathly quiet, seemed to hum with the absence of sound. The door creaked open, light bled in from the street, two shadowy figures entered the room. Out of nowhere a cool breeze. The candles fluttered.

"At precisely 12 midnight, Craig entered the pub," the biographer said into a small tape recorder. "Slowly he made his way across the room and took a seat at the main table."

Craig McManus, his friend Willy in tow, had done just that. Three tables had been pushed together in a quasi-circle. Craig sat at the head of the largest one.

"Be seated," he announced in a low voice. Everyone was. "Please, join hands." Everyone did.

The biographer softly whispered every detail into the tape recorder, but it still echoed in the yawning silence.

Terry sat between Officer Steve and Cathrine as everyone shot suspicious looks across the tables. It was an odd and potentially dangerous array of people.

Terry said, "What the hell..."

"SILENCE!" Craig thundered. The suddenness of it shook the table, "I must have silence."

"Nice," Officer Steve whispered into his left ear.

"Good job," Cathrine whispered into the right.

Go Screw, Terry thought.

"I have summoned you here," Craig continued, his voice growing more overly dramatic with every word. Was that an English accent? "Because I have been contacted by the other side. Others you are all tied to. The victims of the Karaoke Killer."

Someone snickered. Officer Steve jabbed an elbow into Terry's side.

Craig continued, "In a few moments, the psychic energy that flows through us and around us will bring them back. At that time, the killer will be revealed."

This time, no one laughed.

"Willy?" Craig said.

At that, Willy rose and put the hood of Craig's enormous cape over his head, obscuring his face. Craig cast his head downward, grunted, then was silent.

"At precisely 12:04, Craig entered a paranormal trance, quite a remarkable sight..." the biographer-cum-narrator prattled on.

"So," Terry whispered to Officer Steve, "is this it?"

Officer Steve shrugged.

Terry leaned to his right, "Honey?"

Cathrine answered, "Do you think anything you don't say?"

Terry grew sullenly quiet, let go of their hands and folded his arms across his chest.

As the seconds ticked by into minutes, the creepiness factor flew off the charts: 20 people in a candlelit room, holding hands, trying to summon the dead at midnight in a haunted hotel bar. Nope, didn't get much creepier than that.

But after a few minutes, the effect began to fade, and more than one person began to squirm impatiently. It seemed that, on this night at least, Craig's powers would fail him.

After five minutes Terry leaned into Officer Steve, "This is a bunch of bull..."

"AHHHHHHHHHHHHHHHHHHHHHHHHHHHHHH!"

Craig shrieked the shriek of the damned — an icy wind blew through the room, dousing the candles, pitching the room into thick blackness. In the darkness people shuffled. The sound of scraping metal. Frightened murmuring. Hands dropped and groped for an exit.

"Help!" someone, a woman, cried from another table.

It was confusing, claustrophobic, and scary in the dark. The hiss of something slicing through the air dissected the growing din. Something hit the floor. Then all was invisible panic.

"Cath! Steve!" Terry called out.

"That's Officer Steve! I didn't put myself through cop school..."

"I get it!" Terry yelled, "Cath!"

"Here!" she shouted, finding his hand in the darkness.

Terry asked, "Are you okay?"

They both answered, "Yes!"

A few seconds later someone shouted, "Found it!"

And with a click the room was flooded with bright light. Bright, blessed light.

"Much better," Officer Steve announced. "Let's get the hell out of here."

"Couldn't agree more," Terry concurred.

"A drink?" Cathrine suggested.

They funneled to the door, but before they reached it another shriek tore through the night, this time from a man. Everyone turned.

"The hell?" Terry muttered.

Ghost Writer Craig tuned his psychic ear, and they appeared: Edward Kohl, Sal Riggi, Brandi Fossett... all victims of the Karaoke Killer.

There, standing by himself at the head of the table, tears streaming from wide eyes, stood Willy.

Jack Wright was the first to his side. "Willy, what's wrong?"

If the gravity of the situation were not so profound, hearing Jack Wright say, "Willy what's wrong" in his thick Scottish burr would have been comical.

Officer Steve was next to reach him. "What is it?"

Unable to speak, Willy instead pointed down, down to Craig's head. Rather, down to where Craig's head *should* have been. In its place, thrust straight down the neck like a grisly Excalibur, was the steel sword that only moments ago had been attached to the suit of armor behind the bar.

"You," Terry said, sidling up behind Officer Steve, "really suck at this."

Five minutes before...

AS THE hood dropped, Craig closed his eyes and let the familiar coldness settle over him. Each new crossing into the netherworld lessened the shock, but it was never easy. First came the cold, then the heat, then the light, then the dark. The dark was soon followed by the sound of a million voices, some old, some achingly young. As the voices filtered down from a million to a thousand to a hundred, the darkness ebbed and a pale bluish light enveloped him.

Tuning his psychic ear, he filtered the voices down to the only five he cared about at the moment, those of Sal Riggi, Brandi Fossett, Edward Kohl, Ed Henry and Mark Platzer — the victims of the Karaoke Killer.

As the light grew brighter, Craig knew he had arrived, the voices right behind him. Craig's astral self stood and turned to the bar where the five of them sat.

Looking back at his earthly self he thought, *I could lose a few pounds*.

But now was not the time for earthly matters. Ghost Craig went to the bottom of the L of the bar. Seated on the stools opposite him they sat, all still wearing the scars of their encounter with the vicious killer — Sal's skull was split, bits of brain hanging out. Brandi's lower jaw and tongue were gone. Edward Kohl was bald. Ed Henry bore three large holes in his body and was missing an eye. Mark Platzer looked like Mark Platzer, just very unhappy and with a series of red lacerations on his arms and neck.

"So," Craig began, "you asked me here?"

The five of them began babbling all at once.

"Please," Craig raised a hand. "One at a time."

The five of them began babbling at once.

Craig raised both hands: "A moment, please. Bartender?"

The bartender, tall, pretty, brassy, made her way over. "Yes?"

"A cabernet, please."

"Sure thing, sweetie," the bartender answered, pouring the wine.

Craig took a hearty sip. "Thank you, Jilline."

"Pleasure's mine," she retorted and disappeared. Literally.

Craig put the glass down and pointed at Edward Kohl. "You, what's your story?"

"Well," Edward began, flipping back bangs that were no longer there, "I started cutting hair when I was about twenty..."

"You!" Craig pointed at Brandi, "who did this to you?"

Brandi made a series of wet clicking noises. Lacking a lower jaw and tongue made it quite difficult to speak.

"Okay," Craig sighed and pointed at Sal. "You."

"All right, look," Sal began, a piece of skull dripping from his head, "when I was up in North Jersey I was feared. Down here in Cape May I'm too nice to people. I think I gotta go back to being the jerk I was before. Like this buddy of mine and I, we used to go out all the time and raise hell in Jersey City. There is no Mafia, by the way. When we were at

Woodstock we..."

"You!" Craig shouted to Mark Platzer.

"Look," Mark said, raising his hands, blood oozing from his neck, "all I wanted to do was make a buck and have a little fun, you know? Was that so much to ask for?"

"Oy," Craig slapped a hand to his forehead. It was often difficult to get the dead to focus, but it had never been *this* bad.

"Ahem, ahem," Ed Henry cleared his throat, blinked his remaining eye, and addressed the room as if it were a chamber of commerce meeting. "If I may speak for all of us, we asked you here to tell you who killed us. So, if the rest of you don't mind, I'd like to let you know that the killer is... behind you."

"Pardon?" Craig asked.

"The killer," Ed continued, "is behind you."

"What..."

Craig turned. Rising from one of the earth-bound tables was a figure in black. In the netherworld he was safe. So he watched the dark figure slither silently behind the bar, quickly slip the great sword from the suit of armor, and head back to the table.

Hah, Craig thought, *Nothing you can do to me here. The only thing that will bring me back is...*

Craig watched in horror as the dark figure smiled up at him, raised his right foot, and smashed it between Craig's earth legs.

"AHHHHHHHHHHHHHHHHHHHHHHHHHHHHHHHHHHH!" he shrieked, "Why?!"

The dark figure raised the sword as Craig came hurtling back to earth.

"Because I..."

Schwa-TING!

"HATE!"

Schwa-TING!

"KARAOKE!"

Schwa-TING! Thuk!

And it was done.

CHAPTER 11
The End

HERE WAS a pretty decent pre-Oke! crowd at Martini Beach as the restaurant transitioned from dinner to late night. The bar was full of cocktail-sipping customers, most of whom were there awaiting Terry-Oke! The dining room was full of well-heeled eaters finishing off their coffee and dessert. Black-clad, sweaty waiters zigged and zagged. Like every other place in town that booked Terry-Oke!, Martini Beach was seeing a huge spike in business the last 10 days as Terry O'Brien's notoriety grew.

As for Terry himself, he was in the dining room putting his equipment together after the tortuous load-in. Martini Beach was located in one of the prime spots in Cape May — directly above Cabanas beach bar — and afforded the best ocean view in town, but for Terry the location sucked. A second-story bar meant a second-story load-in, which meant going up 16 steps with his heavy equipment. Sixteen steps times eight trips for a guy with a 140-over-80 blood pressure... the math wasn't pretty.

He loved the gig. Martini Beach was the most karaoke-friendly room he played, but the load-in was fiendish, and generally left him short of breath and on the verge of total physical collapse by the time he put the last crate on top of the last box on top of the last speaker.

"My own fault", he constantly chided himself. "Could've gotten the smaller, cheaper system, but nooooo... I had to have the really big, expensive one! For the THIRD TIME! Moron..."

So he had learned to always bring an extra T-shirt — one for load-in, one to replace that sweat-soaked one 20 minutes later. Terry likened his first undershirt to the first wave of soldiers storming the beach at Normandy. His Hanes T-shirt budget had quadrupled in the past year.

Another reason he loved Martini Beach so much was the unusual layout of the restaurant. Once through the red doors and up those accursed 16 steps, one could go to the left, to the intimate horseshoe bar and sip one of Jen McCool's signature martinis. Or you could veer to the right and have a seat in one of the ridiculously comfy, over-sized couches in the lounge room.

The lounge didn't look like much with the lights on — a simple, pleasant, room done in peach and black. But dim the faders, throw on a mirror ball, sprinkle generously with booze and karaoke, and it may as well have been downtown Tokyo.

"Should be a hot one tonight!" Karin Rickard yelled at Terry, a little louder than was necessary. Karin was the manager-operator of Martini Beach, just off her shift and on her second wine.

Terry wiped the sweat from his face, looked down at the was-gray-but-was-now-black-with-sweat T-shirt, and nodded. "I heard it might be."

"You need any help, hon?" Karin asked.

Where were you 25 minutes ago?! "No, I'm all in."

"Okay, sweetie, let me know if you need anything."

A pint of whatever YOU'RE having... "Will do!"

And Karin was off, flitting from table to table, chatting up customers and freshening drinks. Terry followed her out of the room and to the bar, suddenly parched. He liked Karin and her boisterous attitude, and he wasn't afraid to admit it. And if he liked Karin, he *loved* Jen McCool.

"What can I get you, Okester?" she asked him, ignoring the 50 people ahead of him.

Terry smiled. "Your finest glass of cheap red wine."

"You got it." She winked at him. A few moments later he had his *relatively* cheap cabernet, went back to the lounge and once again set to putting his equipment together, certain he was suffering from repetitive stress disorder.

A few minutes later someone tapped him on the shoulder. "Hey, dude."

Terry turned, aghast to see Officer Steve all dolled up in black parachute pants, dark gray sleeveless T-shirt from Merry Go Round, Billy Idol-platinum-spiked hair and fingerless, leather gloves. The only way he could have been more obviously costumed was if he were wearing Spider-Man tights.

Terry laughed. "What the hell are you supposed to be?"

"A karaoke singer," Officer Steve replied. "Why?"

"From 1987?"

"No," Officer Steve responded defensively, then sheepishly added, "1989. This stuff was so deep in my closet I kept waiting to step into Narnia."

Terry smiled. "Doesn't explain the wig."

"This," Officer Steve said proudly, running a hand over his silver-white locks, "is not a wig."

"Huh," Terry said, "I'll be damned. Good look for you."

"Thanks," Officer Steve replied. "It's very freeing."

Terry gave him a once over. "Um... okay."

"I'm going to the bar, can I get you anything?"

Terry shrugged. "Just get two of whatever you're having."

Officer Steve gave him a thumbs-up. "Two cosmos, coming up."

"Wait, I don't..." Terry started, but Officer Steve was already gone, bop-bop-bopping away to the bar.

To each their own, he thought, and went back to plugging in his crap.

Later...

BY 10 o'clock the place was jammed. By 11, it was elbow-to-elbow. By 12 it was insufferable. The restaurant comfortably held about 100 people, and right now there were close to 200, all elbowing and shoving their way into the lounge for the extremely rare pleasure of seeing famous suspected murderer Terry O'Brien and his stupid karaoke show.

Shoved into the far corner, beneath a harsh blue-and-red glare, Terry stood, manipulating the karaoke machine, shaking hands, and signing "I Survived Terry-Oke!" T-shirts. It was hot and sticky and he had just about had it with everyone and everything. His life, so calm and normal a month ago, was now like a bad tabloid story. His friends were dying, his wife was begging him to find a new job, and business was booming for all the wrong reasons. But then there was his new sort-of friend, Officer Steve.

One Cosmo turned into two, two quickly into four, and four into... well, they had lost count after that. Suffice to say both men were feeling all right.

"And now up, for your listening pleasur..." Terry looked to Officer Steve as if to ask, *do I really have to say this?* Officer Steve nodded, so Terry finished, "Esteban Alejandro Maximoso!"

The huge crowd, most of whom were also on their fifth or sixth beverage, erupted. Officer Steve proudly strode to the makeshift stage as the first notes of Billy Joel's "Piano Man" blasted from the speakers. It was Officer Steve's third song of the night. The first two, Elton John's "Your Song" and Jimmy Buffet's "Margaritaville" had been warmly if dispassionately received. But *everyone* loved "Piano Man."

"It's nine o'clock on a Saturday..." he began.

Terry watched him sing and was amazed to see that Officer Steve was blooming right in front of him. Eyes closed, fist gripping the mic, Officer Steve sang with all of his heart and all of his soul, and sang well. The transformation was astounding. Any pretense of being an undercover cop investigating a case was gone. Those hideous clothes had obviously brought something out in Steve that no one, not even he, knew was there. The guy was becoming a performer right before their eyes.

Terry smiled, shook his head, and headed up the ramp into the kitchen for a smoke. He had no idea he only had five minutes left to live.

★   ★   ★   ★   ★

THE dark figure watched in horror as the badly-disguised police officer sank deeper and deeper into the music. It was a shame, really. The dark figure sort of liked Officer Steve, but now that he was morphing into a karaoke whore before his eyes, the dark figure had one singular thought — Officer Steve had to die.

Piano Man, he scoffed to himself. *Even Billy Joel doesn't like that song anymore.*

The dark figure tried his best to block the music out and waited patiently for his opportunity. He had no idea it would only be about another five minutes.

★　★　★　★　★

FIVE minutes and 38 seconds later, the song was over and the crowd responded with a round of thunderous applause. Officer Steve, beaming, left the stage to the handshakes and pats on the back from dozens of people.

"Thanks, thanks..." he said as he waded through the crowd, "appreciate it."

He looked around for Terry, who was just emerging from the kitchen.

"Great job, that was really fantastic," Terry offered.

Officer Steve blushed. "Thanks. It was a lot of fun."

Terry smiled. "You're totally hooked, aren't you?"

Officer Steve looked at the floor. "Yeah."

"Another one bites the dust," Terry commented, "but it's all right. It's pretty cute, actually, watching all of you idiots fall under the throes of canned music."

"You say the nicest things," Officer Steve replied.

"Here," Terry said, grabbing something from his red vinyl bag. "Have one of these."

It was a black Terry-Oke! T-shirt that exactly matched the one Terry was wearing now.

"Hey, thanks man!" Officer Steve said excitedly. "I love it, I'm going to go down to the car and put it on."

"Go nuts," Terry suggested.

"But I've always wondered..." Officer Steve started.

"What?"

Officer Steve waved him off. "Oh nothing.

"No, go on."

Officer Steve held the shirt up. "Well... why does the front of the shirt say 'Terry-Oke!' spelled O-K-E, and the back just says O'ke spelled O apostrophe K E?"

"The apostrophe says 'Karaoke with a bit of Irish Charm'."

"It does?"

Terry sighed. "Sure."

"Well... why doesn't Terry-Oke! have an apostrophe?"

"Look," Terry finished, "you want the shirt or not?"

Officer Steve laughed like a goofy 10-year-old.

"Be right back," he said and dashed away, down the steps, and out of sight. Going back to work, Terry clicked on the cordless mic and announced, "Gracias, Esteban Alejendro Maximoso, for that muy caliente performance. Up next for your listening pleasure, the vocal stylings of Vicky-licious!"

Local newspaper reporter Vicky Samselski stepped up to the mic as Patty Loveless' "Blame It On Your Heart" began. Terry set the cordless mic down on the table holding The Beast, and noticed something, a silver object, someone had apparently left behind. Assuming it was Officer Steve's, Terry picked it up, put it in his pocket, and went after him.

★　★　★　★　★

THE dark figure fondled the silver object in his pocket and made his way down the Martini Beach stairs. It was crowded and the faint smell of cigarette smoke wafted up from the street. His target lay dead ahead, just walking out of the door and on to Beach Avenue. The dark figure felt his pulse jump. The kill always got him jazzed.

★　★　★　★　★

OFFICER Steve was walking on air. He'd just given a breakout karaoke performance and now he had a cool, free T-shirt. A few smokers dotted the sidewalk between Cabanas and Carney's — the other 600,000 people in town all seemed to be upstairs at Martini Beach.

Officer Steve smiled to himself and made his way to his car, which was only about 15 yards away. He stopped briefly, pulled a pack of cigarettes from his tight-tight pants, and turned toward Seaside Sweets, out of the wind, to light the smoke. It was at that moment he saw something that made his blood run cold.

His police instincts kicking in, the world flashed into slow motion. In the window of the candy shop he caught a glimpse of a dark figure hurrying out of Martini Beach behind him. The dark figure held a glinting, metal object in his hand, a hand he was raising over his head as if to thrust it down.

Without thought, without hesitation, Officer Steve acted.

★　★　★　★　★

TERRY dashed as quickly as he could down the steps, which were clogged with people, and out the red door. A quick look to his left, then to his right, and he had him. He pulled the silver, metal object from his pocket and raised it up over his head. As he did this, Officer Steve did the strangest thing.

"Steve!" Terry yelled as the police officer dropped to one knee, pulled something from his sock and spun... BLAM! BLAM!

"Steve!" Terry yelled as the police officer dropped to one knee, pulled something from his sock, and spun on Terry.

"What are you..."

BLAM! BLAM!

Terry stopped, a confused look on his face.

"Here's your keys," he said, and tossed them to Officer Steve. He then looked down at his chest, which now featured two smoking holes and two quickly spreading blooms of blood.

Officer Steve caught the keys, slowly stood, and realized with great horror what he had just done.

"The hell was that for?!" Terry asked, the color draining from his face.

Officer Steve replied, "I thought... you CAN'T... I love karaoke."

"Funny way to show it," Terry gasped, then collapsed to the sidewalk.

Officer Steve was by his side in an instant. "You're going to be okay, I'll call an ambulance."

Officer Steve whipped out a cellphone and dialed 911.

"Hang in there," he told Terry.

Terry, realizing he had little time left, reached up and put a hand on

Officer Steve's shoulder.

He coughed and said, "You... you really... REALLY... suck at this."

Officer Steve took his hand. "You're going to be okay."

Terry looked up at him, an odd smile on his face.

"What is it?" Officer Steve asked.

"So long," Terry answered, "and thanks for all the fish."

Then he closed his eyes.

★   ★   ★   ★   ★

THE dark figure watched from the bottom of the stairwell with a mixture of glee, guilt and sadness as Officer Steve gunned down the innocent karaoke host — not in the dark figure's original plans, but it didn't break his heart.

It didn't take long for Terry to die, about a minute, but any second now there would be a crowd and the authorities, so time was of the essence. Silently the dark figure pushed his way out the door and approached the dead man and the cop.

Officer Steve saw the figure approach. "My God... what have I done? I didn't know you were here... this is... I don't know what to say... it was an accident."

"There, there," the dark figure replied and pulled the silver object from his pocket.

"Why the hell do you have that?" Officer Steve asked.

The dark figure smiled, "Because I..."

Blam!

"HATE..."

Blam!

"KARAOKE!"

Blam!

And it was done.

The dark figure turned and walked away swiftly, trying not to allow anyone to get a look at his face. People were starting to gather.

The dark figure pulled his hooded sweatshirt tighter and hurried up, past the red door of Martini Beach and approached the corner of Decatur and Beach, then a quick left and freedom.

Fifteen feet from the corner, a woman popped out of the corner door of Cabanas. It was Jessica Rose, another karaoke regular.

She saw the dark figure and said, "Hey, I know you! What are you doing..."

BLAM!

Jessica Rose fell dead — the dark figure turned the corner and disappeared into the night.

And the mystery of the Karaoke Killer would never be solved.

CHAPTER 12
A Killer Revealed

Fourteen months ago...

HE dark figure sat at a large round table, ready for the first night ever of Terry-Oke! The host, handsome if a bit of a chubber, finished the interminable set-up of his equipment and was now checking the microphones. The start was only minutes away. The dark figure's heart leapt excitedly as the moment approached. The dark figure loved karaoke.

The host clicked on his mic. "Good evening and welcome to Cabanas for the maiden voyage of the starship Terry-Oke!"

A nice little round of applause broke out. The host, Terry O'Brien, was an affable sort, who came with a bit of a built-in following after his years of local theater and band work.

The dark figure caught Terry's eye, who gave a little wink. The dark figure's heart fluttered once again.

After some opening instructions, Terry announced, "Okay then, enough technicalities, let's get this show on the road! First up tonight, to kick off Terry-Oke! with a doo-wop flavor... Sal Riggi!"

Sal, whom you could always tell by the Panama hat, Hawaiian shirt and screw-you swagger, took the stage and performed "Runaround Sue" to the delight of most of the packed house.

"All right!" Terry shouted excitedly, "now *that's* how you kick off a karaoke business! Thanks, Sal. Appreciate that. Next up, Miss Brandi Fossett with a little country for you!"

Brandi sang her filthy little song and the crowd ate it up.

"Wow!" Terry crowed at the end, "I will never get tired of that song! Thank you, Brandi!"

Brandi smiled, left the stage and sat with Sal.

Any minute now, the dark figure thought, *and it'll be my turn.*

"Okay," Terry said, "Edward's up. He's also going to some country for you, a little Tim McGraw... give it up for Edward!"

And they did, before, during and *after* the song. The dark figure had to admit, it was quite good. But more importantly, they were one song closer to the dark figure's turn.

"And now," Terry continued, the dark figure clenched, "I'd like to do a song for you. It's for my lovely wife Cathrine..." Terry waved to a pretty dark-haired girl at one of the front tables, "and it's called 'Love Changes everything.'"

Terry sang, sang beautifully, fully hitting the top notes, his vibrato strong and clear on the lower notes. It was, in all, fairly astounding. And the dark figure saw it all. Saw him sink deeper and deeper into the music, forgetting all around him. The dark figure was both attracted and repulsed.

It's karaoke, people! the dark figure wanted to shout. *Get over yourselves!*

Four hours later, the dark figure's annoyance had grown into a rage, not only by the delusions of the semi-talented singers, but also by the fact that, despite sitting in plain view all night, the dark figure was never once called up to sing.

A little after 2am, when all was done, Terry made the rounds, shaking hands, accepting drinks. He made his way over to the dark figure.

"Hi," he said, "thanks for hanging out all night."

The dark figure said nothing.

"Something wrong?"

The dark figure simmered. "All night... I was here all night, and you didn't call me up one time."

"Well," Terry answered, pulling a crumpled-up song slip from his pocket. "You didn't fill out a slip."

"A slip?" the dark figure muttered. "A slip! Screw you!"

The dark figure spun and stormed out of the bar.

"Wait!" Terry cried, "I'm sorry! I didn't know..."

But it was too late. The dark figure was gone, off into the night, the first seeds of a diabolical plan planted. All the dark figure needed now was an accomplice.

Present day...

LIEUTENANT Chuck Lear, tall, handsome, silver-haired, stood outside Martini Beach at 2am, yellow highlighter in hand, canarying the hell out of a handful of reports. He felt like a third-grade teacher sometimes, but was it his fault these idiots couldn't spell? At his feet lay two dead bodies: CMPD Officer Steve Pascal, and karaoke host Terry O'Brien, both shot to death an hour earlier.

"So what do you think?" Officer Gus, another cop, asked.

"I'm working on it," Lieutenant Lear answered.

Eyewitness reports conflicted wildly. Some said Officer Steve shot

Terry then Terry shot Officer Steve. Others said the opposite. One person said it was a drive-by. Others still mentioned a third person, a so-called "dark figure," like something out of a bad murder-mystery. Lieutenant Chuck Lear wasn't sure what the truth was, only that an officer was dead and the most infamous serial killer in New Jersey history was likely still on the loose.

"What about this one?" Officer Gus asked, pointing to the tiny, dead figure of Jessica Rose, an avid karaoke singer.

"That," Lieutenant Lear answered, "is wrong place, wrong time."

Pascal and O'Brien were prominent figures in the case of the Karaoke Killer, so in a way their slayings made a sort of gruesome sense. But this Jessica Rose appeared to be just a person who saw something she wasn't supposed to and paid the ultimate price.

Lieutenant Lear was troubled. For reasons he couldn't pinpoint, he felt like this was the end of the trail of the Karaoke Killer.

From Exit Zero magazine...

END OF THE TRAIL OF THE KARAOKE KILLER!

CAPE MAY, NJ—It's been a week since the Karaoke Killer last struck, leading some to believe that the wave of terror may be over. And, in fact, inside police sources confirm that the trail appears cold. Starting a little over three weeks ago, with the bludgeoning death of Sal Riggi outside the Ugly Mug, panic and fear have been the order of the day as person after person joined the obituaries, ending just last week with the shooting deaths of passer-by Jessica Rose, CMPD Officer Steve Pascal and karaoke host Terry O'Brien, the closest thing to a suspect the police had.

We have exclusively learned that documents found on the body of Steve Pascal implicate him and the sitting mayor in a voter fraud scandal that this reporter vows to get to the bottom of. Also, Officer Pascal's police shield was missing.

The life of Terry O'Brien was not nearly so exotic. After years as a middling singer and waiter, he recently started a karaoke business, which also met with middling success until his notoriety grew.

Services for both men will be held this afternoon. — Jack Wright, Editor-in-Chief

The first cemetery...

JACK Wright stood off in the distance a bit, scribbling in his notebook, neither wanting to encroach on anyone's personal space nor enflame anyone that might have a beef. The funeral of Officer Steve Pascal was well attended and quite solemn. Funerals were usually pretty solemn, but when laying a cop to rest things tended to get even heavier. And Steve Pascal was a good cop; thoughtful, brave, sincere. The 21-gun salute, now being fired over Jack's head, had been well earned.

Jack took a few quick photos, jotted another note or two, then went back to his sunburst-orange Honda Element and drove away.

The second cemetery...

CATHRINE O'Brien stood and wept over the casket of her husband. Of all the ways she pictured him dying, none of them included a shoot-out with police in front of a bar. A shoot-out with *someone* in front of a bar, possibly; an angry karaoke singer, an ex-girlfriend... just not the police. So she cried and tried to concentrate on the good times. Unable to think of any, she just cried.

Mostly she was sad for her boys. She knew it had been difficult for Terry to grow up without his father, so she didn't wish the same on them. But then, they probably wouldn't be having that problem. The boys in tow, she left the graveside and piled them into the minivan.

Some time later...

THE dark figure parked in front of the Bank of America in North Cape May, stashed the car keys under the seat on top of a fake beard and mustache kit, and went inside. A few minutes later the dark figure reemerged, opened a cellphone. Clicking through the phone book the dark figure stopped in the "E"s and pushed send.

"Jack Wright, *Exit Zero* magazine, how can I help you?" a voice answered.

The dark figure said, "Hello, this is your 'inside police source.'"

A pause... "Yes?"

"It's done."

A few minutes later, after a brief conversation, the dark figure was home. Going into the basement the dark figure took two items from a jacket pocket and placed them on the small work table. On the shelf above sat a safe. The dark figure opened it. Inside was an array of bottles and containers.

One jar, filled with alcohol, contained a rather large piece of Sal Riggi's brain. In the next floated the big, flappy, dirty tongue from Brandi Fossett's mouth. The small handi-bag next to it contained Edward Kohl's hair. Next was a small vial with an eyeball floating in it — Ed Henry's "eye for business." Next to that was just a wallet, but the wallet of cheapskate rich guy Mark Platzer. And lastly, next to that, pared down from the entire head, was Craig McManus' "psychic ear."

The dark figure smiled and placed the last two objects alongside the others — Steve Pascal's police shield and Terry O'Brien's waist pouch, that Godforsaken fanny pack. The dark figure took one final glance into the grisly curio cabinet and thought, *They're right... serial killers DO like to keep souvenirs.*

A beach...

IT WAS near dusk and the sun was starting to set behind the coconut trees that lined this Caribbean beach paradise. Delaware Bay sunsets were nice — Aruban sunsets with a million dollars in the bank, however, were so much better. On a chaise lounge sat a beautiful woman with long black hair, watching her children play in the sand. So contented was she that she never heard the swarthy-looking Scotsman approach from behind.

"Guess you were right..." he said.

"Jesus jumped up!" she yelped, startled out of her chair.

"They always look at the husband, never the wife."

After a long embrace she said, "Good to see you."

"Ditto," he answered.

Seven months earlier...

THEY sat, the two of them, nervously glancing around. To anyone else it would seem like a harmless dinner with an acquaintance at Cucina Rosa. But to them it was so much more, the culmination of months of flirtation and innuendo, all starting at the *Exit Zero* launch party the summer before, where they first met through, of all things, karaoke.

"Are we sure we want to do this?" Jack Wright asked.

"Positive," she answered.

Cathrine O'Brien's husband had been the entertainment at that party, and while he was busy guzzling free cocktails, the silky Scotsman had moved in.

"Big fun, eh?" he had said then.

"Yeah," she had answered, "big fun."

After a few cocktails of their own he said, "You don't look too happy. What's up?"

"I," she had answered, watching her drunken husband work the room, "hate karaoke."

"Ah," he had replied. With those words a plot, and a torrid affair, were born.

Cathrine didn't particularly hate her husband and it was never written in stone that he had to die — things just sort of worked out that way. But the karaoke had to be stopped. So, over excellent Italian food and a bottle of cabernet, they worked it out.

"We'll start with the doo-wop king."

"Yes," Jack agreed. "Obviously."

"Then the potty-mouth."

"Totally."

"Then that prissy hairdresser."

"Yes," Jack replied, "but a pity, he does such a nice job on my mane."

"Yeah," Cathrine looked up at his slanty bangs, "a great job. After that we'll play it by ear, but I think people will get the message."

"And of course," Jack said, taking a bite of his Chicken Tuscany, "I'll have exclusive rights to all 'inside information.'"

Cathrine smiled. "Ever the entrepreneur."

"Ever," he agreed, "but... um... who's going to do the actual, you know..." he ran a finger across his throat.

"Leave that..." Cathrine downed the rest of her wine and fixed him with a wicked grin, "to me."

And it was done.

The beach again...

JACK and Cathrine sat in the ebbing sun, sipping umbrella drinks as the boys frolicked away. The oldest boy came running up to them, "Hi, Uncle Jack!"

Jack Wright tussled the boy's hair. "Hey there, sport! How you doin'?"

"Mommy, can we go home?" the middle boy asked.

"Sure, buddy," Cathrine answered. "Anybody want pizza?"

The older boys yelled, "I do! I do! I do!"

The baby said, "Goo!"

So they rounded them up and loaded them into the minivan. Car seats buckled, Jack and Cathrine moved to the trunk, where they shared a brief kiss.

"You know," Jack said, "Steve I get, and Terry was an accident... but why Jessica Rose?"

Cathrine drolly answered, "She annoyed me. Thought you might like this."

She handed him a check for a half-million dollars, his cut of the insurance money. Terry, the poor sap, had never known about the $1,000,000 policy his wife had taken out six months earlier. How could he? He hadn't paid a bill or written a check in the five years since they got married.

Jack smiled and tucked the check into his pocket. "See you at the hotel."

She fixed him with a wicked grin. "Not if I see you first."

She winked, got in the van and drove off.

Jack chuckled. It had been a while since he had seen that grin. At first he found it rather arousing, but after a moment, the more he thought about, the more unsettled he became, though he couldn't put a finger on it.

On his way to the hotel it began to dawn on him... *maybe she's got a plan for me, too.*

Jack slept neither that night nor much over the next six months before his charred remains were eventually identified after a suspicious bar fire — a suspicious *karaoke* bar fire — on the island of Aruba.

The culprit was never caught.

EPILOGUE
A Bar, Another Time...

NSIDE the King Edward Bar in the Chalfonte Hotel, things were rocking. A nice crowd had gathered for the King Eddie's first karaoke night.

"Okay!" the host began in a jovial voice, "Welcome to karaoke night here at the King Eddie! Make sure you take care of your wait staff and your bartenders tonight! Looks like I better get started, the place is filling up pretty quick! People are dying to get in here!"

The crowd laughed.

"All right, then, first up tonight... you know 'em, you love 'em, you can't live without 'em! Sal Riggi doing a little Dion for you! Give it up for Sal!"

The crowd did indeed give it up for Sal as Terry handed him the mic. The unmistakable first chords of "Runaround Sue" sounded heavenly coming out of Terry's new speakers. Making his way to the bar he pressed the flesh with Edward, Mark and Ed. Kissed Brandi on the cheek, gave Craig a little noogie. They were all happy and drinking and having fun.

Terry flagged the bartender then waved to Officer Steve, who was three stools away.

"What'll it be?" Jilline the bartender asked.

"Oh, I don't know," Terry answered, "a little red wine?"

"Sure," Jilline replied.

"Hey!" Terry yelled, stopping her, "this room sounds amazing. Is this heaven or what?"

"No," she winked at him, "it's the Chalfonte. Be right back."

Terry scooched through the crowd and took the stool next to Officer Steve.

"How you doing, Steve?" he asked.

"That's officer... ah, never mind. I'm fine."

Terry smiled at him: "I guess things turned out okay after all, eh?"

Steve shrugged. "Guess so."

Jilline gave Terry the wine. Terry raised his glass to Steve.

"To good times," he offered.

"To good times," Steve echoed, clinking his glass.

Terry took a swig. "You're next, by the way."

"Cool, what am I singing?"

"Something from *Rent*?"

"Ooh, it might be a little early for that."

"Well, we're gonna be here for a while, you know."

"I'm just saying, I don't want to peak too early, is all."

"Peak early? Are you kidding me? I'll be happy if you peak at all."

"Now stop that..."

"I can't believe what a diva you've become."

"I'm not a diva, I just want what I want and I want it now!"

"That's the definition of a diva you moron."

"I'm not a moron..."

"You don't smell like cheese any more, by the way..."

The
CELESTIAL

*Up good, down bad... what was the spooky
secret behind America's oldest elevator?*

CHAPTER ONE
Part One: Signs

RENT O'Neil stood in front of the grand old building, looked up at her gleaming columns, and took a deep breath. *I can do this*, he thought and climbed the stairs. The building was the Celestial Dinner Theater and Bed and Breakfast, the oldest in Cape May. Though no one could say for sure how long it had been there, it was widely thought to be the eldest structure in an even elder town. And it was big: four stories tall and almost an acre, a marvel of Victorian architecture. The first two floors housed the theater; the first housing the actual stage, dining room, kitchen, bar and reception area. The second held the dressing rooms, prop rooms, wardrobe rooms and general storage rooms. The immense basement stored most of the stage sets.

In the top two floors were the myriad themed guest rooms; the Egyptian room was adorned with a sarcophagus and a multitude of cat statues. The Wild West room featured swinging saloon bathroom doors and "WANTED" posters of the current guests. The Atlantis room, with startlingly realistic 3-D undersea wallpaper featuring dozens of swimming creatures, also had a scale model of the "lost city" itself in the bathroom. There was also the Medieval Room, the Pirate Room, the Doo-Wop Room, the Shangri-La room, and so on.

The rooms were colorful, plentiful and continuously full. Cape May had long been known as the B&B capital of the planet and The Celestial was the granddaddy of them all, having had nary a single vacancy in recent memory.

But Trent knew none of this as he approached the stained redwood door. All he knew was that, at an old 36, with sore knees, a bad back and an expanding middle, this acting job might be his last. He had no idea how right he was.

With a trembling hand he opened the door, and like a man falling from a plane without a parachute, his theater life flashed before his eyes. *West Side Story* in '93, Riff, more hair, less middle, working knees. *Evita* later that year, Juan Peron, Kristen, bitch. *Annie* in '95, Rooster, fun, Jamie, bitch. And on it went, every memory dripping fresh ice down his spine.

It was right about this time he started having serious doubts. He rightly thought himself particularly ill-prepared for this job for many reasons: the leap back to the stage after a long absence, the meager talent that, fortunately for him, had been overrated by enough people to allow a fairly constant stream of work, the ever-present, crippling self-doubt. Most actors were insecure at their cores — Trent made *them* look like Navy SEALs.

No, this was definitely not going to work out. He quietly took a step back, the door swing closing in a painfully slow arc.

"May I help you?" a voice called from the foyer just as the door clicked shut.

Trent, not wishing to appear rude, quickly pushed it open. "No... no thanks, wrong address. I'll be on my way..."

"Are you sure?" the pretty young receptionist asked, "because you were standing there for about a minute before you slinked out."

"Guh..." he replied gracefully, never much of a liar. "I mean..."

The receptionist drummed her fingers on the big white desk. "Well, we're waiting..."

"Uh, yeah..." His mind groped desperately for purchase, but found none. Defeated, he stepped back inside. "Trent."

"Pardon?"

"Me. Trent. Actor?"

The receptionist replied with a smile, "Me. Joan. Receptionist. Where boy and monkey?"

Trent laughed and relaxed a bit. "Sorry, I'm a little nervous. My name is Trent. Trent..."

"O'Neil," Joan finished. From the desktop she lifted up a sheet of paper and flipped it around so Trent could see; his headshot and resumé.

He flushed a deep shade of red. "You knew."

She nodded with a wink, "We've been expecting you. And don't be nervous, you've already got the job, remember?"

"True," Trent agreed, wiping sweat from his forehead.

Joan came around the desk and offered a hand. "Joan Archer — receptionist, waitress, housekeeper, all-around girl Friday."

"Wow, that's a lot of hats," Trent said, shaking her hand.

"You should see my rack."

Trent raised an eyebrow. "But we've just met."

She chucked him on the arm. "Hat rack, you nerd."

"It's nice to meet you. I'm supposed to find..."

"Tom," Joan finished again, "Tom Ankiel. He's waiting for you. Come, I'll show you."

She casually took him by the hand and gave a tug. The skin-to-skin contact sent a thrill up his arm. It had been a long time since a woman touched him directly. And Joan happened to be an exceptionally *pretty* woman — short blonde hair framing a sharp, bright face. She led him from the reception and through a marvelously ornate bar, replete with gleaming mirrors and fancy bottles and glasses. Behind the cherry-stained bar stood a distinguished gentleman, polishing a glass with a rag.

"This is George, our bartender," Joan explained. "He's been here... forever. George, this is Trent. He's new."

"Pleased to meet you," Trent said and extended a hand.

George glowered at him, gave the slightest, most imperceptible of nods, then spit on the rag and went back to polishing.

"Okay..." Trent lowered his hand, his head, and followed Joan.

"Don't worry about him," she half-whispered. "He'll warm up once he gets to know you."

Trent looked back at George, who was shaking his head. "Sure, sure..." *I'll believe it when I see it.* Two steps from the theater door something caught his eye. "What's that?"

"Oh, that..." Joan hesitated, "why that's one of the Celestial's most historic attractions: the first-ever working elevator in the U S of A, maybe the world. People come from all over the world to see her and take a ride."

"Huh," Trent managed, genuinely impressed, not noticing the melancholy gaze Joan was casting his way. "Neat."

The elevator's burnished brass doors, six feet by eight feet high, were highly polished, but bore the scars of age. Still, it was rather elegant, sitting as it did inside this beautiful bar inside this beautiful building. Trent couldn't take his eyes off it.

"Still works?" he asked.

"In a manner of speaking," Joan answered with a gentle tug at his hand. "Come. This way."

Joan pushed open the big door that led from the bar into the theater and dining room. It was then that Trent decided to make his play.

"Look, Joan," he began, "I hate to bail on you, but it's been years since I set foot on a stage and I'm not sure I can..."

He took three steps more across the soft carpeting, lifted his head, and was suddenly unable to speak anymore.

Part Two: The Theater

"YOU'RE not sure you can what?" Joan asked him.

But Trent didn't hear her. In one breathtaking instant all doubt had been swept from his head. The room was gigantic, easily capable of holding 250 people, and looked as if it had been scooped out of the Titanic and placed here by some magic genie's crane. Hand-lit gas lamps lined the walls, candled chandeliers hovered elegantly over the tables, which shimmered with polished silverware and fine crystal. It was bright and dark at the same time, discordant and beautiful all at once. Silent yet thrumming with energy. Trent felt he had been lifted out of time and dropped into an F. Scott Fitzgerald novel. He half-expected Daisy Buchanan and Jay Gatsby to emerge from the wings and do the Charleston.

"Trent?" Joan tried.

But now he was staring at the stage, mesmerized. It was not the biggest nor the smallest he had ever seen — maybe 30 feet wide by 20 feet deep and elevated three feet off the floor, but it was just... perfect. While the ceiling over the dining room soared some 25 feet, over the stage it was a mere dozen and littered with all manner of high and low-tech lighting. It seemed to Trent as if a thousand years of theatrical evolution had been jammed all at once into this space, willy nilly. It simply oozed character, even though the walls were practically bare and the floor was covered in jig-sawed bits of plywood, chopped-up 2x4 studs and renegade screws and nails.

Somehow he knew he was in the exact right place at the exact right time.

"Wow..." he muttered.

Joan smiled, "Nice, isn't it?"

"Yeah," Trent replied with a chuckle, "you could say that."

"So you were saying?"

"Pardon?"

"Before," Joan reminded him. "You were saying something about 'I really just don't think...'"

"Oh that," he answered, "that was nothing... now."

Joan smiled broadly. "Good. Now I know Tom is around here somewhere. Why don't you sit for a minute, I'll go find him."

Trent nodded, and suddenly realized he needed to sit down, so overwhelming was the moment. Without seeing a script, without attending a rehearsal, he thought, *I want to work here forever.*

Which he would, in the end.

Part Three: The Meeting

A MINUTE later, Joan reappeared from backstage followed by a thin man in a natty suit that looked like tweed. As far as Trent knew, tweed suits went out with the Dodo.

"Trent," Joan perkily announced, "meet Tom. Tom, Trent. Tom is our Artistic Director."

It seemed to Trent as if a thousand years of theatrical evolution had been jammed all at once into this space. He was mesmerized.

Trent took the slim hand offered him and shook it. "Pleased to meet you. I look forward to working with you."

Tom said nothing. He returned Trent's firm handshake and eyed him over for a long moment. So Trent returned the favor.

Here's what Trent saw: a tall, lean man of about six feet. The suit was, indeed, a starchy tweed and looked agonizingly itchy. His face was gaunt and angular, interrupted by a hawk nose, and frosted with a white goatee. He looked a little like what Trent thought Sherlock Holmes must look like, only a little older.

Here's what Tom Ankiel saw — a man of average height, soft build, handsome if doughy face, tragically underdressed in sneakers, jeans and a T-shirt emblazoned with *World Champion Phillies 2008*. Worst of all was the black baseball cap that hid the eyes, for Tom knew the eyes truly were the windows to the soul. But the youngish fellow seemed pleasant enough, so...

"The pleasure," Tom offered in a soft, patrician burr, "is mine."

Joan said, "I was just about to start Trent on his paperwork."

"Excellent," Tom agreed, "then bring him back to me for debriefing.

And no, Mr O'Neil, that does not mean I will be removing your briefs."

Trent was silent.

"That, my young charge," Tom explained after an awkward moment, "is what we refer to around here as 'a joke.'"

"Oh," Trent was red again, "yes... I get it."

He didn't, but he was relieved that the old guy seemed to like him.

"Good," Tom said, "then I shall see you directly."

With that he was off, back to whenceever he came.

"Quite a character," Trent said.

"You have no idea," Joan agreed. "Come on, let's get you started on..."

"Joan!" a man cried from the stage.

Joan turned to see the young man, no more than 21, pushing through stacks of wood that would eventually become a set.

"There you are, good!" the young man continued. "We need to talk. Is Tom around?"

Joan answered, "Can it wait? I have a new actor here and..."

The young man held up a rolled parchment, like a scroll, fastened with a crimson red ribbon.

Joan's face fell. "I see. Let's go get Tom. Trent, would you mind waiting in the bar? George will give you whatever you want."

"Sure," Trent replied, confused, "no problem."

And while he hated leaving this glorious theater, he could tell something serious was going on, so he did as he was asked.

Part Four: The Conversation

JOAN led the young man, Milo, back stage and down the basement steps, where Tom Ankiel was overseeing construction of a wintry, Dickensian village made out of sturdy maple and plenty of cotton snow.

A crew of about 12 buzzed about the project, screwing something in here, hammering something there, applying liberal amounts of glitter and glue, all under Tom's twinkling eyes.

There were few things Tom loved more than designing a new set, watching his minions strip complicated flats and props from the stage, then band together to make a newer, better, even more complicated set for the next show. It had become something of a contest among the Celestial's cast and crew, trying to one-up themselves whenever new shows were mounted, and Tom thought it a healthy competition. Plus there was the bonus effect of each set being more impossibly detailed and dazzling than the last.

"Tom," Joan said, breaking him from his reverie, "we have some news."

He turned. "Yes?"

"Hello, Mr Ankiel," Milo said and held up the parchment, "I got this today."

Tom's eyes momentarily widened as they always did when one of his people got the crimson-bowed scroll. No matter how many times he saw it, he never got used to it.

"I see," he said, blinking slowly. "Well, allow me to be the first to say..." he extended a hand, "congratulations."

Milo shook it with a smile, "Thank you, sir. I couldn't have done it without you."

Joan hugged him briefly. "We're all proud of you. Now you better get moving, you leave in 10 minutes. Get your stuff and meet me by the elevator."

Milo grinned, nodded, and bounded up the basement steps three at a time.

Tom sighed. "Ah, youth... so wasted on the young. Is it not?"

"'Tis," Joan said softly.

"He should do quite well at his next station."

"Yes he should," Joan agreed, "but in the meantime, we're now in a bit of a pickle, are we not?"

"Oh yes..." Tom stammered, "yes indeed. I... I hadn't really thought of... hmmm."

Joan nodded. "Hmmm indeed."

Part Five: The Part

TRENT sat at the bar, enjoying a dry red wine. *First rehearsal isn't until tomorrow,* he figured, *glass of vino can't hurt, right?*

And even though George the bartender was giving him a world class stink-eye, Trent was enjoying every sip. He was always more of a beer-and-a-shot guy, but in this hand-carved treasure of a bar, ordering a beer would seem almost sacrilege. So wine it was. He didn't help himself when, after George served him, he realized he had no cash for a tip.

Oh well, he thought, determined not to let anything spoil his new-found good mood, *he'll get over it.* He didn't know it had been a very long time since anyone had tipped George.

A few minutes later he watched the young man, Milo, enter the bar, a large duffel bag, stuffed to capacity, thrown over his shoulder. He stood by the elevator and, within moments, was joined by Joan and Tom. Trent watched as they quietly exchanged a few words, hugs and handshakes. In a minute Milo was gone, into the brass elevator.

The elevator gone, Joan and Tom now had a quiet, intense conversation, which included more than one glance Trent's way. After a while they seemed to reach an agreement, exchanged nervous looks, then turned their full attention to Trent, who was now feeling a little uneasy.

"Mr O'Neil!" Tom exclaimed in a too-phoney voice as he and Joan made their way across the bar, "so nice we have this chance to chat!"

If the voice was fake, the smile was clip-on. Joan looked at him as she would an embarrassing uncle.

"Knock it off, Tom," she said.

"Fine," Tom relented, "just trying to be cordial."

"Trent," Joan began, in a tone so serious his knees felt weak even though he was sitting down, "we have a bit of a problem."

"Yes?" he asked, mustering all his false bravado, expecting yet another firing.

"Milo," Tom continued, "the young gentleman who just got on the elevator... you see, he was one of our lead actors. And it seems that Milo is going to be... moving on, up the ladder as it were, much sooner then we expected..."

"Which leaves us," Joan continued, "in a bit of a spot."

"Okay," Trent said, "I'm listening."

"Well..." Joan started.

"Allow me," Tom cut her off with a hand to the shoulder. "You see, Mr O'Neil, we hired you based on your potential. Your resumé has some nice things on it, but most of those were over 10 years ago. This is not to say you are without talent; quite the opposite, we see loads of promise in you. However, we were hoping to bring you along slowly, ease you into our methods, our philosophy, our... way of doing things."

"Uh huh," Trent muttered, "and now... you don't need me anymore?"

"No, no," Joan cautioned. "Nothing like that. In fact, we need you now more than ever."

Trent stared at them. "I don't get it."

"Mr O'Neil," Tom put a hand on his shoulder. "How quick a study are you?"

"Fairly," said Trent, taking a gulp of wine. "Why?"

Joan took his hand: "We'd like to offer you the role of Bob Cratchit in *A Christmas Carol*."

Trent was ecstatic. "That's it? You want me to take a bigger part? I was looking forward to playing some of the more minor roles but... Bob Cratchit is a plum! I'd be happy to! Thanks."

"And the Ghost of Christmas Present," Tom continued.

Trent was taken aback. "Oh... uh... two parts. Wow. I wasn't expecting that. But... sure, with enough study time... I should be fine. Absolutely."

Joan continued, "and Jacob Marley."

Trent was silent.

Tom went on, "and a Man of Goodwill, and, possibly, the Ghost of Christmas Future."

Trent swigged the last of his wine and motioned to George for another. When he came back, Tom asked him to leave the bottle and get two more glasses. Silently Trent sat, flanked by his new employer and co-worker, weighing the opportunity. He had played multiple parts in a show before, most notably *West Side Story*, when he played a Jet, a Shark and a policeman, but none of them had any lines. This would be four, maybe five parts, all of which were crucial to the story. It would be a challenge, but one any actor would look back upon fondly and tell stories about to future generations.

Given enough rehearsal time, a week, two at most, he was confident he could pull it off. So emboldened, he downed another glass of wine and said, "Yes, I'll do it."

"Huzzah!" Tom cried.

"Thank you!" Joan concurred.

They filled and clinked their glasses in celebration.

Feeling good, feeling confident, Trent asked, "When do we open?"

Joan paused, "Tomorrow night."

Trent put the glass down. "Go to hell."

"We might, Trent," Tom replied with a hearty slap on the back. "We just might."

CHAPTER TWO
Part One: Meetings

T WAS Trent O'Neil's second day of work at his new job at The Celestial Dinner Theater and Bed & Breakfast, and it was just about the last place on Earth he wanted to be. In a Rube Goldberg-ian twist of fate, Trent was to replace one of the Celestial's lead actors and the five roles he played, all in one day. In eight hours, to be specific.

He had spent the previous night studying his script, running lines and taking notes with stage manager Joan Archer. The memorization of lines completed, today was left to concentrate on the rest of the play, namely blocking (where an actor moves or stands), costumes, music, choreography, props and technical assignments. Other than that, he was almost done.

Head pounding, he now sat at the Celestial's magnificently ornate bar in a pair of torn, dirty sweats and a T-shirt — his common rehearsal attire. Nervously, he drummed his fingers on the bar and tapped a foot on the brass foot rail. Across from him stood George, the bartender, silently arranging and dusting bottles.

"Can I get a soda?" Trent asked him.

George stopped what he was doing, filled a glass with ice, picked up the soda gun and, casting a glance over the bartop to Trent's belly, pressed the 'diet' button.

"Thanks for your concern," Trent said bitterly.

George winked.

It was not new for Trent to make a bad first impression on people. But being intimidated by a 65-year-old bartender who had spoken nary a word to him — that was new.

"There you are!" Joan Archer shouted from the entryway foyer, startling Trent. "Right on time!"

Joan was the heart and soul of the Celestial — smart, young, pretty, full of fire. Walking in behind her, replete with topcoat, top hat and tails, was the brains of the outfit, Artistic Director Tom Ankiel.

"Good morning!" a chipper Joan offered.

"Morning," Trent mumbled. As if the lack of sleep and mountains of stress weren't enough to process for one morning, one other thing was becoming clear.

"Did you get some breakfast?" Joan asked.

"Sure, sure..." he answered, gazing back and forth from Tom, in his high-dollar tuxedo, to Joan, in crisp black slacks, white dress shirt and tailored blazer. "Um, am I under-dressed?"

"No..." Joan started, then actually looked at Trent's ensemble: 12-year-old University of Delaware sweatpants, paint-spattered Nikes, black, bleach-spotted Batman T-shirt and black baseball cap. "Not at all... Tom is perpetually over-dressed, and me? Well, look at me!"

Trent did. Not only was she sparklingly well dressed, but stealthily beautiful.

"Yeah," he said, "I'm gonna go change. Be right back."

But it was too late.

"Oh great!" Joan announced, "here comes everyone else."

"Fantastic," Trent sighed, not even needing to look at them. But when he did his greatest fears were confirmed — they all, about 20 of them, though not quite as natty as Tom, were wearing variations on Joan's outfit — neatly pressed pants and dress shirts, tasteful skirts and pantsuits, an overall uniform of cool professionalism... except for the chubby guy at the bar wearing clothes most people wouldn't use to wax their car.

"No one told me..." Trent started.

"It's okay," Joan assured him, "I should have mentioned something. We have a sort of unofficial dress code here."

"Unofficial?"

"Yeah," she continued. "Not sure when it started... I mean, no one has to dress nice, we just all sort of do."

"Well," Trent hissed. "Nice to know."

Joan scrunched up her face. "I know. I'm sorry. Don't be mad."

Trent couldn't be mad — he was too busy falling in love.

For the next minute or so the bar echoed with the sound of people greeting and swapping stories. Then Tom, his stentorian voice in full affected glory, spoke up. "Thank you!" he quieted them. "Thank you all for coming at this last minute. As many of you must now know, Milo has taken leave of us."

At this there was a small round of applause and more than one dampened eye.

"Yes, I know," Tom continued, "Milo was one of our very best. In fact, one of the best we've had here ever. His absence will be hard for all of us to cope with..."

Oh, good grief, Trent thought, *could you make this any harder?*

As if on cue. "But we have here in his place a most capable replacement, Mr Trent O'Neil from parts north. Mr O'Neil, please stand."

Trent did, to the exact mix of bemused embarrassment and abject horror he was expecting.

"Sorry," he attempted, "I left my good sweats in my other pants."

This drew a few weak chuckles, and nothing more. Trent sat to a thundering silence.

"Sorry..." Joan tried but found herself talking to Trent's palm.

"Mr O'Neil," Tom kept on, "I apologize for not informing you of our informal little dress code here. It is inexcusable and you have my humblest apologies."

Trent was taken aback. "Sure, no problem."

"Ladies and gentlemen, let me assure you," Tom began moving through the crowd. It struck Trent as a football coach giving his big pre-game speech. It was stirring. "Let me assure you, despite Mr O'Neil's appearance at this moment, he is a talented young man and capable of doing great things. As you know, if he were not, he would not be here and neither would any of you. So please set aside this sartorial blunder and take solace in the fact that Mr O'Neil was working with Ms Archer..."

Ms? Hmmm...

"...Until the sun came up this morning in an effort to catch up with the rest of us. Mr O'Neil is a hard worker and we must do our best not to fail him. What we have worked on for 30 days he will have to learn in less than one, and I expect all of you to do your level best to help him. Am I understood?"

He was.

"Now," Tom finished, "if we can make our way into the theater, we have a very long day ahead of us."

Calmly, quietly, the group funneled through the door.

"Guy's got a way with words," Trent offered humbly.

"That," Joan agreed, "is why he's in charge."

With that, they stepped into the theater, where Trent was about to begin his greatest, last adventure.

Part Two: Rehearsal

AGAIN, as it was less than 24 hours earlier when he first saw the theater, Trent's breath was taken away. The stage and dining room had overnight been transformed. Yesterday it was a plain, if elegant, Victorian-era dining room, the stage stripped down to its bare walls, light fixtures dangling, beams exposed. But now...

Joan, seeing Trent's slackened face and open mouth, said, "Cleans up

The stage, rather, the landscape, in front of him that WAS the stage, was a full-scale recreation of an 1860s English street scene.

nice, doesn't she?"

Trent, for a moment, was unable to speak. "It's beautiful."

The dining room, with its intricately laid-out floor plan, a floor plan capable of seating 250 people at once, looked less like a dining room and more like a Dickensian village. The numerous tables were dressed up to look like street vendors carts, or toy shops, or small houses. Trent had to squint to see where the actual chairs and place settings were. It was like having to stare at one of those computer-designed posters for minutes on end before the sailboat or space ship suddenly materialized. And some-how, it seemed as if everything, everything, was covered in snow. Falling snow at that.

"It's unbelievable."

"Nah," Joan said with a dismissive wave of the hand, "it's nothing — a few well-placed fans, a bunch of confetti."

"But where does it..."

At that moment he turned and looked at the stage and was struck mute. He knew, he *knew*, when he saw it yesterday that it was no more than 20-feet by 30-feet, with maybe 12 feet of ceiling clearance. But what he saw before him was a physical impossibility.

"How…" he started.

"Might be better not to ask," Joan finished, giving his hand a small squeeze.

The stage, rather, the landscape, in front of him that was the stage, was a full-scale recreation of an 1860s English street scene, complete with burning gas lamps, heaps of snow, vending carts, butcher shop, toy store… all blanketed in white snow.

Joan gave him a nudge in the ribs. "Look back there."

"What…" Trent looked to the rear of the dining room where, in the back left corner, there seemed to be an office. Actually, it *was* an office, and judging by the wooden sign hanging in front of it, it was the office of Scrooge & Marley.

Joan squeezed his other hand, grabbing his attention, and into a small, wireless walkie-talkie she said, "Test on one, two and three."

"Got it," the talkie squawked back.

"Watch this," she said.

A moment later, Trent watched in disbelief as three different sections of the stage — a vending cart, the butcher shop and a toy shop, — slowly elevated about six inches, then began to turn. In less than a minute the set pieces were turned 180 degrees and, miraculously, came together to reveal the inside of a house. Scrooge's house, Trent assumed by the dark walls and dusty props.

"Test on four," Joan said to the talkie and turned Trent to the back of the house.

Again, he watched in a dreamlike haze as the offices of Scrooge & Marley slowly turned to reveal a brightly decorated living room and kitchen.

"Your house," Joan told him. "I mean, the Cratchit house."

He noted, "It's nicer than my last apartment."

Proudly, she said, "Pretty fancy, huh?"

"It's okay," he ribbed her.

"Re-set," she told the walkie and the setpieces seamlessly returned to their starting positions, the cityscape illusion complete once again.

Trent shook his head, trying to regain his senses. "When…"

Joan answered, "Last night, while you and I were working on your script, the rest of us elves were down here cobbling."

"When did you finish?"

Joan shrugged. "About an hour ago."

Trent was flabbergasted.

"It's okay," Joan assured him, "we're used to long nights. Right now we need to get you ready. So... you ready?"

Trent sighed. "And Tom doesn't want you to let me down."

"Tom is an accomplished motivator. So good, in fact, I give us a one-in-10 chance of actually pulling this thing off," Joan said.

"Your confidence is astounding," Trent replied dryly.

Joan flashed him a mischievous grin, and it was in that moment that Trent fell completely in love with her.

Across the room, Tom stepped to the lip of the stage and cleared his throat. "If we may begin!"

Everyone came to attention.

"First," he continued, "everyone please be sure to say hello to Mr O'Neil and make him feel welcome. Secondly, as it is Mr O'Neil's first, and only, day to rehearse with us, I suggest we take it from the top."

There was no argument.

Over his shoulder and into the tech booth housed above the stage, Tom cried, "Full tech run! Actors to places! Overture to begin on my mark... three, two, one... mark!"

At this the house lights went black and digitally-remastered Christmas bells began keening, throwing Trent into a momentary, blind vertigo. People bustled all around him, unseen. He heard the occasional "Excuse me" and "Good luck." But all he felt right now was nausea. The bells ended, followed by the strains of a virtual orchestra plucking through familiar Christmas carols. Trent was drowning in a cacophony.

Finally, Joan's hand, a port in the storm, found his.

"Follow me," she whispered, "and remember what we talked about. You have all the blocking notes. Don't be afraid to use your script for this run-through. Trust me on that. Other than that, stay out of the way and don't bump into the furniture."

To his, and her, surprise, she pecked him on the cheek.

"Thanks..." he started, but she was gone.

"Over here, Mr O'Neil." It was Tom in the back office set where Ebenezer Scrooge and Bob Cratchit make their first appearance... Act One, Scene One.

"Feeling spry?" Tom asked, eyes a-twinkle in the gloom.

"Spry as I'm likely to get, Mr Ankiel."

"Excellent!" Tom told him. He then popped on a top hat, threw a thick black cape over his shoulders, and furrowed his brow. Face screwed up like a man who just bit a lemon he said, in a croaking British accent, "And please, call me Mr Scrooge. Break a leg."

Trent chuckled and thought, *If only I were that lucky.*

A moment later the overture had ended and the two men stepped on to the darkened set. Trent sat at his counting table, took a deep breath, and tried not to shriek in terror when the lights came up on the offices of Scrooge & Marley, money lenders.

Ninety minutes later, Trent sat on the lip of the stage, holding a towel full of ice to his temple.

"The script said 'Turn left and walk to the toy shop', not 'turn left, walk to the toy shop and watch out for the animatronic horse!'"

Joan laughed. "Oh come on, it wasn't that bad."

Trent smiled. "As far as kicks in the head from horses go, I suppose not. So, how'd I do?"

Joan thought a moment. "On the whole? Not bad. A few rough spots here and there, but overall... good job."

"A few rough spots? Well," he offered, putting down the ice and peering at his watch, "at least we still have... five hours to fix them. A relative eternity."

"Believe me," Joan said, slapping his leg, "we'll use every minute of it."

They sat in comfortable silence for a long minute, before Trent asked, "When is everybody back?"

"About 45 minutes, after lunch."

Silence again.

Then Trent said, "I know it's only been... less than a day, but, despite the current madness, I really like it here. It feels like... home. Too mushy?"

She smiled at him. "Not at all. Most people feel that way when they come here. If they don't, well, they don't last very long, I can tell you that."

"Well, I want to last very long, I can tell you that."

"Don't worry," she brushed a hand across his cheek, "I think you will. Now come on, let's work on the dances. Your first waltz was a disaster."

Trent stood. "Yeah, well, I don't recall putting 'dancer' anywhere on my resumé."

She took the hand he offered and stood with him. "Well it also doesn't say 'two left feet' on there either, does it?"

With a small remote she clicked on the song "Christmas Waltz", featured in Act Two, and danced. It was just about the best time Trent had ever had.

Three hours later, an exhausted Trent O'Neil leaned on an even more exhausted Joan Archer before an ecstatic Tom Ankiel and a weary cast and crew.

"That," Tom announced, "should just about do it for the evening."

A cheer rose forth.

Tom continued, "I am extremely proud of all of you, especially

Mr O'Neil, for holding up quite well the length of this tortuous day with poise and professionalism... despite his rather ratty attire..." He winked at Trent who smiled back, "... and you, Ms Archer, for getting him ready, keeping him focused and suggesting he apply some deodorant some hours ago."

This drew a chuckle from everyone, except Trent, who surreptitiously smelled his pits.

"You have all earned the next hour off, plus I'm pushing call time back an additional half-an-hour as we're expecting a very large house this evening. So you may luxuriate for the next 90 minutes in the manner of your choosing, but all are to be signed in by 8:30 sharp. See you then. Mr O'Neil, a word please."

The cast and crew broke with a minimum of discussion, most too exhausted to do anything but go take a nap, a shower and come back for opening.

"Mr O'Neil," Tom started.

"Trent. Please, call me Trent. Mr O'Neil is my father's name."

Tom nodded slowly. "As you wish. Ahem, Trent, ahem, thank you once again for obviously being a conscientious employee and an obviously quick study."

Trent smiled. "That's my greatest talent: memorizing crap real fast." He then looked at Joan. "Plus, I had a lot of help."

Tom gave him a look that Trent could only interpret as sad. "Yes, well, be that as it may, your efforts here today will not be forgotten. I will see you at curtain."

Trent offered a hand. "Thank you, Mr Ankiel. For everything."

Tom shook it: "It's Tom. And you're welcome."

With that, Joan and Trent were left alone again.

"So," Trent asked, "this is actually the first minute I've been here and not been working... what should we do?"

Joan laughed at him. "For 90 minutes? Gosh, we just have just so many options..."

"We?" Trent said.

Joan hesitated, "Trent..."

And it hit him in the gut. He had done it again, taken a passing interest from a woman as a sure sign of romantic intent. How many times would this be? 100? 200? 1,000? Every episode started with the same certainty, the same heartless butterflies in his stomach, the same baited anticipation of seeing her again, followed by the same crushing realization that, no, pretty girls don't like chubby guys with two left feet, a modicum of talent and little else to offer.

"It's okay," he said, cutting her off. "It's okay if I really like you and you don't really like me. Wouldn't be the first time."

"It's not that," Joan answered. "I happen to find you rather charming in a sweat pants-wearing kind of way."

Trent smiled ruefully.

"It's just... things are different here, at the theater, there's a sort of..."

Trent finished, "Unspoken code?"

Joan chuckled. "Exactly."

Trent stared at the floor. "Is there anything actually spoken around here? Dress codes? Dating policies? Hygienic tactics?"

She lifted his head with a finger. "Trent, we've really pushed you into things here without fully explaining the... situation. There are a lot, and I mean a *lot*, of things you need to know about the Celestial. A new actor's first week is usually spent in orientation meetings, observing shows and rehearsals, generally getting the lay of the land before ever setting foot on stage for a rehearsal, let alone a show. But you... we've had to sort of thrust this all upon you. After tonight, assuming we survive, everything will become a lot clearer. I promise."

Trent nodded, taking mild solace in the fact that this perfect, beautiful creature might like him. "Okay, I believe you."

"Until then..." she leaned in, kissed him on the cheek, and walked away, their eyes locked, Trent's guts quivering, his head spinning.

When she was gone, unable to contain himself, he leapt up on to the stage and, in full Rocky Balboa form, jumped up and down, fists raised in victory.

"She might like me!" he cried, "I think she might like me!"

His elation was quickly dampened, however, when the stage lights were killed, plunging the theater into a complete, impenetrable blackness.

"Um... hello?"

Silence.

"Hello? New guy here..."

He then tripped over an unseen prop and thudded heavily on his ass in front of the stage.

"Ow!"

CHAPTER THREE
Part One: Curtain

I N THE last 90 minutes Trent O'Neil had learned a play and fallen, not only in love, but flat on his ass in a pitch-black theater. After being discovered and rescued some 15 minutes later, he had retired to the men's wardrobe to finalize his costume fittings, headed up to the men's dressing room to apply a little make-up (he hated to admit how much he loved applying a nice base and a little liner to accentuate his round, Disney eyes), downed three cups of coffee and taken his starting place behind the Scrooge & Marley office set.

There was a flurry of activity all around him. From where he stood in the rear of the theater, he could see through a small window and down the length of the theater. In the dining room, waiters rushed from table to table, serving desserts, pouring coffee. It dawned on him what a minor miracle it must be for the kitchen to serve 250 people in less than 90 minutes. To his right and behind him the tech crew tested their wireless headset connections, talking with the lead crew above and behind the main stage. They coolly ran through their lighting cues in a mock run.

Lastly, he saw the children. They were hard to notice at first as the tables and chairs had all been designed to flawlessly resemble a Victorian street scene, but they were there, about a dozen of them, moving from table to table. They were dressed as Dickens-era street urchins, faces blackened with soot, clothes distressed, but their faces were undeniably bright. And the waiters, instead of throwing a hissy fit if one of them got in the way, instead graciously waited for them to pass.

It amazed Trent that what should have been a scene of mass chaos and confusion was indeed quite the opposite. It seemed almost choreographed.

Will this place, he wondered, *ever cease to amaze me?*

With a deep sigh he sat on one of the small chairs backstage and thought of Joan Archer, his newfound theater mentor. It was pathetic how much he missed her after knowing her a day and a half. But the thought of her filled him with the warm and fuzzies and it had been a long time since he had looked forward to seeing a female, so he just went with it.

"It seems to me," said Tom Ankiel, resident theater genius, scaring the bejeebers out of Trent, "that you have grown quite fond of our Ms Archer."

Trying to sound as formal as possible and match Tom's hoity-toity-ness, Trent answered, "Quite. Indeed."

Tom smiled, appreciating the attempt. "Nice try, Mr. O'Neil, but you are many years, hundreds of bottles of whisky and innumerable cigars away from matching my smooth-as-silk, sweet-as-chocolate basso profundo."

Trent cheekily cleared his throat. "Indeed."

At that moment the house lights dimmed three times in succession, the universal theater code for "five minutes."

Tom asked the next question slowly, "Has Ms Archer explained her... situation yet?"

"No, not exactly," Trent answered. "She told me I have all kinds of stuff to learn about her, and this place. Why do you ask? Is there a husband? Boyfriend?"

Tom's voice was flat. "There was, yes, but that's..." With a cough he forced the joviality back into his voice and quickly changed the subject. "I'm sorry, Mr O'Neil, here it is, only moments 'til curtain and here I am distracting you. We shall talk after the show, at which time I'm sure I'll be praising your Olivier-like performance. You and I are due for a heart-to-heart."

"Sure," Trent answered, mildly uneasy. "After the show, I'll buy you a drink."

"Nonsense," Tom clapped him on the back. "First one is always on me."

He turned and walked away. Trent did not see him wipe the tear from his cheek.

Trent stood in silence for a while, trying to decompress. At this point, it was no longer about knowing his lines or remembering his blocking — he either would or he wouldn't. Right now was about bucking up, fastening the chinstrap and going in head first, without a net. Good actors simply got through a show on short notice. The great ones owned it, made it their own. While he had no idea how tonight was going to turn out, it was surely going to be better than falling on his ass.

The lights dimmed thrice in succession once more, then were dimmed to black. Showtime.

"Break a leg," came the quiet voice, followed swiftly by the warm breath.

Trent smiled in the dark. "Joan... thanks, Joan. You, too."

Though it was nearly opaque behind the set, Trent swore he could make out her lovely blonde hair and striking smile.

"What are you doing back here? I though you were running lights tonight?" he asked quietly.

"I was," she answered, "but Shelly, one of the chorus girls, got sick, literally, about five minutes ago… and all over my sneakers. So say hello to Person of Goodwill Number Two."

"Number Two." Trent whistled. "Best damn part in the show."

"Very funny," she said, touching his shoulder, setting him on fire. "But it looks like you're not the only one who will be making their debut sans net."

"Well then, may I wish you the brokenest of legs, Madame."

"You may," she replied and curtsied in the dark.

For a while they said nothing. Then the lights flickered briefly.

"Two minutes," she said hastily. "I better run."

"Ok…"

Before he could finish she kissed him. It was warm and sweet, unexpected, and seemed to draw the breath from his body and fill him with air and light. Lips together, arms entwined, in the dark, Christmas bells ringing. She smelled like a cookie — he hoped he smelled half as nice.

From the office set he heard Tom clear his throat and hiss, "Mr O'Neil… places!"

But he ignored him. This was just about the best damn kiss he had ever had, maybe the best kiss *anyone* had ever had, and he darn sure wasn't going to break it off for some silly old play.

"Mr O'Neil!"

But Trent was gone, caught up in the softness of her.

"MR O'NEIL!"

Nope. Not yet.

"Mr Cratchit!"

"Uh-oh."

Opening an eye he noticed it was suddenly much brighter, partly due to the new fire in his heart, but mostly attributable to the giant klieg lights blazing away above him. Into Scrooge's office. Where Trent was supposed to be.

"Nuts," Trent mustered and pulled away from Joan.

"Sorry," she whispered, grin beaming from her face. She began singing "Hark the Herald Angels Sing" and stepped out into the house, blending seamlessly into the street scene in the dining room

"Mr Cratchit!" Tom as Scrooge thundered.

"A moment, sir!" Trent cried from the wings, frantically trying to put on the rest of his costume and remember his first line.

Tom whaled away, "Your assistance would be greatly appreciated at some point TODAY!!!"

Trent stumbled on to the stage, top hat askew, glasses akimbo.

"Yes, sir. Sorry, Mr Scroo…"

But as the words left his mouth, he stepped on his long, flowing scarf and tumbled, ass over tea kettle, off of the set and swiftly descended the three feet to the hard floor. The puffed cotton snowdrifts did little to break his fall or spare his coccyx. A roar of laughter erupted from the sold-out house.

Tom as Scrooge sneered down at him from above, hint of a smile playing about his lips, and croaked, "Olivier indeed. Bah!"

And this, as it turned out, would be the highlight of Trent's evening.

Part Two: The Show

FOR the next two hours, Trent was lost. Hopelessly lost. His cues were coming too fast, too soon. By the time he figured out where he was in this scene, they were halfway through the next scene, which made for a few awkward moments, such as the one where Trent, in full Ghost of Christmas Present regalia — gigantic Christmas-lighted, velvet robe, soaring golden crown, jewel encrusted cup of "milk of human kindness" and sweat running freely down his face — observed the Cratchit family preparing dinner and blurted out, "God bless us, everyone" instead of "Quiet Scrooge, I'm trying to listen."

And when Tom as Scrooge, trying desperately to conceal his giggles, tried to right him by saying, "Perhaps I should drink a little more of that milk, eh Ghost?" Trent responded with another, hearty, "God bless us, everyone."

At this, Tom burst out laughing. But in true professional manner, he managed to make it sound like theatrical sobbing, burying his face in Trent's sleeve, quivering with laughter. Trent, on the verge of nervous collapse, was unable to say anything other than, "God bless us, everyone" for the balance of the scene. It was a complete disaster, like Jerry Lewis playing Patton.

It was also the funniest scene of the night.

It went on this way for quite some time, Trent trying beyond hope to salvage his character, only to say something completely inappropriate, sending the crowd into another convulsion of laughter, Trent sweating a little more until there was no sweat left. If you had touched his silk vest it would have squished. Then finally, mercifully, it all ended with the entire cast and audience singing "Ave Maria."

It was loud, uplifting and, most importantly to Trent, it meant the show was over.

"Ave, Ave Maria..." they all sang. At the end of the last note the lights went out and the audience burst into applause. The "Choir of the Bells" played as the actors took their curtain calls. Trent, not wishing to face the audience he had just mortified himself in front of, started to slink away from the chorus and backstage — out of sight.

"Not so fast!" Joan cried above the din, grabbing his hand and giving it a squeeze. "You're not getting off that easy."

Trent, red-faced and high-pulsed, was unable to speak. He just gave her a look that pleaded, "Please, let me go!"

But Joan was having none of it. Squeezing his hand they watched and waited as the chorus, then the dancers, then the minor role-players took their bows. Finally it was Trent's turn. He was unable to move, so Joan pulled him on the center of the stage. Suddenly, the lights felt very hot, and too bright — he couldn't see anything beyond their white glare. But he could hear it.

Huh?

It started slowly, tentatively, but it was there. Then it built, and built some more, until the crescendo was undeniable — Trent was getting a standing ovation.

"Huzzah!" someone cried.

Trent held up a hand to block the light and looked for the source of the voice.

"Kudos!" another shouted.

Trent darted his eyes all around, trying to see who was yelling, but it was too late. Now the crowd was hooting and hollering, rewarding his inept performance with the most heart-warming show of acceptance he had ever experienced. He could not help but weep like a child.

After a long moment, Tom as Scrooge emerged, took his hand, and they bowed together.

Tom turned and looked at him as a proud father would his son. "Kudos. Kudos indeed."

Trent could only smile at him as the tears ran down his cheeks.

"And please," Tom said, "do try not to fall off the stage."

Trent laughed. In less than 48 hours he was made to feel more at home in this place than he had anywhere in his entire life.

Part Three: After

SHORTLY after curtain call the theater was empty and the house lights were up. Trent sat on the lip of the main stage, trying to process everything that had just happened. A line of his fellow actors had already come by, offering hugs and handshakes, many of them confessing it was the funniest show they had ever seen, others still admitting they were unable to maintain character as he flailed away from scene to scene. In short, tragedy to him, comedy to them.

Finally, Tom and Joan approached him. They were smiling.

"I must say," Tom started, removing his Scrooge top hat, "that is the most fun I've had on stage in a very long time. For that, I thank you, Mr O'Neil."

Trent flushed: "You're welcome."

Tom tousled his hair, the second fatherly gesture in the last few minutes. "Please, Mr O'Neil, do not feel in the least as if you have let me... us... down."

"I'll do my best," Trent said, unable to meet his eye.

Tom took off his overcoat and set it on the stage. "Remember, I owe you a drink. I'm assuming a very tall, cool drink."

And Tom was gone, with everyone else, out to the bar. Trent couldn't look at Joan, but he felt her there.

"Sorry," he muttered.

"Oh, please," she countered. "Tom is right. That's the funniest damn show we've had in here in ages. Seriously, don't sweat it."

"Great," he said morosely. "I've taken Dickens and made it into *The Producers*. Maybe we can add "Springtime for Hitler" to tomorrow's show."

She took his hand, squeezed it. He looked up at her pretty face, the sharp, sloped nose, the full pouty lips, the eyes like limpid pools... and burst into tears.

Joan cradled his head. "My goodness, what is it?"

He looked up at her again, eyes wet and streaked with red.

"I love it here," he managed through heavy, racking sobs. "This was the worst show of my life, the worst show of anybody's life, and I love it. I don't deserve it. I don't know why I'm here. I don't know what brought me here. I can't explain it. But I'm supposed to be here and I'm terrified I'm going to lose it..."

"Shhh," she rocked him back and forth, stroked his thinning hair, comforted him. "It's all right. You just relax and take a deep breath. It's been a long couple of days. There there..."

She hated lying to him, but she couldn't bear him being like this.

"Come on," she said firmly, lifting his head and looking him in the eye, "let's go get that drink."

"Okay."

She kissed him softly, quickly. He stood and helped her up.

"You know," he said, "for a girl who doesn't want to get involved with anyone, you sure send out some conflicting signals."

She smiled at him, but there was some sadness in it.

"I know, I know," he said, "we'll talk about it later. Gotcha. Now tell

He looked for her in the gloom and saw her, standing by the elevator, holding a scroll of her own, only hers was unbound and quite long.

me, what kinds of vodka do you have?"

Part Four: The Elevator

AN HOUR later they sat at the bar, raucously swapping theater war stories with Tom. Trent, on his third Absolut martini, was feeling much better. Tom had ingested his fair share of red wine, while Joan nursed a beer. Remarkably, it seemed that every member of the audience was still in the bar, carousing, imbibing, having loud conversation.

After a while, Trent said, "This is absolutely amazing! It's like no one wants to leave! It's like no one *can* leave!"

Tom and Joan exchanged a look.

Trent continued, oblivious. "Is it always like this? With such a great crowd?"

Tom answered, "Most of the time, yes."

"Don't you ever have a dead audience?" Trent asked.

Tom laughed. "More often than you can possibly imagine, Mr O'Neil! More often than you can imagine!"

And on they went, another 30, then 45, then 60 minutes. Finally, Trent had had enough.

"Okay," he announced upon completion of his fourth martini, "I better go get some sleep. I'm sure you're gonna wanna put me through the ringer tomorrow."

"Indeed," Mr O'Neil. "Indeed. But pray, do stay a bit longer, there is something I'd like you to see."

"Tom!" Joan scolded. "No, he's not ready."

"Tosh!" Tom retorted. The red wine had his face in full bloom. "And poppycock! He's ready if I say he's ready and I say he's ready to be ready to be... perhaps I've had a bit too much wine."

"Perhaps," Joan snarled.

"But!" Tom continued, "Mr O'Neil did yeoman's work this evening and made this old man laugh harder than he has laughed in years and I say I want him to see it. What harm could it do?"

Joan shot back, "Only the irreparable kind, but if your mind's made up."

"It is!" Tom announced, a little too exuberantly. "That it is!"

"Um, guys," Trent butted in, "any chance you want to tell me what the hell it is you're talking about?"

Joan said nothing. Tom pointed to the big clock on the wall and answered, "Soon enough, my boy. Soon enough."

It was just a few moments before midnight, and for the first time Trent noticed it was growing quiet and a nervous vibration seemed to flow through the room. It was odd, 200-some people going from boisterous to silent in such a brief span. And then he heard the clock begin to chime. Not too loudly, just enough to let you know what time it was. One, two, three... all the way through to 12.

After 12 is when the singing began, softly at first, like a whisper. Trent recognized it immediately as "Silent Night". It was eerie yet oddly soothing. Not knowing what else to do, he sang along.

After a minute or so the bar lights dimmed to black and the only light in the room emanated from the old brass elevator, which Trent had barely noticed before. But now it was all he could look at. Across the bar, Joan grabbed his hand. He smiled at her, she grinned weakly.

"Watch," Tom whispered.

So Trent did. The first thing he noticed was that the golden glow from the elevator seemed to have no source. The elevator itself seemed to be the light, and it was growing brighter. Next he saw, for the first time, that everyone was now holding a rolled-up piece of paper bound with a crimson ribbon, like Milo, the kid actor, had been holding the day before, just prior to leaving on... on the elevator. That had struck Trent as a little strange at the time, but he hadn't though about it since. It now dawned on him that perhaps he should have been paying a little more attention to detail around here the last couple days.

He looked to Joan, but was alarmed to see she was gone, though he hadn't felt her let go of his hand. He looked for her in the gloom and saw her, standing by the elevator, holding a scroll of her own, only hers was unbound and quite long, like a child's exaggerated Christmas list.

He began to speak but she beat him to the punch.

"Miller," she announced, just loud enough to be heard over the signing.

At this, a 50-ish man with a full head of salt-and-pepper hair rose from the bar, finished his drink, shook a few hands and moved to the elevator. The crowd parted before him, still singing softly, and Mr Miller passed through them, a smile (or was it a grimace?) on his face. He approached Joan, gave a nod, opened his scroll. Joan pulled the elevator door open, Mr Miller stepped inside, Joan closed it.

Trent turned to Tom. "What..."

Tom held a finger to his lips and pointed to the elevator, so Trent watched. After a few seconds the elevator made a whirring noise and the light behind the door moved up, and as it did it changed from gold to blue. There was a smattering of applause at this. Trent was still greatly confused and looked back to Tom.

"Up good," Tom whispered, "down bad."

"Why?" Trent asked.

"Stevens," Joan called.

A woman this time, 30-something, pretty, raven-haired, went to the elevator and got on. This time the light moved down and changed from gold to a deep ruby red.

Trent turned to Tom, who said only, "Up good, down bad."

"But why?"

Tom chuckled. "Because heaven's up there, of course."

"Oh, I see," Trent replied. "Heaven."

Trent watched a few more people get on the elevator, some up, some down, then got George the bartender's attention.

"Excuse me," he slurred, holding up his empty glass. "May I have three of these? Thanks."

CHAPTER FOUR
Part One: A Good Week

I T WAS Trent O'Neil's second week at the Celestial Dinner Theater and Bed & Breakfast in Victorian Cape May, New Jersey, and with each successive day the memory of his disastrous (yet hilarious) stage debut eight days earlier grew dimmer. In fact, with extra rehearsal with Artistic Director Tom Ankiel and assistant Joan Archer, it had been several performances since he fell down or set anything on fire.

All in all, a great week — but he was troubled. After his ignominious debut, he had been witness to a bizarre ritual, during which the entire audience, all 200-plus of them, stayed in the Celestial's bar, sang Christmas carols, and one-by-one entered the oldest-known working elevator in the country.

Tom's cryptic words that night — "Up good, down bad" — had been haunting him. But he had not been witness to the ritual in the seven days since, having been ushered out before it began. He felt like he had stumbled into a bad Stanley Kubrick film.

"I'm sorry, Mr O'Neil," Tom had said, in that voice that was part Richard Burton-part Laurence Fishburne, "but I'm afraid Ms Archer was right. I should not have allowed you to see such things before you were ready. It was irresponsible of me to..."

But as ever, at the mention of Ms Archer, Trent slipped away into Stupid Love Dreamland. It had taken him about eight hours to fall in love with Joan that first day, a love that love multiplied ten-fold every eight hours since. He knew it was not going to last. While the present was quite nice — stolen moments and lots of googly eyes — her words to him the week before made it known she had some baggage, some ghosts in her past which were bound to appear at any moment and keep them apart. It was a conversation he dreaded, but for now he chose to ignore the 500lb elephant in the room and instead concentrate on being happy and, more importantly, making *her* happy.

It was all pretty sickening.

Almost as sickening was the look on his face at present as she walked into the dressing room, tightening the love belt on his heart a few notches.

On a scale of one to 10, he was at about 12,382.

"Hi," she said and gave him a squeeze.

"Hi," he replied, applying some make-up, "I missed you."

She chuckled. "We had dinner together half-an-hour ago."

"I know," he smiled at her in the mirror, "an eternity."

She sat down next to him and watched as he took a black eye-liner and drew thick circles around his eyes. "You look like a 10-dollar French prostitute with that stuff."

He winked. "That's nice. Nice talk. And I was trying for five-dollar French prostitute, thank you, so I must be doing something right."

She laughed at him. He loved when she did this — laughed at all his stupid jokes and asides, at the funny faces he made at her on stage, usually during a particularly solemn scene, earning her more than one stern reprimand from Tom. But as Tom knew and Trent did not, it had been almost a lifetime since Joan had displayed such happiness, so he let it mostly slide.

"Now listen," Trent said, "just because someone may make a fart noise during the Tiny Tim's grave scene doesn't mean you have to laugh at it, okay?"

She slapped his arm. "Stop!"

He looked at her in the mirror and again marveled at his good fortune, that a girl like her, so pretty and smart and nice, had decided to let *him* into her life.

She caught him staring. "What?"

"Nothing," he lied, "you just look so smokin' hot in that dress."

"Gee thanks," she replied, standing up. "Head-to-toe starchy wool and lace were the Victoria's Secret of the Dickensian age."

"No wonder that guy was always horny."

At this she said nothing, and instead picked up a powder puff and poofed him squarely in the mug, ruining his make-up.

"Five minutes to curtain," she said as she left, "and you might want to fix *that*."

"Thank you, five," he replied, talcum blowing out his nose like dragon's breath.

Stupid in love.

Part Two: Trent's Last Show

THE show, a musical version of Charles Dickens' *A Christmas Carol*, was going off without a hitch and was, in fact, the most uneventful of the nine Trent had done so far. The crowd, as always, was responsive and appreciative. The songs sounded great, the lights were bright and twinkly, the dances expertly danced. With the show now ingrained and everything coming naturally, there was little to occupy his brain. This was good for him, bad for everyone else. Trent's "idle hands" were a dangerous thing, usually ending up with a cast mate or two as the butt of an elaborate practical joke. And Trent was cooking up a doozy for Joan when they met backstage just before intermission.

"I think I have to quit," he said to her when she ran off stage after Fezziwig's wassail party.

"What?" she replied, panting from the dance, quickly changing out of her "fat mother" costume and into a long, flowing ballgown for the next scene — a "dream ballet" of Ebenezer Scrooge's school days.

"Yeah," he continued, really selling it, "it's really not working out. I think I have to go."

"Well," she said, struggling into the dress, "don't make any rash decisions."

He poured it on. "No. Sorry. My mind's made up. I'm out of here."

At this she stopped, looked him in the eye, and burst into tears.

"Jeez, Joan... I was just kidding."

"I know," she said, wiping her cheeks, "I have to go, that's my cue."

Bewildered, he stood there, trying to figure out just what the hell happened. Usually, people laughed at his jokes.

"That wasn't even the punchline," he said to himself.

In the 45 minutes following the Joan incident, Trent forgot six lines, missed three cues and knocked over a lamp, his Bob Cratchit swiftly becoming Barney Fife.

"Hey," he said, catching her after curtain call, "what happened back there? I was just kidding with you."

She turned on him. "I know. I know you were joking. It was a stupid, hurtful joke. But I knew you were joking."

He tried to take her hand but she pulled away. "Look, I didn't mean to upset you. I never want to leave this place."

She softened a bit. "I'm not upset about the joke, lame as it was."

"Then what..."

Her eyes welled with tears again. "Later. I'll buy you a drink after I get changed. Deal?"

He wanted to grab her and hug her and kiss her until she smiled at him again. He feared that whatever had so upset her had also killed the spark between them, and he just couldn't live with that. But judging by the distance he sensed from her right now, it might already be too late.

"Deal," he muttered, not sure what else to do.

She smiled wanly. "I'll see you in five."

"Thank you, five," he said and trudged away like a 10-year-old who just had his Matchbox cars taken away. He turned to her. "And good luck trying to buy me a drink! Nobody seems to want to take anybody's money around here!"

Part 3: Surprises

SO TRENT sat and waited. And sat. And waited. After an hour he was sure she had blown him off and snuck away. But then Tom appeared, as if from nowhere, and took a seat next to him at the bar.

"Tough night?" he asked, stating the obvious.

"You could say that."

Tom patted him on the back. "Joan will be here in a moment."

"Fantastic," Trent replied, not feeling fantastic at all.

Tom ordered a wine, then said, "I know this has been difficult for you, but everything will be much clearer after tonight."

"What does that mean?"

"It means, Mr O'Neil, that the talk we've put off for so long, we'll be having tonight. You've been doing so well recently it didn't seem warranted." Tom took a sip of wine and poured a glass for Trent. "But after this evening's events, now seems as good a time as any."

"If you say so, but you'd better make it fast, Joan's been kicking me out of here by 11:30 every night." He looked around at the huge throng of people crowding the bar. "Stupid ritual."

"Well," Tom replied, "that won't be necessary this evening."

Trent shrugged. "Whatever. Nothing means anything if Joan is mad at me."

Tom nodded towards the main theater door: "She doesn't look mad to me."

Trent, as always, beamed at the sight of her.

"Hi," she said and walked over and kissed him right on the lips in front of God and everybody. "Miss me?"

"Terribly," he answered, bewildered. Whatever had upset her earlier, there was no sign of it now. She was vibrant, glowing. "What..."

But she quieted him with another, longer kiss.

She looked him in the eye. "I love you."

Trent couldn't move. He couldn't breathe. He couldn't blink. The air was sucked out of his body. His brain was liquefying. His heart was...

"Say something, stupid," she requested.

"I... I... I..."

She coaxed him. "Love..."

"Love."

"You."

"You."

"Too."

"Too."

She smiled. "Altogether now."

He smiled back. "I love you, too."

They kissed again.

"Cheers," Tom said and raised his glass. "Cheers indeed."

Part Four: Closing

"WHERE did *that* come from?" Trent asked.

Joan looked at Tom, who blushed a little. "Well... I had a long talk with someone I greatly respect, and he suggested I lighten up and enjoy the moment. So here we are."

"You?" Trent asked Tom, "said that?"

"I may be old and stodgy," Tom replied, "but I am also an incurable romantic. Mr O'Neil, the effect you've had on our Ms Archer has been undeniable. From almost the first moment you met, there has been a lightness about her I haven't seen in many, many years."

"So thanks," she said and honked his nose.

He answered, "Glad I could help. Are we going to have... the talk now?"

Tom looked at the clock — it was 11:30. "No, it can wait half-an-hour. For now, let's have some more of this delicious wine."

A bottle of Chianti later and it was almost midnight.

With a peck on the cheek Joan announced, "I'm off. I've got work to do. See you in a bit."

Trent smiled as she left. He had never been happier.

"You're good for each other," Tom said.

"She sure is good for me. She off to get the guest list?"

Tom paused, "In a manner of speaking."

A week ago, when Trent first witnessed the ritual, it began with some singing, everyone opening a rolled up scroll with a red ribbon, then Joan calling out their names. One by one they entered the brass elevator. He remembered the eerie light that emanated from it, how frightening and beautiful it was.

"Up good, down bad," Tom said then. Trent wasn't sure what it meant, but tonight he would find out.

"So this list..." Trent started.

Tom finished, "Of the dead."

Trent blinked.

"The list," Tom went on, "is a list of the dead."

Trent tried to speak but could not.

Tom firmly gripped his shoulder, looked him in the eye, "This is the talk, Mr O'Neil. The Celestial is not, how should I put it, an Earthly entity. It acts as a sort of weigh station for the soul."

Trent was dumbstruck.

"The elevator," Tom continued, "is God's instrument. The Celestial, she's a house with many rooms. The scroll, the one with the red ribbon, comes when it is your time to... take a ride, as it were. It comes down from what we like to call 'upper management.' When Joan reads a name, they enter the elevator and learn their fate."

"Up good," Trent managed through his dry mouth, "down bad."

Tom smiled. "Exactly. One has no idea what one's fate is until one enters the elevator, hence our little nightly ritual. The singing, well, that just kind of happened one night some years ago and just seemed to stick. It's a sort of an..."

"Unspoken rule?" Trent asked rhetorically. The Celestial was full of unspoken rules.

"Precisely," Tom answered.

It all made bizarre sense to Trent now — why the huge crowds were different every night, why nobody ever needed money, why he never saw any luggage. Then he thought of the children he had seen in the theater the last week.

"The kids?" he asked pleadingly.

Tom nodded gravely, "I'm afraid so."

Trent suddenly felt very sad, but at the same time, a sort of elation at knowing there was, indeed, *something* waiting for him after death.

"So people who are... on the fence with the guy upstairs, they come hang here for a while, see a show, and wait for the call?"

Tom smiled. "In layman's terms, yes."

"And the children?"

"The children," Tom grinned, "are here to simply enjoy the magic of the theater before ascending. A child is never sent down."

This made Trent feel better. "Okay, but how do you keep this place a secret? I mean, a live dinner theater catering to dead people... You'd think it would be all over the news. Or at least CNN."

Tom smiled wearily. "You don't seem to understand, Mr O'Neil. All of us here, the guests, the cast, the crew, we all... await judgment."

Trent tried to rap his brain around this. "So... we're all..."

"Dead," Tom finished. "Yes."

It was then Trent found out that dead people could still faint.

Part Five: Ritual

WHEN he came to, Joan and Tom were above him.

"Do you think he's okay?" she asked, her words echoing.

"Well, I suppose he can't die again," Tom replied. "Help me lift him."

On wobbly legs, Trent made it up on to a stool.

"You okay?" Joan asked him, cute as a button.

"I think so, it's just a bit of a shock, finding out you're... you know."

She nuggled his chin. "That's why I got upset earlier — you saying you wanted to leave and me knowing you couldn't. It's why we've been need-ing to talk. Usually a new person gets a week of training and orientation before they learn what the Celestial truly is. But with Milo, the person you replaced, leaving us before we were ready, we were forced to skip all that and get you on stage."

Trent asked, "Milo left before you were ready?"

Tom answered, "On average, an actor stays here for 100 years or so before moving on. Milo was here less than 10, much sooner than antici-pated, which is why we didn't have an understudy. But someone upstairs deemed him ready for judgment, and we try not to argue with the people upstairs."

"Good plan," Trent agreed.

There was quiet for a moment, then he asked, "Do you all know how you... you know."

"Lung infection," Tom piped in. "Pennsylvania, 1783."

Trent slapped his forehead, "I knew there was something weird about you, the way you talked and dressed... uh, no offense."

"None taken," Tom harrumphed.

He turned to Joan, "And you?"

"Cancer," she answered, "1987."

Trent smiled, "Explains the Joan Jett haircut."

"I must say," Tom said, "you seem to be taking this all rather well."

Trent replied, "Well, I knew when I got here that this place was dif-ferent, that it was somehow, I don't know, meant for me. I've never felt so accepted before. I knew there had to be something different about it. And while 'haunted-dinner theater-slash-God's-judgment-place-for-souls-in-limbo' was pretty far down the list, I can't say I'm completely surprised. Only..."

"Yes?" Joan asked.

"I can't remember how I..."

"Sure you can," Tom said, whispering in his ear, "just think..."

So Trent did — thought harder than he ever had. Then it happened.

The memories, the pictures of his life burst through his mind like an invisible tsunami. Bad memories pelted him like tiny rocks, good memories flew around in a happy swarm, like bees, sweet-stinging bees, so thick he almost had to swat them away. But they *did* sting. He melted to the floor unable to stand under the weight of seeing himself as a child, loved by his mother and father. Crushed by the sight of the evil he had once done — the jilted lovers, the falsehoods, the wasted opportunities.

But mostly it was unbearably pleasant, watching his life from the outside, from infancy to adulthood, the friends and family. The final, long drive home on the wet, snowy Christmas Eve, trying to beat the weather and get home to his wife and children, up to the last moment, the ice patch and the unforgiving concrete railroad abutment.

A moment of blackness, then a view from above, the long line of people dressed in black, each tossing a lily on to a casket, each grieving their lost friend.

And finally, a whisper, *We'll miss you*, and a final snapshot of his family.

Then it was over. When he opened his eyes, everything was crystal, ephemerally clear. He was a ghost, a long-dead ghost haunting this building so full of dead spirits it was almost alive. Many hands helped him up from the floor, helping hands, the hands of his friends, the hands of those awaiting judgment. He locked eyes with them all, silently offering thanks as they guided him to his seat.

"So?" Tom asked.

Trent answered, "Car accident, 1993."

He felt weightless and leaden all at once. But mostly he just felt tired. So very tired. Remembering one's life and death in 30 seconds takes a lot out of a soul.

"I remember it all," he said, frantically trying to relay it all. "I had a wife, children... a family. I was..."

"Shh," Joan put a finger to his lips, "we'll talk about it later. Right now, just try to rest."

He nodded. The clock struck midnight. Joan gave him a loving smile and left — off to read the list of the dead. By the third chime the crowd had started singing. Last time Trent was here it was "Silent Night". This time it was "Ave Maria". Both times it was beautiful.

Over the singing, Trent asked Tom, "Why Cape May?"

"Excuse me?" Tom asked.

"For all of this," Trent clarified. "This house of many rooms, this elevator to the heavens... why Cape May?"

Tom laughed. "My good man, if you can't be in Heaven, where else would you rather be?"

Trent smiled and took a drink from the wine.

"Sanderson!" Joan cried.

A woman of about 50 rose from the bar, whispered a few goodbyes, and made her way to the elevator, which was now glowing a warm blue. She boarded it and took a last look around. The doors closed. The elevator began to glow gold. Up good.

"Good for her," Trent said to himself.

For the next hour this continued, and though a few times the elevator glowed crimson ("down bad"), for the most part it was a golden evening of indoor sunsets.

By now the bar was nearly empty, three or four people still waiting. Trent finished his wine and instinctively reached into his pocket for a tip. He knew there was no need for money here, but old habits died hard. This is why he was surprised to feel a paper object in his pocket.

"The hell..."

It took a moment to fish out of his jeans – they were a little tight and he was sitting, but he eventually worked whatever it was free and pulled it out.

"Um... Tom?" he said, voice quivering.

Tom turned to him. "Yes, Mr O'Neil?"

In his hand Trent held a white scroll with a crimson ribbon. Joan called a name.

"O'Neil!"

For a long moment, no one answered.

She called again, "O'Neil! I'm looking for a Mr or Mrs....oh my God, Trent."

Trent stood, knees weak, face ashen.

"What do I do?" he asked, frightened.

"No!" Tom slammed a fist on the bar. "This is too soon!"

Trent slowly inched toward the elevator, unable to help it. "Joan?"

Joan stepped in front of him, tears streaming. "It's okay, Trent. It's okay."

Trent was not convinced. "You said 100 years... I've been here a week! What's going on?"

But she shut him up his favorite way, with a kiss. And when she spoke, her voice was all he could hear.

"It's okay," she said, "I love you and it's okay, Trent. If they think you're ready, you're ready."

Now he was crying. "But there's so much I want to do... so many things I want to say to you... so much time I want to spend..."

"Shh," she quieted him again. "I know. But it's okay. Just be brave. Be strong for me."

He was now only a few steps from the elevator.

"I can't stop," he told her.

"I know," she said and hugged him tightly, "I know."

The elevator doors opened.

"It's time," Tom said, also weeping softly, "far, far too soon in my opinion, but it is your time."

The blue light from inside the elevator enveloped him. It was warm.

Tom sang, "Silent night, holy night..."

"All is calm," Joan joined him and let go of Trent.

"All is bright..." the last few bar patrons chimed in.

With the choir singing in his ears, tears streaming down his cheeks, Trent gave one last look around, pausing ever so slightly at Joan, and smiled.

"Round yon virgin, mother and child..."

He turned back to the elevator.

"Holy infant so tender and mild..."

He took the last three steps through the doors.

"Sleep in Heavenly peace..."

He kept his eyes on Joan, who whispered, "I love you."

"Sleep in Heavenly peace..."

The doors slid shut with a soft thud. It quiet as a tomb. Trent sighed, closed his eyes, and waited.

Up good, down bad.

Part Six: Judgement

OUTSIDE the elevator, the singing slowly faded and the small crowd held their collective breath.

"They rushed him," Tom worried to Joan. "He wasn't ready and they rushed him. Rushed him in, rushed him out."

Joan squeezed his hand. "He's better for having been with us, Tom. We need to believe that."

Tom sighed. "I can only hope you're right, Ms Archer. I can only hope..."

The bar filled with a golden light.

Up good.

The Five Stages Of Death

Everyone
around
Jump
Wiggens
was dying...
but HE was
the killer's
target!

Chapter One
Beginning, Intermission, End

IT WAS an unseasonably warm late-spring afternoon in Cape May. While much of the mid-Atlantic seaboard started to warm up in April, Cape May, jutting as it did some two miles out to sea and ever at the mercy of the ocean's constantly evolving atmosphere, did not. The sleepy Victorian town generally traded a "normal" winter of snow and sledding for a brutal whipping by an unceasing 30-knot wind which perma-froze everything to the core rather thoroughly. Ergo, it was usually mid-May before the Cape truly began to thaw and become clement.

But none of that was on Jump Wiggen's mind as he hammered away at the old ceiling beam high atop the stage of the Cape Equity Theater. "The Equity," as the locals called it, sat inside what used to be Cape May's only movie theater, across the street from the ocean, on prime beachfront property. The Ocean Palace, which housed the Equity as well as a single movie house, had gone under some years before when it was discovered that most of its money came from secret, post-midnight showings of decidedly non-mainstream films with words like "Flesh" and "Sins" and "Orgasmatron from Planet G" in the titles.

Though there was currently a movement underfoot to "Save the Ocean!", the organizers were finding it difficult to drum up much interest in saving what amounted to the most beautifully designed, intricately-gingerbreaded porn house the world might ever have seen.

The Equity weathered that storm and was in fact about to celebrate its 20th anniversary — a remarkable feat considering that in none of its previous 19 years had it been able to turn even a fudgable profit. But luckily for Jump and everyone employed at the Equity (a non-profit in every sense of the word), Cape May was full of people both generous and affluent, who liked their oatmeal lumpy and their theater stodgy.

But Jump was not one of those people. At 31 he had led, as actors go, a charmed life. At well under six feet, he fancied himself a poor man's Tom Cruise, though more often he reminded people of a young Billy Joel or Phil Collins. (He could never decide which stung more.) But his non-classical good looks, thick but flexible build and tremendous singing voice left him rarely at a wont for work, or, as a decent-looking straight man in theater, for female companionship. Over the years he had had his (and a few other guys') share of lady friends, all of whom, amazingly, parted as friends. All but one, that is. But still, pretty good stuff for a guy who 10 years earlier was limping his way out of the military on a ruined knee and drinking his way out of college on a ruined psyche.

Jump occasionally quivered with fear at the tenuous connection of sheer and utter chance that led him to Cape May and the thriving theater community dwelling within. He let his mind wander a moment on the "only in theater" tale of the ex-girlfriend's ex-roommate's ex-fiancé's ex-boyfriend's new girlfriend's story about the little murder mystery joint that started the whole thing rolling.

Unfortunately for Jump, the last thing a guy swinging a hammer should do is let his mind wander.

WHAM!

"Dammit!"

His thumb exploded.

"Criminy!"

The waffle-faced hammerhead smashed his thumb, bit into the skin, and sent plumes of white heat streaking up his left arm. Red-faced with agony and embarrassment, he climbed down the scaffolding, thumb in mouth, relieved to see no one was present to see his gaffe.

"How's it coming?" a voice echoed.

Jump started. Waylon Hoag, Artistic Director of the Equity, had apparently snuck in the back. Jump turned, if possible, a shade redder.

"Fine," he lied, a crimson bloom spreading across his gray T-shirt where he had tucked his thumb.

Waylon smiled. "Come with me, we must have a first-aid kit around here somewhere."

A few minutes later they were on the back porch, a lovely plywood-and-2x4 construct put together with all the love and care of a tiger eating its young. The view was also splendid, looking as it did over a row of restaurant dumpsters and barrels of grease. The sea gulls, squawking and fighting over nuggets or rotten chicken, added just the right touch of nuance.

Jump fingered the gauze on his thumb. The bandages and the handful of aspirin had managed to dull the pain down to a gentle throb. Waylon reached into the cooler marked "JUMP" in thick black sharpie and grabbed two bottles of water.

"May I?" he asked.

Jump nodded.

"Feeling any better?"

"A lot," Jump answered, "thanks, Mr Hoag."

"Please," Mr Hoag replied, "call me Waylon."

"Right," Jump replied, abashed, "sorry, just... still getting used to things around here."

"I would imagine. How long were you at Annie's?"

Jump sighed deeply. "Seven calendar years, eight seasons, 63 new shows." He smiled ruefully. "But who's counting?"

Waylon handed him a cool bottle. "It's okay, I understand. Seven months is a long time to be at one theater. Seven years? That's unprecedented. I'm sure you grew roots there that were difficult to unearth."

"The ties," Jump answered, "do bind."

Waylon continued, "I get that it's hard to go into a new environment after so many years of doing things a certain way, but I guarantee," he threw an avuncular arm around Jump, "you give us enough time, we'll be just as much a family here as they were over there."

Jump smiled at the warmth of the comment and at the use of the word "family" to describe Famous Annie's. As he sat and he thought on it, Jump knew that he had indeed found his niche at Famous Annie's Famous Dinner Theater. But a family? Maybe, in a highly dysfunctional, Sopranos/Manson sort of way, but certainly not in the traditional sense. But it was theater, where tradition meant little. He had started at Annie's as a member of the stagehand chorus, worked his way into the acting ensemble, and then into principal cast, where he grabbed many a leading role.

Eventually, more by the grace of the inherent high attrition rate of the nomadic world of theater than by any great talent or vision of his own, he found himself in the director's chair for the final three seasons of his tenure. Trouble was, Jump was the only actor on Earth who didn't want to direct, and the daily/nightly/weekly/yearly grind of putting up six to nine new shows a year wore him to an emotional nub and it was time to go.

No, what you had at Famous Annie's, while certainly a collection of people with a common goal, was not a family, but rather a... well, considering all the backstabbing, bad-mouthing, partner-swapping and bad blood... maybe it WAS a family.

But Mr Hoag meant well enough. "Smoke?" he asked, offering a pack of cigarettes.

Jump smiled. "Ah, been dying for one all day. Trying to quit. Made it almost four hours."

Waylon nodded. "I quit every half-hour or so. Let's walk."

"Sure," Jump said and they ambled down the steps to the sidewalk, walking half-around the block toward the front of the building.

"Tell me again," Waylon requested, "why did you leave Annie's?"

Jump lit the cigarette and diplomatically answered, "It was just my time."

Waylon measured his next question carefully, "And... how do they feel about you working *here*?"

Jump shrugged. "I'm not even sure they know yet."

Waylon took a drag. "Well, if they didn't, they do now. Look."

Jump did. They were now in front of the Equity, and there, directly across the street, sat the gaudy, neon-dripping Famous Annie's Famous Dinner Theater. Even in daylight it looked garish, like a Las Vegas casino working off a hangover. Annie's dwarfed every other building on the blacktop promenade that ran the length of the beach from cove to cove. It was tall, it was shiny and it was relatively new, having been built a scant nine years earlier on the site of the former Cape May Convention Center, which had been tragically pulled out to sea by the tail end of Hurricane Marlene (Marlene being the name of the wife of the guy in charge of naming storms, but that's neither here nor there) in the summer of 2002.

While the town dithered on what to put on the newly vacant slice of real estate, holding the city council hostage to referendum after zoning board approval meeting after IDS sub-committee hoo-ha, Famous Annie's, a theater chain that dotted beach and casino towns all up and down the east coast, swooped in and, citing an archaic, Byzantine law from the Cape May Charter of 1863, grabbed the land on the cheap. Something about "eminent domain" not covering "Acts of God" or some such.

Large, mass-produced theater chains had excellent, fine print-reading lawyers.

The town was stunned and resentful, many letters to many editors were written, much outrage was displayed on many local newscasts, but it was all tilting at windmills — the deal was done.

So up she went, the white and gold monstrosity snidely referred to as "the McTheater" by the spurned locals. And there, on her front porch, clustered (and, Jump was sure, clucking) around a table, was her brain trust — owner-manager Joy Carmichael, her husband Tim Templeton, and his lover Farley Owensby. The three-pronged relationship was odd and difficult to maintain, but was a model of inter-personal dynamic cohesion compared to how they ran their business. But it was such a long story that Jump got weary just thinking about it. All he could muster at the moment was a half-hearted wave.

In response, the three-headed monster stood, turned on its collective heel and disappeared inside for what Jump knew was going to be at least an hour of Jump-bashing over Entenmann's cheese and cherry Danish and Wawa coffee. He'd seen it before, many times — it was not pretty and reflected well on no one.

But there was nothing he could do about it now, so he changed the subject. "I appreciate you letting me help with the renovation. I really need the cash."

Waylon replied, "Hey, we're happy to have the extra help. And the money comes from grants and private contributors, so it's no skin off my nose. We have a lot of benefactors."

"Theater lovers?" Jump asked.

"Tax write-offs," Waylon answered, smiling, "but intentions aside, it all helps."

"Well," Jump said, "I appreciate it still."

Waylon asked, "You really didn't have anything better to do with your Sunday?"

Jump answered, "Not really. The time alone, the labor... it's good therapy. Helps clear my head."

Waylon scratched at his thick, white beard. "Then let me be the first to say..." he offered Jump his hand, "welcome to the Equity. We look forward to a great season and believe you to be an excellent addition to our ensemble."

Jump smiled and shook. "Thanks, it's a pleasure to be here."

"Come on," Waylon took a big swig from the bottle of water and nodded back inside, "I'll give you a hand with that beam."

"I sure could use it. I've been banging away at that thing for an hour," Jump said, and then, unable to help himself: "That's what she said."

"Man, that's good water," Waylon interjected. "Flavored? It almost tastes like... is that... nut? Almond?"

"Well I know how much you love nut water..."

"Ha ha," Waylon said dryly, "you bust them out like that over at Annie's? No wonder you don't work there anymore..."

"You don't know the half of it."

"One of these days."

Jump checked his bottle. "I don't think this is flavored water, I just grabbed a six from the 7-11. But I could be wrong."

Waylon took another long swallow. "Probably just got the labels switched at the factory. Either way, it's really good. Let's go get that beam sorted out."

In they went. Jump's goose-bumped arms registered it was now quite a bit cooler.

Welcome to Cape May, he thought, *don't like the weather? Wait 10 minutes.*

He climbed up the scaffolding, wiped a copious amount of his own blood off the steel spindles with his do-rag, and grabbed his hammer. Something thumped behind him.

A sand bag, he thought, then said, "I think if you can get the claw of your hammer into that joint we can edge it out and..."

But Waylon wasn't there. From his vantage point among the ceiling beams some 20 feet up, Jump could only see a small square of floor. And in that square was a pair of feet. A pair of feet that looked like the body they were attached to was lying on the floor.

"Waylon?" Jump called.

Nothing.

"Mr Hoag?"

The words echoed. Jump's stomach fell and his mouth went dry as he descended the scaffolding. Step-by-step his fears were realized.

"Oh boy..."

There, on the floor, lay Waylon Hoag, Artistic Director of the Cape Equity Theater, water bottle in hand, deader than a doornail.

There, on the floor, lay Waylon Hoag, Artistic Director of the Cape Equity Theater, water bottle in hand, deader than a doornail.

Chapter Two
Bitch, Moan And Bitch

JUMP sat on the lip of the Equity's stage, numb amid the flurry around him — a crime photographer took Polaroids of the scene, police officers mingled about, and slowly, the cast and crew of the Equity were starting to gather. He could see them in the lobby through the double doors. The old building used to be a movie theater, built in the 1940s, and the lobby still looked it — ornate marble concession stand, velvet-draped walls and a magnificent chandelier. It was the kind of place you expected horse-drawn carriages to drop off men and women of means in tuxedos, fancy evening gowns and long-stemmed cigarette filters.

The assembled actors and stage hands in their cut-offs, flip-flops and T-shirts seemed an architectural affront. They hugged, exchanged condolences and cast furtive looks Jump's way. He was the new guy, alone with their beloved boss on his first day of work, and now their beloved boss was dead.

Nice first impression, he thought.

He didn't know them well enough to join their little circle of grief, but neither could he waltz out with a, "Hey, how you doing? Sorry the big guy's dead. See you at rehearsal tomorrow?" It was going to be awkward and Jump was dreading it, between a rock and a hardening corpse. Unfortunately for him, though, that awkward exchange would never take place.

"Pardon me. Got a sec?" a voice asked from the orchestra pit.

Jump looked down and saw the detective. Or rather, saw what looked like a TV parody of a detective — cheap gray suit, worn tan overcoat, three-day stubble and beaten brown fedora. The face beneath resembled a weather-worn Dennis Quaid that, sadly, in a few years would start resembling *Randy* Quaid.

Jump answered, "I guess not."

"Name's Curtis, Detective Ike Curtis," he said and stepped on to the stage.

"Wiggen," Jump answered, "Jump Wiggen."

"Jump?" Curtis made a face. "The hell kind of name is that?"

Jump smiled. It was his favorite question. "Granddad was a paratrooper in the big one, 101st Division Screaming Eagles. Shot down over Italy. Survived three years in a work camp. Dad was a paratrooper, 173rd Airborne Brigade Sky Soldiers. Got pinched in 'Nam, spent 18 months in a Tiger cage."

Curtis looked impressed. "And you?"

Jump tapped his left knee. "High School Division Championship Game, 1996. Cleat got caught in the dirt sliding into third. Blew out the ACL, ruptured the meniscus. My knee turned to dust. I'm a 4-F."

Curtis sincerely said, "Sorry to hear it."

Jump waved him off. "Don't be. If you hadn't noticed, my ancestors had a lousy habit of becoming POWs. My great-granddad went down with *The Lusitania* for chrissakes'. "

Curtis smiled. "I see your point."

Jump picked up the bottle of water next to him — it was cool and sweaty and he suddenly realized how thirsty he was. He'd been trying to drink that water for an hour. He was twisting the cap when Curtis interrupted.

"I'm sorry, but... have we met before?"

Jump answered, "No, I don't think so."

"Huh... you look awfully familiar."

Jump replied, "I get that a lot. I guess I've just got one of those faces," then, with a bit more pride than was necessary, "or maybe you saw the regional commercial I did for Ron's Car Barn last summer?"

"No, that's not it."

Jump slumped. "Then sorry, I've never seen you before today. And I told the other officer — one minute Mr Hoag and I were talking about the renovation, the next he was... gone."

Curtis nodded at Jump's hand and the gigantic bloodstain on his REM T-shirt. "What's with the thumb?"

Jump flushed. "A little trouble with my aim. Hammers hurt."

"REM?"

"Love their music, hate their politics."

"I hear you. And you were working on the ceiling?" Curtis asked, poking a finger skyward.

"Yes," Jump answered and wiped the cool plastic bottle across his forehead. "He was going to help me with a beam I was banging away at and..."

His faced turned a ghostly pale.

"You okay, Mr Wiggen?"

Jump barely heard him. "Not... don't... my head..."

What he couldn't say was that his head, much like his ruined thumb, was now a white-hot Jacuzzi of roiling agony.

Curtis eased him down. "Take it easy."

Jump convulsed as a heartless wave of nausea rolled through his guts like a tasty breaker. Why was this happening? Why did he feel unhelmeted in deep space? And why was he so damn thirsty?

"Here," Curtis said above him, "drink some water."

Through blearing eyes Jump watched Curtis grab the bottle and it struck him. *No! The water!* He tried to shout but his jaw had clenched shut.

He remembered Waylon's last words — *Mmm, is that almond?* It didn't seem odd at the time, but now...

"Easy!" Curtis shouted, grabbing him. "Medic!"

Jump had had this dream as a child — leashed to a post, offered to a giant monkey, or stuck on a frozen lake as the ice monster approached. Terrified and paralyzed, he could not get away from the bottle of water Curtis was intent on feeding him.

"Hold still, dammit!" Curtis shouted.

But Jump did no such thing. He began to thrash, anything to escape the deadly liquid. On the last spasm he slammed the back of his head into a bank of footlights, which exploded with an electric flash. Jump just as quickly succumbed to the lights in his head and an imaginary curtain fell. All was black and smelled of burnt hair and flesh.

And he may have soiled himself.

One hour earlier...

CAN you believe him?" Joy seethed, "sitting over there, rubbing our noses in it?"

Joy Carmichael was the owner-operator of Famous Annie's Famous Dinner Theater, a franchise with over 30 branches dotting the east coast, which, with its gaudy architecture and neon accessories, would not have looked out of place on the Vegas strip, or at the very least, Branson. And the "him" in question was Jump Wiggen, ex-employee of Annie's, current employee of the Cape Equity Theater, Annie's biggest rival.

At that moment, Jump was standing across the street in front of the Equity, staring at them and waving weakly.

"I never did like him," Tim Templeton, Joy's husband, chimed in. "He just never seemed to get it. Know what I mean?"

"I do," offered Farley Owensby, Tim's lover. "Remember how he fought me on his medieval costume?"

"Well," Tim interjected, "it was a fur stole and a sequined leather codpiece. I don't really blame him for that."

Farley was aghast. "It was ART, Tim, or have you forgotten what that looks like?"

Tim retorted, "To you art is anything with a naked man and some sort of lubricant..."

Farley stood. "Oh no you dih-int..."

Tim rose. "I think I did..."

"Boys!" Joy hissed and they dutifully sat. "Not where he can see us!"

In unison, the town's oddest trio stood and went inside.

Famous Annie's sat on the most prominent lot on the most prominent block of Cape May's beachfront. And if she looked like a casino on the out-side, inside she more resembled a kind of theater-based gift shop-slash-brothel. At Annie's, art regularly took a back seat to commerce. Large 8x10s of the half-naked cast adorned the black-and-white leopard-print walls. An obscenely huge TV played clips of the current show, something about pirates and booty and laser beams, on an endless loop.

It was the literal embodiment of the figurative migraine.

Joy, Tim and Farley took their places around a bar table. Joy looked out the window and watched Jump converse with Waylon Hoag, soon-to-be late artistic Director of the Equity.

"The nerve..." she muttered.

It was a slap to Annie's management that one of their loyal own, a seven-year veteran no less, would leave them. And not only leave them but jump ship to their biggest competitor. It was an absolute affront. People didn't just leave Famous Annie's — they jumped or were pushed. And never to a more prestigious gig — the post-Annie's demonization drill took care of that. Actor is hired, actor works a summer, actor realizes he'd rather work in salt mine, actor quits/resigns/is fired. Actor seeks next job, potential new employer calls for reference, potential employer is told how awful said actor was to work with, how he/she was a raving sex fiend/alcoholic/kleptomaniac. Said actor moves to west coast under assumed name.

And it wasn't just references — the local campaign was even *more* dev-astating. Rumors would begin to float about the actor's sexual preferences and/or desire to be intimate with animals/underage kids/inanimate objects. More than one born-and-bred local had been driven from town by such insidious lies. And now... now it was Jump's turn.

"Listen," Joy said firmly and the boys stopped chirping, "here's what we're going to do..."

And it was on.

Three hours later...

WHEN Jump awoke in the ICU wing of the University of Pennsylvania-backed Cape Regional Medical Center (unjustly referred to as "Cape Fear" by the locals) the pain in his thumb took a distant back seat to the gnawing heat in the back of his head.

"Jeez-US!" he croaked.

"Easy..." Detective Curtis said from the chair. "They pulled about a hundred shards of glass from your noggin. Was quite the little light show you put on."

Jump nodded gingerly. He was relatively comfortable in a soft hospital gown, bootie slippers and warm, fuzzy blanket.

"How did you..."

Curtis tapped a pen to his skull and held up a mirror. "Your forehead. Take a look."

"My forehead? Oh, right, my forehead."

Jump's forehead, usually a model of dermal perfection, now looked like it had been boiled into a blister, the blister rudely popped, then gently massaged with rusty steel wool.

"You wiped that bottle across your head and a few seconds later your skin literally started to bubble," Curtis told him. "That's when I figured something wasn't right..."

"Wow," Jump said, "you ARE a detective."

"I know, I know," Curtis replied with good humor. "Anyway, my hand started to burn, too, after I picked it up. You could say I had a bit of an epiphany."

Jump couldn't help but smile. The cop, though a walking stereotype, was agreeably self-deprecating and, apparently, pretty bright. He said, "I remembered Mr Hoag said something about the water tasting different, like almonds, which I remembered is a sign of arsenic poisoning. Thank you, Weblo Scout training."

"Not only that," Curtis continued, "but we sent the water down to the lab. For safe measure it was diluted with about 25% carbolic acid. It was sweating through the plastic, that's why you're skin melted. Mine, too. If it hadn't..."

But no more needed to be said. Jump knew he had narrowly escaped a terrible fate. What he didn't have was any idea how this could have happened.

"Any idea how this could have happened, Mr Wiggen?"

This guy is scary. "No, none at all."

"No idea why someone would want to hurt Mr Hoag?"

Jump considered this. "Today was my first official day on the clock. I'd been in a few times the previous couple of weeks to audition, meet the producers, fill out some paperwork... I've been in the building five, maybe six times. Rehearsals were scheduled to start tomorrow... I was working on the renovation. Mr Hoag was the only person I really knew at all."

"Okay," Curtis said, "I believe you. For now we're going to treat this as a freak accident. We'll trace the bottle back to the manufacturer, the rest have already been pulled from the shelves... maybe there was some kind of computer mix-up at the bottle factory or something, though I think that's highly unlikely. But Jump, can you think of any reason why somebody would want to hurt you?"

"Um..." Jump was smacked. He'd pissed off a few people in his day, but who hadn't? But he was generally well liked around town and amongst his past and present co-workers. He could think of no one. Except...

"Well, I did just leave my last job after seven years. It wasn't, how should I put it... it wasn't a friendly parting, but it never is with those people."

"Which people?"

Jump sighed. "Famous Annie's Famous Dinner Theater on Beach Drive. It didn't end well, but I swear to God, nothing ever ends well there. I mean, they're pretty rotten, but I don't think they could do anything like this. Why do you ask?"

Curtis looked him in the eye. "Mr Wiggen, was anyone else scheduled to work with you today?"

Jump shook his head. "No, it's Sunday, everyone else has lives."

Curtis smiled: "Did you tell anyone else you were working today?"

"Just my mom, in Pennsylvania."

"Because I'm trying to figure out, Mr Wiggen, how not one, but two bottles of water laced with enough acid and arsenic to kill a small army ended up in your lunch cooler."

Jump was stunned. "My lunch cooler?"

"Yes," Curtis answered, "if you or Mr Hoag had bothered to look inside you would have seen that everything else was, I think the word is... emulsified."

"Emulsified?"

"Melted," Curtis finished. "Chemically."

Jump's stomach turned. "Even my chicken salad sandwich?"

"Especially your chicken salad sandwich."

"Damn. That was a really good sandwich. Curried, Indian-style, from Depot Market."

Curtis replied, "I prefer the cutlet, but the curried is quite good. But I want you to understand what I'm saying. If there wasn't a manufacturing error it means someone, presumably not yourself, put them in there."

Jump turned paler. "Uh-huh."

"And as bad as your face looks..."

"Thanks."

"...And as much as my hand hurts, I'd sure hate to be the county medical examiner cutting open Waylon Hoag right now. His insides must be totally liquefied. And organ soup, while nifty for worms and such, can't be a very pleasant encounter for a human being."

"I see," Jump said, then swiftly barfed into a little plastic basin.

"Sorry," Curtis said, then barfed into his own little plastic basin.

Everyone knows that barfing, like yawning, is contagious.

After a moment, Jump asked, "Is it possible for me to get a goddamned drink of water now?"

I T WAS very quiet inside the Equity — the worn, red velvet seats empty, the stage a pale blue wash. The cast and crew sat in fold-out chairs, scripts in hand. Backstage a radio softly crackled some oldies from 1230AM WCMC. The soothing voice of DJ Jim Mac-Millan did little to dispel the pall that had settled over the place.

"And now," Jim intoned in his light New England drawl, *"a little Sam Cooke for you on this beautiful Wednesday afternoon..."*

Darling you... send me. Darling you... send me...

The cast absently flipped through their scripts, ironically enough an Agatha Christie-type murder-mystery called *The Five Stages of Death*, about a theater company plagued by seemingly unsolvable homicides. The author was a local fellow by the name of Stanford Whitley, and as his name might suggest, he was obsessed with the minutiae of Victorian-era drama. As such, it was he who would be directing this new production in lieu of the late Waylon Hoag. And it was Stanford Whitley who presently threw open the great double-doors of the theater and entered with all the pomp of a drunken peacock.

"Greetings all!" he announced, the 'r' slightly rolled. "Pardon my tardiness, but the horse drawing the carriage in front of me looked to be about two years too late for the glue factory."

This drew nary a chuckle from the crew. Stanford bounded down the aisle undeterred, with great energy and panache. In a vintage three-piece pin-striped suit and bow tie, black velvet cape, with a silver-topped wolf's head cane, wire-rimmed glasses, salt-and-pepper goatee and, worst of all, a black beret atop his balding head, he was a walking picture saying a thousand words.

"In case you don't know" — everyone did — "my name is Stanford Whitley and I will be... filling in for our dear, departed Mr Hoag as director of *The Five Stages*."

He was thin, reedy, and his voice seemed perpetually on the verge of breaking, like a 45-year-old 13-year-old.

"I trust you've all had a chance to read through the script." They hadn't. "And I expect this to be a relatively painless process, provided you take my direction to heart and trust that I know this play better than anyone in the world. After all..." he paused for dramatic effect, "I wrote it."

The round of applause he was expecting never came. After an awkward beat he cleared his throat and continued.

"Now, I assume you all know Ms Greeley, our stage manager..." They did. Vicky Greeley, a mousy sort with stringy blonde hair and a baggy sweater, gave a wave, "whom I hope has supplied you with all the prop and wardrobe notes you'll need..."

She had not and she began to sweat.

"...So we'll start with a cold-reading and then get into blocking the opening..."

The doors opened again, interrupting the director, whom most had already pegged as insufferable, and someone else entered. Slowly. Gingerly.

"Hi all," Jump croaked, his throat still scratchy from his three-day hospital visit. "I'm really sorry I'm late. They wouldn't discharge me until my urine... they wouldn't discharge me."

"Ah!" Stanford announced, whipping off his cape with a flourish. "This must be the esteemed Mr Wiggen. Greetings to you, Jump, and condolences on your recent hardship."

"Um... thanks." *Asshole*, thought Jump.

"Please," Stanford motioned to an empty chair with a spindly arm, "take your rightful place among the boards. You are one of us now."

Oh, brother. "Thanks."

Jump stepped onstage. Small pieces of broken lightbulb, which he had shattered with the base of his skull three days earlier, crunched under his sandals.

"Sorry," Vicky whispered, "the small pieces were really hard to sweep up."

Jump gave an understanding nod. "It's okay, I still have a few shards in my noggin... I'm feeling a little light-headed."

Jump stared at them. It took a moment but they eventually got the stupid joke and everyone chuckled. A 50lb weight came off his chest.

"Yes, well," Stanford continued, smarting at his stolen thunder. "Why don't we get on with the reading."

As Jump moved into the pale blue light, the extent of his ordeal became apparent. The bandage covering his forehead, though mercifully flesh-colored, was still Frankenstein-ish and looked as though he had gotten a skin graft from The Fantastic Four's Thing. Angry, sore-looking needle marks dotted the crook of his right elbow. And what they didn't see under his Gap T-shirt were the large patches of missing chest hair where EKG patches were heartlessly applied and ruthlessly ripped off on at least six occasions. He now knew exactly how *The 40-Year-Old Virgin* felt.

"Just a sec," he winced as he limped to his chair, because also unseen, under his cut-offs, was the bruise in his right groin that was the approximate size and color of an overripe eggplant, where they had run the cardiac catheter into his right femoral artery and taken iodine pictures of the inside of his heart, to make sure the poison he'd ingested caused no lasting damage. Finally, with a protracted sigh, he took his seat.

"If we're all ready," Stanford said with a hint of bitchiness, "let's begin." Then, in a breathless hush, "Page one, act one, scene one... Lights up on an empty theater. The stage is set as the library of an old, Victorian mansion on the Jersey Shore. In the distance, a boat horn wails, and an ever-vigilant lighthouse keeps constant guard..."

More than one person rolled their eyes. Jump instead chose to give in to the Percocet buzzing through his head and drifted away, the events of the last three days replaying fuzzily in his head...

Hours earlier...

IT TOOK some doing in the dark and with an injured thumb, but the dark figure finally made it to the top of the scaffolding, a dizzying 20 feet above the stage. The thumb had been thoroughly mangled some hours earlier and under great duress beneath the head of a flesh-eating, waffle-faced, 12lb hammer and was now thumping like a Jay-Z record, but the pain was manageable and the plan had to be followed to a tee, no matter the physical sacrifices.

His Spider-Man act completed, he did the unthinkable and looked down. Fortunately, it was too dark to get full vertigo, so he blinked the sweat from his eyes and carried on. Making things more uncomfortable were the array of tools and gadgets in the black work pack around his waist. She called it a fanny pack, which he despised, but what did she know about espionage?

Putting her out of mind he set to work. It was going to be a delicate job getting it just so, but he'd learned some things in his years working with tools – in his line of work it was often required that one learn every aspect of production.

He started with the chisel and hammer. It was slow going, having to keep quiet, but he eventually got the notches big enough. Next came the small handsaw, one of those $1.99 ones from Swain's Ace Hardware, where the handle looks like a gun. He'd have liked a cordless electric one, but funds were limited at the moment, since he'd recently left his job. But again, with time and patience, the work got done.

Next came the weights. They had to be placed perfectly, otherwise the timing would be screwed. Lastly, he planted the small, remote-controlled blasting caps. He hoped he wouldn't have to use them (they were infinitely more traceable than sawdust), but the job had to be done right the first time, no matter what the cost. There would be no second chance.

The last part was his least favorite, so he chose not to dwell on it and instead just did it. He bit down hard on the thick carpenter's pencil and picked up the cheap saw again. Bracing himself, he placed it on the mark and slowly began sawing back and forth. It hurt, and his blood spattered quietly on the metal like a soft rain in the dark theater, but in a few seconds it was over. Ignoring the new white-hot pain in his head he swiftly slapped the flesh-colored patch over the fresh wound. He wobbled a bit on his perch due to the pain and loss of blood, but after a few moments steadied and girded himself for the climb down.

The steel scaffolding was slippery with his blood and he was seeing little white spots behind his eyes, but he was still unable to suppress a little smile at the thought of the carnage to come.

"This should be good," he whispered to himself, stepped to the ground and scurried out the back stage door.

Later...

AN UNEVENTFUL week had passed since Stanford Whitley took over the reins at the Equity and, despite his obvious shortcomings as a director and insatiable need for attention/approval, the show was shaping up quite nicely. It wasn't the best show Jump had ever been in (that would be *West Side Story*, 1999, when, 30lbs and half-a-head-of-hair ago, he played an agile, wily Riff) nor the worst (that would be the *Big Apple Christmas Spectacular*, 1996, a holiday show that cut-and-pasted bits from *Scrooge*, *The Muppets' Christmas Carol*, *Miracle on 34th Street* and, inexplicably, *My Fair Lady*, into one giant, incohesive mess), and the cast proved easy to work with and versatile – each actor played at least two parts.

And so it was that after seven solid 12-hour days of rehearsal, *The Five Stages of Death* was chugging along on time and under budget. At the moment, Jump sat backstage, fidgeting nervously in his butler costume, watching through a slit in the main curtain as several hundred people filed into the Equity for tonight's preview/dress rehearsal performance.

"How you feeling?" Jimmy Fuentes asked.

Jump nodded vigorously. "Good. I'm good. You?"

"Scared shitless," Jimmy answered.

"Good," Jump replied. "Then it's not just me."

Jimmy asked, "How's the leg? And the thumb... and the forehead..."

Jump smiled. "All good, thanks. I'll tell them you asked."

"Do that," Jimmy said and walked away.

Jimmy was a good guy and one of the first at the Equity to befriend Jump. Most of the others quickly followed suit, but Jimmy was the first. A portly fellow with jet-black, over-jelled hair, and jovial demeanor, he always made Jump smile. The Jimmy part of him was All-American – he loved football, movie sequels and Pearl Jam. The Fuentes part was all surface – sharp, Latin features and olive-hued skin that seemed perma-tanned.

Jump thought it perfectly reasonable that Jimmy and the gang would have trouble warming up to him — he was the last person to see their old boss alive and a small cloud of suspicion still hung over him. But after their second grueling day of rehearsal all bad thoughts were forgotten and they all got drunk together at the Pilot House.

Vicky Greeley announced in her tiny voice, "Five minutes, everyone."

"Thank you, five," the cast reflexively answered.

Now all eight of them were there, nervously pacing or going over their lines, perfecting any last-second dialect changes. Jump did none of this — he either knew it or he didn't. So he just sat on the hard wooden stool and waited for curtain.

He had no idea that death lingered around the corner.

"A moment, please," Stanford announced, gathering the cast. "We have a few moments now and I want you all to know how proud I am of all of you."

He was sincere, and Jump found it hard to to remember why he didn't like him.

"Shortly we shall tread the boards as millions have done before, from Cleveland to the Great White Way, and enter ourselves into the yawning chasm of theatrical history..."

He suddenly remembered why.

"So good luck to you all, or as they say... break a leg!"

The cast dissipated with a mumble.

"Mr Wiggen," Stanford said to Jump. "A moment of your time please."

"Uh... sure." Jump followed him to a quiet corner.

Stanford half-whispered, "I know this is very last-minute and a complete breach of professional theater protocol but, well, you see... it is the debut of my new play and, well, there's a woman I'd really like to... the point is, I wonder if I may impose upon you and take the butler scene from act one, scene three for myself. I wouldn't ask, but..."

Jump considered this. Scene three got probably the biggest intentional laugh in act one and he'd been looking forward to doing it in front of an audience to get a true gauge. But he was playing one of five butlers and there were other unintentionally funny scenes, so what the hell?

"Sure," he answered. "Why not? You want to impress a girl, I understand. But I'll have to cover your tech."

"Oh, thank you, Jump," Stanford exhorted, "you are too kind. The tech is simple. When the butler yells the word 'Cucamonga!' simply set off the air cannon by flipping the red switch next to the light board."

"Got it," Jump answered, "and give 'em hell out there."

"Mr Wiggen," Stanford said with a deep bow, "I am in your debt. I hereby owe you one. You are indeed a good man."

Maybe this guy's not so bad after all. "Don't sweat it, I'm here to help."

A few moments later the lights dimmed and *The Five Stages of Death*

A gigantic ceiling beam fell from the sky and crushed him where he stood... in unceremonious, Wile E. Coyote fashion.

made its world premiere.

Fifteen minutes later...

JUMP sat in the tech booth awaiting his cue. He watched the action onstage via the small TV monitor mounted in the corner. The show was going fine, a few snags here and there, the odd missing prop or dropped line, but nothing major.

He watched as Stanford strode on stage and announced, "Lords and ladies, it is my pleasure to announce the arrival of Lord and Lady Hummerdinger from Cucamonga!"

Jump smiled, the line was funny, and flipped the red air cannon switch.

Only the air cannon didn't fire. Instead there was a series of sharp pops, like firecrackers going off under a wet towel, and a gigantic ceiling beam fell from the sky and crushed Stanford Whitley where he stood.

He was thoroughly smushed and quite dead in unceremonious, Wile E. Coyote fashion.

In the booth, Jump flipped the red switch several times. "Huh... I don't think that wasn't supposed to happen."

UMP sat blinking, not believing what he just saw on the TV monitor. Did a ceiling beam really just fall from the sky and drive Stanford Whitely into the floor like a Brad nail? He pulled his finger from the red switch like it bit him.

"Flip the red switch," he said to himself. "He told me to flip the red switch. I flipped the red switch."

The theater was quiet and nobody moved — not the ushers, not the audience and not the actors. The giant THUMP of the beam hitting the floor still reverberated through the building. Looking like one of the Muppets in the "Mahna Mahna" bit, stage manager Vicky Greeley stuck her head out from backstage and surveyed the scene.

"Oh my," she uttered as a small rivulet of blood began seeping from under the beam.

Meanwhile, on stage, confusion ruled. The other seven actors, in various forms of starchy Victorian dress, looked back and forth at each other like lost sheep. The crowd, for the moment, thought the falling beam some spectacular new effect like the chandelier in *Phantom of the Opera* or the helicopter in *Miss Saigon* or Rosie O'Donnell in *Grease*. But an unsettling chatter was rising

Upstage center, dressed in regal garb, Jimmy Fuentes, Jump's best friend in the cast, looked at Elspeth Anne, company hottie, and whispered, "Is this part of the show?"

Elspeth replied with a blank stare and the mildest of shrugs. She looked awesome in her French maid outfit. "Dunno."

Jimmy, sensing the panic in the audience, did what all actors do when they don't know what to do — he went on with the show.

"Yes, it is I!" he announced, a tremor and hitch in his voice. "Lord Thurmond Hummerdinger, and my wife, the lovely Summer Hummerdinger!"

Amanda Kaulich, at his side, greased with sweat in an ill-fitting, beaded dress, took a deep bow. *Too* deep. The zipper seam on the back of the dress burst, spilling hundreds of little plastic balls on to the stage and 14lbs of hidden back fat into plain sight. "Oop!"

This did little to calm the stirring crowd. In typical smacked-ass nature, this all took about 15 seconds, but felt eternal on stage.

"Is that blood?" came a voice from the crowd.

Jimmy looked closer at the fallen beam and he, too, now saw the growing crimson stream oozing from beneath it.

"The hell?" He moved in for closer inspection, but in doing so stepped on several dozen silicone beads. Coupled with his slick leather-soled shoes, prodigious girth and the normal effects of gravity, he went tumbling ass-over-teakettle, face coming to rest mere inches from the growing pool of blood. What he saw when he opened his eyes he would never forget as long as he lived.

"Mommy," he whimpered as he stared at Stanford Whitley, half of whom was squashed flat. Worst of all, as Jimmy looked at his squished face, it seemed as though Stanford was staring back, eyes bugged, shocked, surprised. Jimmy began to weep. Then Stanford blinked.

Jimmy ran screaming from the stage. It was, and forever would be, the fastest he ever moved.

Earlier...

DETECTIVE Ike Curtis, 20-year veteran of the Cape May Police Department, was pretty sure he'd never met worse human beings than the ones that sat before him now.

"And you're sure," he continued, rubbing a hand across his throbbing forehead, "the he's... what did you call him... a she-he?"

Joy Carmichael, owner-operator of Famous Annie's Famous Dinner Theater, snapped back, "Or a he-she, we're not really sure of the terminology."

"I understand," Curtis said. "Why would you be?"

He sat at the large, round table in the theater's dining room, with Joy, her husband Tim Templeton, and his lover Farley Owensby. His trademark tan overcoat was coming in handy: the AC was cranked — it was about 57 degrees in the theater.

He asked, "You always keep it so cold?"

Tim answered, "Once you get 350 people in here it will go up to about 65."

Farley winked. "And it helps to keep the actors at attention... if you know what I mean."

Curtis asked, "The men or the women?"

"I don't care," Farley laughed.

"I see," Curtis said, then wrote 'Sexually Hostile Work Environment' to the laundry list of violations he'd already jotted down in his notebook, among them: expired liquor license, disabled sprinkler system, unsafe wiring, overpriced tickets, and really bad taste.

But Ike Curtis was not here today as an agent of the state liquor control board, the pipe fitters' union or the better business bureau. He was here to find out why somebody might want to kill Jump Wiggen. Ten days earlier, two bottles of poisoned water found their way into his lunch cooler, killing his boss, Waylon Hoag.

He continued, "And you say you fired Jump because..."

"First of all," Joy piped in like air leaking from a big balloon, "he was nowhere near worth the money we were paying him — $350 a week to act and direct? Please, I could've gotten some college kid for half the money."

"And what a fine production that would have been," Curtis replied, dripping with irony.

"Exactly," she said stupidly.

"And," Tim said, "he really wasn't much of an actor — terrible with accents, his singing voice was okay, but he couldn't dance his way out of a paper bag."

"Really?" Curtis asked, then cast an eye to the far wall, which was festooned with plaques and awards from different theater groups, four of which read, "Cape May County Theatrical Organizations' Annual Triple-Threat of the Year Award to... Jump Wiggen, Famous Annie's."

"And," Farley continued, "he was terribly difficult to work with, wouldn't wear any of the costumes I designed for him..." Tim rolled his eyes. "...At great expense to the theater and Joy in particular."

"Yes," she agreed.

Geniuses, Curtis thought.

At that moment one of the actors, in a leather thong and some kind of feather boa/pirate costume thingy and knee-high boots, approached the table. The actor looked embarrassed.

"Excuse me, Mr Owensby?" the actor said.

"Yes love," Farley answered. "Scoot your little butt over here, and tell me what's the matter."

The actor turned a deep red and approached. "The clasp on my... pants... is broken... again."

Farley hissed, "Seems like all I do is repair these things."

The actor looked at Curtis with eyes that said, *He's not fixing them at all.*

Farley continued, spinning the young man around, producing a needle and thread from his pocket, casually resting a hand on the kid's exposed buttock. "I'm sick to death of fixing these things... but I never get tired of a good codpiece in my face. HEL-LO! There you go love, all done."

Detective Ike Curtis had seen a lot of things in his 20 years on the force, but this place was the strangest of them all. And even though no crime had been committed per se, he felt an undeniable urge to toss all of them into lock-up for 36 hours or so.

"Thank you for your time," he told them.

"So, um..." Joy started nervously, "you'll remember what we told you about Jump and spread the word?"

"It's important people know about his... affliction," Tim said.

Ike Curtis rose from the table and said, "I will do nothing to spread this web of lies you've been feeding me for the last 45 minutes. I don't believe one word you've told me about Jump Wiggen." He stared at Tim, "and the only 'affliction' he suffers from, as far as I can tell, is having been exposed to three heartless, soulless succubae like yourselves."

"Well I never..." Joy exclaimed.

"Easy, dear," Tim cautioned.

"And furthermore," Curtis continued, "despite the fact that I think you're all too stupid to get out of each other's way and far too dumb to have dreamed up a plan to poison Jump's water, I'm still keeping an eye on you."

Farley threw a hand to his cheek. "Us? What did we do?"

"If I see or hear of any of you getting within a mile of Jump I'll have the health department on your head so fast it'll make your collective ass spin."

"Wait a minute," Tim interjected, "were we suspects?"

"Were," Curtis stressed, "till I discovered you're dumber than a sack of hammers."

"Now just a second..." Tim tried, but Curtis cut him off.

"I mean it — I see or hear about any trouble between you and Wiggen I will shut this place down, got it?"

Their silence sufficed.

"Now get me out of here. I need a shower."

Later...

JUMP felt an eerie sense of déjà vu as he sat on the lip of the Equity's stage and watched the police activity around him. Upon seeing the fleeing Jimmy Fuentes, the audience, some 200 of them, finally caught on that what they had witnessed was not a special effect and was, in fact, an actual person being flattened by an extremely heavy piece of wood, and left. Quickly.

Once again, Jump gazed at the cast, gathered in the lobby, telling their tales to anyone who would listen (despite the minutes-old tragedy, they were actors, and every actor loved having a new a story to tell). Once again he found himself confronted by the TV cliché of a cop, Ike Curtis. Only this time each, unbeknownst to either, respected the other.

"So you just flipped the red switch?" Curtis asked.

Jump shouted, "He told me to flip the red switch, I flipped the red switch!"

"Okay, calm down," Curtis said. "I'm just trying to get a feel here."

"Okay, sorry."

"What happened when you flipped it?"

Jump looked at Curtis, then over his shoulder at the mess behind him, then back to Curtis as if to say, *Do you not see the man they're squeegeeing off the floor?*

Curtis corrected himself, "I mean, did you see or hear anything unusual? Was there anyone backstage who shouldn't have been?"

Jump shook his head. "I was in the tech booth, it's kind of over and behind the stage. I couldn't see backstage but... I don't think so. And I didn't hear or see anything... wait!"

Curtis prompted, "I'm waiting."

Jump thought back. He had flipped the switch and then, what was it? *Yes! It sounded like firecrackers.* "I heard firecrackers!"

"Firecrackers?"

"Firecrackers!"

A few minutes later, they were in the cramped tech booth, which fit roughly one full-grown human being, and smelled strongly of stale BO. They sat next to each other, butts squinched together on the hard wooden seat.

"It's all pretty standard stuff," Jump explained. "I did some of the wiring myself last week during rehearsals. Made sure this was plugged into that and whatnot. I had nothing to do with the air cannon, though. That was all Mr Whitley."

Immediately upon reaching the booth, Curtis noticed another smell — the acrid scent of burnt wood mingled with a metallic tang, like a roll of paper caps after you've shot them off in your old plastic six-shooter. And he knew what must have happened.

"Okay, up you go!" came a voice from the stage.

Jump and Curtis' eyes shot to the small TV monitor.

On stage they had secured a vinyl strap around the errant ceiling beam, connected it to the small backhoe that Clyde Stickle of Stickle Construction had skillfully driven into the theater, and were preparing to lift it.

From his seat on the machine, Clyde announced, "One... two... three!"

With the slightest bit of resistance and the knee-buckling sound of a wet suction cup, the beam rose. Mercifully, the resolution of the aging TV monitor was so poor all Jump and Curtis saw was an opaque circle on the floor. They looked at each other, visibly relieved.

"Thank God for small favors," Jump offered.

"Indeed," Curtis agreed. "Now let's trace this wire."

Jump nodded, "It's gonna get dusty — we have to go up over the acoustic tiles."

Thinking back on his experience at Famous Annie's, Curtis replied, "I've been dirtier."

★　★　★　★　★

A FEW minutes later, covered in sweaty black dust bunnies, they were back on stage, examining the gigantic beam as it hung before them. Thankfully, the remnants of Stanford Whitley had been removed.

"So," Jump said, "whoever it was bypassed the power from the air cannon to these?"

"Right," Curtis told him. "See these little black marks? That's where the blasting caps were. The perp chiseled his way in, expertly I might add, wired the caps, and sawed through and weakened the cross joists just enough that the whole thing would give way with the blast."

Jump whistled. "Impressive."

"It is," Curtis agreed unhappily, "which means whomever we're looking for is no amateur, probably did some time, has a sharp knowledge of tools and..."

"Excuse me, Detective Curtis, sir?" a voice said behind them. It was a young CSI.

"What is it, son?" Curtis asked.

"Sir," the CSI said, "we found some blood and tissue samples on a metal scaffold backstage upon arrival, sir. A lot of blood and a lot of tissue."

"What's your point son," Curtis urged. "I'm in the middle of an investigation."

"The point, sir," the CSI continued, "is that we crossed and typed it against everyone who works here and everyone we have on file, and it was all from the same donor."

"Get to it, man," Curtis ordered.

"Sir," the CSI informed him, "the donor is one Jump Wiggen."

Curtis looked to Jump, who could only stare back.

The CSI continued, "His blood type and DNA are on file at Cape Regional from his last hospital visit. They automatically enter it into the BCI just in case of... well, in case of instances like this."

Curtis kept his eyes on Jump. "I understand. Thank you. You can go."

The CSI went. Curtis cocked an eyebrow.

"What?" Jump asked. "So my blood and skin are all over the crime scene. It'll never hold up in court."

Curtis was silent.

"That was a joke."

Curtis did not smile.

Jump paused. "This is bad, right?"

Curtis nodded.

"Should I run?"

Curtis shrugged.

"I think I'll run."

Jump turned, sped off... and promptly tripped over a CSI tool bag, smashing face-first into the stage, flattening his nose, and blackening his eyes.

"Maybe I'll stay."

"Good call."

CHAPTER FIVE
Higher Than A Mountain, Thicker Than Water

UMP felt foolish as the blood from his crushed nose dripped down the back of his throat, a product of his ill-fated, ill-conceived escape attempt. Upon hearing that a copious amount of his own DNA was discovered all over the crime scene (a three-ton ceiling beam and a three-foot square piece of stage) he had stupidly decided to run for it, only to trip and smash his face into the stage.

"Feeling any better?" Detective Ike Curtis asked, handing him another fistful of aspirin.

Jump answered, "Physically fine, emotionally crippled."

"Well," Curtis comforted him, "it was a really bad idea."

"Yeah, you don't have to remind me."

They were quiet for a moment. Finally, Jump said, "Oh-for-two."

"Pardon?"

"The killer," Jump informed him. "Oh-for-two so far."

Curtis regarded him kindly, "I was wondering when you'd catch on."

"I'm not that stupid. Once is an accident, twice is a trend. The poison in the water... that could have been an accident, a manufacturer's error... but a giant ceiling beam crashing down on the exact spot where I was supposed to be at the exact moment I was supposed to be there? You don't have to draw me a map."

"Well," Curtis consoled him, "looks like you're handling it pretty well."

Jump looked up, bloodshot, raccoon eyes watery, white tape holding his shattered nose together, twin streams of blood leaking from his nostrils. "Does it?"

Curtis said nothing. Jump looked pathetic — black eyes and red nose accentuating his patched forehead, which was now seeping blood after his jarring cranial encounter with the hard, wooden floor.

Curtis shook himself and said, "Mind explaining to me how your blood and skin got here?"

Jump held up his left thumb, which bore an ugly green and black bruise, half a fingernail and a loose, blood-soaked band-aid. "Remember this?"

Curtis did and now began to wonder if there was any place in Cape May that Jumps' blood *wasn't*. He claimed to have smashed the thumb the day

Waylon Hoag died.

"That was 10 days ago. This stuff is fresh."

"How fresh?"

Curtis held up a crimson finger: "Still wet."

"Lovely."

"Your blood is all over the scene."

"So is half my thumb."

"Old news," Curtis said, sounding perturbed now, avuncularity gone. "You need to tell me how this blood got here today."

Jump looked him in the eye: "Detective Curtis, I have no idea."

Curtis hesitated. "Where were you last night?"

"I was here 'til midnight for rehearsal then went home and caught up on my DVR. Are you watching *Jericho*?"

"Your point, Wiggen?"

"I went straight home from rehearsal, ate a sandwich, watched some TV and was asleep by 3am."

Curtis asked, "Can anyone verify this?"

"Pfft... I wish."

"Did you go anywhere, Wawa for coffee or a shorti? The Ugly Mug for a crab cake? Pilot House for some nachos?"

Jump shook his head. "No, it was late and I was tired. My apartment is five blocks from the theater, above Freda's Café. I walked down Beach to Ocean. It was dark, I didn't see anybody."

"Um..." a voice said from behind them, "that's not exactly true."

Jump turned to see his friend Jimmy Fuentes, looking a little scared and very uncomfortable.

"What do you mean?" Curtis asked him.

"Yeah, what do you mean?" Jump echoed.

"I'm sorry, Jump, we're tight and all, but... I saw you at the Jackson Mountain around two."

"Is that so?" Curtis asked.

Jump was flabbergasted.

"Sorry, dude," Jimmy offered. "I remember 'cuz the rest of us went to the Pilot House to get a bite, run some lines, and we wondered where you went. A couple hours later, I'll admit we'd had a few, but we were all walking Elspeth home..."

Jump chimed in, "One pretty girl needs seven escorts home?"

"... And when we walked past the Mountain I saw you sitting at the bar. You looked pretty drunk, all hangdog... I think you were hitting on the bartender... anyway, that's what I saw, we all saw you there, we tried waving but you were too far gone. I'm sorry, Jump, but you're just not telling the truth."

Jimmy, looking like his puppy just died, slinked away.

Curtis turned his gaze to Jump. "Care to explain this?"

Jump, jaw agape, said nothing.

Curtis stood. "Jump Wiggen, you have the right to remain silent, anything you say can and will be used against you in a court of law..."

"Frak!"

"*Battlestar Galactica!*" Curtis chirped. "Now *there's* a good show."

Earlier...

IN THE confusion, no one saw the dark figure sneak backstage. There would only be a few minutes until the police arrived and swarmed the place, so he had to work quickly. Blast his luck! The remote detonation device worked perfectly, the beam falling swiftly after a series of crisp *Pa-Kows!* But he'd failed to notice one tiny detail — the wrong actor was on stage. That minor nuisance aside, the dark figure took pride in the fact that he'd managed to crush another human being into something you could fit into a bread box.

"Is that blood?" a voice from the audience asked, bringing the dark figure back from his reverie. Time to move.

The dark figure was very glad now that she had recommended having a PLAN B, just in case, though what did *she* know about PLAN Bs? He could already hear what she would say.

"See?" she'd say, "I told you you'd need a PLAN B, didn't I? Aren't I always right about these things? I'm always right about these things. Some day you'll appreciate that. Not like... not like him."

And on and on she would go, about him, about this, about that, until he was ready to throttle her. Then she would take her shirt off and he would forget what she was talking about. That's how it always went.

"Hummerdinger!" one of the actors shouted.

This again broke the dark figure from his trance and prodded him to act. Unseen in the darkened theater, he slid against the rear wall to the tech booth. It was short work removing the access panel, monkeying with the few wires that needed monkeyed with, and making his way out the stage door. Once outside in the cool night and safely away, he once again allowed himself to think of her with her shirt off. As sirens wailed in the distance, the dark figure found it increasingly difficult to walk.

The next day...

JUMP was in no mood. He'd spent all night trying to fall asleep in the CMPD's holding cell, and all morning drinking coffee, trying not to fall asleep. It was quite a miserable quandary. Agitated, annoyed, face throbbing from its meeting with the floor and his other injuries all itchy and achy, he sat and waited for the new new director of the Equity to arrive.

They were all there at the theater, the eight of them, Jump alone in the house, everyone else on stage, shooting the breeze, running lines. Jump mopily sipped a tall Wawa coffee and felt sorry for himself. He looked up – his friend Jimmy Fuentes looked back forlornly, but Jump wasn't ready to forgive him just yet, it being pretty much Jimmy's fault that Jump spent the night in the clink to begin with. So, as any good 12-year-old would, Jump ignored him.

It seemed odd and a little disrespectful to be performing on the same stage where, barely 12 hours earlier, Stanford Whitley got pile-driven. But this was theater, and the show, as they say, must go on. So the last bits of Mr Whitley were sponged away and a small orange cone placed over the divot in the stage, Stanford being the same minor inconvenience in death that he had been in life.

No one yet knew who would be replacing him, so a minor current of anticipation coursed through the air. Jump assumed it'd be some other regional musical theater lifer that New Jersey seemed lousy with. And 99 times out of 100 he'd have been right.

But not today.

"Sorry I'm late!" the stunning redhead announced as she strode through the theater doors. "Whose idea was it to let horses and carriages set the pace for summer traffic? Don't answer that, it's rhetorical. Everyone onstage. Now. That includes you, Mr Wiggen. I don't care how nervous or scared or sore or bruised or bleeding you are... this play has some serious pacing issues that need fixing quick and we're not going to get it done with you moping around in the shadows."

Jump was stunned.

"And I think, all things considered," the mystery woman continued, "most of us would prefer to see you in the light."

Jump was shocked.

By now she was on the stage, removing her jacket, dropping her purse on a chair. "So hop to! We've got a show to unlearn."

She and the cast stared down at him. Jump rose, the mask of hurt he wore making his battered face, if possible, even less appealing. He made his way to the aisle. He felt shaken, stirred, violated – yet... something else was brewing up inside of him as he stared at the statuesque, fire-haired woman before him. Something he couldn't quite pin down, but...

Oh crap, he thought. *I'm falling in love.*

"Today!" she shouted.

Jump smiled and climbed on to the boards.

★　★　★　★　★

A FEW hours later, act one was in much better shape and they took a break.

Jump went outside and listened as the ocean pounded away at the surf across the street, behind Famous Annie's Famous Dinner Theater. Jump thought it a crime that something as beautiful as the ocean was blocked by something as hideous as Annie's, a blinking tin-and-neon monstrosity blighting the Jersey coast.

It was early evening now and dusk was just beginning to bruise the edges of the sky when she walked out — the newly widowed Diane Hoag. Jump was not completely shocked to learn Waylon had been married, despite what his gaydar told him, but he was surprised to learn he had landed someone as seemingly together and no-nonsense as Diane. Not that Jump didn't believe someone like Waylon couldn't land someone as together as Diane — rather, Jump didn't really believe women as together as Diane actually existed despite working his way through a few.

He looked at her as she lit a thin, narrow cigarette, one of those "ladies" brands that was the equivalent of smoking a plastic straw, and conversed loosely with a few of the actors. He lit a Marlboro Light and tried not to notice her, how pretty she was in an unfussy way, how her sharp features belied her true age, how her auburn hair was leisurely tousled and billowed softly in the cool breeze. And he tried not to notice that she was now staring at him staring at her.

"Crap..."

She said some quick parting words to the actors, snuffed her smoke, then made her way over. His heart pounded and his stomach gurgled, an unfortunate nervous habit, and he quickly tried to check his breath, only to end up snorting a few of his own ashes. He was coughing violently when she stopped in front of him.

"Attractive," she said.

Jump coughed some more.

"Goes well with the rest of your ensemble — bruises, blood and camouflage..."

He knew she was busting his chops, making fun of his cameo shorts and myriad injuries, but he could think of nothing to say besides "Thanks."

Swift too," she said, her tone light yet still mocking.

"Sorry," Jump offered. "I think I just collapsed a lung."

"Take your time."

A few hacks later and he was calm. He looked at her closely, for the first time really, and his heart skipped a beat. *Dammit!*

"Better?" Diane asked.

He nodded. "Much, thanks. If I may, I'd just like to say you've done an amazing job streamlining act one."

Diane smiled. "You don't have to kiss my ass. I don't think you killed anyone."

"Well, that's a relief."

She continued, "My husband spoke very highly of you, and Waylon spoke very highly of no one. That tells me something. May I have a cigarette?"

He gave her one and lit it. "About Mr Hoag... I mean Waylon..."

"Was queer as a three-dollar bill, but we really liked each other and the tax breaks for a husband and wife heading up a non-profit theater were enormous, so..."

"Not really where I was going, but... okay."

She didn't skip a beat. "...We decided to partner up. It was Waylon's idea to open dress rehearsal to the public, demystify the theater for the general public. Plus, people always enjoy watching an actor screw something up."

"There is that," Jump agreed.

"He also thought to finance the renovation by selling bricks and benches and anything you could engrave someone's name on. I kept waiting for that annoying carpenter to jump out with his megaphone and yell, 'Move that bus!'"

"He was smart."

She blew a thick plume of smoke from her perfect lips. "Exceedingly so. But I want you, especially, to know that, even though I'm all business right now, I'm grieving heavily inside. I'd like someone to share that grief with when we're done here tonight and I'd like that someone to be you."

"Um..."

"Pardon my forwardness, but we haven't much time. And right now we need to get back to work. Just say 'okay' and we'll go from there."

"Okay."

"Good, now back inside."

In they went. Jump wondered if anyone noticed he was walking on air.

★　★　★　★　★

TWO hours later, they were on the last page of act two, all the slamming doors, innuendos and misunderstandings coming together in a delicious *Three's Company*-style finale. Backstage, Jump smiled as his friend Jimmy Fuentes delivered a killer comedic monologue. He was good. Funny. A talented guy. And Jump decided right then to make nice with him.

"I bid you adieu!" Jimmy said and stomped off the stage, cape trailing behind dramatically. Those on stage broke character and applauded.

"That was great!" Jump told him as he stepped behind the curtain.

"Yeah?" Jimmy asked. "It felt good."

"The cape," Jump said. "The cape action is... it's bringing sexy back."

Jimmy smiled, then the two of them were silent a long moment.

"Look..." Jimmy started.

"Forget it," Jump stopped him. "We're good. Let's talk after. Right now I just want to get through this damn play once without anyone dying."

"I hear that."

Jump started away, "Be right back, I have to hit the... OW!"

"Quiet backstage!" Diane shouted from the house.

"Criminy!" Jump hissed.

"What is it?" Jimmy whispered.

Jump lifted his right foot, which now had a large chunk of 2x4 sticking from it.

"Yeah?" Jimmy asked. "So?"

"What you can't see," Jump winced, "is the very large nail that is securing it to my foot... by sticking through it."

"Oh," Jimmy said softly, "that must hurt."

"A bit," Jump agreed. "Can you..."

Jimmy went to the tech booth stairs. "Don't sweat it. What do I have to do?"

Jump tried not to pass out. "When the clock strikes 12, kill channel six and punch channel eight three times, when the rooster crows."

"Got it," Jimmy said, bounded up the steps and squeezed into the booth.

"Thanks," Jump said and pointed to the ratty, backstage couch. "I'm going to go over there and faint."

Jimmy chuckled. "Wuss."

Jump step-clonked to the far wall.

"Quiet backstage!" Diane yelled again. Behind the curtain, Jump flipped her the bird.

He'd experienced a lot of new pain in the last week and a half, but this pain, a sharp metal spike jutting up into the soft fascia tissue of his foot and grinding against the bones on top, may have been the winner. On stage, the grandfather clock began to strike 12.

Jump laid himself down on the couch and his pain-addled mind began to wander. *Have I eaten? Why does my ear itch? Is that coffee I smell? Didn't Stanford Whitley die filling in for me last night? Why is stage right left and stage left right?*

He bolted up on the couch. Stanford Whitley had indeed died while taking his place. "Jimmy! Wait..."

The rooster crowed, the lights flashed. Jimmy poked his head out of the booth.

"What?"

"Quiet backstage, dammit!"

Jump was sweating. "Nothing, I thought... never mind."

"Jeez, dude," Jimmy said, "you're losing it."

Then the tech booth erupted into a ball of flame.

CHAPTER SIX
As Time Goes By

Eight years ago...

JUMP Wiggen, a spry, handsome young lad, sat stunned in the lobby of the Three Blind Mice Dinner Theater and Country Club in Wilmington, Delaware. The cast list for the next show, *Hello Dolly*, had just been posted, and he was shocked to find his name absent not only from the lead roles, but from the list altogether.

"I don't understand," he said to his girlfriend, Kirsten Hopwood. "Did I do something wrong? Did I piss somebody off?"

Kirsten, whose sharp face sat atop a voluptuous dancer's body, answered, "I don't know, did you?"

Jump could only shrug.

He and Kirsten had only been an item for a few weeks, and already, for him, the spark was fading, which was a shame. He'd lusted after her for years, having seen just about every show the Three Blind Mice had produced since his adolescence, and Kirsten's name was always at or near the top of every Playbill. Nailing her was a huge score. But like the dog that catches his tail, once he'd gotten it he really didn't quite know what to do with it and found it rather more boring than he'd anticipated.

"I should talk to Doug," Jump said to her. "He'll know what's going on."

Doug Feoli was one of the Three Blind Mice's producers and had been, up to that point, pretty square with Jump.

"Oh don't bother him," Kirsten warned. "You know how busy he gets when one show is ending and another going into rehearsal."

"I have to," Jump said. "Something's not right. I've done a good job here. My Riff is solid and this entire run of *West Side Story* has been sold out. I'd like to think I had a little something to do with that."

Kirsten nodded slowly — she knew Jump was right. After a week of previews the local reviews started hitting the Philly and Wilmington papers. Jump's performance in particular had been singled out as "energetic" and "buoyant" and "against type," leading to the 1200-seat venue having barely room to stand for the last nine weeks. With three weeks left in the run, the next show was about to go into production and Jump expected to have, if not the lead role, at least have *a* role.

So, with Kirsten trailing him spewing feeble verbal warnings not to bother Doug, Jump strode purposefully to his office and bothered him.

"Doug," he announced, throwing open the door.

A surprised looking secretary scuttled from Doug's lap, and Doug looked none to pleased.

"A knock," Doug said, "would be nice. Thank you, Charlotte, you can go now, we'll finish... dictating that letter this afternoon."

It was awkward for a second, then Jump got down to business: "Why am I not in the show?"

Doug smiled calmly. "Well, Jump, not every actor gets every show he thinks he's entitled too."

"True," Jump replied, "but I'm entitled to this one. You read the reviews, you know I helped turn *West Side* into one of your biggest hits in years."

"Ah," Doug said, remaining placid, "the reviews... has someone been believing their own hype?"

Jump paused. "Yeah, a little. So?"

Doug waved a hand. "It's no matter. You're correct, the reviews were good, the show is good and the Three Blind Mice is making money. Please sit."

Jump and Kirsten sank into the deep leather chairs before Doug's desk.

"I hear you two are seeing each other," Doug said.

This made Jump a little uncomfortable. "About seven..."

"Six," Kirsten corrected.

"About six weeks," Jump concluded.

"Things going well?" Doug asked.

"Sure," Jump answered.

"Great!" Kirsten said with zeal.

"Well that's very nice," Doug continued, stroking a hand over his trim beard. "But what I'm going to say next is not very nice, and you may not want to be here to hear it."

Confusion reigned for a moment.

Jump asked, "Me or Kirsten?"

Doug looked at Kirsten and said, "You."

Alarmed, she grabbed Jump's hand tightly.

"Ow!"

"It's okay," she said firmly. "Whatever you have to say to Jump you can say in front of me."

"Um... sure," Jump muttered.

"Suit yourselves," Doug said with a shrug and opened a drawer on his huge oak desk. From it he produced a manilla envelope teeming with disheveled papers.

"What the hell is that?" Jump queried.

"I'm glad you asked me that, Jump," Doug said with a smile. "Because this is what I like to call the Jump Files."

Kirsten said, "The Jump Files?"

Jump chimed in, "What exactly are the Jump Files?"

Doug's smile grew wider and he began to look like an Italian, bearded Tiger Shark. "The Jump Files began approximately five minutes after Mr Wiggen here walked through our doors as an employee of the Three Blind Mice. You know those little suggestion boxes we have posted at various spots around the building?"

They did. The Three Blind Mice was gigantic and there seemed to be as many suggestion boxes as electrical outlets.

"These," Doug continued, pulling a handful of sheets from the folders, "are all the suggestion slips we've received over the last seven weeks that mention Jump in any way, shape or form. For example," he picked a random slip and read it, "'Please ask Jump Wiggen to wear proper footwear.'"

Jump defiantly said, "Well that's not so..."

"'Jump Wiggen needs to wear clean clothes to rehearsal, he smells like a homeless person.'"

Jump fidgeted in his seat. "Well, when I got here I was a little down on my luck and didn't have..."

"'Jump Wiggen raped me in the wardrobe closet last Friday.'"

Jump said nothing. Silence filled the room, the last few words seeming to echo in the still air.

"Can... can you repeat that?" Jump asked.

Doug's smile was gone. He looked Jump in the eye and said again, "'Jump Wiggen raped me in the wardrobe closet last Friday.'"

Kirsten pulled her hand away. "Jump... how could you?"

"What?" he protested. "I didn't! That's a lie... who wrote it?"

"Sorry," Doug said, his smile returning. "They're all confidential, no names."

"Well that's..." Jump stammered, "this is just... I can't believe... you really think I..."

Kirsten shifted as far away from him as she could. Doug kept his dark eyes fixed on him.

"Wait a minute," Jump said, anger ebbing, fear rising. "You... you believe this? You think I raped someone here?"

Doug sifted through the pile of slips. "Jump, I have at least 17 different complaints about you in here, forcing yourself on women... and one man."

Behind him, a half-dozen firemen busied themselves with the mechanics of pacifying the heat of the just-extinguished blaze.

Jump was out of his chair now, apoplectic. "Doug, this is ridiculous! You know me..."

"Do I?"

"Yes," Jump said firmly. "You do. This is someone's idea of a sick joke. I mean, sure, I've dated a few of the girls here... a couple of waitresses, a chef, about half the chorus... but force myself? Never. It's a lie. Someone's trying to get me fired."

"Well," Doug said, "unfortunately for you, it's worked."

"What?"

"Jump Wiggen?"

"Yes?"

"You're fired."

Kirsten Hopwood burst into tears, her eyes locked with Doug's.

Present...

JUMP Wiggen, no longer spry, not quite as handsome as eight years ago, sat yet again on the lip of the stage inside the Cape Equity Theater. Behind him, a half-dozen firemen busied themselves with the mechanics of pacifying the heat of the just-extinguished blaze, laying down coats of foam and keeping a fresh flow of water running over the charred bits.

"Got him!" one of them announced and Jump turned to watch them do their grisly work.

From inside what used to be the tech booth they pulled the smoking remains of what appeared to be a human being, then laid it down in the black vinyl body bag on the floor.

"Jimmy..." Jump muttered and choked on his emotions.

It was Jimmy Fuentes, Jump's best friend in the company, now lying in that bag, little wisps of smoke still rising from his blackened flesh. Mercifully, another of the firemen zipped it up.

"I'm sorry about your friend," Detective Curtis said. "Really."

Jump nodded and wiped the back of his hand across his face, forgetting how much pain that would bring him.

"Dammit..." he hissed through clenched teeth.

Twenty minutes ago, too late realizing what was about to happen, he tried to warm Jimmy that something terrible was going to happen. As he neared the tech booth it erupted into a gigantic ball of flame, singeing the hair on Jump's face and giving him second-degree burns all over his mug. His eyebrows now resembled clumped eyeliner, his goatee looked like the iron filings you might find inside a children's "use the magnet to put a beard on the clown" game.

This, on top of the acid burn on his forehead, the thumb he savaged with a hammer two weeks ago, the face he shattered the day before on the stage, and the giant nail now sticking into the bottom of his foot, made him more than a little irritable.

As if on cue, Curtis asked, "How you feeling?"

Jump looked up at him, lacking the proper words, and said, "Great."

Detective Curtis eyeballed him. The kid needed to answer some questions and he needed to answer them now, but he just couldn't bring himself to toss this physical wreck of a man under the hot lights of the interrogation room just yet, even though a night in jail might be the best thing for him. So he decided to use a different tack.

"You know," he said to Jump, "I never asked you what brought you to Cape May to begin with?"

Jump hesitated. It had been a long time since someone asked him that and it was one of his very favorite stories. The twists, the turns, the oohs and ahhs... it was a wing-dinger, and he smiled widely in anticipation of telling it. Then his fire-dried lips split and blood shot from them like someone stepping on a ketchup packet.

"Ow!"

Seven years, 342 days ago...

JUMP was miserable. In the three weeks since his unceremonious firing by the Three Blind Mice, he'd sunk into a deep depression, stopped eating, and stopped performing up to his usual level of excellence in the boudoir. Kirsten, like a mother hen nursing an injured chick back to health, was quite attentive and doting and understanding of his... shortcomings.

If he heard her say, "It's not your fault, it happens all the time" one more time he was going to scream and break something.

"We're almost there," she announced from the driver's seat, giving his thigh a reassuring pat. This would normally stir him up in certain regions, but today... nothing.

"Okay," he said absently.

The "there" in question was a Troika Productions audition for a national tour of *Oklahoma!* It was a show Jump had no business auditioning for — he was certainly not the Oklahoma type, and he was doing it mainly to quiet Kirsten, who'd been prattling on to no end about his need to "get back out there."

So, here he was, forking over $20 for two hours of parking in an insanely-overpriced Manhattan parking garage, putting his jazz shoes on to try out for a show he was never in a million years going to get.

Once inside he found himself surrounded by the usual array of hopefuls — leg-warmer clad, '80s-denying dancer folk, cowboy hat-wearing, too-eager actor folk, and everything in between. If it wasn't real and happening right in front of him, he wouldn't believe that such people existed and never in numbers this large... there must have been a thousand people crammed into the un-air conditioned studio.

So he and Kirsten shoved their way to the front of the line, signed up on the big call sheet and waited with the rest of the rubes.

"Let's see," Kirsten yammered, "it's 8:30 right now, we're number 756 and 757 on the list... we should get to go sometime around 5 o'clock."

"Wonderful," Jump answered listlessly.

"Oh, cheer up, poopy pants," Kirsten goosed him. "At least we get to spend some quality time together."

He smiled wanly at her beaming face. He decided not to be a total prick and resisted breaking up with her then and there.

"Kirsten!" a voice called from the crowd.

They craned around, looking for the source of the voice. About 15 people deep and to their right, a thin hand waved through the air.

"Kirsten!"

"Oh my God, I don't believe it!" Kirsten cried.

From the crowd burst a rail thin, curly-haired blonde, her mane as wild as her eyes.

"Bonnie!" Kirsten cried and the two girls squealed with delight as they embraced. "I don't believe it!"

A moment later they had composed themselves and Jump noticed that Bonnie had someone in tow — a sandy-haired man of slight build, but handsome nonetheless.

"You have to meet my boyfriend," Kirsten announced and dragged Bonnie over. "Jump, this is Bonnie Cartwright, my old college room-mate... Bonnie, this is Jump." She gazed up at him adoringly: "My fella."

Jump suddenly felt nauseous.

"Nice to meet you, Jump. Classic name." She shook his hand, then suddenly juggled Kirsten's breasts. "You having fun with these bad boys? Oh man, the guys back in college... anyway, we had our own fun with these guys, didn't we, K?"

Bonnie winked at him and Jump was suddenly much more intrigued by Kirsten Hopwood.

"But I'm being rude," Bonnie said, pulling the sandy-haired man over rather forcefully. "This is my friend Mark, Mark Summers. Mark, this is Kirsten and Jump."

"Pleased to meet you," Mark said softly.

Jump asked, "How do you two know each other?"

"Well," Bonnie started, "Mark is living with my ex-fiancé, Louis, who discovered he was gay as he was walking up the aisle."

"Wow," Jump said.

"You're telling me," Bonnie replied. "But it was very convenient... Mark was his best man."

"Guilty," Mark said with a smile.

"So Jump," Bonnie started, "do you act, too?"

Jump's mood darkened. "I did..."

Kirsten squeezed his hand. "He's between jobs right now. We met at the Three Blind Mice almost 10 weeks ago and have been so happy. But I'll be a lot happier when I get my man here back on stage. He's so talented."

Mark said, "Yes... Jump... Wiggen... I read about you in the *Inquirer*, you got killer reviews... what happened? Why aren't you there any-more."

Jumped weighed the many options he had to answer with and chose the least complicated. "It's political."

"Oh..." Bonnie and Mark moaned in unison. If there was anything a theater actor despised more than bad reviews or lousy direction, it was intra-theater politics. Every actor understood this and it went unques-tioned as a one-word answer to the most complicated of questions.

"Well, if you're looking for work, I just left this place in Cape May,

New Jersey... it's right on the shore," Mark offered. "Famous Annie's something or other. It's a big chain that's popping up all over the east coast. I hear the salary is pretty lousy but hey, a job's a job, right?"

"Hmm," Jump said, curious, "Cape May, eh? Never been, but I hear it's nice."

Mark grabbed his hands. "You should totally audition there, like, tomorrow. Here," he pulled out his cellphone. "I'll give you the number..."

Present...

DETECTIVE Curtis was riveted. "So whatever happened with Kirsten?"

Jump answered, holding the antiseptic gauze against his seeping lips, "We auditioned here together, got hired together, lived together, worked together, ate together, slept together, showered together... it was like cramming five years of real-life couplehood into six months. That's how long we lasted before we broke up. She moved away. Last I heard she was in California in real estate, but that's third-hand info from an internet site for Three Blind Mice alumni."

"Huh," Curtis mumbled, "that's a pretty good story."

Jump chuckled. "You shoulda tried living it."

At that moment, Diane Hoag, widow of the late Waylon Hoag, first Artistic Director of the Equity, approached.

"How are you gentlemen doing?" she asked.

"Fine," Curtis answered. Jump just nodded — it hurt to talk.

"Are you through with our young friend here?" she asked the detective.

He really needed to talk to him further — for Pete's sake he was the only real suspect they had — but it looked like he'd had enough for one night.

Curtis said, "Promise me you'll come by the station first thing tomorrow and I'll send you home tonight."

"Done," Jump replied.

"Okay, see you at nine," Curtis said, then noticed that Diane had tenderly taken Jump's hand. "Make it 10:30."

Jump nodded, the policeman left, and Diane led them away. It was that evening that Jump discovered that a man with less than half his working body parts could still pleasure a fellow human being.

CHAPTER SEVEN
O Brother, Where Art Thou?

UMP Wiggen pulled open the heavy front door of his apartment building and stepped out on to the fringe of the Washington Street Mall. It was 10:15 and he had a 10:30 appointment with Detective Ike Curtis of the CMPD. He'd been up since 8:30, which was right about the time the kitchen staff at Freda's Café, above which his apartment sat, arrived and started pounding chicken. It was an odd-but-effective alarm clock.

It was a short block-and-a-half walk from his room to the police station in City Hall, and in that short time he was unable to wipe the goofy smile from his face. His charred, poisoned, smashed face.

He half-walked/half-be-bopped through the light at Ocean and Washington, the longest red light known to man, and skidoo-ed past Celebrate Cape May, 39 Degrees and the numerous other shops that popped up in the Acme parking lot about 10 years before. His favorite had been the Bethel's newsstand, the only place in town he could grab a pack of smokes, the *Philadelphia Daily News*, some comic books and the latest *Penthouse* and/or *Hustler*, depending on his mood.

He was now closing in on City Hall — policemen in various garb entered and exited the busy building, lawyer types in dark suits jogged up and down the front steps, one judge, robes held up to reveal board short covered legs, scampered out and fed his meter. Jump was about to enter and face perhaps the most important day of his life, his one and possibly only chance to clear his name of these inexplicable coincidences. He should have been terrified. Instead he couldn't stop grinning stupidly, recalling the passion of the previous evening. Despite his bruised and punctured limbs, his flash-fried face and various other ailments and injuries, it had been the best horizontal throwdown of his life.

Bow-chicka-bow-wow!

Diane Hoag, recently widowed, was a patient, tender and inventive partner, much more so than he had expected. But perhaps three years of being married to a gay man had repressed a few things in her. Jump wished Waylon Hoag was still alive for him to thank.

So he tried to block her pretty face out of his mind as he climbed the steps. Tried to forget how her scarlet hair fell lazily over one eye. Tried to forget her soft hands on his face as they applied the medicinal burn ointment. Tried and failed.

"Morning!" he chirped to the undercover detective going down as he went up. He thought the quizzical look the detective gave him was a little off but decided to ignore it.

"How's it going?" he asked another passerby, a bailiff, drawing yet another surprised stare. This was a little more disconcerting. Had he missed something?

He pulled open the door to City Hall and proceeded down the stairs to the police department.

"Wiggen," he told the duty guard through the thick plastic window. "Got a 10:30 with Detective Curtis."

But before the guard could respond, Detective Curtis walked up behind him, carrying a cup of coffee and apple fritter from Wawa.

"What the hell..." he said. "You're early."

"No," Jump corrected, hungrily eyeing the fritter. "You said 10:30, it is now..." he glanced at a big clock on the wall, "10:23... technically I'm early. Very early for me."

Curtis eyed him for a moment. "Are you feeling all right?"

Jump eyed him back. "Fine, thank you."

"The pain medication they put you on... not having any side effects, are you?"

"No," Jump answered, "but you're, like, the third person to act weird around me this morning. Maybe my meds are giving you people the side effects."

Curtis nodded to a door down the hall. "Let's go sit."

"Fine," Jump replied, the coffee smelling like heaven. "You get any donuts around here? I know it's cliché, but..."

Curtis opened the door and motioned for Jump to sit. "I need you to be quiet now and stop joking around."

Jump stopped, mildly alarmed. He'd been feeling a bit of camaraderie with the old cop over the last few weeks as they worked together to solve the mystery of the theater deaths, but now he was thinking that perhaps he had over-sentimentalized the guy, for there was nothing friendly in his tone at the moment.

He asked, "What's wrong, Detective?"

Curtis snapped on the little tape recorder on the table and gravely said, "Detective Ike Curtis interviewing one Jump Wiggen, 10:24am, Wednesday morning..."

"Detective, what's going on?"

"Mr Wiggen seems to be in an altered state given his behavior earlier this morning."

"Earlier this morning... what?"

Curtis clicked off the recorder and snapped, "Dammit, Jump! Stop messing with me! I want to believe you didn't do these things but you have to start making it easier!"

Jump was stunned. "Detective Curtis, I have NO IDEA what you're talking about."

Curtis began to pace impatiently. "I can look past your dead buddy..."

"You mean Jimmy?"

"Yes, I mean Jimmy!"

A giant fireball in the theater's tech booth had consumed Jimmy the night before. "What about him?"

"I said I can look past your buddy seeing you somewhere you said you weren't the night of the second murder."

Jump scratched his goatee. "Oh yeah... that."

The night before a huge ceiling beam fell and squashed director Stanford Whitely into the floor, Jump had truthfully claimed to be home sleeping. Jimmy said he'd seen him at the Jackson Mountain. While it seemed weird at the time, Jump had simply written it off as mistaken identity.

"Still no explanation?" Curtis prodded.

"No," Jump said defiantly, "because I wasn't AT the Jackson Mountain that night. I was home in bed, like I told you."

"And you were the only one with Waylon Hoag when he died!"

Jump was irate. "Lots of people are the last people to see people... not all of them are in jail, are they?"

"Do all those people bang the other people's wives after they die?"

This stung Jump. "What business is it of yours?"

"None," Curtis said, "if I wasn't a cop. But perhaps you can cut through your Percocet haze long enough to see how things are stacking up here — time, opportunity, motive..."

"Motive?"

"The girl, jackass! The girl!"

"Oh yeah..."

"And now this act you're putting on today!"

"About that," Jump said. "What the hell are you talking about?"

Curtis flipped the recorder back on. "Mr Wiggen, do you recall you and I setting up a meeting for 10:30 this morning to discuss the recent string of deaths at the Equity?"

Jump nodded.

Curtis rubbed his temple. "Can you answer verbally, please."

"Oh, sorry... yes. Yes, I remember."

"Do you recall my initially making that meeting for nine then changing it?"

Jump answered, "Yes. Yes I do."

Curtis continued, "And do you recall showing up here at 9 o'clock anyway and agreeing to surrender yourself at 5pm tonight?"

Jump nodded, "Yes. Yes I... pardon?"

Curtis looked him in the eye. "Do you remember coming in here 90 minutes ago and offering to surrender yourself into my custody?"

"That... WHAT? I don't... I was in bed at 9 o'clock."

"Sleeping?"

Jump began to smile.

"Never mind."

"Detective Curtis, I'm sorry, but I was not here this morning."

Curtis pushed *play* on the crappy VCR hooked up to the cruddy TV on the far side of the room. "Then would you mind explaining this?"

With great trepidation Jump looked at the screen. What he saw he could not explain — a man, a man who looked exactly like him, dressed exactly like he had been the night before, bearing the exact same injuries to his face, hand and feet, sitting down at the table, confessing to the murders and offering to surrender himself at the end of the day after tying up some personal loose ends.

When it was over, Jump had to sit.

Curtis said, "So now you can see why I'm a little confused."

For a long while Jump said nothing, his head was spinning too fast. Finally he asked, "Did you check his DNA?"

Curtis nodded, "A match. Just came back from the lab."

"I..." Jump started, but stopped, unable to think of anything coherent to say.

Curtis took a long sip of coffee, broke off a piece of the fritter and offered it to Jump, who declined, appetite suddenly quashed.

"So," Jump muttered, "if I'm supposed to surrender at the end of the day, where am I now?"

Curtis chewed on the pastry, "I assume you're at home, making some phone calls, filling out some paperwork, getting your affairs in order."

"You assume?"

"Well, obviously, as I'm not with you, I can't be 100% certain."

Jump was aghast. "So a guy walks in, confesses to three murders, and you let him walk out, willy-nilly?"

Curtis answered, "I'm not an idiot, Jump. I've got two of my best guys with him."

Jump was suddenly very concerned. "And where are they now?"

"Last time they checked in they were getting coffee and donuts at

Wawa. That was about 20 minutes ago. In fact, that's where I last saw you, in the back of a police Jeep, putting Splenda in a French Vanilla latté. Yuck."

"Dammit, Detective! Don't you see?"

"What?" Curtis stammered, spraying bits of fritter on the table.

"How could you have left me there then meet me here a few minutes later?"

"I, well... I walk slow."

"Slow enough for me to beat you here? And don't you think the two-guys guarding me would have LET YOU KNOW they were dropping me off here?"

Curtis was stumped. "Well, I haven't really thought..."

Jump stood, knocking over his chair: "Where am I right now? Detective... RIGHT NOW!"

"Now Jump, just calm down." Curtis flipped on his walkie-talkie. "This is Curtis to Marion and Butts. Status please?"

The radio squawked and a tiny voice came over the air. "This is Marion, subject entered his apartment approximately 15 minutes ago, alone. Requested several hours to use his computer, contact family and friends, get a lawyer... the usual."

Curtis asked, "You have eyes on?"

"Negative," came the answer. "Butts and I are stationed directly in front of the building, all exits covered. He's not going anywhere, sir."

"Thanks, Curtis out." The detective turned off the radio. "Satisfied?"

"Absolutely," Jump answered. "Except for one thing — if I'm in my apartment right now using my computer then who the hell is standing in front of you?"

Curtis paused, unable to answer.

"And he's not alone."

"Excuse me?" Curtis asked.

"Whoever is in my apartment is not alone. Diane Hoag is in there."

Curtis grabbed the bracelets from his belt. "Why don't I just secure you here and go check it out. You won't mind, will you?"

Jump's mind raced and he sat at the table and offered his wrists. "Of course not, I just want to get to the bottom of this, just like you."

"Thanks," Curtis offered. "I knew you'd understand."

Curtis opened the handcuffs and prepared to slap them on Jump's wrists, but Jump leaned quickly forward, grabbed the hot cup of coffee, and threw it in the detective's face. Curtis yowled.

"Sorry," Jump yelled sincerely as he dashed from the room. "I'll see you over there, I guess!"

And he was gone.

★ ★ ★ ★ ★

IT TOOK Jump all of 30 seconds to traverse the block-and-a-half back to his apartment. The adrenaline and pharmaceuticals in his veins blocked out the pain from his ravaged body, and he fairly flew across the pavement.

In their police Jeep, Officers Marion and Butts could only stare in wonder as the Frankenstein-looking man ran-hobbled in front of them and entered the apartment building they were meant to be guarding. They looked at each other like two guys in a bad buddy cop movie and flipped their radio on.

"Detective Curtis!" Marion shouted into the walkie. "Detective Curtis are you there!"

"Here," they heard Curtis' strained voice answer.

"Detective, the subject has escaped! Well, hold on... he was escaped, but just went back into the... wait... Detective Curtis, what's going on? Detective Curtis? Detective Curtis, are you there?"

At that moment Detective Curtis, red-faced from exertion and searing hot coffee, pounded on the hood of the Wagoneer, causing Marion and Butts to jump out of their skins.

"Out of the car!" he screamed.

Officer Butts could have sworn he smelled like hazelnut.

★ ★ ★ ★ ★

JUMP, having slipped by the startled police, huffed and puffed up the 21 steps to his apartment door. Breath ragged, head light, pain creeping into the edges of his mind, he fumbled for the keys. Finding the right one he slid it into the lock and opened the door.

Dammit! he thought. *A smart guy would have listened in first. Oh well...*

The living room was empty, though the TV was on. Dr Benton was moping about something or other on an old *ER* rerun. Jump slowly, silently padded across the yellow-orange shag carpet and peered into the open kitchen — a half pot of coffee, fresh, sat on the burner. A few dirty plates and utensils were piled in the sink. Broken eggshells sat atop the trashcan and the toaster was still warm. He made his way to the bathroom — empty. As he looked into the tub he heard it, the distinct sound of mattress springs in use.

Just outside the bathroom was the spare bedroom. Jump quietly opened it and peered in — his computer was unused, the Spider-Man screensaver shooting webs all over it. A small fan blew in the window, futilely trying to pull all the hot air out of the room. It was then it dawned on him.

He'd left Diane alone, in bed. She had no idea what had been going on for the last 25 minutes. For all she knew it was him that came back, brewed them a pot of coffee, made breakfast and took it to the bedroom. Therefore, it was probably him who was...

Jump threw open the bedroom door, and in the most surreal moment of his life, saw himself on top of her, in flagrante delicto, and the surprised look in her eyes as she realized something was not quite right.

"The hell?" she managed.

"Diane," Jump said wearily, crestfallen, "I'd like you to meet my twin brother, Land."

CHAPTER EIGHT
Tangled Webs

ETECTIVE Ike Curtis stood, red-faced and furious, outside Freda's Café on Ocean Street, atop which sat the apartment of Jump Wiggen, local actor and only real suspect in a series of gruesome murders, all revolving around the Cape Equity Theater. In the last 20 minutes the case had taken a surreal, only-in-the-movies veneer, with one man being in two places at once and police so comically inept they made Jackie Gleason's Smokey look like Peter Falk's Columbo.

"How did he get past you?" Curtis demanded of Marion and Butts, the two cops assigned to guarding the man they thought was Jump Wiggen.

Butts, a large African-American man of about 30, answered, "We just... he was... we thought he was upstairs!"

"Yeah!" Marion, a scrawny white kid of maybe 23, agreed. "He was upstairs!"

Curtis was impotent with rage. How could he not have seen this? There were two Jump Wiggens running around town! Or at least, there were two people who looked very much like Jump Wiggen running around town. It explained Jimmy Fuentes seeing him at the Jackson Mountain when Jump claimed to be at home sleeping, and why he looked so damn familiar to Curtis from their first meeting.

"It's all right," Curtis told the other cops, sounding as conciliatory as he could muster. "It's me I'm mad at, not you. He played us all for suckers. Well... somebody did, anyway."

"Don't sweat it, sir," Butts told him.

"You had no way of knowing," Marion assured as well..."20/20 hindsight."

The pity with which this beefy, mentally deficient Michael Jackson and Paul McCartney combo now looked at him made Curtis' skin crawl.

"Do me a favor," he told them, "stop trying to make me feel better. Call in some back-up and meet me in the restaurant."

Marion and Butts tucked their tails between their legs and did as they were told.

Curtis fished deep in the pocket of his trench coat for the pack of cigarettes he knew was in there. They had to be — he put them there 20

Detective Curtis paced in front of the restaurant, pondering his next move, muttering to himself.

years ago, the night he decided to quit. He left them as a constant test to himself, an exercise for of the will, and for 20 years they stayed wrapped in cellophane.

Until today. Being duped by a doppelganger framing the wrong man for murder could drive one to light up.

He packed the smokes, tore them open and lit one, and it was like he'd never quit — it was that great and disgusting. He paced in front of the restaurant, pondering his next move, muttering to himself.

"For someone to pass themselves off as Wiggen, they'd have to know an awful lot about him — where he worked, where he lived, the circles he moved in... when he was in, when he was out... his habits and mannerisms. And it means..."

He now remembered the DNA matches at the theater and the copious amounts of blood.

"It also means the same DNA, a family member, but to leave that much DNA behind he'd have to have... no..."

Detective Curtis could hardly bring himself to believe.

"He couldn't have..."

Upstairs...

JUMP could hardly bring himself to believe it: "You sawed open your forehead and smashed your thumb with a hammer?"

"Yes!" Land, his twin brother, answered while rising from the bed and putting on his pants, "and I had to drive a nail through the bottom of my foot... you know how hard that is to do?... and smack my face with a shovel and stick my head in a burning oven and cook my head, thank you very much! If you weren't so accident-prone this whole experience would have been a lot more pleasurable for me."

"You didn't have to do anything," Jump replied. "You chose to... idiot."

Land threw on a shirt. "Don't call me an idiot."

Diane Hoag, who was naked as a jay bird on the bed, pulled up a blanket and looked at them – both handsome despite the myriad of facial injuries, both in decent shape but both could stand to lose a few pounds, and the only way to tell them apart was the different T-shirts they were wearing – Jump's white, Land's black.

"Excuse me," she interrupted, clutching the Philadelphia Eagles blanket tight, "but exactly whom did I just have... relations with?"

"I told you," Jump answered testily. "This is my brother, Land."

"Jump and Land?" she said. "You've got to be kidding me. Don't tell me... he's a long-lost twin?"

"No," Jump replied, "he's a long-ignored, wished-forgotten, EVIL twin."

Diane said, "And I just..."

"Yes, you just..." Jump said.

"With your brother?"

"Yes, with my brother."

"Huh," she muttered. "I thought that was a little... unpracticed."

"Hey!" Land protested.

Jump winked at him. "Truth sucks, no?"

"Yes," Land answered and pulled a gun from the boots he had just slid on, "but I have a gun."

"Touché."

Diane asked, "Can you go back and explain the brother thing again? I'm a little behind."

Jump replied, "Land and I were born to the same parents, that's about where any family resemblance ends. I did pretty well in school, Land didn't. I had a lot of girlfriends, Land didn't..."

"'Til about 10 minutes ago..."

"Gross..."

Jump continued, "I was good at sports, singing, acting... all that stuff.

Land wasn't. And this drove Land crazy."

"That and all the jail," Land offered.

"Yes," Jump carried on, moving closer to the bed. "Land spent most of his young adulthood in the clink — stealing cars, knocking off 7-11s, a little light B&E, but now it seems he's graduated up to murder. Is that about right, bro?"

Land shrugged. "You're leaving out a lot of the details — how mom and dad always liked you best, what a goddamned teacher's pet you were, how you basically had everything handed to you on a silver platter... but you got the gist of it, yeah."

"Again with the 'you got all the breaks' stuff? That is such a tired piece of crap. I've worked for everything I've gotten. You're just jealous. Always have been, always will be."

"Not true," Land argued. "Not true at all."

Jump looked to Diane. "It's the oldest story in the book, real Shakespearean stuff... brother hates brother, brother goes insane, brother kills some theater people and sleeps with the brother's girlfriend..."

"Girlfriend?" she replied. "Let's not get crazy."

"But I thought..."

"You're a nice kid and all but... I'm not really ready for a relationship."

"Ha!" Land cried.

"You shut up," Jump told him.

"I've got the gun, so... YOU shut up."

"I'm sorry, I didn't know we were still 11..."

At that moment, there was a knock on the door. A loud one.

"Police!" a voice called. "Open up!"

"That's Curtis," Jump informed them. "He must be pissed at me."

Land said, "Line forms to the right."

Jump looked to Diane. "I have to explain to him what happened..."

Land cocked the gun. "Don't move."

Jump was shocked. He knew his brother was sick with hate, but he never thought he'd actually kill him. "Seriously?"

Land nodded. "'Fraid so. Move back."

Jump sidled up to Diane who, during all the talking, managed to get herself fully clothed. "You really led me on you know."

Diane shrugged. "I was horny, what can I say?"

"Talk later, lovebirds," Land ordered, brandishing the firearm. "Right now I got some thinking to do."

"Why start now?" Jump could not resist.

Land leveled the gun at his face. "I swear, one more sound..."

Jump got the hint and zipped it.

"Police!" the voice from the door cried again. "Open up or we're coming in!"

Land peeked out of the bedroom into the living room. The front door rattled as the cops beat their fists on it. He needed a plan and one came to him.

"It's me, Jump!" Land lied loudly, "I'm in here with my brother,. Doesn't that explain a lot? I can't believe how smart he was about everything!" *That'll show 'em.* "I'm trying to talk him out of his brilliant plan!" *Heh-heh...*

After a brief pause, Detective Curtis shouted back, "You've got five minutes!"

Land savored the moment to himself internally. He'd out-thought his brother and now the police. Five minutes would be plenty of time to get his hostages tied up and take them out through the window and down the...

"Fire escape!" he screamed into the empty bedroom. "Dammit!"

Jump was, apparently, one step ahead.

Seconds earlier...

AS SOON as Land poked his head out of the room, Jump acted, nudging the widow Diane Hoag to the window, soundlessly sliding it open and stepping out on to the fire escape. If Jump knew his brother, he would think of some stupid plan he thought was genius, gloat to himself for a few seconds, forgetting why he was thinking of a stupid plan to begin with, then realize he really should focus.

His brother politely followed the script to a tee and by the time he was shouting out the window after them, they were on the ground and sprinting toward the busy Washington Street Mall.

"Wait!" Land shouted.

This was swiftly followed by the sound of a crashing door and, "Police! Down on the ground!"

Jump braced for the gunshots but they never came. A few seconds later they were running into the Pilot House.

Seconds earlier...

LAND had done it again... thought himself into quite the pickle.

He ran to the window and shouted, "Wait!"

That second, the door crashed open in the living room and the sound of angry feet on ugly shag rug filled the apartment.

"Police!" the older detective shouted at him. "Down on the ground!"

Then Land really DID have a good idea.

Sliding the gun into his pants he turned to the detective with red eyes and a pretty convincing fake sob. "Detective Curtis, thank God you're here! He took Diane!"

"Jump?" the detective asked.

"Yes," Land answered, his hysteria rising, "it's my brother Land, he made me put on his clothes and gave me this gun. Here, take it. And he took Diane... they're going to get away! Please detective, I love her!"

Curtis snatched the pistol and turned to Butts: "Watch him. I'm going after them."

"What about me?" Marion asked.

"Are you the one I asked to make sure all the exits were covered?"

Marion stared at the floor and nodded, "Yes, sir."

Curtis told him, "You stay here, too, numb nuts. The rest of you, follow me."

Curtis and the rest of the detail filed out the window and down the fire escape. When they were gone, it was eerily quiet in the bedroom.

Land plopped down on the bed. "Man, this is some kind of crazy, huh?"

"Quiet," Butts said. "Just sit there."

"Come on," Marion said quietly, "we're the ones that screwed up, don't yell at him."

Butts was clearly in a lot of psychic pain over the blunder. "It's the simplest thing... cover the exits... and we screwed it up."

"I hate to be a stickler," Marion said, "but technically he ordered *you* to do it."

Butts looked sternly at his partner. "But you were with me."

"Yeah, but..."

And on the argument went for several more seconds. Sitting on the bed behind them, Land slowly inched his duffel bag closer with his foot. This done, he even more slowly reached down into the side pocket and produced his spare side arm and raised it at the two bickering men.

"Hey!" he yelled. "It was both your faults."

He then shot each man in the face and followed the others out the window.

Seconds later...

PANTING and red-faced, Diane and Jump staggered into the Pilot House restaurant, a favorite gathering place of locals after work, which was now packed with tourists, as it often was just before noon.

"To the bar," Jump whispered, and they half-shoved their way through the three-deep lunch hour martini crowd to the furthest end from the door.

The bar at the PH (as the locals liked to call it) was Jump's favorite

— nicely-sized, removed enough from the dining room for a bit of soli-tude if one needed it, and adorned with three huge TVs, each showing a Philadelphia sports team in action, unless, of course, a bunch of New Yorkers took over the place and made them put on a stinking Jets game or something.

But sports were the furthest thing from Jump's mind at the moment. Rather, he was growing ever more interested in his brother's actions. In the back of his mind he'd always known that some day he'd have to face the long-cast shadow of his crazy brother, but figured he had a few more years, at least. Three-to-six, to be precise. Land must have been a good boy in his last stint to get out so soon.

"You okay?" Diane asked.

Jump smiled wanly. "Aside from my brother trying to kill me, the cops thinking I'm a murderer, and you just using me for my body, I'm fine."

"Listen," Diane started, "it's not that I don't like you. I do, it's just..."

"I'm over it," he cut her off, "so you can save me the 'it's not me it's you' routine. All I'm worried about right now is trying to stay alive. Wanna help?"

Now it was her turn to feel smacked.

"I'll take that as a yes," Jump said. "Now, I have to figure out why he's here now. He can't have done this all by himself — he's not that smart. He must be working with somebody."

Diane squeezed his hand. "But whom?"

The tender gesture took Jump by surprise. "That's the question."

"Jump!" a voice cried from the dining room... "Diane!"

"Great," Jump muttered and plastered on a happy face. "Hi Vicky!"

Diane did the same, hooking her arm through Jump's. "Hi, how are you?"

Vicky Greeley, a small, mousy woman and stage manager of the Cape Equity, sat eating nachos with the rest of the cast and crew at a large round table near the fish tank in the rear of the dining room.

"Join us!" Vicky called over the din of the busy restaurant.

"We can't!" Jump answered. Then he saw Detective Curtis at the side door. "Love to!"

He pulled Diane along beside him, staying out of Curtis' sight line.

"Jump? What are you doing here?" another female voice asked from behind.

It was Joy Carmichael, owner/operator of Famous Annie's Famous Dinner Theater and Jump's hated former employer.

"I'm, uh... having lunch... with my new co-workers. You?"

The Equity cast and crew rose from their table, scowls on their faces.

Famous Annie's was the enemy.

"The same," Joy said, then, in a voice loud and shrill enough to cut glass, "but the last I heard you were being questioned by the police about all those murders over at your theater."

"Keep it down, will you?" Jump implored, keeping one eye out for Curtis.

Joy's right and left-hand men stepped forward.

"Don't... don't you talk to her like that!" Tim Templeton, her husband said, voice trembly.

"Or we will smack you down!" threatened Farley Owensby, his lover.

The rest of the cast of Famous Annie's now stood from their chairs, and even more theatrically scowled. It was like *West Side Story*, a very bad, very gay *West Side Story* in which it was impossible to tell the Jets from the Sharks because everyone was wearing a different shade of fuchsia. You could cut the tension with a feather boa.

"Listen..." Jump started, but at that moment both the front and side doors of the Pilot House burst open.

From the front door, Detective Curtis drew his gun and shouted, "Nobody move!"

From the side door, Land Wiggen did the same. "Yeah... do what he said!"

Jump slapped a hand to his forehead and said, "Crap!"

I T WAS tensely quiet inside the Pilot House restaurant. What seconds before had been a bustling, lunch crowd now sat in stunned silence as not one, but two men stood before them with guns drawn. One of them was Detective Ike Curtis, who looked down the barrel of his .38 snub nose at a very frightened-looking Jump Wiggen, whom he thought was Land Wiggen trying to escape.

Ten feet to Curtis' left stood Land, whom Curtis believed to be Jump, and who also looked down a gun barrel, his a .45, at his terrified brother.

Curtis glanced warily back and forth from Jump to Land, thinking each was the other. Jump, who was now shielding Diane Hoag, inched over to the giant fish tank at the end of the dining room.

"Stop moving, Land," Curtis finally said. "There's nowhere to go."

Curtis was right — the detective blocked the way to the side door, Land the way to the front door. Behind them was a wall and a kitchen door, which was blocked by several very confused-looking waitresses, unsure if they should serve their trays of food before they got cold. They wisely chose not to.

Curtis continued, "Just let the girl go and let's talk about this."

"Yeah, Land... you heard the cop, let Debbie go and everything will be all right."

Curtis looked at him. "I thought it was Diane."

Land never hesitated: "That's what I said."

Jump caught on. "Wait... you think he's me?"

"I think who's who?" Curtis asked.

Land said, "I'm me all right. No doubt."

Jump ignored him and looked at Curtis: "You think I'm Land? Is that it? Is that what's happening here?"

Curtis felt a doubt. "Until I learn otherwise, yes, that's what I'm going with."

Jump hooked a thumb at his brother. "And he told you I was him? The crazy insane person with a gun standing next to you? Who just called his girlfriend Debbie instead of Diane? *That* guy?"

Curtis shrugged. "Sure, why not?"

Land jumped in. "Don't listen to him detective, he's just trying to confuse you."

"Well, he's doing a pretty good job," Curtis replied, slowly turning toward Land, whom he now sort-of thought was Jump. "Why don't you give me that gun and we can sort all this out?"

Land remained calm. "It's okay, Detective, I've got them covered for you. You can go cuff him. I got your back."

Curtis now had his gun pointed directly at him and spoke slowly, "I'd really, really like you to hand that..."

BLAM!

BLAM!

The two gunshots pierced the air and hung there. The smell of cordite filled the room. And the 100 or so diners, who sat so quietly only moments ago, now shrieked and panicked, leaving their tables and rushing for the nearest exits.

Jump watched in dreamlike horror as Land, half his head gone, fell to the floor.

"Land?" he started, but was too cotton-mouthed to continue. His ears rang. His heart pounded.

On the other side of the dining room, Detective Ike Curtis staggered toward the door, blood seeping from a hole in his chest, the life dripping out of him.

"Detective?"

Ike Curtis turned, looked at Jump, his breath ragged, then fell to the floor. He did not move.

"Let's go, Jump," he heard a voice command him. "The rest of them will be here soon."

The words echoed in his ears as if spoken from very far away in a deep valley. The world began to recede. He looked over to see Diane Hoag holding a large pistol that still had smoke wafting up from its barrel.

"You? What..."

She grabbed his face by the chin. "There isn't time, Jump, we have to move."

She tucked the gun away in her pants, took Jump by the hand, and headed for the kitchen. They'd never get out the main doors now — they were crammed with people trying to get out. So she pushed past three stunned waitresses, into the kitchen and out the back service door.

Cool air rushed across their faces as they stepped outside on to the periphery of the Washington Street Mall. They could clearly hear more panicked screaming coming from the front of the building. Across the mall, the church bell rang 12 noon.

"Follow me," Diane said and pulled him along.

Jump's legs had turned to rubber and he was pretty sure he was going to faint.

"Keep up!" she hissed.

Sirens began to wail in the distance.

"You had a gun..." Jump offered meekly.

"Yup."

"The whole time..."

"Yup."

"You killed my brother."

"He was going to kill you."

"I know, it's just... it's still kind of a bummer."

"I understand."

For the next half-hour they wound their way silently up and down the shady, tree-lined side streets of downtown Cape May. A few times they had to duck for cover behind a fence or bush as a police car crossed at a side street, but they went unnoticed. It was some time in here that it all became too much for Jump. For a week now he'd handled being the prime suspect in multiple murder investigations with his usual droll aplomb, but deep down it was brewing. And now it bubbled to the surface in the form of the stream of tears that ran down his cheeks.

"Okay, it's okay," he heard Diane say. She still sounded far away, but her squeeze of his hand reminded him he was still on Earth. And without noticing or really caring, she had led them to the beachfront and the Equity.

"What are we doing here?" he asked.

"I'm not sure," she answered. "Just seemed like the place to go, I guess. Let's get inside so no one can see us."

"Okay..." Jump answered wearily.

Once inside, Jump started to feel a little better, physically anyway. He instinctively walked down the aisle and up on to the stage, where he'd hoped to spend the next part of his life doing serious plays for serious people. But now it looked as though the next part of his life was going to include a lot of time in jail.

"You feeling okay?" Diane asked, handing him a bottle of water.

"A little better, I guess."

"Good," she said perkily. "I want my man in perfect health."

"I'm your man now?"

She nuzzled his cheek. "If that's okay with you."

"Sure," he said uneasily. Something wasn't right.

"Here," she said and handed him a couple aspirin. "These should help. They were all I could find in the first-aid kit."

"Thanks," he responded, popped the pills in his mouth, and took a big swig from the bottle of water. "Mmm, that's good water... what is that... almond? Oh no..."

"Oh yes," Diane countered. "Sorry."

Two seconds later, Jump was writhing on the floor in agony.

★　★　★　★　★

WHEN he awoke later, night had fallen and the theater was very dark. A single white bulb, a work light, burned on stage, illuminating Jump and the 10 feet around him. All else was pitch.

"Hello?" he tried to say, but his mouth was covered, so it came out more like, "Hmblow?"

The memory of the last half-day buzzed around his head like an incessant mosquito, everything jumbled together, bits and pieces flying here and there. He was only sure of one thing — that he was still alive. Diane had only given him enough poison to incapacitate, not enough to kill. Apparently it was far more enjoyable for her to watch him roll around on the ground in constant agony than look at his still, lifeless body. After six hours or so, though, his body just quit and he fell into a dreamless near-coma for several hours.

And now it was dark and scary and he was bound to a chair with what felt like six rolls of duct tape, with the obligatory strip across his mouth that was going to hurt like a sumbitch when whomever pulled it off.

He struggled futilely with his bonds for a moment and, finding himself securely strapped down, gave up. He racked his brain for any idea on how to get out of here alive and why on Earth Diane would be a part of this, for he was quite certain he was not going to live beyond this day and that it would be Diane who would plant him.

"Awake?" came a voice from the blackness, somewhere behind him.

He twisted and mumbled, unable to answer.

"Sorry for the tape," Diane said, "but I couldn't have you waking up and screaming bloody murder if you woke up while I was at dinner."

Jump cocked an eyebrow.

"Oh yes, I had a lovely Cuban Pork Chop at Lucky Bones followed by drinks at Martini Beach... it was quite lovely."

How, he wondered, could the woman that 100 witnesses saw shoot and kill two men in broad daylight go bar-hopping the same night and not get picked up?

"Maybe next time," she said, her voice getting closer, "I'll take you with me."

This was followed by a haunting little laugh. Then, without warning, the duct tape was ripped from his face.

"Gah!"

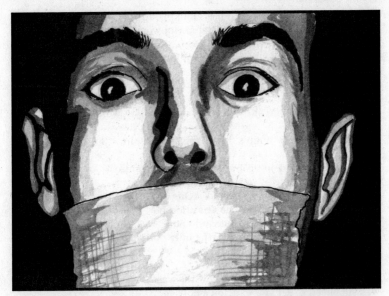

He was only sure of one thing — that he was still alive. She had only given him enough poison to incapacitate, not enough to kill.

"Shh..." Jump felt something sharp against his throat. "Not too loud now, hear?"

He nodded.

"Good. Now, let's have a look at you."

Her heels clicked softly on the stage as she walked around him. And when she stepped into the light, he felt a familiar stirring in his groin, but more importantly, a sense of something wrong.

"Figure it out yet?" she asked.

"Tip of my tongue," he managed, barely above a whisper.

"Maybe this will help."

She reached up behind her head and, with a few flicks of the wrist, her auburn wig came off, revealing a head of shiny blonde hair, pulled tightly back into a bun.

"Well?" she asked.

He shook his head. "Not yet."

With an impatient sigh she now set to work on her face. To Jump it looked like she was giving herself a facial massage, but when she lowered her hands and dropped the half-dozen facial prosthetics and false teeth on the floor, he knew whom he was looking at.

"Kirsten?" he whispered. "Kirsten Hopwood?"

"Ding, ding, ding! You win!"

Kirsten Hopwood... the ex that Jump had let go after they moved to Cape May together.

"But... last I heard you were in California somewhere with some guy..."

She answered, "Yeah, well, that didn't really work out, so... here I am!"

The wheels in Jump's head began to spin, "So you and... my brother?"

She smiled and Jump's arousal stirred again, the one part of him impervious to terror.

"He was easy," she answered. "One look at these bad boys..." she ripped open her shirt... "and he was all mine."

Jump tried to look away but could not.

"And so you know, you were the only one that was meant to die. All the rest were unfortunate accidents."

"Comforting."

"And Mark, well, he didn't know the water was poisoned, only that he was supposed to get you to drink a bottle..."

"Mark?" Jump asked.

"Yes, you remember Mark, my ex-roommate Bonnie's ex-fiancee's boyfriend?"

Jump's mind reeled. "The guy at the Troika audition? What about him?"

Kirsten smiled at him. "Picture your buddy Waylon Hoag without the beard and glasses and age make-up... voila! Mark Summers!"

"Jeezly crow... anyone else?"

"No," she answered and began taking off the rest of her clothes. "Just the three of us."

"And I'm the only one who was supposed to die?"

"Well, yes," Kirsten answered matter-of-factly. "Mark drank the water by accident, that Stanford Whitely twit was standing in your spot when the beam fell and crushed him, and Jimmy Fuentes was covering your tech when the booth blew up because you stepped on a nail, you clumsy idiot."

"What about my brother?"

Her face darkened. "A shame, I agree... but he was going to shoot you, and I couldn't have him robbing me of my revenge, now could I?"

"Revenge for what?"

"For you dumping me, silly."

Jump paused. "I take it you were a little more invested in our relationship than I was."

"A lot more," she said, stripping off her pants. "Who do you think put those slips in the suggestion box at Three Blind Mice, accusing you of rape?"

Jump gritted his teeth.

"I saw all those other girls checking you out, sweetie, and I couldn't have you around all that. I loved you."

"Kirsten..."

"Shh..."

"Whatever you're thinking of doing, don't do it. We can work this out."

"I'm afraid not," she said, slipping on a black outfit from her gym bag. "I'm a bit of a hot commodity right now. They've got our pictures all over the news, even CNN! We're a national story, baby. No, I'm afraid that if I'm going to get away, you have to die."

Jump began shaking. "Come on, you're not really going to kill me... are you?"

She nodded. "Looks like."

What felt like all his blood rushed to his face and he screamed, "No, dammit! You're NOT going to do this! If I weren't tied down I'd... I'd rip you limb from limb!"

"Easy, sugar, you're going to hurt yourself."

Jump calmed. "Listen, we can fix this. You let me go and I don't say a word. I'll tell them you had me blindfolded. No one will know..."

She considered this for a moment. "Good try but sorry, no."

Out of ideas, Jump began to weep. "I don't want to die, Kirsten."

"No one does," she answered, "but everyone has to."

She raised the large pistol to his head and cocked it.

Jump, knowing this was the end, took a deep breath, looked Kirsten in the eye, and made his peace. "I'm ready."

"I love you, Jump."

BLAM!

Kirsten's right eyeball exploded into a pink cloud and she fell to the ground, dead.

"You okay, kid?" someone asked from the back of the house.

"Yes, Detective Curtis," Jump answered, "yes I am."

A minute later the theater was lit up and crawling with police and ambulance crews, and Jump Wiggen was safe.

EPILOGUE...

NE year later, Detective Isaac "Ike" Curtis retired from the CMPD with full honors and started his own private investigation business, which immediately flourished — there were lots of people in Cape May who didn't trust their spouses. And 25% of every dollar he made went into a college fund for the children of officers Butts and Marion, who were both struck down in their prime in the line of duty.

In the wake of the "The Equity Murders" as they were now known, the Equity itself, in the glow of all the press (good and bad) was finally turning a profit under the direction of former stage manager Vicky Greeley who, though mousy in appearance, had the heart of a lion.

Famous Annie's also suffered a reversal of fortune, having to shudder its doors after founder Annie Jewel, a former beloved child star, admitted to a years-long substance abuse problem beginning at age 10 in 1942 that shrank her vast fortune and forced her to liquidate all of her business holdings. Joy Carmichael, Tim Templeton and Farley Owensby now work the 11pm-7am shift at the Bank Street Wawa.

And Jump Wiggen, who'd always dreamed of stardom but never dared think it possible, was now living his dream on the west coast. After the murders, his name and face were plastered over TV screens and news-papers across the county. He was a household name by the following week, then pegged to write and star in a cinematic version of his story, called *The Five Stages of Death*, a title he purchased from the estate of Stanford Whitely, which then set up the Jimmy Fuentes Memorial Fund for Underprivileged Actors.

The movie was a smash.

The Reindeer, the Elf and the Attic Vent

'Twas the night before Christmas... when a terrible thing befell the Flynn family

Chapter One
Christmas Eve

LIVER was excited, naturally, but an almost imperceptible anxiety pecked away at the edges of his brain. Something was not quite right. At six years of age and a full 16 months older than his brother John, he'd used those solo months to train himself to be aware of stuff that others weren't, to sense when things were out of order, to almost smell a bad thing about to happen. And he smelt that smell right now. That, or his brother needed a diaper change.

"I don't like this, Mommy," Oliver said, matter-of-factly, to the raven-haired beauty sitting on the sofa. But at six, matter-of-fact still sounded awful cute.

"Oh, stop it," Mommy said. "Try to relax a little and have fun."

"YES!" his little brother John screamed, spinning in a circle and inadvertently punching his Daddy in the testicles. "FUN!"

John was a darling, physically the opposite of Oliver — tow-headed with a round, puckish face, a fun-loving and carefree disposition. Oliver was more circumspect, dark-haired with a sharp face, wise beyond his years. It was John's duty in life as a four-year-old ("four anna HALF!" he would correct) to spin in circles, bump into things, and be a huge, cute pain in the ass.

He had long ago ceded the talking and arguing to Oliver, who gladly took the mantle. This was fine, except that, not speaking as much, he didn't know as many words as Oliver. This was not what others considered "normal," so John was labeled a Late Talker. This led to much underestimating of John, who may not have talked as much as his brother but was just as smart. John figured that he could talk and argue more if he wanted, but why bother Oliver? He was so good at it and clearly enjoyed it more than John.

So John the Quiet, as Daddy liked to call him, continued spinning and dancing and bumping into things. The last thing he bumped into was soft and squishy and made a big "OW!" when John's elbow connected with its head.

From under a pile of pillows, baby Harry emerged, wailing, a fresh red welt rising over his eye. He rushed across the room and into the arms of his Mommy, who kissed him where it hurt.

"John…" Mommy said, casting an admonishing eye, one expertly imitated by Harry, little tears rolling down his cheeks.

"DON!" Harry cried. "Now! No! Don!"

At two, Harry was neither slow nor circumspect. He knew exactly what he wanted to say, he just had no idea how to say it.

When things settled, Mommy said, "Okay boys, in front of the tree."

Oliver relented, but not without some consternation. "I still don't like this, Mommy."

At that, Mommy stuck out her tongue and raised a digital camera, an early Christmas gift from Daddy.

"Okay, now smile and look cute... on the count of three... one-two-three!"

With a whir and a flash the moment was pixelized for all eternity. Or until someone accidentally hit the *delete* button, whichever happened first (the latter being far more likely, given Mommy's ham-fisted knowledge of all things digital). But what appeared on the little camera screen at that moment was both precious and priceless — the three Flynn boys in their custom-made "Naughty Boy: Return to Santa!" pajamas, John and Harry grinning stupidly, Oliver looking like somebody just told him the Earth was flat.

"Ha!" Daddy cried.

"Perfect!" Mommy agreed.

"Me look, me look," John stammered and ran over.

Harry followed with, "NEE NOOK! NEE NOOK!"

Oliver quietly joined them, but not before taking one more moment to try to put his finger on exactly what it was that was bothering him. Something was definitely out of kilter, and though he couldn't nail it at the moment, he would not have to wait much longer.

"Come, Oliver," Mommy urged him. "Join your brothers."

So Oliver did, and for the next 90 minutes they reveled without a care, Mommy and Daddy sipping a peculiar-smelling egg nog drink, the boys dipping their buttered toast in hot chocolate. This was followed by a viewing of *How the Grinch Stole Christmas* on DVD (Oliver had it practically memorized, but Harry and John seemed to enjoy it, and that was enough for him... seeing his younger brothers watch Chuck Jones' devilish holiday creation in wonder was like watching it himself through new eyes), the annual reading of *'Twas the Night Before Christmas* by Daddy, with sound effects by Mommy, and interpretive dance by John — and a final round of kisses and hugs before hitting the hay.

For 364 nights of the year the boys slept in their own beds, save the occasional bad dream or wet accident, but every Christmas Eve they "camped out" in the living room on the off-chance they might stay awake long enough to spy the guy in red. Oliver was 0-for-6 so far but number seven was feel-

Ian Burkholder had never been much of a driver of earth-bound vehicles,
let alone this flying, red, jet-propelled contraption,

ing lucky.

He had no idea *how* lucky.

By 10 o'clock they were tucked snugly in their Spider-Man, SpongeBob and Disney Princesses sleeping bags, and were heavy-lidded, yet wired with anticipation. But by 10:30pm, even the forever-juiced Quiet John was blinking very slowly, and Mommy and Daddy knew it was safe to go wrap more presents in the bedroom. At least, that's what they told Oliver they were doing, — he suspected it was code for something else.

So Oliver watched blearily as his brothers dozed and Daddy blew him a kiss as he shut the bedroom door.

Daddy looks happier than WE do, Oliver thought, and it was just about the last thing that went through his waking mind. For an hour-and-a-half he dreamt of *High School Musical* and *Lego Star Wars*.

Then things grew a bit more terrifying.

Fight Or Flight

IAN Burkholder had never been much of a driver of earth-bound vehicles, let alone this flying, red, jet-propelled contraption, which made every second in it a borrowed one. The navigation seemed simple enough at first, but it was that rare thing that actually got harder the *more* you did it. To Ian, it was like stepping cold into the cockpit of a Boeing 747 and being told, "Okay, now fly."

But he somehow managed to keep the laden sleigh upright and plow on. He was freezing half to death in his skimpy elf outfit. He had forgotten that today was Delivery Day and he'd be miles above the Earth traveling at an insane rate of speed. His ultra-lycrex parka and sub-nuclear thermographic long johns were tucked away in his closet. The work-a-day elf outfit left little to the imagination and did even less for one's personal warmth. So Ian was lucky that he remembered the silver flask of amber liquid to keep him warm.

He flipped open the lid of the flask and drained the last of it. For a moment, it was fire in his gut, then the burn eased to a gentle warmth that climbed up through him. He tilted it a few more times, making sure he got every drop from the flask, then tossed it atop the other seven empties under his seat.

"Ah," he muttered and smacked his lips, "much better."

His Daddy taught him at a young age, more by example than by ever taking any real interest in him, that booze, though the cause of many of life's problems, could also be a sort of solution.

"Criminy!" he yelped as the sleigh nose-dived through a dense cloud-bank, the 437th time that night he was sure it was THE END, but the auto-Santa kicked in and righted things .

"Ha!" he shouted, "I'd like to see the boys upstairs do THAT!"

Ian was more bitter than usual this Christmas Eve, as only a few hours earlier everyone in his department had received a promotion. Everyone, that is, but him. Why was life so cruel?

As he pulled an eighth flask from the seemingly endless array of hidden pockets on his elf suit, a beacon on the dash started to blink — he was in position. He was working the United States: East, which, as he rapidly descended, began to twinkle beneath him.

It was his cousin Reginald who had gotten him into the Santa business. Reginald, the good cousin, whom everyone adored, who did well in school, and who invested in SantaCorp from the beginning and was now one of a dozen CEOs running it. Dear, great Reginald, who extended a pompous, sanctimonious hand to aimless, wandering Ian.

"I'll tell you what," Reg had said to him, "I've got some pull on the factory floor, now that I'm one of the youngest CEOs in the history of New Great Britain..." He announced the last part loudly and with great emphasis, at which the rest of the gathered cousins ooh-ed and ahh-ed like star struck sheep. "How would you like a job at the North Pole?"

Ian wanted to tell him to slag off and yell, "No fanks!" in his ruddy little face, but it really *was*, despite Reginald's sneering condescension, a great opportunity. Many a time had he heard tales of men, younger than himself, who had started on the factory floor and, over time, climbed the corporate Santa ladder into cushy, low-work, high-yield jobs at One Santa Plaza high over London (it was a literal ladder). Apparently, attrition was very high at SantaCorp, especially among the pilots. Most normal people found it impossible to be THAT happy all of the time.

Ian was beginning to know how they felt.

And as he had just flunked out of wizard school, which was okay with him, it seemed just as good a gig as any. Ian had never taken to the magic world — the school was swarming with nasty ghosts and strange critters. And word was that the headmaster was a bit of a poof — and who needed that?

So off to SantaCorp it was, where, after three weeks of paid training, he was named a clock manager. Three weeks after that he was bumped up to flight coordinator. And a scant three weeks after that he was "promoted" to pilot. Sitting now, atop the swerving, zigzagging, merry bundle of death, it was also dawning on him exactly why attrition among pilots was so high. It was suicide.

But none of that was here nor there at the moment. It was now just a few strokes before midnight, when a year's worth of work and planning was about to, Lord willing, pay off. He was assigned the Eastern Seaboard. Among pilots this was considered a "starter" route, which was code for a "shite" route. But you had to start somewhere. He slowed his descent and, as the lights below drew nearer, cast an eye at the clock mounted on the sleigh's considerable dashboard, which made the space shuttle look like a Tonka Toy.

Ian was not sure exactly how it worked, but at the stroke of midnight, the entire world would slow down... or he would speed up. (The process was confusing and very hush-hush.) Either way, he and the rest of the pilots would move imperceptibly, and in immeasurably quick time, to roughly a million homes each. For Ian, this meant all of New Jersey. And Delaware. A "shite" route indeed.

So he watched the clock make its inexorable arc towards 12 and hovered over the Jersey Cape. Then 12 struck, the world went red for a moment, and Ian heard nothing but his own heartbeat for a few terrifying thumps. But the red quickly turned to green, which quickly turned back to normal, or at least a much slower or faster version of normal.

Diving towards Earth and drawing from the flask, Ian, now almost as high as his sleigh, made his final descent into the Jersey Cape.

A Rough Landing

MORE than three hours had passed since Ian began ducking in and out of chimneys, but in regular time it had been only a minute or two, such was the way Santa time worked. What would be an agonizing, back-breaking 12-hour shift to Ian, would take about five minutes in the real world.

Nice for THEM, Ian thought bitterly. Things were going swimmingly until the tell-tale ache began to throb behind his left eye. He reached for the flask but found it empty. This was not good. Without more booze, in a few minutes his head would be pounding, and he was barely a third of the way through his route. He now had two priorities in life: deliver presents, get whisky.

With this mantra, he fought the brutal, howling oceanfront wind and fluttered wildly over a row of Victorian, gingerbread houses like a kite caught in a hurricane. He pressed a red button and the sleigh stopped with an enormous *THUD!* over the middle home, a green-and-yellow affair that made Ian's stomach turn a little. Were it not for the ClausTech Sound Regenerator 3000 turning the cacophony into the sound of frolicking reindeer hooves, the neighborhood would have been awakened and the gig would have been up.

It was a rough landing. The contents of the flask that Ian's brain was now swimming in both peaked and began to ebb at almost the exact same moment. Alcoholics know this feeling, hence the saying, "One is not enough, two is too many."

He throttled back the engines (reindeer had been outlawed as a propulsion device since the mid-1970s after they were deemed an Endangered Species, despite their overflowing numbers in New Great Britain... most chalked this up to their powerful package-carrying union and its head, the sentimental favorite Rudolph, whom insiders knew was about as loveable as Jimmy Hoffa, but who was portrayed by the mainstream media as the heroic scamp from days of yore), threw the gigantic sack of toys over his shoulder and bounded to the only visible means of entry, an attic vent, which led either to a laundry room or a septic tank. Ian didn't care. He needed to get inside and raid the liquor cabinet.

He emerged into a tiny laundry room packed with dirty clothes and some kind of musical equipment. From there, it was a short jaunt into the living room where he distributed a dozen parcels, and into the kitchen, where he could almost smell the booze on the top shelf of the pantry. He filled his flask with Irish whiskey then stuffed the bottle in his sack — it was amazing the things people didn't notice missing in the euphoria of Christmas morning. Emboldened, he snatched a bottle of vodka, too.

Satisfied, he turned to make his way back to the laundry room, ready for the next home, when something caught his eye. There were three darling little boys lying on the floor around the tree as if they were presents themselves. For a moment, Ian allowed his blackened heart to swell a little. He was nearly on the verge of tears when... WHAT?!

He leaned closer to examine them, to see if he really saw what he thought he saw. He blinked, rubbed his eyes, and looked again. And there, on the shirt of each boy, was a message printed, clear and unmistakable: *Naughty Boy: Return to Santa!*

Ian was vexed.

★ ★ ★ ★ ★

OLIVER dreamt he was inside a giant Santa sack and that, as his head poked out of the top, a deranged-looking elf was cursing and spitting and drinking frequently from a silver flask as the sleigh flew through the night. This wasn't really the kind of good dream he expected to have on Christmas Eve. In fact, this wasn't a good dream at all.

And when the elf turned to him and said, "'Ello guv'nah!" in a raspy voice, he realized that it was not a dream in the least.

Then he screamed for 20 minutes.

Chapter Two
Good Dream Gone Bad

IGH over the Atlantic Ocean, Oliver Flynn was having the most lovely of dreams. Or at least as lovely as they get for six-years-olds who have not yet discovered women. He was at a birthday party, inside a giant bouncy castle, the kind he so loved at all his friends' birthday parties but, sadly, had never had at one of his own, despite the constant gentle reminders. Sometimes, moms and dads were a little slow on the uptake.

He usually loved his bouncy castle dreams and couldn't wait for them to come — sometimes he even went to bed early in order to wait for them (a habit strongly encouraged by Mommy and Daddy). But there was something different about this one — it was getting a little too vivid, a little too real for comfort. The bounces came hard and fast, and the castle grew very cold and very windy. Plus, it was very dark.

Had it been this dark when he took his shoes and socks off and first felt the cool vinyl beneath his feet, before that first glorious jump? It was probably shady, to be sure, but this darkness was a little advanced for his tastes. And why was it so windy? It was only now he noticed that high-pitched whine of a whipping wind just outside the castle. He touched the wall, and the vinyl rippled beneath his touch — ice cold, as if an electrical charge ran through it. But it wasn't electricity making the synthetic fabric dance — it was the howling wind on the other side of it.

Oliver then looked around. The door of the castle was gone! Now, he was scared and confused. What happened to the happy birthday party? When did it get so dark and cold and windy? And why hadn't he noticed?

"Mommy?" he called, tentatively.

But Mommy was not there. His little six-year-old heart began to pound. Then he noticed the wind seemed to be rushing upward, toward the roof of the bouncy castle. Looking up, he saw a small, round hole in the roof. He somehow knew this was the only way out, so he did what any kid trapped in a bouncy castle would do — he bounced. Only, it wasn't quite as super-bouncy as it had been just a minute ago. In fact, it was barely

Had Oliver's brain been mature enough, he most likely would have gone insane on the spot.

bouncy at all. And the smooth, helium-filled floor had been replaced with things far more lumpy, round and pointy. This floor *hurt*.

But away he bounced nonetheless, each bounce bringing him nearer and nearer the hole in the roof, and freedom. As he drew nearer to the hole, he was sure he could see stars whizzing by at an alarming rate.

On his final bounce, his feet pushed off something soft and squishy and covered with hair.

"OW!" his little brother Quiet John screamed.

And as Oliver grabbed hold of the opening, it was at that moment he realized he wasn't dreaming any more at all.

"Oh dear," he said and inadvertently released his hands. After a short fall he landed on something else that was soft and hairy, only a little smaller than Quiet John.

"NO!" screamed baby Harry in shock and fear. "NONONONONO!"

"Oh my," Oliver muttered.

Now he was *very* afraid. So he began to kick and pull and climb. The whipping wind made the walls of... whatever they were in... bloom in and out, like giant bellows, like they were inside a giant balloon, mid-blow-up. He scrambled upward, followed the sound and taste of the rushing air, and reached the opening once more, his face full of wind. He took a deep breath and poked his head out of the tiny hole. For the rest of his life he would wish he hadn't.

"Mmm-hmm..."

The sight that greeted him was more terrifying than anything he had ever encountered before or ever would again, and was more terrifying than anything he could imagine: a deranged, mad-looking dwarf, spitting and cursing to himself, fought the controls of the flying contraption they were on, which leapt and bucked like an angry Palomino. Oliver looked over the side — the Atlantic Ocean zipped beneath them at what had to be 1000mph.

Then the deranged elf did the worst thing it could possibly do. It turned to him, cocked an eyebrow and offered a raspy, "'Ello guv'nah!"

Had Oliver's brain been mature enough, he most likely would have gone insane on the spot. As it was, his six-year-old noggin was simply unable to process this information all at once, so instead of losing his mind, he began to scream. Then he caught his breath and began to scream some more. Then he ducked back down into the sack, for he knew that that's what it was now, and continued screaming.

Quiet John and baby Harry, who had scooched beneath their brother in an effort to see what was going on, saw him screaming and began to do the same. In their eyes, their big brother Oliver was a pretty cool customer, and if he was screaming like this, they knew they must be in a world of hurt.

Outside, on the driver's seat, Ian Burkholder, the enraged dwarf in question, heard what sounded like leaking balloons inside his SantaCorp sack. He regarded it briefly, fought against another wild dip from the sleigh, shrugged, and continued on.

"Eh," he thought, "we'll let Santa deal with it in the morning."

And, like so many drunks before him, the next morning would be the worst of Ian's life.

Into Every Rain...

ANTHONY "Big Prune" Pruoli loved his job. He loved being at SantaCorp. He loved the constant mood of cheerfulness and joviality. He loved the slimming effect his Elfin Night Watchman's uniform had on his backside. And it was the one place, the one time in his life, he loved being a dwarf.

"Morning Ella!" he said happily to the young dwarfette manning the check-in table. He'd always liked Ella, and from her lingering look at his magically-reduced posterior, perhaps she was warming up to him, as well.

"Morning!" she chirped back cheerily, as if someone had spiked her coffee with helium.

A bit flushed, Big Prune continued on his rounds. Being a night watchman at SantaCorp wasn't a big deal to the muckety-mucks, but for a guy with the hardscrabble background of an Anthony Prunoli, it was pretty big stuff. He was born a Brooklyn dwarf, Brooklyn recently being named in *Elf Quarterly* as one of the three worst places on Earth to be born a dwarf (after Detroit and Philadelphia), and only discovered (was rescued by?) SantaCorp by chance, via the drunken ramblings of a dwarfen conquest late one night at Flaherty's Pub.

"You gotta get under Grand Central," the unfortunately named Herminagelda Rubin-stein had muttered under her breath and over a fifth of gin that fateful night. "Track 29½, the North Pole Express."

She went on to say she had been expelled from SantaCorp for inappropriately propositioning the big man himself, which wouldn't have been a big deal (Santa was forever dealing with groupies and chubby chasers) if Mrs Claus had not been in the room, just cooked dinner and poured the cognac that emboldened her to grab his... mistletoe in the first place, all at Herminagelda's "Welcome To SantaCorp" dinner.

She went on about lousy pay, memory wipes and slave labor, but all Anthony heard was the part about a world where people like him were the rule, not the exception, and so he sought out this mystical Track 29½, finding it a few months later in a real Indiana Jones moment. But this is not Anthony's tale, so that must be saved for another time. Suffice it to say, Anthony "Big Prune" Prunoli was as happy as any dwarf had a right to be.

"Grandma got run over by a reindeer..." he sang to himself. He could not shake the song from his head, no matter how much he despised it. He was currently on attendance rounds. It was a shade after 6am and D-Day was coming to a close. All pilots, flight control, and package dispersal personnel had to be in their racks by 7am or there would be trouble.

The 7am rule had been implemented a quarter-century earlier, when oil supplies were scarce and it was discovered, through a drop-by-drop inventory of gas rations, that several dozen pilots, after delivering their cargo, were routinely taking the newly-built R-850 jets out for joyrides, often with female dwarfs either underage or close enough to to make many a grown man nervous. The R-850s were renowned for their sleek handling and very shiny noses.

So Big Prune moseyed to the hangar/flight control area and watched the big board as jet after jet landed, the pilots disengaging the engines, then making their way to their bunks. Big Prune carried a kind of computer clipboard. When each jet was docked, a red light would turn green, and when each pilot climbed into his bunk, a green light turned red. It was an ingenious yet remarkably simple process of keeping stock of the inventory.

At 6:53am Big Prune threw a glance at his watch, sighed deeply, and looked at his board. The last R-850 was yet to check in and it was getting close to curfew.

"Burkholder," Prune said with resignation and very little surprise.

At that moment a red blip appeared on the big radar screen, a very wobbly-looking red blip, and made its way toward the hangar. Big Prune, anxious to finish up check-in and get back to Ella at reception, headed over to the hangar bay and cast an evil eye at Ian, whose own eyes were 10 times more evil without even trying.

The R-850 roughly touched down, skidded to a halt, and Ian dismounted with some difficulty.

"Burkholder," Prune announced, a little too full of himself. "Why am I not surprised? Last one out, last one in."

Ian tried to ignore him and flung the almost-empty sack over his shoulder. It squeaked, but Prune didn't hear it.

"Off to the nearest pub?" Prune continued, really laying it on thick, "Off for a quick nip? A pint? A yard? Or did you take care of that while you were flying, in direct violation of the Elfin Code of Ethics, part three, sub-paragraph six, line J?"

Ian was a drinker, no doubt. But if there was a close second anywhere here in Munchkin Land, Big Prune was it. Ian was dying to point this out, in a loud voice, to as many people as possible, but instead he said, "Toss off, Prune" and shuffled toward the dorms.

But Prune, feeling undeservedly superior, could not let it go: "Yes? Got to get off to bed, do ya? Head starting to pound a bit, is it?"

Ian kept walking, through Flight Control, to the check-in table and Ella, whom he'd always been rather fond of, Prune unrelenting in his slagging all the way.

"Morning, Ella," Ian said.

"Good..." Ella started, but Prune, seeing a chance to humiliate a rival in front of his crush, interrupted...

"Watch out, Ella," he proclaimed loudly, "you never know when this one is going to go off half-cocked."

Ian turned. "Speaking of half-cocked..."

"Boys!" Ella tried.

By now security had taken notice, and Slim Catching, the other night watchman on duty, made his way over. This made Ian very nervous. "A problem, gentlemen?" Slim asked.

Ian looked at the floor. "Nope, no problem, just trying to get to bed."

"Yeah," Prune announced. "No problem here, the old sot just needs to go and sleep it off is all, isn't that right?"

Ian turned up a furious, rheumy eye.

"All right, all right," Slim interceded, "you've made your point Pruny, leave him be. Off to your rack, Ian."

Ian began to leave.

Slim stopped him. "After you check in that sack."

Blast!

Ian hesitated. "The fing is, Slim, I've gots all me change of underwears in there."

Slim eyeballed him. "You used your Santa Sack, on Christmas Eve, to pick up your laundry?"

Ian gave a throaty chuckle. "Yeh, two birds, one stone and all that..."

"Well," Slim said, "all right then. Get to your room, empty that sack and get it back down here forthwith, yes?"

"Much obliged," Ian said to Slim, then to Prune, "You and me, we'll pick discussion up later, neh?"

The look in his eye caused the much larger Big Prune to wilt a bit. This did not go unnoticed by Ella, who at that moment decided she would never go out with him. Ian, on the other hand...

"Night all," Ian said and ambled away.

Everyone said goodnight, Ella a little louder than the others, and started back to their posts.

Help! Ian said.

Slim stopped and turned. "Pardon?"

"Nuffin', nuffin'," Ian lied. "Frog in me throat is all, g'night."

They all said goodnight again.

Again, *Help!* from Ian.

Slim was perturbed now. "Look you, just go to bed and sleep it off before I write you up."

"Course, of course," Ian muttered quickening his step, followed by, *Help!*

It was louder this time, more distinct, and it clearly was not coming from Ian — they all saw that now. The voice, actually now it sounded like voices, were coming from the Santa Sack.

Slim gave a sad look and drew his light-baton. "Ian, tell me you didn't..."

"Wish I could," Ian replied.

"Hands up, sack down," Slim ordered, and Ian complied.

Ian, Slim, Prune and Ella all watched as the big brown Santa Sack wiggled on the floor. After a moment, a little hand appeared in the opening. A moment after that, three very young Earth boys were standing before them.

Slim asked, "Ian?"

Ian put his hands out pathetically. "All right lads, here's what happened..."

While Ian told his story, the youngest boy strode purposefully across the room, walked right up to Ian, and kicked him in the shin. Hard.

"BAD!"

"Ow!" Ian cried and rubbed his shin. "I think that one's Harry."

Chapter Three
Happy New Year

AN Burkholder, flyer of dangerous, present-delivering red sleighs and consumer of tasty brown liquids with unfortunate side-effects, sat in complete supplication, as many drunks are wont to do, on the cold steel bench in the SantaCorp security office.

Please God, get me frew dis and I'll never pick up again... he thought, along with other such thoughts concerning church every Sunday, the swearing off of cheap women and no more gambling.

He looked through the wire-filled window as night watchmen Slim Catching, a decent fellow by all accounts, and Anthony "Bug Prune" Prunoli, a right bastard, talked to Ella, the receptionist. Their faces were twisted with angst and worry, the source of which sat three feet to Ian's left.

"You're not going to get away with this," said source #1, the oldest of the three young boys being held by security. His name was Oliver and he was six years old. Next to him sat his brothers, Quiet John, four, and Baby Harry, two. All three of them looked at Ian in a very cross manner, as they had every right to — it was Ian who snatched them from their living room in a drunken stupor, mistaking their adorable *Naughty Boy: Return to Santa!* pajamas as a direct order from on high. From where on high, Ian had not the slightest idea, being sober and all, but it had made perfect sense at the time.

"So I dids what any good, Santa-fearing elf would do," he told Slim and Big Prune earlier. "I picked 'em up and put 'em in me sack."

Ian looked at the boys now and felt quite bad.

"My Mommy and Daddy will find us," Oliver said. "They love us very much and will find us."

Ian had to smile at the little guy's spunk. Cute as it may be, Ian could tell he was serious.

"Yeah!" Quiet John piped in, "dat wadn't berry nice."

Ian now felt terrible as the weight of what he'd done slowly sank upon him. "I know, I know... look, I mades a mistake, awright? I didn't means to..."

"Burkholder!" Slim chirped, popping his head in the door.

Ian jumped, composed himself, and answered, "Yeah?"

Slim, Big Prune and Ella all entered the claustrophobic holding room.

Slim spoke first.

"We've come to a decision."

"Yeah?" Ian asked hopefully.

"Yes," Slim carried on. "We've decided..." he cast an admonishing eye at Big Prune, who lowered his eyes to the floor, "...that since none of us has acted with great honor this morning, and that allowing these children to enter the heart of SantaCorp is an unimaginable breach of company security... we've decided not to report you."

Ian felt a two-ton weight lift off his chest. It would have been bad had they reported him. Losing your job and going to prison bad. From the grapevine, he'd heard Santa prison was only a half step up from Mexican prison. They were basically the same, except Santa prison had mistletoe. Lots and lots of mistletoe.

So Ian, in the most gracious voice he could muster, which was not very, said, "Fanks," and began to shuffle off.

"Aren't you forgetting something?" Slim asked.

Ian snapped his finger. "Of cor', how could I..."

He slapped a hand to his forehead and made his way back to the boys on the bench. He took Oliver by the shoulders, stood him up gently, embraced him in his thick arms... and stepped away, a shiny silver flask in his hand.

"Almost forgot, I stashed one on the kid."

He drank from the flask and started away again. Only Ella's disapproving eye stopped him.

"Wha'? Dids I do something?" Ian protested, noticing Prune and Slim's glares as well. "Why is you all lookin' at me likes that? I fought we all agreed that... oh, right. The wee ones."

"Yes the wee ones," Slim said, agitated. "We've got to figure out what to do with them."

The four grown-ups regarded the lads, who sat quietly, staring at them. Baby Harry sniffled.

"Oh, poor dear," Ella said. "He's got a bit of a cold."

She grabbed a blanket from a nearby locker and wrapped it around the two-year-old.

"Coal!" Quiet John, four, shouted at the sight of the coarse blanket. "Me coal too!"

Oliver interpreted, "He says he's cold, too. My four-year-old brother is speech delayed. It's quite common in younger siblings as close in age as we are, 16 months, and should not be mistaken with any kind of mentally-challenged stuff."

Prune whispered to Slim, "Did you say he's only six?"

Slim nodded slowly. "Creepy, isn't it?"

Oliver said, "I am also a little chilly. You have more blankets?"

"Of course we do," Ella answered. "Boys, in the bottom drawer of my desk are some homemade Afghans I've been working on.".

Slim, Prune and Ian all bolted for the reception desk, each trying their best to impress Ella with their kindness, each failing miserably, elbowing the other out of the way.

"There you go, boys," said Ella, wrapping each child lovingly. "These will keep you warm. Why don't you have a lie down on the bench. We'll fetch you pillows."

"That would be nice," Oliver told her. "Thank you."

"Tank you," Quiet John repeated.

"TANKS!" Harry shouted.

"Weckome," Ian slurred. And for the first time in a long time, he smiled.

Santa Claus is Coming to Town

SLIM, Prune, Ella and Ian all sat in the break room adjacent to the room the Flynn boys were now sleeping in. For half-an-hour they'd been poring over ideas on how to right the wrong.

"I could always takes 'em back," Ian offered, his headache almost visible to the others.

"Good idea," Big Prune replied, sarcastically. "No one will ever notice the big honking red flying sleigh zipping around the old neighborhood, will they?"

"It's a good thought, Ian, but the sleighs are only invisible on D-Day," said Ella.

"Rights," Ian said, red-faced. "I forgot 'bout that."

Ella smiled at him sweetly. She patted his hand and the rest of him turned as red as the elf outfit he was wearing. Big Prune noticed this and turned a slightly different shade of red.

"I'm afraid there's only one thing to do," Slim said gravely. "We've got to tell the big man."

It was the option they were all dreading and trying their hardest not to come around to, but it was screamingly obvious.

"No," protested Ella, "there must be another way."

"'Fraid not," Ian replied, rising from the table and trying to sound brave. "It's my mistake, my fault, I'm ready to own up to it."

Ella squeezed his hand again, not knowing it was she who had spurred Ian to such noble actions with her attentions. A faint glimmer of hope flickered to life inside of Ian that perhaps she, this Ella, might be able to polish this turd of a life.

"That's big of you, Ian," Slim told him. "I'll ring the office and let them know we need an appointment upstairs as soon as possible. In the meantime, Ella, would you mind keeping an eye on those boys? I'm sure they're going to need a Mommy figure."

Ella blushed and did as she was asked. But before she could cross the room, a great to-do was being made in the reception area.

"What the hell is all that?" Big Prune asked, making his way to the big window.

"You got me," Slim answered, craning to see down the hall.

Ella said, "It's 7:45am the morning after, I don't know who could be... oh dear."

At that, a great flood of people filled the hallway outside the break room and a hearty "Ho-ho-ho!" rattled the windows.

"Oh, sweet jumpin' Christ," Ian stammered. "It's him!"

And him it was. Appearing amid the wave of humanity, a giant man in a red suit stood out.

"His annual After-Delivery appearance!" Ella half-whispered, half-shrieked. "I forgot!"

Though the big man in the hall wasn't wearing the red and white suit of lore, it was close enough to send the Flynn boys, in the next room, into a tizzy.

"Santa!"

"Santa!"

"PANDA!"

The sight of three non-dwarf children pressing their noses against the glass and screaming his name gave Santa pause.

"Ho-ho... ho?"

Santa stopped, Ian, Ella, Prune and Slim stopped breathing. Santa, a quizzical look in his eye, opened the holding room door.

"Ho-ho-ho! And what have we here?" Santa asked, rhetorically.

"Santa!"

"Santa!"

"PANDA!"

The Flynn boys screamed again and threw themselves around his legs.

"And what have we HERE?" Santa asked jovially.

"I'm Oliver," Oliver answered. "These are my brothers. John is four. Harry is two. Santa? What's that smell?"

"Well, uh..." Santa tried, "you see, uh, Santa was at a little party earlier and..."

"You smell like my daddy on Sunday morning," Oliver continued. "Santa stinks!"

"FART!"

Santa, unamused, shot a glare at Ella.

"Ho-ho-ho," he muttered through clenched teeth, with strained joviality, "and who might these boys be? I don't remember hearing about new children at SantaCorp."

Ella started, "Well you see Santa, there was a bit of a mix-up this morning..."

"A mix-up?"

Slim continued, "Yes, sir. You see, one of our pilots made a mistake and..."

"What kind of mistake?"

Ian took a deep breath, puffed out his chest and stepped forward. "It were me, Santy. It were me what did it. See, what happened was, I've gots a little trouble with the drinky-drink now and then..."

Santa's eyes went soft. Ian carried on.

"And sometimes I don't use me best judgment, and, well, in this case it seems I..."

"They're my nephews," Big Prune said, startling everyone.

Ella, Ian and Slim stared at him.

"My sister's boys," Prune continued. "Actually, my sister-in-law's boys. They desperately wanted a tour of the factory. I told them it was off-limits to all non-SantaCorp personnel and, well, they were so crestfallen, sir, that I crumbled."

The room was silent.

"So," Prune went on, "I brought them in and asked Ian to look after them while I did my rounds. They got away from Ian, who was only doing me a favor, sir, and raised a little havoc. All's well now. Ian, Ella and Slim here rounded them up and we were just about to take them home. When you came in, sir."

Santa regarded them all with a squinky eye, then leaned in close to Prune, who could smell the stale egg nog and brandy on the big man's breath.

"Is your sister-in-law," Santa asked, "an elf?"

Prune lied, "Yes, sir, born and bred. Third generation, actually."

Santa gave him an up-and-down. "All right then, see to them."

With that, the noisy celebration resumed and Santa left the room.

"Yeesh," said Ella. "I've never seen Santa so pissed."

Young Oliver blinked. "What? He didn't seem mad to me."

"Not mad!"

"HAPPY!"

"No dear," Ella corrected and threw a Mommy-like arm around the boys. "Where we come from 'pissed' means, inebriated, besotted... drunk."

"Oh," Oliver said. "I know that word. Drunk."

"Beer!"

"POOPY!"

"Come now," she told the children. "Let's get you somewhere safe and warm. How does a nice breakfast of milk and cookies sound?"

The boys' eyes widened. Oliver said, "You have cookies for breakfast?"

"Oh yes," Ella answered, leading them away. "We do lots of fun stuff here at SantaCorp."

An hour later the boys were fed, sleeping, and dreaming of home.

Happy New Year!

OVER the next several days, Slim, Prune and Ella went to great pains to keep the boys within earshot yet out of sight, even harder to do than it sounds, especially when one of them was two years old and very opinionated — but keep them hidden they did. Then, after a week or so, when it became clear that Christmas morning was going to be Santa's one and only visit of the season, they grew a bit more lax, allowing the boys full access to the break room and all the goodies held within.

It was also around this time that others at SantaCorp began to notice strange things around the factory: the odd child-size shoe (which wasn't much of a surprise, considering everyone working in SantaCorp had child-sized feet — rather, it was the Spider-Man or SpongeBob design that caused more than one eyebrow to be raised), the occasional flying Lego, the mysterious appearance of Chicken McNugget boxes. However, they were overlooked.

The New Year came and went. To the employees of SantaCorp this second, less important holiday, was best left to the amateurs. (It was run by the Mayor Grinch and the much-chagrined Who's in Whoville, who learned shortly after the Grinch's "transformation" that it was all just a political ploy to seize power... the Grinch was a Democrat... and were now chafing under his totalitarian rule.) And in the days and weeks that followed, the existence of the Flynn boys living in SantaCorp became common knowledge.

However, no one reported them, or Ian or Ella or Slim or Prune, because they all loved having the boys around. At first they were just a pleasant distraction from a tedious workday, but by the time spring rolled around, they had become something like the company mascot and were loved and well cared for by all. Eventually, the charade of hiding them slipped away.

The Flynns had initially taken up residence in the break room, the three of them sharing floor space in a large closet. Now, after a lot of hard work by a lot of SantaCorp employees, they lived in the employee gym locker room, somewhere they knew Santa would never look if and when he ever popped in.

And finally, by the time summer returned, the boys were taking regular shifts on the factory floor, at first just helping with clean-up and going for supplies, but eventually taking their own turns at building and boxing the toys they themselves hoped to receive next Christmas.

They had almost entirely forgotten about Mommy and Daddy. But that was about to change. Abruptly.

T WAS with a heavy, yet elated, heart that Santa peered from the control room down at the factory floor. As his (mostly) merry band of elves plugged away at their last-minute Christmas Eve workload, he stroked his sizeable beard and mentally prepared himself for their pre-flight pep talk. It had been a year of change at SantaCorp, with many new policies enacted since the previous year's near-disaster. Most importantly, he had introduced the 12 Bells support group for any elf with a substance abuse problem — it was known as the 12 Steps Of Christmas. Alcoholism rates among elves were the second-highest on record — a bit higher than those of the American Indian, and only slightly lower than the Alaskan Inuit.

It was a centuries-old issue, one that the big guy himself suffered from. He had been able to function for a long time, decades in fact, but every year it became a bit harder to get through the day. But, with the help of 12 Bells and its 500 or so other members, he had been able to maintain sobriety for nearly nine months.

It had also been about nine months since he had come to accept that Ian Burkholder's "nephews" were anything but. In the haze of alcohol, he could convince himself to carry on as if nothing was different. But after a nasty, booze-induced episode involving himself, several female employees and a snowman, he began to face facts — SantaCorp was slowly falling apart. And, as his Italian cousin liked to say, a fish rots from the head down. Santa vowed to do something about it, hence 12 Bells.

He also decided to take better care of his employees. He opened a world-class daycare facility, with beds for the children of elves who had to work the overnight shift. Under this guise, he was also able to build a nice living space for the Flynn boys.

Santa also built an on-site movie theater, optioned a McKringle's restaurant with a pimped-out playland, added a gym and spa, and karaoke bar. And upon reflection he realized that the catalyst to almost all of these changes were the Flynn boys, who by now were taking regular shifts on the factory floor, sweeping up, running for supplies, and helping to make the children's toys.

The Flynn boys were loved at SantaCorp. It was through them that many good things had happened. But all the good things in the world would never be enough to offset the one bad thing: them being there in the first place.

Santa wasn't stupid, he had cable, and he saw the frantic news reports in those early days, and he would have righted the wrong that same day had he been able. Unfortunately, Santa Time, that brief window that stopped the world and allowed he and his pilots to fly unseen every December 25 at midnight, worked only once a year.

So he waited. And waited.

Until now.

"Okay, Joffrey," he said to the little elf with the giant clipboard standing next to him. "It's time."

Joffrey hit the red button on the wall, a brief siren keened, and all work on the factory floor ceased. Santa, resplendent in his red outfit, made his way down the stairs. All eyes were on him.

Below, Ian and Ella emerged from the break room with a cup of hot cocoa, and Big Prune and Slim Catching popped out of the security booth. It was these four who were most responsible for the Flynn boys debacle. They found each other among the throngs and stood side by side.

"My loyal employees," Santa began, "that time is upon us."

The gathered group burst into spontaneous applause.

"Thank you," Santa continued. "Now, time runs short, and I have a few things to say before we take to the skies..."

There was a collective gasp from the crowd. Santa smiled.

"Yes, we... I will once again man a sleigh and do what I should have been doing for all these years — delivering the goods. Not above you, but with you."

This drew another spontaneous round of applause.

"Yes, thank you, but please... we haven't much time. Where is Ian Burkholder?"

Ian threw a cautious glance at his friends and stepped forward. "'Ere, sir."

"Ian," Santa requested, "come stand here next to me... Mr Burkholder, as some of you may know, came to us two years ago with a spotty past, very little flying ability, and a taste for liquor."

The crowd chuckled, Ian turned three shades of red.

"I am proud to say tonight that Ian, one of the founding members of 12 Bells, has had nary a drop in nine months and has helped me, through the power of his example, do the same."

There was a brief pause, then a great cheer rose up.

Over the din, Santa said, "Ian, with your future so bright, would you please guide our sleighs tonight as new squadron leader?"

The big man pinned a ribbon to Ian's jacket, an arrow with a red point, and shook his hand.

Ian wiped away a tear he hoped no one saw. "Be glad to, sir." He peered through the crowd and saw Ella was bawling, too.

"What do you think of that ribbon, Ian?" said Santa.

"That there, sir, is a slice of fried gold. Fried gold, my friend."

Santa laughed and quieted the crowd. "Now, where are Anthony Prunoli and Slim Catching?"

They stepped forward.

"You two, as such keen observers of the rules of SantaCorp security measures," he winked at both men, who looked terrified, "will now be the first sheriff and mayor of SantaCorp Village, a free housing development that breaks ground on the first of the year."

The crowd fell silent.

"SantaCorp Village is where you will ALL live, rent-free, and where the Hall Of Congress, headed by Pruny and Slim, will meet once a week to discuss town issues. It is my great hope that in the shadow of Santa-Corp a utopian society will arise, working together... though I'm sure a few obstructionists will rise up, as is to be expected in a free society."

Another great roar erupted as Santa pinned impressive-looking medals on the men's chests.

"And Ella Fontaine," Santa called. "Quickly now, time is shorter than you lot..."

Ella emerged.

"Ella, as the heart and soul, the very face of SantaCorp... I'm expecting you to keep these boys out of trouble."

"Gladly, sir," she curtsied and scampered next to Ian.

"Finally," Santa announced, "where are the Flynn boys?"

Another collective gasp as Oliver, John and Harry appeared.

Ian said, "You... you know about them, sir?"

"Ian," Santa answered. "I was a sot, but I was never stupid."

"Yes, sir."

"What do you want with us, sir?" Oliver asked in his usually blunt manner.

"Whatchoo want?" John echoed.

"WHAT!" Harry shouted.

Santa laughed. "Boys, I've been in the Santa business a little over two millennia, and in none of those years have I had as much fun and personal growth than in this one. I have you three to thank."

"Yeh... me too," Ian added.

"Yes," Ella said quietly. "Caring for you boys... well, it made me happier than I've ever been. And... you helped bring Ian into my life."

"Us too," Slim said, stepping forward with Prune. "At first I thought it was going to be a huge pain in the arse looking after a bunch of brats..."

Prune finished, "But we'd wake up each day for work looking forward to seeing you."

Oliver stared down. "Well, um, you're welcome, I guess."

"Oliver," Santa said, lifting the boy's chin with a chubby finger, "you don't seem to understand... every person in this room could tell you the same thing — that you and these precious brothers of yours have made SantaCorp, despite what those Disney twits might say, into the happiest place on Earth."

Oliver smiled. "Well, sir... I'm glad we could help."

"We helped," John chimed.

"Poopy!" Harry cried.

"But now," Santa went on, "it must end."

Oliver asked, "What do you mean?"

Santa answered, "As much as we all love having you here with us, as much as you've made us all happier, you should never have been brought here in the first place."

Ian, Slim, Prune and Ella all shrank.

"I forgive the mistake," Santa said, and the four eased, "for all the joy it has brought us, but it was a mistake. It's time to take you home."

"I think," Oliver said, with a bit of a quiver, "I think we'd rather stay, sir."

Santa smiled warmly. "I know you would. And, perhaps in a few years, you will come back to visit. But right now I need the three of you to bundle up, you're riding on my sleigh."

A minute later the boys were ready to go. They walked through the silent crowd toward the sleigh hangars, shaking the occasional hand, accepting the occasional hug. By the time they reached Santa's sled their faces were wet with other people's tears.

"Time to go, boys," Santa told them.

Ian, in RED-2, was the second sleigh in line. As he looked at them in their pajamas and puffy winter gear, he found it near impossible to speak. But when he did he said, "Fanks lads."

Oliver asked, "For what?"

Ian took his hand and knelt before the boy. "For making me want to be a better man."

He hugged them all and went to his sleigh, sobbing. The boys turned to the gathered elves, waved, and climbed aboard.

"You boys ready?" Santa asked.

*By the time they reached Santa's sled, the faces of the Flynn boys
were wet with other people's tears.*

"I think so," Oliver answered. "You've been doing this for over 2,000
years?"

"That's right," Santa answered.

Oliver went on, "So, like... like you're over 2,000 years old? Like Jesus
or something?"

Santa smiled. "Well, we're all kind of the same guy. It's complicated.
I'll explain on the way..."

With that, Santa put a finger to his nose, jerked his head, and the fleet
of sleighs took to the skies to bring a Merry Christmas to all and to all a
good night. A few minutes later, Santa had an idea.

Home

GEORGE and Helen Flynn, as they had every day for the past 364 days,
stood vigil outside their lovely gingerbread home near the ocean in Cape
May. It was from this house, exactly one year earlier, that their children
had been taken away from them, the now-world famous Flynn boys. Two
things made this day different from all the others. First, it was midnight,

Christmas Day. Second, they were not alone.

What had started as a solemn memorial to their missing children had escalated into a full-blown cause with a capital "C." In the days after the boys' disappearance, all the big talking heads on all the big talking news channels decried the sad state of humanity that such adorable, young (white) children had been taken from their homes. For a good six weeks there were daily updates, and the inevitable suspicions projected on to the parents. It always seemed that, in the absence of a logical explanation, these things happened. It was an almost natural part of the process.

But that eventually fell by the wayside, as did the daily coverage. By early spring they were a once-a-week mention in the local papers, and come summer the missing Flynns were but an afterthought.

And so it was on this Christmas Eve, a year later, that George and Helen Flynn sat on their porch, while about three dozen locals assembled on the sidewalk holding candles, singing carols, passing cookies and cocoa and doing their level best to comfort a friend and neighbor in need.

"Silent night," they sang, "holy night..."

On the porch a small wooden replica of a grandfather clock began its solemn chime, the Bong-Bong-BONG-Bong... Bong-Bong-BONG-Bong announcing the arrival of midnight, which would be followed by 12 single bongs.

"All is calm, all is bright..."

The first two bells chimed without incident.

"Round yon virgin, mommy and child..."

At bells three, four and five, a small wind blew up, oddly.

"Holy infant so tender and mild..."

On bells six, seven and eight, the Flynn parents and a few on the sidewalk would have sworn they could hear sleigh bells.

"Sleep in heavenly peace..."

On bells nine, 10 and 11 they could all hear the unmistakable sound of not only sleigh bells, but clattering hooves.

"Sleep in heavenly..."

On the 12th bell of Christmas voices stopped, jaws dropped, and all hearts skipped a beat.

"Ho-ho-ho," Santa said quietly as the people parted and his giant sleigh landed on the sidewalk.

As silence hung over the crowd, the nine tiny reindeer chuffed and beat their hooves against the cold. A few of the sidewalk sections cracked.

"Sorry," Santa said. "I don't usually use the reindeer... it's a union thing... but when they heard what we were doing tonight they insisted."

In the quiet, dozens of other sleighs began appearing in the sky, blotting out the moon.

"Um," Santa continued, unsure of what to say, "I know this is pretty unusual, we've only done it once before, and that was at a little manger a long time ago," he gestured to the surrounding sleigh, "and there were only three of us then... oh I do go on, don't I... what I'd like to say is both thank you and sorry. I think the boys can explain the rest."

"The boys?" Helen Flynn said from the porch.

George stood, "You mean..."

From the back of the great sleigh, Oliver, John and Harry stood and climbed over the great sack of toys.

"Hi mom, hi dad," Oliver said.

"Hi!" John echoed.

"HI DARE!" Harry screeched.

Their words rang in the stillness as heavy snow began to fall. George and Helen walked slowly from the porch and drank in the sight of their boys. Wordlessly, they embraced their children. A moment later the entire congregation joined them, and in their communal joy, a year's worth of despair dissipated into the night.

Epilogue

IN THE years that followed, life returned to normal. Amazingly, though, no one who was there that night ever talked about what they saw. To them, it seemed, just knowing something to be true was enough. Sure, they would share a knowing glance and a nod while about the town, but no one ever spoke of it.

Oliver, John and Harry grew to be fine young students and men of business, and their year of living merrily soon became a faded memory, until one year, quite unexpectedly, they each received by post a copy of a book. It was called *Return To Santa* and authorship was credited to an Ianella Slimprunoli. Though this tale of young children absconded in the night by a drunken elf was written off by critics as nothing more than an amalgamated rehash of *Peter Pan* and *The Chronicles of Narnia*, consumers thought it was quite spiffy and snapped it up for the holidays.

Coincidentally, Oliver, John and Harry's bank accounts became quite large and the rest of their Christmases were very merry indeed.

The Jetty

Forty years after that fateful night on Cape May beach, the man in the black trenchcoat stood on the jetty for the final time...

HE tall man in the black suit and hat stood motionless in the ankle-deep surf that rolled in, clawed at the beach with a sizzle, and rolled back out. The day was blazing hot, and the bikini and Speedo-clad cavorters who filled the beach threw long, curious glances at the man in the black suit and raincoat, which outlined his rail-thin frame as the clothes worked like a bellows in the stiff, undulating ocean breeze. He looked to be about 50. The coat and suit were Italian, handmade, and clearly very expensive, as were the brushed leather loafers now soaking in the corrosive salt water.

He was a curious sight indeed amid the Frisbee-tossers and paddle-ballers, though he seemed oblivious to them all. Let them look — he knew what this stretch of beach really was and damn the rest of them if they didn't. They would know soon enough.

He took a deep breath, let a momentary burst of anger fade, then stepped from the surf and up on to the jetty, which rose up out of the water like the spine of some great, ancient beast. The doing would be treacherous in his now-sopping shoes. He stepped gingerly, yet confidently, on to the giant, craggy rocks, a nearly imperceptible smile on his thin lips.

The large black-brown rocks glistened under the midday sun and a fine spray wetted his face as he climbed. The manmade, beach-preserving formation jutted some 100 yards out into the water, the surf sounding ferocious as the small waves crashed into the rocks and the noise echoed all around and through it. The man took another deep breath, coughed a bit, and smiled placidly out at the ocean.

It wouldn't be long now.

Forty years ago...

A WARM mist blew in from the Atlantic on the sweltering Saturday afternoon. It had been dark, cloudy and damp all day, the expansive beaches empty — a true rarity on a summer weekend in Cape May. It was in this setting that Jerry and the Pirates stormed the jetty that lay directly behind the crumbling convention center on Beach Avenue.

"Ahoy!" Jerry cried in his best shiver-me-timbers growl. It hurt his throat if he did it too much, but he wanted to sound authentic, so he ignored the rusty razor blades drawing across his vocal cords and screeched away. "Prepare to be boarded! Yahr!"

This was met with the assorted yells and "Avasts!" from his mates, who ranged in age from eight to 12. Jerry was 10, and though younger than the biggest boys, he was their unspoken leader, their ideas man. It was summer, and summer meant no school and loads of free time. After a few weeks the thrill of playing stickball on the lawn of the Christian Admiral had lost its allure. Hide and seek at the South Cape May train depot had also grown boring. Even sitting on the beach and looking at the summer girls in their newfangled, midriff-bearing "bikinis" was growing tiresome. NEVER dull, but a little same-y.

It was Jerry who, one bored afternoon, cast an eye toward the newly installed rock jetty and was thunderstruck with perhaps the single greatest idea of his young life. Rocks. Waves. Water. PIRATES!

With the abandon of newborn pups they tore off to Wilbraham Park and fashioned swords from the many fallen tree limbs that littered the ground. Fortunately for them, the night before a mild nor'easter had blown through town, loosing many fine instruments of pillage and plunder. They tore the sleeves from their T-shirts and cut the legs off of their pants with seashells (much to the chagrin of their working-class parents, to whom a $5 pair of Levi's represented a large chunk of their paycheck) to make bandanas and eye patches. It seemed every piece of junk they could lay their hands on was turned into some kind of weapon or finery. A few had even dared to pierce their ears, using water ice and thin beach reeds, and strung bottle cap earrings through their swollen lobes, though a few nasty, pus-filled infections quickly threw the damper on that.

Still, these boys were serious about their pirating. These boys, and one brave girl.

"Ye'll never take us alive!" Kelly shrieked as Jerry climbed atop the rocks.

She lunged at him with her sturdy twig — he dodged and slapped her on the hindquarters with his own wooden epee.

"Hey!" she cried, breaking character. "No butts!"

Jerry shrugged. "You didn't call it, so..."

THWAP! "Ow!"

Although the only female among this group of rogues, Kelly was a "girl" in only the loosest sense of the word. At 10, and a few months younger than Jerry, she was tougher than most of the other corsairs.

"Ha! Good one, Captain!" Butchie cried from his side.

"Yahr! Twas!" Jerry agreed and they clanked "swords."

Butchie was the youngest of them at a shade over eight. He was, to put it kindly, a fat child. He was game enough in their little adventures, be it pirating or hill-climbing or football, but he was easily winded and, as nice as this group of friends was, he was often picked on to the point of tears. But he was never deterred and always the first one back the next day, eager for another adventure.

Kelly thwacked him on the ass.

"Hey!"

"Doesn't feel so nice, does it, tubby!" she yelled through a wide grin.

Butchie looked down and Kelly immediately felt ashamed. But they exchanged a quick look, he saw the sorry in her eyes, and on they went.

"Well, avast, me hearties," a bigger boy yelled from the far, beach end of the jetty and over the crashing waves. "If it isn't Captain Jerry Blackhat and his band of merry men."

"Yahr," Jerry replied, "there be no merry men here, this be not Nottingham Forest. But what be it to you, Toothless Tommy Tuck?"

"Hey," Tommy whined, also breaking, "I told you my tooth fell out, no making fun."

"Yeesh," Jerry said, smiling, "why be ye all so sensitive this fine morn? Be I surrounded by a bunch of twee women?"

The other boys, and Kelly, said, "Oooooooooh…"

Stung, Tommy bowed up and replied, "The only woman I see here stands afore me, and I ain't talking about HER!"

This last bit was emphasized with a furious sword jab in Kelly's direction, and was followed by another long, "Oooooooooh…"

This seemed a bit much to Jerry and he was about to call time-out to calm things down, advise everyone to stop getting personal and thwapping asses, but before he could, Kelly leapt forward with a growl and jumped on poor, defenseless Tommy Tuck with an urgency he would only come to appreciate some five years later on his second date with Suzie Atkins.

"What the…" he started, but Kelly brought him down, hard, on the rocks. Tommy Tuck squealed as his head hit the stone with a *crack!* audible over the angry surf.

All fell silent, except for the moaning Tommy.

"Jesus… time out! Time out!" Jerry cried and rushed to the boy's side.

Kelly stood, aghast. "I didn't mean…"

"Out of the way," Jerry commanded and knelt over Tommy. "Tommy… Tommy! Can you hear me? Can you see me?"

"Yes," he answered, rubbing the back of his head. "I'm not deaf, dumb or blind."

The gang visibly relaxed.

Tommy stood, a bit wobbly at first, then righted himself. Kelly rushed toward him. "Tommy, I'm so sorry, I didn't mean to…"

He held her at arm's distance. "Yeah, I know. What I said was mean. I'm sorry."

"Let me see your head," she ordered and would not take no for an answer.

He bent and lowered his head, and they all gasped at the rivulet of blood that slowly trickled down the back of his neck.

"Blood..." Butchie uttered in a hush.

The other kids said, "Cool..."

"That looks nasty," Jerry observed. "Maybe we should call it quits."

"Maybe," Tommy shrugged, then grabbed his sword, "or maybe I should make you walk the plank ye scurvy dogs! Yahr!"

He roared, turned, and nailed many of them with firm raps across the knuckles and buttocks and the battle was made afresh. Their keening laughter and howls of delight were audible as far as the Beach Theater, which was playing a curious little film called *Planet of the Apes*, starring a snarling, shirtless Charlton Heston, the living symbol of all that was manly.

And on and on they went, stopping intermittently to replenish their energies with Zagnut bars and purple Kool-Aid, brought in plastic-y smelling Tupperware pitchers and warmer than the ocean water. Jerry suspected, as he swilled the violet concoction, that the combination of Kool-Aid and Tupperware would immediately cause cancer of the body. Minutes passed, then hours. Eventually, exhausted and exhilarated, they noticed the sun beginning to set over the now-placid ocean.

Sweat cooling on their brows and bodies, the feeling settled in that their day of fun and adventure was drawing to an end. Jerry felt like a Lost Boy. Butchie pulled his Mighty Mouse watch from his pirate satchel and eyed it. "It's getting late, I better get home. Mom said before dark. Kelly?"

Kelly smiled at him. "Yes, I'll walk you."

Butchie beamed and stuttered, "Mom said... mom said if you wanted to you could stay for dinner. She's... she's setting an extra place."

"That sounds nice, but I'll have to ask my dad."

"Okay," Butchie replied calmly, but inside his heart was leaping.

Jerry saw the elation in his eyes. He knew, heck, *everyone* knew, that Butchie was smitten with Kelly and, in his eight-year-old eyes was having a first date with her, and so he did not have the heart to tell him that he and Kelly had been sweethearts for the better part of the summer.

Instead he said, "Stickball tomorrow? Noon at the Admiral?"

This was met with general grunts of assent and the matter was settled. Stickball was hardly the most original idea, but he knew that stickball was a secret code for he and Kelly to get there 15 minutes early and practice their kissing in the giant hotel, under her great, stained-glass dome.

Only Jerry knew why Kelly turned a bright scarlet.

"Are you okay?" Butchie asked her.

She nodded vigorously, averting her eyes from Jerry, who was smiling at her and a little flushed himself.

"Okay then," Jerry announced, "see you all then."

They began to meander slowly off of the rocks, chatting about the sad state of the Phillies, the goings-on at the Ponderosa Ranch, and about that

The young pirates' keening laughter and howls of delight were audible as far away as the Beach Theater.

slightly oily guy named Nixon who was all over the TV these days. They got as far as the sand leading up toward the promenade when Jerry, sensing something amiss, cast a glance over his shoulder.

Tommy Tuck was standing tall, arms folded, still midway down the jetty's length.

"You coming?" Jerry called.

Tommy slowly shook his head.

"Well... what?"

Tommy deliberately removed his pirate garb, placed it at his feet, threw his sword into the water and said, in a clear, loud voice, "King of the Beach."

The group stopped in their tracks and regarded each other, an electric chill passing through them all from the now-cool breeze and from the implication of what King of the Beach meant.

King of the Beach was much like the regular King of the Mountain, except that instead of trying to scale a hill while your friends pummeled you, the first person to reach the furthest rock of the jetty was declared champion of all the world. It was a foolish game fraught with peril and a good chance of permanent injury, but it was also just about the funnest game they had ever invented.

Without a word, Jerry tore off running back toward the ocean, slipping momentarily on the slick rocks. A moment later they were all tearing haphazardly on to the jetty. Tommy Tuck, with his sizeable lead, turned to run, a little too quickly, and his feet skidded out from beneath him. He flopped on to the rock, badly skinning his knee. But what was a skinned knee when the championship of the world was on the line?

He regained his footing and looked back. The rest of the gang had quickly closed the distance between them. Ever the strategist, Tommy knew his best chance of winning now lay in his size advantage. The jetty was narrow, so narrow in fact that Tommy often imagined the 300 Spartans holding off a million screaming Persians upon it.

He planted his feet as firmly as he could on the wet rocks and braced himself for impact. He knew if he could keep them from getting past, he could slowly back his way to the furthest rock and bask in his hard-earned triumph.

The gang huffed toward him — Tommy opened his arms and embraced them in a violent hug as they slammed into his body, a body that would eventually grow into one of exceptional power and grace, both of which he would use in 15 years as the owner of the Everlasting Tuck Construction Company.

"HA!" he screamed as the bodies pushed and ducked and pushed and crouched and pushed and jumped and pushed against him, but Tommy Tuck would not be denied. He was the immovable object to their irresistible force. And he was winning.

In the middle of the pile, Jerry probed and prodded for a way past, to no avail. The others ones swarmed around him, a pulsating collection of flesh and sinew, all working in vain toward a common goal. It was then that Jerry had an idea.

Feeling like the smartest kid in the room he began to climb, on to and over the collected mass of human bodies. And as he rose he saw, over Tommy's head, the furthest rock. The thrill of impending triumph gripped him. He pushed with his little legs and pulled himself higher atop the rugby-like scrum of squirming limbs. He looked down and smiled. Suddenly, the mass of bodies below him began to rise as Tommy, the biggest and strongest of them all, found new purchase on the slippery rocks and stood, lifting the pile with him, looking for all the world like a miniature Hercules completing one of his seven feats of strength.

Jerry was impressed, and for a moment stopped to admire his friend, half-expecting a lion to appear out of nowhere... but no lion materialized. But it was here, now almost 10 feet in the air above the suddenly jagged looking rocks, that Jerry realized how extraordinarily dangerous his current situation actually was.

"Guys..." he started, but then the most unexpected thing happened.

The ocean, which for the better part of the last three hours had been as calm as glass, quickly and silently unleashed an enormous wave. To his right, Jerry could hear the delighted whoops of joy from the surfer boys on their long boards, ecstatic at the tasty boomer that was finally rolling in, their hours of waiting and paddling around finally being rewarded. Jerry was filled with a different emotion altogether.

Fear.

"Guys!"

Too late.

The wave, which now rolled majestically toward the beach on either side of the rocks, crashed violently into the end of the jetty, exploding into an angry spray of hungry ocean. Like a freight train it plowed into them. None knew that Jerry had climbed on top of them and so shrieked with delighted surprise as the chilling water slammed into them. But above, the rogue wave lifted Jerry off the pile and into the air.

In slow motion, Jerry got that stomach-pulling feeling he always got when he had flying dreams — that he was leaving the Earth, rising inexorably toward space, unable to control his ascent and headed for certain doom in an airless vacuum. Those dreams invariably ended with Jerry waking with a gasp, his sheets soaked with sweat. But here, in this moment, he knew that he was indeed going to come back to Earth, and that it would not be pleasant.

"GUYS!"

His friends looked up at the boy impossibly suspended above them on a cloud of water, a cloud that quickly dissipated and left their friend dangling, for just a split-second, in mid-air, like Wile E. Coyote running off a cliff in pursuit of the Road Runner. Meep-meep.

And it was in the same sickening slow motion that they watched Jerry fall. It was not graceful. The young boy clutched at the air, arms pinwheeling, feet seeking invisible purchase. He landed with a gut-wrenching thud, the air expelled from his punctured lungs with a whoosh. He did not move.

Stunned, his friends gathered round and stood over the pitiful, ruined boy lying on the rocks. Blood gushed from a crack in his head. His legs were all right angles.

All was silent for a moment. The wave was gone, dissolved into the rocks and into the air and sand, like the ruinous cacophony of the last three seconds never happened. Water dripped off of them and landed, unnaturally loud it seemed, on the rocks.

Butchie spoke first, "Is he... is he dead?"

Kelly answered, "I... I don't know."

As if in answer, Jerry drew in several ragged breaths.

"Well," Tommy said softly, "I guess he's breathing."

They stood there, the lot of them, without an inkling of what to do next.

Present Day...

THE man in the black suit maintained his perch atop the jetty. All day he had stood there, enjoying the breeze, squinting against the sun, watching with an inner joy as the occasional pod of dolphins swam by, some of them breaching proudly, drawing a round of applause and many a hoot and holler from the beachgoers.

It had been a spectacular beach day and so he'd had to wait it out, the accursed Cape May weather, unpredictable until you needed it to be unpredictable. But now, as evening approached, the man in black was alone. If you saw him from afar, you wouldn't know why, but you'd feel a little sad.

He reached into the deep pockets of the trenchcoat and fingered the items inside. Without looking at them he could see them simply by touch now, so often he'd felt them in his pockets, almost like Braille.

Almost time.

With a deep sigh and a shudder he began slowly walking the jetty's length, the ever-present wind at his back.

Forty years ago...

WHEN Jerry came to, it was dark. Dark and chilly. The night was warm enough — the chill came from his deepening shock. He took a moment to do a mental self-inventory, and the results were not good. For a moment he thought the side of his face lay on some unseen pillow, it was all warm and soft. He soon realized that there was no pillow on the unforgiving rock. Rather, the left side of his face had been so thoroughly pulverized that the bones felt like down feathers. The warmth emanated from the blood slowly leaking from his ear and mouth.

Despite this, he smiled and chuckled to himself.

Funny, he thought, *the rocks never look that hard when you're just sitting on them, but smash your head into one and all of a sudden you've got an earful of sand and a busted skull...*

He wanted to laugh at this, to fight off the fear with a good guffaw, but he sensed even the slightest movement would bring freakish agony. A college boy he once knew, a neighbor who was now in Canada to avoid the draft... which Jerry didn't understand because didn't they have wind in Canada?... anyway, he remembered this boy was studying to be a doctor,

The man in the black suit maintained his perch atop the jetty. All day he had stood there, enjoying the breeze, squinting against the sun...

and he once told Jerry that, if you feel like your body is "telling you something", like "don't turn that way" or "don't walk on that ankle" or "don't TOUCH me there" that your body was probably right and you shouldn't do whatever that thing was.

That's how he felt at the moment, so he chose to laugh on the inside, but promised himself he'd laugh his ass off out loud in a few days.

Something to tell the grandkids...

Fishing around his mouth he found a few holes where teeth should be, and the coppery taste of blood told him he'd bitten his tongue pretty good, too. So to go with his busted head and smashed face, he was now looking at the very real prospect of months of painful dental work. Joy. And he didn't even want to THINK about his leg.

His self-assessment done, he tried to lay as still as possible and let his mind wander over the day, the pirate games, and the comical look on Tommy Tuck's face when Kelly had attacked him.

THIS started him laughing.

Don't do it... he told himself, too late.

The slight tremble and rise of his chest sent white-hot flashes from every part of his body through every other part, all centering somewhere for an instant before settling somewhere else. It was the worst pain he could imagine imagining, and he could imagine a lot.

STOP!

After a few moments he willed himself still and the pain ebbed and finally tapered off. Jerry unclenched and began to sweat.

"Better not do THAT again," he whispered to himself, only it came out more like, *Eggs nog chew fat amen.* Again, laughable if not for the utter anguish of it. And he wasn't sure if it was good news or bad news that he couldn't feel his leg anymore — he only knew that it didn't hurt, and that was okay with him.

With his open eye he stared out over the ocean, which twinkled with the light of a billion stars as the placid water lapped gently against the rocks. All in all, quite lovely, except for the ruined boy.

It's okay... you're okay, he told himself and almost believed it. *Think of something else...*

Was it always this quiet and peaceful out here and he was always too loud to notice? Perhaps. Every time he and the gang were here it was a constant barrage of "Yahr!"-ing for their pirate games or "Pow-Pow!"-ing for their war games, and very little quiet introspection — 10-year-old boys did that rarely.

Jerry was getting very sleepy now, and while he sensed that was bad, there was very little he could do about it. What sounded like a dozen moths fluttered in his ear, swarming at his consciousness, barely audible over the pounding of his heart. It was very quiet and suddenly he missed his friends very much. As the blood hissed out of his ruptured skull he was all hot misery and floaty dreaminess.

Yes, it had been quite a fall.

Present day...

THE man in black was nearing the end of the jetty. The surf had picked up in the last hour or so. Though he wore no watch he knew it must have been approaching 10 o'clock — behind him the noise of people talking and dining at Tisha's and Henry's on the Beach were dying. In the distance he saw the lights of Rehoboth Beach, Delaware, a scant 17-mile, 80-minute ferry ride away.

The man had summered once in Rehoboth and had twice nearly melted off his hands in the hot grease fryer of the little donut shop he worked in that summer during college, and it was not an experience he repeated. Through the rest of his college and grad school summers he chose to remain in calm Cape May. In those days it wasn't the tourist Mecca it was today, but an enterprising young man with a bit of drive and the ability to mix a fine martini could always find a good summer job if he so chose.

"Hey, mister."

The tiny voice from behind startled the man. He turned to see a young boy, maybe nine or 10, standing behind him.

"Yes?" the man replied.

"You're all by yourself out here."

The man nodded. "I am."

"Well... why?"

The man smiled. "Long story. I used to play out here... when I was about your age, in fact."

"Was it fun?" the boy asked.

The man paused, then answered, "It was the most fun any of us ever had."

An adult voice came from further inland. "Billy! Billy get back here! Leave than man alone!"

Billy said, "Welp, I gotta go, mister."

The man replied, "Yes, well, a little boy like you shouldn't be out here all by yourself."

Little Billy turned and ran back to the promenade, and when he was gone, the man felt very much like a little boy out here all by himself.

Forty years ago...

A DULL pounding woke Jerry, streaking from behind his eyes and into his teeth. It hurt like hell, but it was good to know he was alive still.

Must have passed out, he thought, then flushed: *hope nobody saw me...*

It was very dark now, and quite a bit cooler, then it slowly dawned on him that he couldn't feel *anything* anymore. Aside from the throbbing in his head, the rest of him was numb.

If my brain doesn't want me to feel it, it MUST be bad.

And the realization struck him, a fact so obvious he wondered why he hadn't thought of it before. It was not in any way a good or pleasant thought, but oddly, it did not make him feel frightened, just mildly resigned.

I'm going to die out here. As if on cue, thunder pealed in the distance and a few, fat raindrops tickled the rocks. He bore a wide grin as the rain splashed more heavily. He was tired and just wanted to close his eyes again, get some sleep. *Just a little rest, so tired, the rain is so warm, just a little rest...*

"Jerry," a voice said out of nowhere, "don't go to sleep, Jerry."

Jerry blinked the water out of his good eye and strained to find the speaker.

"Don't move," the voice said, "you're hurt pretty bad."

Jerry had no argument.

"Here," the voice said and lifted Jerry's head up, placing it back down on a soft blanket, "this might help."

"Fanks," Jerry managed. "Who..."

"Mike," the voice answered, "I'm Mikey. I'm here... a lot. I watch you guys play pirates and stuff, but... you never invite me in. But it's okay."

Jerry was flabbergasted. *We invite ALL kids to play! I'd never leave you out! You don't know what you're talking about...*

"Wuffum puh miggabreck..." was what came out.

Mike stopped him. "Don't talk. Your jaw's busted. But I know what you're saying, that you let everyone play because you know how much it stinks, and you're right. I want to play with you guys, I just... can't is all. But it looks fun."

"Fizz..."

"I'll bet. How do you come up with your games?"

Jerry answered with a string of incoherent grunts.

Mike replied, "Really? All my dad did was drink. Drink and hit my mom. He's gone now, though. Has been for a while."

"Phorry..."

"Not your fault. No one's, really."

They went on for a while that way, the two of them, Mike asking a question, Jerry grunting away, Mike somehow understanding. After a while Jerry forgot about the dark and the cold and the rain and they were just two guys talking.

Then something bad happened.

In the middle of a conversation about baseball, Jerry's body seized up and he spat a copious amount of blood from his pulpy mouth. He looked like a swordfish on a taut line, fighting the reel. After a few seconds he was still again.

Mike somberly asked, "Are you all right?"

Jerry spat and righted his brain. "Mmm'kay."

The numbness that had claimed his body was now creeping into his brain, it felt. Thoughts were difficult to arrange, speech was a near impossibility, broken jaw or no. He knew, he just knew his time was coming, if only Mike would shut up long enough for him to close his eyes.

"You stay here..."

Duh...

"I'm going to get someone to help," Mike told him.

Jerry nodded slightly in understanding. Finally, some peace and quiet.

"But do me a favor while I'm gone."

Anything, just leave...

"When my friend comes back I want you to tell him who your three favorite baseball players are. Deal?"

Jerry blinked in disbelief. He had just rearranged his sizeable baseball card collection the night before in order of favorite to least favorite. Though Jerry didn't know it, he had a mild form of OCD which manifested itself in the constant rearranging of his baseball cards — first by position, then by team, then by age, batting average, home runs, RBIs and on and on. But last night... last night was the most agonizing yet — from favorite to least favorite. And somehow this kid *knew*.

"Deal?"

"Kneel..." Jerry managed.

"I'll be back in a jiff, Jer-Bear."

Jer-Bear? Nobody's called me that since...

Mike wiped the rain from Jerry's eye and patted him on the cheek: "Hang in there, buddy. Remember, three favorites."

Jerry managed a nod and a smile, that odd sleepy feeling faded as he concentrated on the task at hand, the ridiculously easy task at hand.

1. Dick Allen.

2. Willie Mays.

3. Carl Yastrzemski.

Done and done. Except...

Except how do I leave out Pete Rose and Willie McCovey, they're both great hitters, and what about Joe Morgan? Or Lou Brock?

NO! The list is solid. Dick Allen is going to win five MVPs before he's done so don't even THINK about taking him off. I mean, he's great... right?

Sure, sure he is, Jer-Bear, you tell yourself whatever you need to to keep Allen on your stupid little list. You know damn well there are 10, no... 20 players better than him in the NL alone.

Really? Name one.

How about Johnny Bench?

Bench is a great CATCHER, dummy, but he's not even close to Allen all-around.

Oh really?

Look, I'm allowed to like Dick Allen if I want. It's my list — I can put who-ever I want on there.

I know, but it's a fraud list, a FAKE list...

It is NOT!

Is TOO!

All his internal arguments ended this way, in the brainpan numbing OCD ritual of he said, he said, he said louder.

Is NOT!

Is TOO!

Is NOT!

"Hello?"

"Gah!" Jerry screamed and winced at the pain in his jaw

"Jeez, sorry, dude."

"Uhnnnnn..."

"I hear you. My friend Mike told me you were here. I'm Tommy, I'm from around here. Yeesh, Mikey wasn't kidding, you're in a world of hurt."

Thanks for letting me know...

"Mikey's going for help, he asked me to hang out with you 'til he gets back."

Great.

"So, mine — Frank Howard, Ken Harrelson and Bob Gibson."

"Baaah..." Jerry scoffed.

"I know, I know," Tommy defended himself. "Gibson is a pitcher but, you know, he's pretty tough, too."

"Muhnever."

"Mikey shouldn't be too long, he's a real fast runner. He loves to run. What's your thing? Running? Baseball? Surfing?"

"Mrrighting..."

"Writing? Huh, really? That's cool, I guess."

"I knoge," Jerry said defiantly.

"Easy, buddy, easy. Writing is definitely cool. Chicks really go for that sensitive artist crap. Trust me, I know." Tommy lay down sideways and winked at his good eye.

Jerry could barely see him through the rain and the grey fog that was growing in his eye, but there was something vaguely familiar about Tommy. He knew him from somewhere, and it was going to drive him crazy, like having a word on the tip of his tongue, until he figured it out. Tommy, and Mikey before him, they both rang a bell in the inner recesses of his brain.

Tommy continued, "I can't really move you or anything but... can I do anything for you?"

Just leave — I'm getting tired again. Just want to get some sleep.

Tommy clicked his teeth. "Sorry, Jer-Bear, 'fraid I can't do that. Tell you what I can do, though, is help get rid of some of that pain in your jaw."

Jerry's eye went wide. Tommy laughed. "I'm not going to hurt you. Just try to relax, you won't feel a thing."

I haven't felt anything in hours. I don't need YOU to tell what I am and what I'm not going to feel...

CRACK!

"Ow."

"Better?"

Jerry said nothing for a moment, a little dazed from the white-hot spark of pain that just zipped through his jaw and dispersed like a shot. Something definitely was different.

"I can talk," he said, opening and closing his mouth, testing the rusty hinge of his jaw.

Tommy wiped his hands on his pants. "Yep. Your jaw was dislocated, not broken. Figured I'd pop it back in for you."

"That hurt."

"Kind of the least of your problems right now. No charge, by the way."

"How did you..."

"Pre-med, State College. First thing you learn is anatomy, then how to fix it."

"Huh," Jerry chuffed. "Well... thanks."

Tommy nodded. "Welcome."

"You have no idea how frustrating that was not to be able to..."

"Yeah?"

Jerry blinked. "Not to be able to..."

"You all right?"

Jerry blinked again, something was wrong, "To be able to..."

"Jer-Bear?"

But all was black.

★　★　★　★　★

IT WAS a nice dream, all white lights and soft linens. It was warm in the dream and there was no rain splashing in his eye, no annoying kid or med student to keep him from sleeping. He still couldn't move very well, but all the pain was gone, the numbness replaced with floating, and floating was nice, much better than walking or running or even riding a bike.

In the dream he couldn't talk anymore but that was all right — floating was an even trade for talking (and a real steal in Jerry's book, like the Lou Brock trade). It took a moment to orient, but after a few moments he had it figured out. Up was light and warm, down was cold and dark and rain. He did not want to go down, so he let himself be carried up, up like a dandelion seed caught in a breeze, or one of those little spiders that makes a parachute out of its web, or like a...

"Jer-Bear..."

Like a... like a... he was running out of analogies...

"Jerry?"

And that stupid voice was making it hard to concentrate.

"It's not time yet, Jerry, so why don't you come back down here with us?"

But I WANT it to be time. Down there hurts — up here I get to float.

"I know, floating is fun, but not yet."

But...

"Jerry, there will be plenty of time to float later, but now I think you better come back here.:

The thought of leaving the dream made him profoundly sad. This was the best place he could ever imagine being. But...

"What about your mother? If you leave there will be no one left. And she'd really miss you."

Well, I miss people too and THEY never come back.

"I know, Jerry, but your mom needs looking after, and she loves you more than anything on Earth. Do you want her to be all alone?"

It was a lame trick, but Jerry knew the voice was right. He knew what he had to do. So, with one more longing look up into the soft, warm light, he turned and floated back to the cold, hard down. The light grew dimmer as he went and he passed through a thick fog. Once through, he could make out some objects below. To his great surprise it was HIM. Him surrounded by three people. And everybody was right — he did NOT look good all twisted up on the rocks like that. His heart grew light and giddy as he neared himself. This was the coolest thing EVER! He could not WAIT to rub it in somebody's face.

★ ★ ★ ★ ★

"THERE you are!" a gruff voice boomed into his upturned ear. "Good boy!"

Jerry felt hands rubbing his chest. Funny — he was laying face down a few seconds ago, and now he was on his back.

"I wasn't supposed to move," he said.

"I know," the gruff voice replied, "but things had to be done, no time to be gentle."

"If you say so."

"Name's Leonard, Lenny if you prefer."

Jerry coughed. "I'm meeting all kinds of people out here on the jetty at night. Any more of you out there?"

Lenny laughed, a deep grumbling laugh. It did not sound healthy. "You've still got your sense of humor I see. That's good. You get that from your mother, I bet."

Jerry snickered. "Yeah, she's a riot. She's gonna LOVE seeing me here like this."

Leonard chuckled. "I doubt that very much."

Jerry tried to lift his head but could not. Instead it flopped with a squish on the now-sopping blanket Tommy had given him. "Leonard, do you know where Tommy is?"

"He went to look for help."

"I thought that's what Mikey was doing."

"He is, but not very well, apparently. Your friends are out there. They

It was HIM. Him surrounded by three people. And everybody was right — he did NOT look good all twisted up on the rocks like that.

didn't abandon you."

Jerry sighed. "That's nice to know. It'd be nicer if they decided to ever come back."

Leonard, smiled. "Patience, Jer-Bear, patience. You get that, or your lack thereof, from your father, I'm certain."

Jerry quietly said, "I wouldn't know. He died when I was a baby."

Leonard paused. "I'm sorry."

"Not your fault... cigarettes."

Leonard sighed. "Nasty, dangerous habit."

Jerry craned his neck to see the man but couldn't really get a good look at him. He saw enough to know he was wearing a black suit and trenchcoat. And now that he thought of it, he had never gotten a real good look at Mike or Tommy, either.

He asked Leonard, "So what're you, like... Mike and Tommy's dad or something?"

Leonard considered this. "You could say that."

Jerry was confused. "What does that mean?"

"Well, we're related."

Jerry said, "This has got to be the weirdest night of my life."

"JERRY!"

This voice belonged to neither Jerry nor Lenny. It was Butchie.

"Butch!" Jerry quickly sat up... and immediately regretted it. The pain in his torso was beyond description and he was pretty sure he could HEAR his broken ribs grinding against each other inside his chest.

All went white, then black, then white again, then it was stars. He tried to breathe but it felt like a giant hand was clamped on his chest. He was all panic. His heart thumped in his ears and he could feel consciousness ebbing away once again. Then he felt a warm hand on his face and heard a soothing voice in his ear.

"Listen to me, Jer-Bear," Leonard said. "I don't have much time so I need you to listen."

Jerry managed a weak nod as he sipped air.

"You're going to pass out in a moment, and that's okay... a perfectly normal response to the distress your body is in right now. Your brain knows how hurt you are and sometimes it just shuts you down when it's too much. Okay?"

Another weak nod. Leonard's voice sounded like it was echoing off some unseen wall.

"Jerry! Jerry!" It was Butch, still in the distance, but closer. "It's me! Butch! I got your mom! And the doctor! We're almost there!"

Leonard continued, "You're going to come out of this all right, Jer-Bear. You're going to heal up and be fine. Maybe a slight limp in your kicking leg, but you were born to play baseball, so I wouldn't worry about it."

Jerry smiled at this, smiled and shook as his body started shutting down.

Then came the other voices, much closer now. "Jerry, it's mommy! Be strong, honey! Be strong, we're coming!"

They were so close now he could hear sand cascading across the jetty rocks.

Leonard squeezed the boy's hand: "I have to go now, Jerry, but I want you to know that I'll always be here for you."

A siren keened from Beach Drive and Jerry could hear paramedics scrambling. Beams of light now bounced off the rocks as the rescue party neared.

Leonard then said the last words he would ever say to Jerry: "Everything is going to be all right. I'll see you in about 40 years, champ."

It was then that Jerry finally saw the man's face in the light and it all made perfect sense.

His mother was the first to reach him: "Jerry, thank God, oh thank God, thank God, thank God, it's okay now, sweetie, mommy's here, hold on, sweetie, hold on..."

Jerry took a deep breath that rattled in his lungs and said, "Goodbye."

He watched as Leonard smiled and walked away.

Then it was darkness.

★ ★ ★ ★ ★

HE OPENED his eyes slowly, his eyelids weighing a thousand pounds each, it seemed. He blinked away the fuzz and saw he was in a hospital room. This did not surprise him, given his condition, which was still grim but certainly improving. Around him were dozens of flower arrangements and gifts and baskets of fruit.

Have to whack my head on a rock more often, he thought.

He was warm and dry and pleasantly foggy. The events of the previous 36 hours or so came to him in brief flashes like a skipping record. Images halted, stuck for a moment, then zipped by too fast to recognize. He saw his mom's face, then Butchie, then the ambulance crew. A gurney, a big, fat IV needle, being lifted on a stretcher as the paramedics grunted across the heavy sand. There was also a vaguely pleasant recollection as he remembered Mikey, Tommy and Leonard on the jetty. He couldn't wait to talk to them again, to thank them.

"Look who's awake," his mom said from the side of the bed.

Jerry smiled. "Hi mom."

"Hi Jerry," Said Butch, who sat anxiously in the corner. He was terrified of hospitals.

"Hey buddy. Looks like I owe you one."

Butch blushed a deep red. "You'd have done the same for me."

"I'd like to think so."

Kelly appeared at the foot of the bed and Jerry's heart raced.

"We got you this." She handed him a banged-up old motorcycle helmet. "For next time we play."

"Funny..."

His mother said, "Yes, but there's going to be no next time. If you ever go back out on that jetty, STAY there."

They all laughed a little.

Then Jerry asked, "So... what exactly happened? You guys were all gone when I woke up."

Butch answered, "We saw you were hurt pretty bad, so we all went to get help. We left that Mikey kid to look after you."

Kelly continued, "It was Butchie who got everyone to calm down and came up with the plan."

Butch was now a never-before-seen shade of crimson.

"My man..." Jerry said. "Who was Mikey? Did you guys see him before."

"No," Butch answered.

"It was weird," Kelly added. "It was like... one second he wasn't there, then he was. I guess he was with us all day and we just didn't notice him."

Jerry nodded: "And what about Tommy and Leonard — did you see them?"

Butch and Kelly shook their heads and looked oddly pained. His mom spoke up, "Would you kids give us a minute, please?"

Butch and Kelly left the room, as Jerry's mother looked at him steadily.

"What?" Jerry asked. "Are Tommy and Lenny here?"

"Jerry," his mom started, "when we got to you it seemed like you were having a conversation with someone."

"I was. Lenny."

"Jerry, you were alone on the jetty."

Jerry blinked. "No, Lenny... Leonard was there. He talked to me. And before him it was Mikey and Tommy. Tommy fixed my jaw."

His mom was silent.

"What?" he asked, impatient.

"Jerry," she started, "dozens of people walked past the jetty while you were out there, and none of them saw you and none of them saw anybody else because there *was* nobody else."

Jerry laughed. "What are you, crazy? There were three of them, like I told you..."

His mom stopped him. "The doctors believe you were hallucinating, Jer-Bear, because you hit your head so hard and lost so much blood. It's nothing to be ashamed of."

"You're right," Jerry agreed, "I'm not ashamed because there's nothing to be ashamed of, because Mikey, Tommy and Lenny were there. I'm not making it up!"

"No one thinks you are dear, it's just that..."

"What? This is bullshit."

"Language."

"Sorry."

She placed a cool hand on his. "The names, dear."

"What about them?"

She took a deep breath and gave him that patient mother look he hated so much. "Honey..."

Here we go...

"Honey, do you remember your dad?"

Jerry shrugged. "A little. He had a deep voice and smelled like smoke."

"What about his name?"

"Sure, Michael."

"Michael what?"

"Michael Leo..."

His mom sighed and a tear rolled down her cheek. "Jerry, the ambulance people and police have all looked for these people you were talking about and nobody can find them. There were no traces of anyone else being on the jetty with you, no footprints or anything."

"The blanket. Tommy put a blanket under my head!"

"Darling, your head was resting on a mound of sand. You must have gathered it yourself somehow. And son, Thomas was your father's middle name."

Michael Thomas Leonard.

Mikey. Tommy. Lenny.

Jerry's heart sank. "No, they were there, I saw them, I talked to them!"

His mom wept freely now: "No dear, they weren't..."

"THEY WERE!"

But he knew the truth now. It was right there in front of him. That whole night, the feeling of having met those boys before, of somehow knowing them, was all clear now. His face grew hot, his breath heavy, and his eyes welled. How could it all have been in his head? It was too real. He didn't want to believe it, so he chose not too.

"It was dad."

"There, there sweetie..."

Jerry smiled and looked at his mom who was stroking his hair. "It was dad, don't you see? He was there with me. He kept me alive until you guys got there. Can't you see that? It was dad all along. How could I not have figured it out?"

She said, "Shh, it's okay now, sweetie, you get some rest..."

He could see that she was in complete "mom" mode now and that arguing would be futile. So, despite the thousands and thousands of thoughts and words banging around in his head, he simply said, "Okay, mom, okay."

And she was right — everything *was* going to be okay.

Present day...

JERRY Leonard, Jer-Bear as his dad used to call him as a child, took one last, long look up at the Cape May promenade and turned back toward the sea. From his pockets he drew the two objects he'd been absently fingering all evening and held them before him.

In the pale moonlight he could barely see the faded pictures. The first was a weathered, old baseball card which read: *1st Base —Philadelphia Phillies — Butch Knotwell*. Beneath it was a photo of a strapping young lad in red pinstripes, far removed from the baby fat of his pirate-playing days. Jerry and Butch had remained close into high school, at which time his athletic prowess raised him to a level of popularity Jerry could never hope to attain. And while they always remained friendly, gone was the chubby little sidekick of his younger years. It was only two years ago that Butch, being inducted into the Philadelphia Sportswriters' Hall of Fame, credited Jerry Leonard with being the first guy to give him a chance and a little confidence.

But Jerry was not at the ceremony — he was in Switzerland, trying an umpteenth different holistic cure for the aggressive cancer that now permeated his entire body. He had continued with his writing through grammar, high school and college, had sold a few novels, and had a few of those novels turned into crappy movies, for which he was paid a princely sum, thus affording him the luxury of flying to places like Switzerland on the off-chance the magic, cancer-killing bullet might actually exist.

He ran a finger over the baseball card, then flicked it out to sea.

Next he looked at the other photo. It was of Kelly MacDonald, his 10-year-old crush. They, too, had remained friendly over the years, but it was Butch who ended up with the girl. She grew more and more beautiful, he more and more athletic and popular. They were the classic homecoming king and queen, head cheerleader and captain of the football team, high school sweethearts who got married straight out of high school and would remain so until they died.

The last time Jerry saw them was three years ago and 30 years into their marriage, in some whistle-stop town on some old-timers', goodwill baseball function on the banquet circuit. The years had been kind to them, and when Kelly got up to get them both a cup of coffee, Butchie had watched her with the same pink flush on his cheeks Jerry had seen more than 40 years ago, on that fateful morning, when Butchie thought they were having their first date.

Turned out he was right.

He gave her photo one last look then it followed Butchie's Topps card into the water.

Jerry looked up at the stars and took a great lungful of salt air. He'd lived a solitary, almost monastic life. He had the odd girlfriend here or there, but none of them lasted. They, like his old group of pirate-playing school friends, were unable to grasp the concept of his unshakeable faith. The idea that he had a certain amount of time on this Earth to do good things... and he had *done* them.

"See you in 40 years, champ," his dad said that night, and as he grew older Jerry took that as a subtle message that he shouldn't screw things up while he was here. And so, with his movie money, which he had invested wisely in the then-blooming home computer market, he had anonymously donated millions to various hospitals for cancer research and treatment.

His donations increased as his own condition worsened — after all, you really *can't* take it with you.

It was mildly terrifying, yet oddly freeing, to know when the end was going to come, and while the cancer was painful and the treatments nearly unbearable, they both served to keep him focused on the doing of the good.

Forty years ago, he had tried and tried to convince his friends that what had happened to him that night on the jetty was real, that someone was looking out for him and therefore somebody must be looking out for all of us. But after a few weeks he stopped. He couldn't convince them — they did not want to be convinced. And though he didn't know it then, that night on the jetty and the faith it instilled in him was the spike that eventually split his childhood friendships.

Out on the jetty, the water splashing against the rocks, he enjoyed the last few seconds of his mortal life. He closed his eyes, shuffled carefully to the end of the furthest rock, and tensed to jump into the water for the last time. And there, on the precipice, he felt something he hadn't felt in 40 years — a spark of doubt.

Maybe it all was in his head. Maybe his experience that night was nothing more than the random firing of synapses in the crushed skull of a dying boy, the fevered dream of a kid with a busted body, the all-too-understandable delusion of a panicked brain desperately clinging to life.

He suddenly felt very scared and very alone.

From behind him a voice asked, "You just can't do the things the easy way, can you, Jer-Bear?"

Jerry smiled, closed his eyes, and felt a hot rush of tears stain his cheeks as relief flooded him. A nearly literal wave of warmth, like a giant, gloved hand, surrounded him.

"Ready, son?"

Jerry nodded but did not open his eyes. He did not have to. Rather, he lifted his face to the growing warmth of the light above him, and took a step.

The two discarded photos bobbed in the water below, faces up, as if peering into the sky.

Then it was dark.

Acknowledgments

N JANUARY, 2004, following yet another frustrating, debilitating Eagles playoff loss, I wrote what turned out to be the first of many emails to Jack Wright, who six months prior had launched *Exit Zero* magazine in Cape May (and whom I'd briefly met while serving him at Elaine's Dinner Theater that summer).

My first email read as follows:

I'm writing mostly because it's the off-season, the theater is closed and I'm really bored, but also because I'd like you to consider "hiring" me as a writer of some kind. My background is in theater and acting so I could be an entertainment reviewer... I have been in two local bar bands, so I could be a music writer/critic. Or as just some kind of "opinion" column in which I share my witty insights on life in general. Or, you know, some combination of all of the above.

Several, long (very long) emails later, we had a deal. A column, called Undertow, was born. Within weeks of its launch, it became a local touchstone and something of a Cape May phenomenon, if you'll excuse my hubris — and lack of modesty. Undertow is a weekly chronicle of who I see doing what, where, and with whom, and sometimes why (I moonlight, serious moonlight, as a karaoke host and singer for Acoustic Mayhem).

Undertow, which I was sure was going to cost me friends faster than being a guy who voted for George W. Bush (twice!), instead helped me make many more. Most days brought a constant barrage of, "Ooh, can you put me in your column this week?" The answer was always, "Yes", though many of those people came to regret it later (myself chief among them).

In 2006, from the bowels of Undertow, my first short story sprang: *Murder-Oke!*, the catalyst for this book. Unsure how my friends, employers and patrons would react to being slaughtered and/or ridiculed in the story, my reticence soon faded as, soon after its publication in the pages of *Exit Zero*, the requests of, "Ooh, can you put me in your column?" turned into requests of, "Ooh, can you kill me in your story next week?"

And thus, a second Cape May phenomenon was born, if you'll excuse my hubris — and lack of modesty.

So, all that said, welcome to my first book! And on the off-chance it also turns out to be my LAST book, I'd like to thank some people.

I thank my regular readers, who were, quite literally, the inspiration for many of the characters contained herein.

I thank my new readers. By purchasing this book you support the idea of Cape May as a genuine center of arts and literature (though calling these stories "literature" is a bit of a stretch), and not just architecture.

I thank my editor, Jack Wright, for his countless hours spent putting this project together. It was he who gave my first chance as an untested writer, and he whose boundless enjoyment of, and affection for, these stories helped me see them through new eyes. Words fail me.

I thank Mike DeMusz, whose illustrative work in these pages adds more to the printed word than I could have hoped. He also drew me thinner, and I didn't even have to ask.

I thank author David Stern, whom I've known for 30-plus years, and who has been unwavering in his support as I try to become a "real" writer. He has the patience of a Vulcan.

I thank author Orson Scott Card, who is the reason I write in the first place (though I'm not sure how much credit he'd like for *that*). His work has helped shape my life. That he contributed to our little endeavor (see the back page blurb) astounds me.

As ever, I thank my siblings, Mike, Chris, Greg, Dan, and Erin. Without them, the murderous tendencies exhibited in these stories would never have come to fruition. And to my mother, Marlene, who had me, taught me, raised me, and set me loose on the world. So really, it's all *her* fault. And to Gene. We all miss you.

Lastly, I thank Cathrine, Owen, Jackson and Henry O'Brien for being the reasons (literally) that I rise each morning, and the reasons I continually strive, though often fail, to be a better husband and father. I've learned to write what I know, and what I know is that my life would be nothing without them in it. If nothing else, this book will stand as a lasting testament of my love for them, though this may be a funny way of showing it.

Until next time, don't get caught in the Undertow.

— *Terry O'Brien, Cape May, March 31, 10:50am*